GW00992860

WELCOME TO MEANTIME

WELCOME TO MEANTIME

MURRAY DAVIES

First published in 2014 by Old Street Publishing Ltd,

Yowlestone House, Devon EC16 8LN

www.oldstreetpublishing.co.uk

ISBN 978 1 908699 80 0

Copyright © Murray Davies, 2014

The right of Murray Davies to be identified as the author of this work
has been asserted by him in accordance with the
Copyright, Designs and Patents Act 1988.

Every effort has been made obtain permission for all illustrations, but
in the event of an omission the publisher should be contacted.

All rights reserved. No part of this publication may be reproduced,
stored in or introduced into a retrieval system, or transmitted, in
any form, or by any means (electronic, mechanical, photocopying,
recording or otherwise) without the prior written permission of the
publisher.

10 9 8 7 6 5 4 3 2 1

A CIP catalogue record for this title is available from the British
Library.

Printed and bound by CPI Group (UK) Ltd, Croydon, CR0 4YY

Typeset by JaM Book Production

WELCOME TO MEANTIME

DAY ONE

Wednesday

'YOU TRIED TO kill Terry Rich. You tried to drown him.'

'No, sir.'

'No? You held Mr Rich's head under the water until he confessed to a crime he did not commit.' Defence counsel paused for effect. 'A confession that you tortured out of him.'

'That's not true, sir.'

I'd been trying to kill the bastard.

Something that Detective Chief Inspector Patsy Chalke could not admit. Especially as she had just denied it on oath.

The jurors were looking at her with a mixture of admiration and disbelief.

If only they knew.

Coppers seldom won foot chases. While the villain was fuelled by fear and adrenalin, the police officer was propelled only by a sense of duty, and at the same time handicapped by the weight of his equipment. Poor old plod didn't stand a chance.

Even though Chalke had been in civvies, Terry Rich had been getting away from her when he'd spotted the uniforms coming down the towpath towards him. Rich had doubled back towards Chalke, taking what he'd thought was the soft option.

Except that Patsy Chalke was not a soft option – especially if you were a shit of an evil child molester like Terry Rich.

Chalke had waited until Rich was alongside then hurled herself at him, sending them both into the Grand Union Canal.

What had happened next was now the subject of cross-examination in Court 12 of the Central Criminal Court.

Patsy Chalke glanced at Rich. He leered back.

'In fact, Detective Chief Inspector,' continued the rich tones of Mansel Daley QC. 'You have a record of taking the law into your own hands.'

'Objection.'

'Sustained.'

But the damage had been done. The seed had been planted in the jury's mind.

'Why did the defendant run back towards you?'

'I assume because he'd seen that uniformed officers had cut off his escape.'

'Why would the defendant fear a police officer?'

'Why was he running away from a woman?'

Gotcha, you bastard. That'll teach you to ask a question without thinking through the answer.

'You were angry with the defendant, DCI Chalke,' said Mansel Daley. 'You wanted to do him damage.'

Chalke turned to face the jury. 'Any decent person who had seen what Terry Rich had done to that little girl would be angry.'

'But Mr Rich had done nothing to that unfortunate little girl, had he?' Mansel Daley was at his most silky – and his most dangerous. Chalke braced herself. 'Apart from the confession you tortured out of him, the police have no substantive case against the defendant.'

That was more or less true. No DNA, no forensics, nothing to tie Rich to the attack on eleven-year-old Vicky Gresham apart from one unreliable witness – and the knowledge that Rich had done exactly the same thing before.

A fact that the jury was not allowed to know.

'I did not torture Terry Rich.'

Chalke caught sight of her boss, Commander Alison Begley,

at the back of the court. Begley refused to make eye contact. Patsy would have appreciated a quiet thumbs-up, rather than being blanked.

Mansel Daley continued, 'You claim that the defendant said, "Okay, I did it. I couldn't help myself. Don't let me drown."'

'Yes, sir.'

'In fact, you told the defendant that you were going to hold him under water until he confessed.'

'No, sir.'

'And what the defendant said was, "Please, I'll say whatever you want but don't let me drown."'

Chalke glared at Rich.

The lying toerag!

What she'd actually said to Rich was, 'I'm going to kill you, you fucker, and save the courts the trouble.'

He spluttered, 'I'm sorry. I didn't mean to do it. Let me go.'

She said, 'Not until you're fucking dead.'

And then the bloody uniforms had arrived.

Mansel Daley paused to consult his notes. Chalke tried to seize the initiative.

'I'd chased the accused for a quarter of a mile. I was too tired to try to drown anyone – certainly not someone twice my size.'

'How deep is the water in the canal?'

'About five foot where we fell in.'

'The defendant cannot swim. You pulled his jacket back off his shoulders so that he could not move his arms. You had him by the hair and kept forcing his head under the water. Each time he tried to regain his balance, you kicked his legs away.'

Had she really done all that? God, she was good.

'Oh, come on, Mr Mansel Daley. I'm five feet seven and weigh nine stone. The defendant's six foot and fourteen stone. You really think that I could drown him? It was all I could do to hang onto him until my colleagues arrived.'

Sodding uniforms – dragging her off Rich.

Rich was staring at her again, his piggy little eyes blazing in hatred. Chalke felt the hairs rise on the back of her neck.

Bring it on, pond life. This time I'll really do you damage.

'Members of the jury, you can see that the defendant wears his hair long – with good reason,' intoned Mansel Daley. 'Mr Rich, please lift the hair over your left ear. Thank you. You can see that a portion of Mr Rich's ear is missing. It was bitten off by Detective Chief Inspector Chalke.'

This was the part Patsy had been fearing. She wasn't going to be able to talk her way out of this easily.

Mansel Daley pressed his advantage. 'You don't deny that you bit off Mr Rich's ear.'

'Apparently, I bit his ear.'

'Apparently!'

'These things happen quickly. It's nothing like the choreographed fights you see on TV. We fell in water. I went under. I was fighting to survive.'

'You bit off half the ear. Hardly using necessary minimum force, were you?'

It was worse for me. I could have been poisoned.

And Rich had bled like a stuck pig, a swirl of claret in the chocolate water.

'No further questions, m'lud.'

Patsy Chalke stood outside court feeling the adrenalin drain away. Her blouse was sticking to her back with cooling sweat. She shivered.

One of her new team, Detective Sergeant Bobby Leyden, was weaving his way through the Old Bailey's crowded foyer towards her. Or rather – a battered and bruised version of Bobby Leyden.

His face was a mess. His left eye was almost closed. A livid purple bruise covered his left cheek.

Chalke was about to ask what had happened when Alison Begley, her boss as head of the Homicide and Serious Crime Command, appeared looking as if she sucked lemons for a hobby. Begley didn't beat about the bush.

'That was a less than convincing performance,' she told Chalke. 'If Rich walks, we'll know who to blame.'

Thanks a bunch. You should be here rallying your troops, not slagging them off.

Begley, battleship-grey hair lacquered to within an inch of its life, recognised Leyden. Her eyebrows rose. 'What happened to you?'

'Fighting, ma'am.'

'Fighting?!'

'I was boxing last night for the Met against the RAF.'

'Should you have been boxing when you knew you were due to give evidence the next day?'

'Assistant Commissioner Branson insisted, ma'am.'

Begley opened her mouth, decided that it would not be politic to criticise a senior officer, turned on her heel, and stalked off back to her desk at Scotland Yard.

'I hope you won,' said Chalke.

'Banjaxed him in the last round. Just as well. The cack-handed bastard had me on points. Bloody southpaws. I couldn't get my left hook working. You should come and see a fight some time, guv. We've even got women boxing now.'

Chalke shuddered. 'Not my thing, sergeant, but the commander's right. You're not in a fit state to give evidence.'

'That's okay – I'm not being called. My bloke copped a plea. And me in my best whistle, too.'

'Sorry?'

'Suit. My best suit.'

If that was Leyden's best suit, God help the others, thought Chalke.

'Are you going back to Greenwich?'

'Yes, ma'am.'

'I'll give you a lift but first I need a drink and a cigarette – not necessarily in that order.' Patsy checked her mobile phone. One missed call. She hit the return call button. 'DCI Chalke. I've been in court… Say that again… Where's the body? On my way.'

Barely one week into her new job, still trying to get to grips with a new team, a new set-up and a new part of London – and now this.

She closed her phone. 'After a drink and that fag.'

Muriel Figgens plucked at her coat, an angry, black-clad sparrow of a woman, sitting to attention in the back of the funeral car. 'I still can't believe your father could go like that.'

'Leave it, Mum. Dad's dead. Move on.'

Muriel's daughters sat either side; her three granddaughters in the row in front. There was room for the sons-in-law in the big Ford Dorchester but Muriel had made them drive themselves – and warned them to stay sober to take the women home after the wake.

'Just think of the insurance money, Mum.'

'Puh.' All the money in the world couldn't assuage her resentment. To be married for fifty-two years – and then for him to die like that!

They were approaching Hither Green cemetery. Stan had always said he wanted to be buried here.

Payback time.

The hearse in front slowed. Panic engulfed Muriel.

'This isn't it,' she shouted. 'We're not stopping here. We're going to Falconwood Crem.'

The funeral car came to a halt behind the hearse.

'I told you, it's the wrong place,' repeated Muriel.

'It's all right, Mrs Figgens,' called the driver. 'We've just stopped to let a cortège pull in.'

Muriel sighed in relief then she flung open the car door and ran up to the hearse.

'Look, you bad bastard,' she shouted at her husband's coffin. '*This* is where you'd've been buried if you'd kept it in your trousers. Look. Look.'

She pointed at the cemetery, rapping on the glass side of the hearse as if to gain her dead husband's attention. Her daughters hurried up to try to calm her.

'What was that about?' asked the driver as Muriel was led back to the car.

'You never knew Stan Figgens?' asked the funeral director Herbie Bell. 'Owned the fishmonger's in Eltham. Great one for the horses and the women.'

'He must have blown it all, judging by this shitty little send off.'

'That's where you're wrong, my son.' Bell brushed dandruff off the shoulders of his black overcoat. 'Couple of weeks ago, Stan got a Yankee up at Ascot and went off celebrating with some dolly bird. Trouble was, Stan was seventy-three and needed a bit of help. He took one Viagra too many. Instead of coming, he went, so to speak.'

'At least he died with a smile on his face.'

'Yeah, but the widow's pissed off because everyone's laughing at her. She's getting her revenge by burning him on the cheap.'

The basic £1,355 funeral plus hire of one limo at £170. Any cheaper and they would have had to put Stan on a handcart and wheel him to the crematorium.

The hearse pulled in through the gates of Falconwood cemetery. The chapel was full. Stan had been popular with everyone – except Muriel. The coffin was borne to the catafalque. Bell escorted Stan's widow and his daughters to their place in the front row, bowed solemnly – and left for a cigarette.

He was on his second roll-up when he heard the opening bars of 'Mairzy Doates' – Stan's choice of recessional music. It was Bell's cue to accompany Muriel to view the floral tributes.

Muriel barely glanced at them. The only card she bothered to read was attached to a fish formed from blue irises and yellow chrysanthemums. Her eyes hardened.

'Let's get on with it,' she said.

'Would your daughters like to accompany you?' asked Bell.

'Wouldn't have thought so.'

'Right.' Bell went to take the widow's arm then thought better of it. He led the way past the carefully tended flower borders around to the back of the chapel and into the committal room.

'If you look through these glass panels, Mrs Figgens, you'll see your husband's coffin being charged into the cremator.'

'That oven-like thing?'

'Yes.'

On cue, an attendant appeared manoeuvring a metal bier carrying the coffin. A second attendant slid up the metal door of the cremator. A red glow pulsed out. Once the bier was aligned, the men slid the coffin into the cremator and closed the door.

Muriel continued to stare, her arms folded, until she demanded, 'Is that it? That's all there is?'

'That's it.' Bell nodded solemnly. 'Have you given any thought to what you're going to do with the ashes?'

'I'm putting them into an hourglass so I can turn the sod over whenever I feel like it.'

Bell didn't think Muriel was joking.

On the way back to the car, Muriel asked, 'Why didn't the Dim Reaper do the funeral himself? He's known Stan for years.'

The Dim Reaper was the nickname for Dave Shine, who owned the funeral parlour, and seven others across south-east London.

'Mr Shine spends most of his time in Spain nowadays.'

'That may be so, but one of my daughters saw him in Eltham a few days ago.'

'Mr Shine doesn't have much to do with the day-to-day running,' said Bell, who himself had been wondering why the Dim

Reaper hadn't been in touch for a while. Not that Bell minded. Things ticked along very nicely without him.

'He used to be a right villain,' continued Muriel, dripping with bile. 'He could be as nice as pie to your face but you never knew what was going on in his head. I remember when he was starting out and he thought Charlie Pearce in Charlton had deliberately undercut him.'

'What happened?'

'He only forced Charlie's hearse off the road, didn't he?' Muriel clutched her handbag tightly to her body. 'And there was a coffin in there. Didn't do to cross Dave Shine.'

Bell was relieved not to be invited into the Downham Tavern where the wake was being held. Word was that Stan had left £1,000 to each to his girlfriends. There were going to be fireworks – especially when Muriel discovered that her closest friend was one of the recipients.

Bell and the driver were the first to arrive back at the funeral parlour in Lee Green, the hearse having gone to the Sydenham branch for a funeral next morning. They parked in the yard at the rear. Bell unlocked the back door. Their receptionist had the morning off to go to hospital so the offices were empty. Phone calls were being automatically patched through to another branch. Bell walked through to the front door to collect the post, thinking of Stan Figgens – a small wiry man in a straw boater and blue-striped apron, a twinkle in his eye – always with a line of chat for the ladies.

Muriel was going to go mental when she heard about the bequests. Stan was taking the piss from beyond the grave – or, in his case, the flames.

Bell pushed open the door to his office.

A silver-haired man in a dark suit was sitting behind the ancient wooden desk. He appeared to be asleep, his head resting on his chest.

It took Bell a few seconds to realise he was staring at the body of Stan Figgens.

And a few more seconds to think that if Stan was here – who was in the oven?

Herbie Bell reached for his whisky flask.

DC Carl Cochrane glanced at his notes. 'Stanley Arthur Figgens. Died a week last Saturday and was due to be cremated at Falconwood at 10.30 this morning.'

'Has anyone moved the body?' asked Chalke.

'No, ma'am. The undertaker took one look and did a runner,' replied Cochrane, a sandy-haired Scot with a permanent scowl.

Not surprising, thought Chalke, as she looked at Figgens.

Bell's office was crowded with photographers, fingerprint specialists and scenes of crime officers in their white hooded overalls and lilac gloves. Chalke felt at home.

'And someone's been cremated in Figgens's place?'

'Looks like it. The crem people say they can see bones in the ash but the oven needs to cool down before we can get at them. Uniforms are securing the site.'

The funeral parlour was larger than it appeared from the outside. The public areas consisted of a reception area, coffin showroom and chapel of rest, while behind the scenes there was a wash and dress room, the embalming room and the workshop where various coffins stood against the wall. Chalke ended her tour in the cold room where a large cabinet with metal doors held three bodies awaiting funerals.

'Let's talk to the funeral director,' Chalke said to Leyden.

Leyden was surprised to be included. He'd first met his new boss when she'd arrived in Greenwich a week last Monday, but since then he'd been pounding the pavements on a pub stabbing that was going nowhere.

Chalke had been friendly enough in the wine bar near the Old Bailey but that was because she'd wanted to talk about the Greenwich squad. Leyden wasn't prepared to discuss his mates with the new guv'nor, and had been politely uninformative. Good to know she hadn't held it against him.

They found Herbie Bell in the yard, still in his frock coat, high wing collar and grey-striped dress trousers, screwing shut a hip flask.

'DCI Chalke, Homicide and Serious Crime Command,' said Patsy. 'And this is DS Leyden.'

Bell found he was looking at a beautiful woman in her thirties; expensive business suit, good legs, high cheek bones, chestnut hair well cut. A woman who stood out in a crowd; perhaps a high-flying business executive or TV news reader.

In contrast, with Leyden what you saw was what you got – a burly street fighter with a battered face and a number-one haircut, bristling with attitude.

'Is it possible you could have put the wrong body in the coffin?' asked Chalke.

'No way,' replied Bell.

'Why not?'

'When someone dies, a doctor has to certify death before the body can be released to a funeral director. A second doctor re-examines the body at the funeral parlour. Every corpse is logged and an identification tag attached to the ankle. The ID travels with the body at all times. It's impossible to cremate the wrong body.'

'Impossible?'

'There's always the exception to prove the rule, but –'

'What happens to the body when it's here?'

'It's kept at a constant temperature of five degrees centigrade. The body will be embalmed a couple of days before the funeral.'

'Are all corpses embalmed?' asked Leyden.

'They'd whiff if they weren't,' said Bell. 'Anyway, they need to be embalmed if the family wants to view the corpse.'

'Did Stan Figgens's family view his body?'

'The widow didn't. It was the daughters who brought his

clothes. The coffin was sealed last thing yesterday afternoon.'

'How do you dress a corpse with rigor mortis?' asked Leyden.

'Rigor mortis wears off after two or three days.'

'I didn't know that,' said Leyden. Nor did Chalke – though she didn't admit it.

'How was the coffin sealed?' she asked.

'I'll show you.' Bell walked back into the workshop. 'This is the sort of coffin Stan had. Chipboard with a maple veneer, taffeta lining and three plastic handles either side. The lid's secured by four screws.' Bell held up a 2-inch screw. 'Known as a plume screw. Looks metal but it's plastic.'

'Where was the coffin last night?'

'On a bier in the cool room.'

'Who has keys to this place?'

'I do. The receptionist. One of the FSOs might take the spare key if they've an early start.'

'FSOs?'

'Funeral service operatives.'

'Who runs the business?' asked Chalke, wondering why the world was so full of acronyms.

'Bloke called Dave Shine. I'm the senior FD.'

'Where's Mr Shine now?'

'He came back to Britain about ten days ago but I've not seen him since lunchtime Monday. He called in for half an hour. Nothing special.'

'What time did you arrive this morning?' asked Chalke.

'About eight. The drivers and bearers got here just after.'

'And the coffin was exactly as you left it?'

'I think so. I didn't look closely. It had Stan's nameplate on it.'

'Did the coffin feel different when you put it in the hearse? Was it lighter or heavier than yesterday?'

Bell shook his head, releasing a shower of dandruff. 'The bearers didn't notice anything.'

'Where's the widow?'

'At the wake in the Downham Tavern.'

'Go and talk to her, sergeant,' Chalke ordered Leyden.

'Did you know the Downham Tavern used to have the longest bar of any pub in England?' asked Leyden.

'Fancy that.'

'It's shorter now.'

'Then you won't have any trouble finding Muriel Figgens, will you?'

Bobby Leyden looked around the crowded back room of the pub until his eye settled on a black-clad, angry woman holding court.

'Mrs Figgens. I'm DS Leyden. May I have a word in private?'

'Why?' She was instantly alert, spoiling for a fight.

'It's regarding your husband.'

'What's that bleeder done now? Sold my own house behind me back?' Her lips contracted into a bloodless line. 'Leaving money to those trollops. I'll fight it, that's what I'll do. I'll fight it.'

Leyden didn't have a clue what she was talking about.

'May we talk in private?'

'Whatever you have to say, say it here,' said the widow.

'I'm afraid I have some bad news.'

Muriel gave a mocking laugh. 'That'll be a change, won't it? Bad news, dearie? I've had nothing but bad news since I married that worthless bastard. What is it?'

The room had fallen silent; the mourners straining to hear what was happening. 'It's your husband Stanley Arthur Figgens –'

'I know his bleeding name.' Muriel took a gulp from her gin and tonic. 'We're seeing him off, ain't we? And not a moment too soon.'

'That's just it, Mrs Figgens. He's not gone, exactly.'

'What do you mean, not gone? You're having a laugh, ain't you, son? I saw the coffin go into that oven with my own eyes.'

'Your husband wasn't in it.'

'Jesus Christ!' Muriel Figgens slammed down her glass to stare at Leyden. 'But he is dead? Tell me he's dead.'

'He's dead all right but he wasn't in the coffin. We believe there may have been another body in there.'

'So where's Stan now?'

'Back at the undertaker's.'

Muriel Figgens emptied her gin and tonic in one. 'I'll tell you something now – I'm not going through that again.'

'Mrs Figgens –'

'And I can tell you something else – if that wasn't Stan, I want my sodding money back.'

Patsy Chalke was not in good humour. Having missed the turn-off to Falconwood Crematorium, she'd got stuck on Rochester Way until the Danson Interchange and then been forced to crawl back through heavy traffic on busy suburban roads. She hated wasting time.

She hoped the crematorium manager would turn out to be a shitty little jobsworth so she could work out her frustrations but Deirdre Stone was large and jolly – like so many who spent their time dealing with the dead. Coroners' officers were the best joke tellers in the Job. Perhaps laughter was their way of coping.

'You wouldn't believe the paperwork I'll have now,' said Deirdre Stone cheerfully. 'And we're already the busiest crematorium in the country.'

'In that case, why isn't there a better road link?' demanded Chalke, determined not to succumb to Deirdre's motherly charms without a struggle.

'There are clear directions on our website.'

'I didn't have time to look at your website.'

Chalke didn't mention that she had failed to program her satnav – again. According to that gadget, she was currently somewhere west of Fishguard. She'd have to get round to reading the instructions – some day.

'Take me through what happened at the funeral,' she said brusquely.

'I'll show you.'

Chalke followed Deirdre into a light, airy chapel. Two of the four walls were made of glass. The catafalque was surrounded by lovat-green curtains.

'You must understand that every coffin arriving here is sealed and accompanied by an authority card which stays with the body every step of the way,' began Deirdre.

'Okay.'

'This is the smaller of our two chapels. This morning was a little unusual because the widow asked to see the coffin being charged into the cremator.'

'I didn't know you could do that.'

'Members of some religions – Hindus for example – need to witness the moment.'

Deirdre escorted Chalke to the committal room sandwiched between the two chapels.

'The catafalques are just the other side of those soundproof doors,' explained Deirdre. 'Our attendants monitor the service on CCTV, then once the congregation's left, they go in, place the coffin on a bier and wheel it in here. If a cremator's free, the coffin's disposed of immediately. If not, by law it has to be cremated within twenty-four hours.'

She led Chalke into a side room containing a bank of five blue cremators with stainless steel doors.

'Which one should Stan have been in?' asked Chalke.

'Bottom right.'

Chalke peered through the small window at the intense red glow.

'Once the ashes have cooled, they're raked out and put in a

cremulator where the larger bones like the tibia and fibula are ground into a fine ash,' continued Deirdre.

'Do the jaw and teeth survive?' asked Chalke.

'Not a chance. It gets up to 850 degrees centigrade in there. At that temperature all the DNA's destroyed as well.

'Any chance of fillings or anything like that being left?' Chalke was thinking of a bullet.

'Metal melts. We run a magnet through the ash to find things like false hips.' Deirdre pointed to a collection of dull metal objects in a bucket. 'We recycle as much as possible.'

Chalke's mobile phone rang. 'Yes, Sergeant.'

'I'm back at the undertaker's, ma'am,' said Leyden. 'Two things. The SOCOs have found fibres in the cool room cabinet that could have come from Stan's suit.'

'Right.'

'And Bell's just coughed that Dave Shine keeps a bird on the side. He comes back to London to get his leg over.'

'The Dim Reaper's doing well for himself,' observed Leyden gazing up at the sand-coloured block of modern flats overlooking the river Thames. 'Not a bad drum.'

'Drum?'

'Drum and bass. Place.'

'Why don't you speak English?'

'It is English where I grew up.' Leyden bit into the battered sausage he'd bought at the local chippie.

'Where was that?' Chalke knew that she needed to learn more about her squad but her own secretive nature made it difficult. She hoped that if she wasn't curious about others, then they wouldn't be curious about her.

It never worked.

'Ferrier estate in Kidbrooke,' said Leyden, his mouth full.

'I've heard of the Ferrier.'

'Everyone's heard of the Ferrier,' said Leyden.

The Ferrier was an infamous sink estate a few miles away which was shortly to be knocked down by Greenwich Council. Not before time, said those who lived there.

The early cloud had cleared, leaving a glorious late summer afternoon, the sun turning the Thames blue. In the distance the skyscrapers of Canary Wharf rose from the Isle of Dogs. To their right, an aircraft climbed out of City airport.

Chalke flicked the butt of her lunch into the Thames. 'How did Mrs Figgens take the news about her husband?'

'She got the petrol that he wasn't toast,' replied Leyden, brushing crumbs off his lapels.

'I haven't a clue what you're on about.'

'Mrs Muriel Figgens found the idea that her husband hadn't been cremated distressing.'

Chalke grinned. 'Let's go and talk to the girlfriend. Just hope she speaks English – unlike some around here.'

Leyden refused to rise to the bait. As they walked towards the block of flats he observed, 'There must be money in the death business. I wouldn't mind living here.'

Chalke made a doubtful noise. 'Wouldn't kill for it.'

'It's better than my shoe box.'

When would she learn to keep her mouth shut? Just because she lived in a penthouse.

Lucymar Varenos was a 23-year-old Venezuelan with sallow skin and the sort of pinched face that went with a drug problem. She wore shorts and a T-shirt, a get-up which accentuated her bony frame.

There was starved chic and there was malnourished, thought Chalke. This girl belonged on an Oxfam poster.

Definitely more atrophy than trophy.

The third-floor apartment was filled with cheap contemporary furniture. A flat-screen TV filled most of one wall.

Chalke perched on the mock leather sofa under posters of Caribbean beaches while Leyden prowled next to the picture window looking downriver towards the old Royal Naval College – now Greenwich University.

'You speak English?'

'Some.'

'Is this your apartment?'

'*Si*. I live here.' The girl's dark eyes stayed fixed on the floor.

'Do you own it?'

'It belongs to Mr Shine.'

'When did you last see him?'

Lucymar gave an elaborate shrug. Chalke fixed the girl with a hard stare. 'Think.'

Forget the *good cop, bad cop* routine. If this girl was going to be a pain, she'd get the *two pissed-off cops* routine.

'Maybe yesterday.'

Chalke held out her hand. 'Your passport.'

Lucymar's face tightened. 'I don't know where it is.'

'If you can't show me your passport, then I'll have to assume you're an illegal immigrant. You want to spend the night in a detention centre?'

Lucymar stalked off to the bedroom.

'Do Venezuelans need visas?' Chalke whispered to Leyden.

'Not if they're staying less than six months and not working or studying.'

'How do you know that?'

'Doesn't everyone?'

Lucymar returned. Inspecting her passport, Chalke saw that the girl had first entered Britain twelve months ago. Last Christmas she'd gone home to Caracas, returning in January. It was now September. She had overstayed by two months.

'You don't mind if we have a look around, do you?'

Lucymar's eyes flashed with anger but she nodded meekly.

Chalke didn't have a clue what she was looking for, but something might turn up. She was disappointed. The flat was practically sterile. There were no smells, even. No scents of polish or coffee, no stale sweat or cat's piss.

The bedroom was spotless. It put Chalke's to shame. She told herself she must tidy up when she got home. Make the bed, hang up the clothes she'd strewn everywhere, put her dirty underwear in the laundry basket. Then again… life was too short.

She checked the bedside drawers. No sign of Shine's passport or wallet. A photograph on the bedside table showed a man in a black shirt, open to reveal a gold medallion, leaning on the bonnet of a silver BMW Series 6 coupé. The man, in his early forties, had dark swept-back hair and a heavy jaw.

Chalke took the photo into the living room. 'Is this Dave Shine?'

'Yes. That's his car. He's very proud of it. He keeps it in the garage here.' Lucymar was sitting at the table, her left foot pumping up and down.

'What time did you last see him yesterday?'

'Maybe midday. He went to see someone in the West End. I don't know who.'

'How did he get up to London?' Chalke handed Leyden the photograph.

'He drove. He says public transport is for people who haven't made it.'

'What was he wearing?'

'He always wears black. Like in the photo.'

'Did you know that Mr Shine has another house in Blackheath?'

'That's for his wife. He doesn't often come to London when she's here.'

I bet he doesn't, thought Chalke. 'How did you two meet?'

In a bar on the Costa del Sol where she was working, said Lucymar. When Shine found out that she was saving to come to Britain to learn English, he suggested that she enrol at one of Greenwich's language schools. He'd buy her a flat nearby. She could live there. It suited them both.

'What happened to your studies?'

'Dave wants me here when he's in London.'

'And when he's in Spain?'

'Then it's different.' Lucymar gave a secret smile.

'As soon as you hear from Dave, ask him to phone me.' Patsy Chalke handed the girl her card. She took it unwillingly.

Back in the corridor, Leyden made a dart for the closing lift door.

'I was going to take the stairs,' said Chalke.

'Old Chinese proverb. Never run when you can walk, never walk when you can stand, never stand when you can sit, never sit when you can lie.'

'Okay, we can check that the Dim Reaper's Beamer's not in the car park,' said Chalke, as if to justify taking the lift. 'Just in case.'

They rode down to the basement. The lift opened onto a dusty concrete lobby leading to the underground car park. It was chilly, damp and badly lit. They walked along the bays, checking the cars. The last bay was occupied by Dave Shine's BMW coupé.

'He came back,' said Leyden. 'Why didn't he go up to the flat?'

'Who says he didn't?' countered Chalke. 'Lucymar never once asked why we were asking her questions.'

The car doors were locked. Leyden tried the boot. It too was locked. But now that he looked closely he saw that there was a tiny smear on the lip.

'Blood?' murmured Leyden.

'Blood,' agreed Chalke.

*

Patsy Chalke's office looked over the police station yard towards the back of Gloucester Circus. Two centuries ago, the Circus had been planned as an oval with sweeping crescents enclosing a formal garden. Then the architect Michael Searles had run out of money, leaving the last third a hotchpotch of buildings that had been flattened by a V1 rocket. After the war, first council flats and then the police station had been built on the bomb site. Now residents of Gloucester Circus either lived in the flats facing Georgian houses or in Georgian houses looking out at the flats. Neither was perfect, thought Patsy.

Her bare office depressed her more than the view. Next door, her immediate superior Detective Chief Superintendent Des Weaver had photos of his wife and daughter on his desk, commendations around the walls and cacti along the window ledge.

The only personal touches in her office were a wooden model of a man with jointed limbs and a sheep in wellington boots. On the sheep was written, *Smile. It confuses people.*

Both were presents from former lovers. The one who'd given her the model man had told her, 'Put him in whatever position reflects your mood, then I'll know where I stand.'

Patsy had arranged the wooden arms in surrender.

After the Terry Rich incident, she'd been transferred to the south-east task force of Homicide and Serious Crime Command, Specialist Crime Directorate, based in Greenwich. She hadn't been surprised. Greenwich was the traditional dumping ground for coppers who cocked up or gave trouble. Those who did not conform.

Chalke had found a depleted squad and a backlog of unsolved cases, including a fatal stabbing during a brawl outside a Woolwich pub – the case Leyden had been working on. A second murder involved the mugging of a pensioner that had gone wrong. Detectives knew the killer's identity. Proving it was another matter.

In addition, a series of brutal post office raids was grabbing local headlines while police intelligence indicated that Greenwich was the terminus for a people-smuggling racket.

Chalke needed the Stan Figgens mystery like a hole in the head.

She pressed the bridge of her nose between thumb and forefinger and asked Des Weaver, 'Any chance of drafting in a few extra bodies?'

'No chance. The budget's all gone on the war on terror.'

'Begley could request more resources.'

Weaver, grey haired, broad-shouldered, florid and avuncular, gave Chalke a knowing look. 'You don't think Alison's going to rattle cages for us, do you?'

'But we've a DI on long-term sick leave and two sergeants on secondment.'

'More glory for the few,' said Weaver.

While others were posted here to get them out of the way, Des Weaver had spent his entire career in south-east London. Never mind how much the brass had tried to move him to other duties, other areas, Weaver had always managed to wangle his way back. As a result there was nothing he didn't know about local villains.

He could have retired twelve months ago, after his thirty years – the optimum length of service to get the maximum pension – but he'd stayed on. He claimed he didn't fancy working for a security company, he didn't play golf and his wife Brenda didn't want him under her feet at home. Chalke suspected that he was waiting until his only daughter – on whom he doted – qualified as a doctor. Young Annie Weaver didn't have a student loan around her neck. Instead she drove a newish VW Golf and spent her vacations in Thailand.

'How are you getting on with Bobby Leyden?' asked Weaver.

'Fine – when I can understand what he's saying.'

Weaver chuckled. 'Bobby's got his *sarf* London act off to a tee. He's much sharper than he lets on.'

'I'll remember that. Shall we run over today?' she asked. 'See where we're going?'

'Of course. Get Leyden in if you like. A bit of responsibility might get him thinking about his inspector's exams.'

'Okay.'

Chalke walked along the corridor into the Incident Room filled with rows of metal desks, each with a phone and a computer monitor. The monitors not being used had blue screensavers bearing the Met motto – 'Working Together for a Safer London'. The blinds were down against the late afternoon sun, making the atmosphere in the room even heavier than usual, with its smells of stale sandwiches, paper, warm dust, and deodorant. The small offices of the statement reader and action allocator lay to one side.

Chalke paused in front of the whiteboard, absorbing the ongoing lines of inquiry. She would never be Weaver's equal as a thief-taker, but she did have a photographic memory.

Leyden was putting down the phone.

'No reply from Dave Shine's number in Spain,' he told her. 'I'll try again later.'

'Come into my office. Mr Weaver and I are about to review the day's events.'

Leyden followed her, looking as if he suspected he was walking into a trap. He took the small chair against the wall. Weaver entered seconds later.

'How's it going, Bobby?'

'Fine, thank you, sir.'

'Right. It's fair to say that at the moment we're treating the case as a suspicious death.' Chalke sat behind her desk. 'Are we certain that it's a human body that's been cremated? It wasn't a dog or some other animal in the coffin?'

'The doc reckons that it was a man, from what's left of the pelvis,' said Leyden. 'We'll know more tomorrow when a forensic anthropologist examines the remains. There's definitely amalgam from teeth fillings and something that looks like a belt buckle.'

'No bullet?'

'Not so far, ma'am.'

'Okay.' Chalke steepled her fingers. 'So, someone broke into the funeral parlour between six last night and eight this morning with the body of an unknown male. They opened Stan's coffin, took out *his* body, hid it in the cool room and put the other body in the coffin. Then, between 9.30 a.m. and midday, while Bell was at the crem, they returned to position Stan's body behind the desk. Someone went to a lot of trouble. Why?'

'Also, who's been cremated?' asked Weaver, looking at the mystery from the other end.

'We've checked mortuaries, hospitals and undertakers right across London and the south-east,' reported Leyden. 'No one's missing a body.'

'Bell said the funeral parlour was unoccupied only because the receptionist had taken the morning off. That suggests inside information,' said Chalke.

'Maybe chummie didn't leave and return this morning,' suggested Weaver. 'Maybe he was hiding in the cool room with Stan all the time.'

'Bit gruesome.'

'Not if you're used to working with dead bodies.'

'Like Dave Shine,' said Chalke, trying to manipulate her wooden man to imitate Rodin's *The Thinker*. So far she'd only succeeded in making him look as if he was on the lavatory.

Leyden asked Weaver. 'Have you had any dealings with Shine, sir?'

'And the rest. I first nicked him in the early nineties. He took it personally. The man's got the memory of an elephant – a rogue elephant. Never forgets, never forgives. Six foot of muscle on a short fuse. Worked as an enforcer for the Jolly crime family for a while. For some reason, Shine always wanted to be an undertaker. When a funeral director in Eltham retired some time back, Dave acquired his two shops. Now he's got eight. Word has it he got the nickname the Dim Reaper when he tortured some Albanian who'd upset the Jolly family. He'd got this guy strung up with electrodes clamped to his balls. Shine couldn't understand how the Albanian could stand the pain. In the end Shine got so angry that he beat the bloke to death. Only then did someone point out that he'd forgotten to switch on the power.'

'Charming,' said Chalke.

'His wife Crystal is a golf fanatic. About three years ago, they bought a villa near a golf course outside Alicante. No children.'

'How do you rate him, sir?' asked Leyden. 'Killer or victim?'

'Killer, every time,' replied Weaver. 'But we do need to know who he's topped.'

Chalke's phone rang. She listened. 'Thank you. Anything else let me know.' She replaced the phone. 'That was blood on Shine's Beamer,' she told Leyden. 'There's more in the boot. The car's on its way to the labs.'

'We need to check Shine's associates, see if they can provide a lead as to who was in the coffin,' said Weaver.

'Who normally acts as statement reader in a major inquiry here?' asked Chalke.

The statement reader searched for the lie in the paper. He sat undisturbed reading every word of every statement from every witness. Boring as hell – but that was the way murders were solved. And you didn't have to go out in the cold.

'The Eternal Flame,' said Leyden.

'He likes the shiny bum jobs,' agreed Weaver. 'And he's good.'

'Who're we talking about?' asked Chalke.

'Les Blunt. The guy who looks like Billy Bunter without the glasses,' explained Leyden. 'The Eternal Flame. Never goes out.'

Weaver glanced up at the wall clock. 'I reckon that's my lot for the day. Anyone fancy one in the Tolly Shop?'

'I'll join you, sir,' said Leyden. 'I'll just try Crystal Shine one more time.'

This was a chance for Chalke to get to know her team better but she didn't like beer and wasn't that keen on pubs. Anyway, she'd had enough for one day.

'Coming, Patsy?' asked Weaver.

'I'm afraid I've arranged to see my sister,' she lied. 'Another night.'

Leyden tried the number in Spain. This time he was in luck. Crystal Shine had just returned from the golf course, but she couldn't talk. She needed a shower and then she had to dress to go out. She wasn't particularly concerned that her husband hadn't been seen for a few days. Dave was like a bad penny. He'd turn up. She didn't know of any enemies nor had she any idea what he did when he was in London. Dave had no money worries, as far as she knew. She couldn't think where he could be. She had to go. She wasn't going to miss a night out for bloody Dave.

Leyden got to the pub to find Weaver in the garden with Carl Cochrane and Les Blunt.

The pub's real name was the Richard the First but old hands knew it as the Tolly Shop. According to Weaver, it had once been owned by the Tolly Cobbold brewery when the small bar had been the off-licence – hence the name Tolly Shop. Weaver liked it because it had no TV, no jukebox and no fruit machine. A good old-fashioned boozer, he called it.

But no sooner had Weaver handed Leyden a pint of lager than his phone rang. Weaver moved away to take the call. He returned looking solemn.

'Problems, sir?'

'My daughter's bringing her new bloke for supper and I'm under commander's orders to get home soon and sober.'

'One before you go?'

'Better not. I'll catch up tomorrow.' Weaver stood, drained his glass in one and slouched away.

'You don't think of the guv'nor being under the thumb,' commented Cochrane.

'He's doing it for his daughter,' explained Blunt. 'If you made more of an effort at home, you wouldn't be on wife number four.'

'Number three,' corrected Cochrane. 'It's not my fault I marry bloody-minded old battle-axes.'

'Whose fault is it, then?'

'They change, you know,' muttered Cochrane darkly.

Tell me about it, thought Leyden.

'Hey, Bobby, what does Karen think about you coming home with a face like a well-smacked arse?' asked Blunt.

'Don't think she notices,' said Leyden in a neutral voice.

'Women get like that,' said Cochrane. 'I rest my case.'

'Well, while you're resting your case, Carlo, you can shift your arse and get us a drink. It's your round.'

Leyden and Blunt stared in silence at Cochrane, still nursing the last of his lager.

'No, it's not.'

'Yes, it is,' said Blunt. 'I got one. The guv'nor got one.'

'And I bought you two pints last night when you said you'd no money on you,' remembered Leyden.

'I've not had a chance to go to a hole in the wall.'

'The pub takes plastic, Carlo,' prompted Leyden.

'Pints or halves?'

'Fuck off and make sure it's Stella and not that Foster's shit.'

Cochrane scowled and headed inside. Watching him leave, Leyden noticed how other drinkers had given their table a wide berth. Was it was that obvious they were coppers?

'Do you think he'll do a runner?' asked Blunt.

'Wouldn't dare. He knows I'd hunt him down.'

'He's getting worse. He never used to be this tight.'

'Oh, I don't know.' Leyden remembered Blunt had landed the statement reader's job. 'Who's becoming the station cat, then?'

'You don't have to walk off the shoe leather to be a decent copper.'

'Bollocks. You're just a shiny-arsed flub.'

'Just because your lips ache when you read.'

It was a well-worn argument between the two. The idea of being stuck in a small office, undisturbed, day after day, reading statement after statement, was purgatory to Leyden. He enjoyed being out on the streets.

Blunt – five years older and two stone heavier – was keener to take life easy.

'You're well in with the new skipper.' Having enjoyed the spat, Blunt moved on to more important matters. Like all desk-bound coppers, he was finely tuned into office politics; tracking who was in and who was out, who was a rising star, who was going to leave a crater when they crash-landed.

'I bumped into her at the Bailey this morning,' said Leyden. 'She was really decent about last night's fight – unlike Begley.'

Blunt looked towards the doorway. 'He has done a runner, you know.'

But even as he spoke, Cochrane emerged, three pints in his hands.

'Christ. Look at that! Well done, Carlo.'

Cochrane sat down. He did not appear very happy.

'I tell you who's looking good,' said Blunt, taking a pull at his lager. 'Sue Bigtits.'

'Don't let Begley hear you say that. Not only is Sue Jones a woman but she's a black woman.' Leyden put on his Begley voice. 'It's officers like you, DS Blunt, who give the Metropolitan Police its reputation for institutionalised racism.'

'Begley's a tosshead who couldn't catch a tea leaf if he was running down a street bollock-naked with an old lady's handbag, hollering, look at me,' said Blunt.

'No one's arguing with that, but you're right – Sue is looking good,' said Leyden. 'Perhaps she's got a new bloke.'

'Got to be better than that Darren.'

The squad were fond of their administrative assistant. Sue Jones was a bubbly black girl in her late twenties with an infectious giggle and an incongruous West Country burr. She had made herself indispensable: fetching sandwiches, buying presents and flowers for wives and girlfriends, helping book holidays, and – not least – resolving IT problems.

In return, they were fiercely protective of her. And, behind her back, called her Sue Bigtits.

Her last bloke, Darren, had been a wastrel who'd made the mistake of treating Sue like dirt in front of Leyden. The next day, Leyden had stopped by the building site where Darren worked as a brickie and marked his card. Darren and Sue had split up soon after.

'If Sue Bigtits is looking good, what about Patsy Chalke then?' asked Cochrane.

'Don't even dream, mate. You're not in her league,' scoffed Blunt.

'Do you know what she did last weekend?' asked Leyden.

'I'm a copper, not a fucking clairvoyant.'

'Went to see Elton John in concert.'

'So? My Moira's been to see Elton John.'

'Not in New York, not for the weekend. And flying business class.'

'Shit!'

'I thought she looked knackered on Monday.'

'I've never flown business class in my life,' said Cochrane.

'You're so fucking mean, Carlo, you'd wing-walk to save money.'

'How do you know she'd been to New York?'

'She mentioned it on the way back from the Bailey. I think she regretted telling me afterwards.'

'Christ! I'd tell everybody,' said Blunt.

'That's the difference between you and Patsy, mate,' said Leyden. 'She's got class. You ain't.'

Patsy Chalke decided to leave her car at the nick and take the Docklands Light Railway home. It was a toss-up which of Greenwich's two stations was closer.

She thought the town centre one was, but then there were steps and a long escalator. On the other hand, if she went for the DLR at the main railway station, she'd have to walk almost the whole length of the platform.

Chalke decided on the town centre, detouring through St Alfege's churchyard, an oasis of tranquillity away from the snarl of traffic. She promised herself that she'd bring sandwiches and a book here for lunch one day – if she ever had time.

She left the DLR at Heron Quays on the Isle of Dogs. It was a short walk to her penthouse flat overlooking the river. The porter bade her a respectful good evening and held the lift. The apartment smelled musty and tired after the day's sunshine. She opened the windows, stripped to her underwear and poured a glass of Bandol. The bottle was less than half full. She must have drunk more than she'd thought last night.

She really must cut back on her drinking. She said the same most nights, usually as she was going to bed. The vow had come early tonight.

She wrapped herself in a silk kimono and went onto the balcony for a cigarette.

Even in her own home, she felt guilty about smoking.

To avoid the Terry Rich trial preying on her mind, she started thinking about Stan Figgens. It would have been nice not to think about work at all but Patsy couldn't help it. Patsy was a worrier, although she hid it well.

She thought of herself as a swan. On the surface all elegance and unruffled plumage, while under the water, out of sight, two huge ugly webbed feet were working like the clappers just to stay in the same place.

It looked as if the Dim Reaper had killed someone and disposed of his victim in such a way as to conceal their identity. Clever. But why had he left Stan Figgens behind Bell's desk? Had he been interrupted? Did he have a warped sense of humour? Was he trying to give Bell a heart attack? It didn't make sense.

Patsy sipped at her wine and tried to relax. From her sixteenth-floor eyrie, she could see all the way downriver, past the O2 Arena, to the Thames Barrier and beyond. Closer, at the entrance to Greenwich Creek, she picked out Lucymar's block.

Poor girl. She'd sold her body and her soul to get to London but she wouldn't last long once the Dim Reaper discovered that she was partying in his absence. Out on the street, visa expired, no money, drug habit to fund. Only one way – down. She'd find a pimp or a pimp would find her. Pimps and drugs went together like flies and shit.

Patsy decided to call Lucymar.

'Hello.' The girl answered on the third ring. She sounded flat and tired. There was a TV on in the background. Patsy found she didn't know what to say.

'Hi, Lucymar. It's Patsy Chalke. I was just wondering how you were.'

'I'm okay.'

If Patsy had binoculars, she'd be able to see in the windows of Lucymar's apartment. She didn't tell the girl that.

'Not heard from Dave?'

'No.'

'Is this normal for him when he's in London?'

'No. He's only ever stayed away for one night before.'

'Has Dave been having business problems? Anything been worrying him?'

Lucymar was slow to reply. 'There was a phone call a day or two after he arrived,' she said. 'From Cyprus. He was quiet for a while then he cheered up.'

'How do you know the call came from Cyprus?'

'Because Dave asked where this man was calling from. Then Dave said, "North Cyprus! Christ! You sound as if you're just down the road."'

'What did they talk about?'

'I don't know. Dave took the phone into the bedroom.'

Chalke made a note to trace the call. 'When Dave gets back, ask him to call me. You've got my mobile number.'

She rang off. The sun was beginning to set and the evening stretched ahead. Now she was home, she felt restless. She wished she'd gone for that drink with Weaver. She needed to shake herself out of her torpor. There was a swimming pool and gym in the basement. She'd go and work off the tensions of the day – and stop her bum getting bigger.

Before she left, she checked her mobile phone.

It was dark by the time Patsy returned, glowing and virtuous. She poured herself another large glass of wine, telling herself that she'd earned it. She took the drink back onto the balcony and lit a cigarette. She enjoyed London at night, the million pinpricks of light, the orange reflections on the river; the laser beam from Greenwich Observatory along the line of the meridian. A river disco boat could be heard rounding Limehouse Reach.

She finished off the Bandol, opened another bottle and put her meal in the microwave. Eastern spiced chicken with apricots and bulgar wheat, courtesy of M&S. Sometimes she thought she kept their ready-cooked foods department in business. She was glad she had shares in the store.

It was almost eleven when she took the last of the wine and the new Anita Shreve novel to bed.

She had made herself comfortable with Joni Mitchell on the Be-oSound when her mobile rang. She checked the number.

'What time do you call this?' she asked.

'Sorry. Difficult to get away. I had to say that I was –'

'Where are you?' she interrupted.

'Outside.'

'Letting you in now.'

DAY TWO

Thursday

'THANKS FOR COMING in,' said Leyden as a uniformed officer escorted Muriel Figgens and her younger daughter Maureen into the exhibits room.

'Didn't think I had any choice,' sniffed Muriel.

Leyden indicated the clothing laid out on the table. 'This is what Mr Figgens was wearing. Could you confirm that these garments are his?'

'Why?'

'Come on, Mum.' Maureen was embarrassed by her mother's truculence. 'Just do what the bloke asks.'

'You took his clothes to the undertaker's,' retorted Muriel. 'You do it.'

'By the way, do you know of anyone who might have had it in for your husband?' asked Leyden. 'Anyone with a grudge?'

'Only half the bleeding husbands in south London.' Muriel Figgens squinted up at Leyden. 'Those bruises ain't going, are they, son? How'd you get them?'

'Boxing.'

'Oh.' She curled her lip in disappointment. 'Thought some bloke might have given you a hiding.'

'Mum!' Maureen tugged at her mother's sleeve.

Leyden tried to lower the tension. 'Would you like a cup of tea or coffee?'

'Nah. Let's get this over with. I get nervous if I'm in a police station too long.'

'Everything's here,' said Leyden. 'Although it seems he wasn't wearing any underpants.'

'Why would he?' demanded Muriel. 'He was going to his funeral, not a game of strip poker.'

Maureen gave Leyden a sympathetic smile.

'You recognise these items?'

'Yeah, yeah.' Muriel hardly bothered to look.

'Maureen, will you confirm that these are the clothes you took to the funeral director's?' asked Leyden. 'Blue suit bought in Matalan. White shirt, blue tie. Primark.'

'Mum wouldn't let me bring his best. She said it'd be a waste.'

'Black Oxford shoes, black socks. Tie pin.'

'That's his National Federation of Fishmongers tie pin. He was very proud of that.'

'The cufflinks –'

'What cufflinks?'

'These.' Leyden pointed to a pair of cufflinks, shaped in a rough rectangle with the top right hand corner elongated to a point.

'I don't think they're Dad's,' murmured Maureen. 'Are they, Mum?'

'What?'

'These cufflinks.'

'Never seen them before.'

'You're certain you didn't take them to the funeral director's?' asked Leyden.

'Yeah.'

Muriel Figgens turned the cufflinks between her fingers. 'These are gold. No one in their right mind sends gold to the crem.'

Chalke didn't like funeral parlours, didn't like their patina of sanctity or the way they made you want to talk in whispers. Above all, she didn't like the way Herbie Bell had been lying.

Because Bell was not being allowed into the Lee Green parlour, he was running the business from the East Greenwich branch, opposite the site of the old hospital – currently a hole in the ground while developers bickered with the council over the number of affordable homes they had to include.

'Must have been useful being this close to the hospital,' observed Chalke.

'Suppose so.' Bell, in a black jacket and striped trousers, was shorter than Chalke remembered. The dandruff was the same.

'Got in with the mortuary staff there, did you?'

'Dave saw they were looked after.'

'How long have you worked for Dave Shine?'

'About seven years. Dave had just expanded, bought a load of shops and wanted an experienced FD to run them.'

'And it's a going business?'

'Dave's planning to go properly international with a shop on the Costa del Sol and another in Gibraltar.'

'How do you get on with him on a personal level?'

Bell froze. 'Don't, really. He doesn't mix business and pleasure.'

'Do you like him?'

'We have… a professional relationship.'

'You must have formed an opinion.'

'You wouldn't want to get on the wrong side of him.'

Chalke's phone rang. 'Yes, Bobby?' She listened intently. 'Okay.' She asked Bell, 'Who dressed Mr Figgens?'

'Paul Ingrams did most. I helped him put on the jacket and tie.'

'Neither Stan's daughter nor his widow recognised the cufflinks on the corpse. Did anyone else bring clothing?'

'No. Just the daughters.' Bell frowned. 'I don't remember any cufflinks. I think I did up one cuff while Paul did the other. It'll be on the computer.' He tapped at the keyboard with one finger. 'There.'

No mention of cufflinks. Odd.

'Anything else?' asked Bell.

Plenty, sunshine.

'We're not clear who had access to the funeral parlour. You've told us that only you and the receptionist carried keys. Does Dave Shine have one?'

'Of course. It's his business.'

'Anyone else?'

'There'll be a few knocking around the other branches in case anyone needed to get in early.'

'Why didn't you say this yesterday?'

'No one asked me.'

Bell was pissing off Chalke. She was beginning to see him for what he was – a master of dumb insolence. He hadn't volunteered a single fact. Everything had to be extracted.

Her phone rang again. 'Stay there,' she told Bell as she walked outside. 'Yes, Bobby.'

'I thought you should know that the commander's been on.' A heavy lorry churned by. Chalke pressed the phone to her ear to catch what Leyden was saying. 'She wanted to know why you're not at the Bailey.'

'Because I'm investigating an active case.'

'That's what Mr Weaver told her. He reckons Begley's looking for someone to carry the can if Rich walks.'

Chalke sighed. She didn't need to be at the Bailey. She wasn't the senior investigating officer in the Rich case; she was just the one who'd collared him – and the one who was going to get the blame if he was acquitted.

'How does Bell explain his alibi?' asked Leyden.

'I haven't asked him yet. I'm saving the best until last.'

Leyden had been right. Les Blunt was good. He'd found the first lie in the paper in the first hour. Bell frowned impatiently as Chalke returned.

'One last thing. Why did you lie about your movements after work two nights ago?'

The veins in Bell's cheeks darkened. 'I don't know what you're talking about.'

'You said in your statement that you'd spent two hours drinking with Paul Ingrams. He backed you up.'

'So?'

'According to his wife, Ingrams was playing soccer with his son in the garden at 6.30 p.m.'

'This is rubbish.'

Chalke had had a gutful of Bell. His broken veins, his dandruff – and especially his little games. 'There's only one person with the means and opportunity to swap those bodies over – and that's you.'

'Me?' Fear flooded into Bell's rheumy little eyes. 'Honest! Not me, chief inspector.'

It was the first time he had addressed her by rank. It showed he knew he'd gone too far. Chalke regarded him silently.

'Okay,' continued Bell. 'I went for a drink – but not with Paul.'

'Who, then?'

'No one. I just fancied a drink. My missus goes potty if she knows I've stopped for a jar on my tod–'

'Where were you drinking?'

'The Railway in Lewisham. The barman knows me. He'll tell you. I had three pints, whisky chasers.'

'And then you drove home?'

'It's no big deal. I can handle my drink.'

Shorthand for admitting he was an alcoholic, thought Chalke. 'Do you know any of Dave's Shine's friends? Did any come to the shop?'

'Never. I don't think he kept up with many people after he moved to Spain. He's not the easiest of blokes to get on with. To put it mildly.'

Chalke's first task back at the nick was to try to sweet-talk BT liaison into prioritising the trace on the Dim Reaper's Cyprus call. When she'd failed in that, she turned her attention to the overdue study of her squad's personal files. She was thinking they made depressing reading when there was a tap on her door and Weaver entered, looking pleased with himself.

'How are you getting on with the Dim Reaper inquiry?' he asked.

'The blood on Shine's car boot is type O. Shine's AB. It looks if he used the car to transport his victim.'

'Still no motive?'

'No.'

'What if Shine's involved with a Colombian cocaine cartel shipping drugs into Britain in expats' coffins.'

'*What?*'

'Shine regularly sends back coffins containing expats who die in Spain,' explained Weaver. 'He only accompanies them when they contain drugs. He arrived with one ten days ago.'

'How do you know this?' asked Chalke. 'I've not seen it in any intelligence site I can access.'

'SOCA play their cards close to their chest.'

'SOCA!'

When SOCA – the Serious Organised Crime Agency – had been set up, it had been hailed as Britain's FBI, amalgamating the National Crime Squad, the National Criminal Intelligence Service and investigators from Customs and the Home Office's Immigration Service. The idea was to bring together 4,000 experts, give them extra powers and set them loose to make life hell for the Mr Bigs of crime.

Except it hadn't happened.

Two years after its inception, the agency had failed to prosecute a single crime baron. Instead the Home Office had cut its budget, sacking 400 officers. Another 148 had quit or fled back to their forces.

'I've got a mate in their drugs liaison,' explained Weaver almost apologetically. 'He gave me the heads-up.'

'And will SOCA be telling us officially what they know about Shine?'

'Only if they feel they have something to gain.'

Chalke controlled her temper with difficulty.

'Stuff them.' At least she had Weaver on her side – and with his contacts, he was worth twice any SOCA hotshot.

'How come sniffer dogs don't detect the drugs at the airport?' she asked.

'Air-freighted coffins are hermetically sealed and zinc-lined.'

'Is Herbie Bell in on this?'

'Wouldn't have thought so, otherwise Shine wouldn't need to come back.'

Shine's drug trafficking could be the motive they needed, thought Chalke. It would be just like Shine to have killed a rival and then put Stan Figgens behind the desk as a warning to others.

DI Andy Butterfield knocked and put his head around the door. Butterfield, good-looking with a head of thick wavy hair, was the office mannequin, favouring smart blazers and highly polished shoes – the antithesis of Leyden.

Butterfield was nominally Chalke's number two in the ab-sence of the senior DI but she had already decided that he was a waste of space. He was also a devout follower of the Alison Begley school of political correctness. 'Sorry to disturb you, ma'am. But I thought you'd like to know the judge is sending out the Rich jury first thing in the morning,' he said.

'Fingers crossed, Patsy,' said Weaver.

Weaver's news about SOCA made Patsy decide that she'd had enough for one day.

She needed a drink but she wasn't in the mood to be gregar-ious. She asked Leyden about decent local watering holes. He didn't know about wine bars, he said, but if she fancied a drink on the river, there was the Cutty Sark on Ballast Quay. Having sought his advice, Chalke then felt she had to invite him to join her.

Consequently, Leyden was now fetching drinks while she sat on the river wall wondering if Soca had not passed on Shine's drug links because they had reason not to trust the Greenwich squad.

The personal files made sorry reading.

It was St Augustine who said that there was no saint without a past, no sinner without a future.

But then St Augustine had never met the Awkward Squad.

Cochrane had been a member of the Serious Fraud Squad, where he'd been close to a corrupt insider dealer who'd walked free after a trial where the defence had been suspiciously well briefed about the prosecution strategy.

Les Blunt, lazy and overweight, had twice been suckered by the same con-man into releasing him. Supposedly he'd convinced Blunt that he had arrested the man's twin brother.

Butterfield had caused a major prosecution against a terrorist cell to fail by contaminating the evidence.

One detective had a history of getting into drunken fights and then using his warrant card to avoid arrest. Other officers had abused their power in different ways. One had tried to fit up a local villain after discovering he was shagging his girlfriend; one had refused to break up a fight for fear of getting hurt; another had failed to make a note of a vital interview, leaving a serial rapist free to rape again.

There was a reference in Leyden's file to an incident at Millwall football ground, but nothing else that would see him banished to Greenwich – other than his general surliness.

Chalke felt like Snow White with the Seven Limping Dwarfs. Maybe those bastards in the Met's HR thought they'd got the last laugh after all.

In their dreams.

She looked up to find Leyden standing in front of her holding a glass of wine, a pint of lager and a packet of crisps.

'Thank you.'

'Did you see *Big Brother* last night?' he asked, sitting down next to her.

'Sorry?'

'*Big Brother.*'

'I don't watch much television.' Chalke took a crisp.

'Not even the football?'

'Especially not the football – though I have been known to take a structured sickie during Wimbledon.'

'Tennis?'

Chalke bit into the crisp. 'Christ! What the hell are these?'

Leyden inspected the packet. 'Roast turkey, cranberry and stuffing.'

'God, It's bad enough having to eat turkey at Christmas. They're disgusting.' Chalke lit a cigarette.

Leyden waved away the smoke. 'You're killing yourself.'

'My choice.'

'But you're damaging my health as well.'

'And what are you doing eating those crisps? Don't be an old woman.' Chalke swivelled around to look at the river Thames.

'When I was a nipper, there was a bloke who used to row across from the Isle of Dogs for a pint here,' said Leyden. 'One night, my brothers nicked his boat. He got in a right two and eight.'

'How many brothers have you got?'

'Three and a sister.'

'And you're the only copper?'

'We'd have been kicked off the Ferrier if any more of us had gone moody.'

'Gone moody?'

'Gone straight.'

'Is the Ferrier estate as rough as they make out?'

'The Rottweilers go round in pairs. The fire brigade hates the place because of all the chip pan fires on Christmas Day.'

'This is the first time you've served back in the area?'

'Yeah. The brass didn't want a copper from the Ferrier policing the place. I don't know how Mr Weaver has managed to stay here all those years.'

'Nor does anyone else,' smiled Chalke.

'You were at the Yard?'

'SO 1. Specialist Protection.'

'Can I ask… is the story about the American true?'

'Depends what you've heard.'

There were no secrets in the Met. The more the brass tried to hush up things, the more the rumour mill went into overdrive.

Patsy had been in charge of babysitting a party of American senators and businessmen attending a London arms fair. The hospitality had proved too much for some. Patsy had managed to get them back to the Ritz hotel where the senator from Alabama tried to grope her. She warned him off but the senator wouldn't listen. In the Rivioli Bar, he'd stuck his hand up her skirt. She'd laid him out.

Both sides had tried to cover up the incident but the damage had been done. Chalke had been moved to borough policing at Chingford – where she'd chased down Terry Rich.

In the fallout from Rich, Human Resources had suggested that she might like to resign before she was fired. Patsy had suggested that Human Resources might like to go fuck themselves. In retaliation, they'd sent her to Greenwich.

To head off further personal questions, she said, 'That buckle we found in the ash is odd. It's too small to come from a man's belt. Where else would you wear a buckle?'

'On clothing? Some leather jackets have belts with buckles at the back.'

'Or a buckle from a handbag.' Chalke held up her shoulder bag. 'That buckle's about the same size.'

'Why would a man carry a handbag?'

'Some men do.'

'Not where I come from.'

'They do in some countries,' said Chalke. 'What if the dead man was a foreigner, maybe an illegal immigrant?'

'That could explain why no one's missed him – and might fit in with the drugs connection,' said Leyden. 'Did Begley say anything about getting the press involved?'

'I reckon she won't do anything until she can be seen to be on top of the situation.'

'Begley wouldn't know how to pour piss out of a boot if it said tilt on the heel.'

Chalke knew she should slap Leyden down for coming out with something like that. But what the hell. It was a sore point among murder detectives that the current head of the capital's Homicide and Serious Crime Command had made her name in Diversity Strategy and Citizen Focus – whatever that was – and not at the sharp end.

'What are you doing this evening?' she asked.

'I should go to training but it's a schlep to the gym in Abbey Wood. I'll probably go for a run. What are you doing?'

'Having a quiet night in.' Patsy remembered to praise her new team to Leyden, knowing that word would get back. 'Les Blunt did well.'

'Yeah, TF2 doesn't miss much.'

'I thought he was called the Eternal Flame.'

'There's more to Les Blunt than you think.'

'Okay, TF2?

'You really want to know?'

'That's why I'm asking.'

'Too Fat To Fuck.'

'But he's not, is he? He's not that gross.'

'Don't know. His wife has this thing about not letting anyone watch them.'

'Thanks for that.' She had a lot to learn about working in Greenwich.

But by the time Leyden got home to his small terraced cottage in Grove Park on the wrong side of the South Circular, he'd convinced himself that it was too soon to begin training. He needed more time to recover from the fight. He'd run tomorrow.

Karen was out at a birthday bash for one of the girls at the hospital – or so she said.

He went to hang up his jacket in the bedroom. Karen's hospital trousers, tunic and a pair of knickers lay on the floor next to the laundry basket. It would have been just as easy to drop them in, thought Leyden. It would have surprised his colleagues to learn that Bobby was a tidy person. You had to be when you lived in a doll's house – a doll's house with a cupboard of a box room where he could work out.

Bobby had met Karen, a physiotherapist at Queen Elizabeth hospital, after he'd wrenched his right knee jumping over a wall chasing a drug dealer. He'd asked her out during his second appointment. Within six weeks, she'd moved in. They'd talked of marriage and where they'd go on their honeymoon. But the wedding never happened. The excitement faded. By the time they had both realised that they weren't right for each other, habit and convenience had taken over. A year and a half was a long time in a failing relationship.

Back downstairs, Leyden found the fridge empty apart from four cans of 1664 lager and a bottle of wine. Karen had been going to shop on the way home. He could call her to ask why she hadn't, but what was the point? He inspected the TV listings. *Was Dr Crippen Innocent?* Of course he bleeding wasn't, but Bobby liked those sorts of programmes. There was *Big Brother* later. He'd phone for a curry – and that was the evening sorted.

Bobby remembered how Chalke had turned up her nose at watching TV. She went to theatre, ballet, opera. Not his cup of tea.

He was fascinated by his new guv'nor. She was clearly posh, well educated and well off – but flying to New York for a concert… Bobby had thought he and Karen had been adventurous when they'd gone to Brussels for a weekend. He knew Chalke wasn't married and wondered if she had a bloke. She wore what could be an engagement ring on the third finger of her right hand. Maybe an indication of a broken romance. If so, he'd bet good money that Patsy had been the one to break it off. No one in their right mind would turn her down.

Chalke seemed to have taken a shine to him. He didn't know why. He was just a south London lad who'd always wanted to be a copper.

That was all he could do.

But Patsy Chalke – what the hell was she doing in the Job?

Leyden was in bed, pretending to be asleep when Karen finally got back. He carried on pretending.

DAY THREE

Friday

SUE JONES LEFT the new Co-op carrying a pint of semi-skimmed milk and a box of Yorkshire tea bags. In her purse was DS Leyden's receipt from the dry-cleaner's. She'd offered to pick up his suit. If she didn't do it, she'd told him, it'd stay there for weeks, and he'd known it was the truth.

Sue walked past the Roma woman selling the *Big Issue*, past the burger bar and the charity shop, to the dry-cleaner's.

She stepped on the mat in the doorway and walked to the counter. There was no one there. She pressed the button to ring the bell, and waited. No one came.

The drum on one of the machines was going round, making a heavy clunking noise.

Sue glanced at it, then walked around the counter, past the rack of garments awaiting collection, and looked into the back room. She couldn't see anyone.

'Hello?'

She returned to the front door to look up and down the scruffy 1960s precinct, then went back into the shop.

The machine was really making a dreadful noise, as though it was about to come off its bearings.

Sue peered closely at the machine.

A hand appeared behind the circular, thick-glassed window. Then a face stared out.

Sue turned and ran back to the police station.

*

'He must have been a midget to fit in there,' said Leyden, peering at the small circular door.

'Lee Finch was five foot four and weighed eight stone dripping wet,' replied Weaver.

'Was that why he was called Minicab, sir?'

'His father was a taxi driver known as Ron the Cabbie. The son was nicknamed Minicab. Turned out it suited him.'

'Knew him well, sir?'

'Not really. Once upon a time he was a promising rally driver but that ended when he married his first wife. She was an unpleasant piece of work. When she left him, she took everything. Finch had built up a chain of booths in the West End – dry-cleaning, key cutting, engraving, that sort of thing. People joked that she was the only woman in south London to have cleaned out the dry-cleaner's.' Finch looked around the linoleum-floored, machine-filled room. 'This is all that's left of Minicab's empire,' he said.

'Do we have anything against him?'

'We had him down for the getaway driver on a security van heist ten years or so ago but there was nothing we could make stick.'

Weaver left to brief the area press officer. The shopping precinct had been sealed off, a canvas screen hiding the dry-cleaner's itself. A police officer logged everyone passing under the blue and white crime scene tapes.

Leyden watched as Minicab's body was lifted out onto plastic sheeting. Once the photographers had finished, Dr Will Brennan, the forensic medical examiner, moved in. He took his time inspecting the body.

'What do you think?' asked Leyden after a while.

'I can tell you one thing straight away–'

'Yes?'

'It was a clean death.'

'You're a great help, doc.'

Brennan stood up. 'Phew, that solvent's evil. Could kill someone.'

'You think Finch was asphyxiated?' asked Leyden.

'There're lacerations on the back of the head and a bruise on the right temple, but we'll have to wait until the post-mortem to find out if they were caused by a blunt object or by being thrown around in the drum.'

Leyden pulled on latex gloves and began going through Minicab's pockets. There was £140 in sodden notes in his jeans while a windcheater hanging in the back room contained a wallet with credit cards but no keys or phone. The till was empty.

DCI Chalke came in.

'How's Sue?' asked Leyden.

'She'll be all right. Blunt's feeding her sweet tea and biscuits.' Chalke wrinkled her nose. 'God, what's that smell?'

'Perc,' replied Will Brennan. 'Or to use its proper name, tetra-chloroethylene or perchloroethylene solvent.'

'How do you know that?'

'It's what they use in most dry-cleaners – despite mounting evidence of its carcinogenic effects.'

'This machine has a forty-minute cycle, so Lee Finch couldn't have been put in there before nine o'clock,' said Leyden. 'The Co-op opens at eight so we should be able to find some witnesses. What about that woman outside selling the *Big Issue*?'

Chalke glanced along the pavement. 'She's not there now. See if anyone knows where she can be found. And find out if any of the supermarket girls had a break between nine and nine-forty. What's out the back?'

'A door leading to a service access. No sign of forced entry. I'd say Minicab just walked in, took off his windcheater and got ambushed.'

'Perhaps we should first establish time of death? Ask his wife what time he left home this morning, perhaps, that sort of thing?'

'Yeah, I guess so.'

'Work the theory around the facts, sergeant. Not the other way round.'

'Sorry, ma'am.'

Chalke left to brief the canvassing teams.

'That's what happens when you let your brains go to your head,' said Brennan once she was out of earshot.

Chalke had been in her office less than five minutes when BT liaison called with the Cyprus number that had phoned the Dim Reaper.

'No subscriber's name?' asked Chalke.

'It's in the north of the island. I'm afraid you'll have to speak to the police there.'

'That's a problem?'

'Well, for a start we don't have an extradition treaty with the Turkish Republic of Northern Cyprus. If you're lucky, a dozen faxes, half a dozen emails and three Hail Marys will get you to a guy who'll explain regretfully that nothing can be done until a week next Thursday.'

'Terrific.'

Chalke dialled the number, but it was unobtainable. She left the number on Cochrane's desk with a note to phone the Cyprus police. Let him deal with the tosspots.

The uniforms outside Minicab's home called to say that Mrs Finch had just arrived. She'd been carrying a vanity case. And hadn't been heartbroken at the news of her husband's death.

'See you at my car in five minutes,' Chalke told Leyden.

'Do you want a bacon sarnie from the canteen? I've not had any breakfast.'

Nor had Chalke – if you didn't count black coffee and a

cigarette. She could kill for a bacon sarnie. 'No, thanks. And you're not eating one in my car, either. It'll smell for days.'

She found Leyden beside her red Mercedes SL Roadster in the overspill car park, wolfing down his sandwich. Chalke had raised eyebrows when she'd turned up in the sports car. Coppers were petrol heads. They didn't need to look online to find out that her wheels had cost over £62,000. They knew – and tongues wagged.

She was glad she hadn't bought the Porsche.

'Did you know this car park's on an old railway line?' asked Leyden.

'What, here?'

'It was the line from Greenwich Park station to Lewisham. The station – where the Ibis hotel now is – was opened in 1888.' Leyden took another bite. 'Trains stopped running in the First World War. It was another eighty-odd years before Greenwich and Lewisham were directly linked by railway again.'

'Fascinating,' said Chalke. 'Can we go now?'

Leyden crammed in the final mouthful and put the wrapping paper on the front wheel arch of Cochrane's Lexus.

Minicab's home turned out to be a detached bungalow on a lane into Oxleas Woods off Shooters Hill. The door was answered by a WPC family liaison officer.

'How's the widow?' asked Chalke.

The WPC rolled her eyes. 'She's not what you might call grieving. She just told me to bog off, doesn't want me in the house.'

'Charming.'

The WPC pointed to the door to her left. 'She's in the kitchen.'

The kitchen was dark with an upright cooker and huge fridge-freezer, a cheap Formica table and four matching chairs. The only modern item was the microwave oven. The smell of toast made Leyden hungry again.

Lorraine Finch was in her thirties, scavenger thin, wearing jeans and T-shirt, no bra. Her bottle-blonde hair framed her hard face like a coalscuttle helmet. Leyden took an instant dislike to the woman.

'Mrs Finch, we're police officers,' began Chalke. 'It's regarding your husband's death.'

'Yeah?'

Lorraine picked up a mug of tea and leaned against the draining board. The detectives were not asked to sit down.

'I gather you weren't home last night,' said Chalke.

'So?'

'Were you with your husband?'

'No. Not that it's got anything to do with you.' Irritation and impatience were etched on the woman's face.

'When did you last see your husband?'

'Yesterday morning. When he went to the shop.'

'You don't know what time he got home last night?' Chalke paused. 'Or if he did come home, even?'

'He wasn't back when I left at half past seven.' Lorraine Finch took a sip of tea, added more sugar and stirred until Leyden's nerves were on edge.

'Did you speak on the phone?' asked Chalke when Lorraine finally stopped.

'Nah.'

'Where were you last night?'

'What's it to you?'

'Mrs Finch, your husband has been murdered. We're asking everyone connected with him to account for their movements in the past twenty-four hours.'

'Can't help you.' Lorraine Finch feigned a yawn.

Chalke had had enough. 'Get your things, Mrs Finch. We'll continue this at the police station. You are free to call a solicitor.'

'What would I want with a solicitor?' Lorraine Finch was rattled. 'I was seeing my bloke. Me and Lee, we got a sort of understanding, if you get my meaning.'

'An open marriage?'

'Yeah, if you like.'

'And Lee was comfortable with that?'

'He didn't get no choice.' Lorraine examined her nails. 'He had to like it or lump it.'

'Did he… play away?'

'Don't know.' Lorraine Finch shrugged. 'I never asked him.'

'Would you say yours was a happy marriage?'

A barking laugh. 'You've got to be joking.'

'This other fellow?'

'He ain't the sort to settle down.' Lorraine Finch threw the dregs of her tea into the sink. 'Listen, there wasn't much love in our marriage to start with. None at the end. The sod led me up the garden path. There weren't no money. A poxy little dry-cleaner's. Puh!'

'Your husband is dead,' Leyden reminded her.

'Yeah, well. Perhaps now I'll live a bit.'

'Where were you last night?'

'At the fights in Woolwich.'

'What fights?'

'The cage fights. That's what my man does.'

Leyden could picture her at the ringside, lips drawn back, screaming for her man to batter someone.

'What's his name?'

'What's it to you?'

'He's all that's standing between you and a cell, sweetheart.'

'Tony. Tony Yayale.'

'Guinness!' said Des Weaver.

'She said he fought under the name Sandstorm,' said Chalke standing in front of the whiteboard where she had written the names of Lorraine and her lover.

'He might do, but Tony Yayale's known as Guinness on account of the fact that his mother's Irish and his father was West Indian. He owns the Stag pub with the gym in Bermondsey. We fancied him for the killing of Giz Washington, the Brixton dealer, six years back, but a gym-full of witnesses swore Guinness had been there at the time.'

Sue Jones appeared with a box of canteen sandwiches. The detectives had tried to persuade her to go home, but she seemed determined to carry on. She put the sandwiches down on an empty desk near the whiteboard.

'So far, all a search of Minicab's home has found is that Lorraine has a thing about leather and restraint,' said Chalke as detectives gathered around the sandwiches.

'If there's a cheese and pickle, it's mine,' said Weaver.

'Here you are, guv,' said Leyden, taking charge.

'Don't suppose there's any tongue?' asked Cochrane.

'There's bacon and egg, corned beef, ham and tomato–' Leyden picked up a sandwich. 'I'm not sure what this one is.'

'I'll take the ham and tomato,' said Blunt.

'Make sure it's just the one round,' growled Cochrane.

Chalke cleared her throat. 'If you've quite finished–'

'Sorry,' said Weaver. 'Aren't you eating?'

'I'm not hungry.' She ignored her rumbling stomach. Perhaps she was carrying this diet thing too far. One throwaway remark the night before last about a spare tyre and now she was fasting like a Tibetan monk. If Tibetan monks fasted.

'Preliminary post-mortem puts time of death between 9 p.m. and 1 a.m.,' she said. 'Cause of death was two or more blows to the head. We don't know where Minicab was killed but he was dead when he was put in the drum. No signs of a struggle at either the dry-cleaner's or his home.'

'I think that one's fish paste,' decided Leyden.

'Finch's wallet and phone are missing,' continued Chalke, glaring at Leyden while at the same time wondering how many calories there were in fish paste. Not too many, surely. 'Neither the Roma woman nor the supermarket staff saw anything. Tomorrow morning we'll stake out the precinct.'

'How come I'm left with egg?' protested Leyden.

'What if Lorraine and Guinness killed Minicab, dumped his body in the shop, then went back to Guinness's place to establish an alibi,' said Blunt.

'But why did the killer bother to start the machine this morning?' asked Chalke.

She watched as Blunt reached out a pudgy hand to take the fish paste sandwich. It was probably for the best.

'Ground and pound, you tosser. You got him on the floor. Smash his face into the canvas.'

Chalke stood at the doorway of the squalid gym reeking of stale sweat and embrocation. Two men were fighting in a cage made of netting hanging from the ceiling while a mulatto-skinned man with a bull neck roared instructions.

'Elbow him. Again. Beat the fucking granny out of him. Jesus!'

Two other men, minders by the look of them, were watching the fighting. They noticed Chalke and Leyden, and strode towards them. Leyden took a step forward.

'What do you two think you're doing?' said the larger one. 'Fuck off out of it.'

Patsy Chalke held up her warrant card. 'Police. We're looking for Tony Yayale.'

'That's me.' The bull-necked man turned on the minders. 'You were supposed to have locked that fucking door. Piss off and take those ponces with you.'

The fighters were already scuttling away, past a miniature treadmill. The minders followed.

Yayale swaggered over to the detectives, picking up a dumb-bell in each hand on the way. He began a series of hammer curls.

Despite himself, Leyden was impressed.

Chalke saw Guinness differently. She saw a shaven-headed lout with bulbous skull that no doubt contained little by way of a brain, walrus fat rolling down the back of his neck, a Union Jack tattoo on one bicep and a couple having sex on the other. The knuckles of his left hand were tattooed with letters HATE. Large tufts of hair protruded from the armpits of his sleeveless vest.

Not someone you'd take home to meet the parents unless you wanted to be orphaned or disinherited.

'What was going on here?' she asked.

'I've a stable of cage fighters, ain't I?' Yayale squinted at Leyden's bruised face. 'Someone clattered you, then.'

'Not as much as I clattered him,' said Leyden.

'Ooh, big talk from the big man,' sneered Yayale.

'Do you cage-fight yourself?' Chalke asked him.

'That's what they say.'

'Is it as violent as it looks?'

'There're rules covering things like gouging or hair pulling.' Guinness sounded regretful. 'Other than that, it's all down to sending your opponent a message.'

'What message?'

'Be fucking afraid because I'm going to hurt you bad.'

'Are those blokes in the cage due to fight any time soon?' asked Leyden.

'Streatham. Tomorrow. Want a ticket?'

'I was thinking I might have a bet.'

Yayale gave Leyden a hard stare. 'Nah, you don't want to be doing that. Here–'

He offered Leyden the dumb-bells. Leyden resisted the temptation to take them and show the pond life what he could do.

Yayale snorted derisively and continued his curls.

'We're investigating the death of Lee Finch,' said Chalke.

'Yeah, I heard he was dead.'

'When did you last see him?'

'He used to come to the fights but I've not seen him for, what, four moons.'

'You admit you're having an affair with his wife?' asked Chalke.

'I could hardly deny it, treacle. Every face in the fight game knows. Loves the tear up, does Lorraine. Goes off like a two-bob clock every time she sees blood.'

'Must have an interesting time with her periods,' murmured Chalke.

'Do me a favour.'

Leyden noticed how while Chalke was the one asking the questions, Guinness was replying to him. Women occupied a low place in Yayale's world.

'She watched you fight last night?'

'Then we went back to my place on Bostall Hill. Listen, if that no-mark of a husband couldn't hang on to his missus that was his problem.'

'Did he say anything to you?'

Guinness gave a mocking laugh. 'Wouldn't dare. He'd know he'd get a smacking.'

'But you and Lorraine aren't living together?'

'And have some slapper tell me what to do in my own home? She stays the night – when I let her –and that's it.'

'Can you prove the pair of you were there all night?'

'I've got a video if you want to see it, treacle, timed and dated. That'll show you where we were at three o'clock this morning – and what we were doing.'

'A video?'

'Her idea. Listen, why would I want to kill Lee Finch? I've got what I want.'

'What was going on there, Bobby?' asked Chalke as they walked to her car.

'I reckon that if we went to Streatham tomorrow night, we'd see those two guys fighting each other,' replied Leyden. 'They were going through the moves to make it look good for the punters.'

'What was that little treadmill for?'

'Pit bull fighting. That's one reason why they didn't want us nosing around. They use the treadmills to get the dogs fit. Did you spot the harness?'

'No.'

'They harness the dogs to tyres and make them haul the tyres up hills to get them strong.'

'By the way, well done for not rising to the bait when Yayale offered you those weights. I didn't know you had it in you.'

'Yeah, well, it wasn't easy.' As they got into the Mercedes, Leyden asked, 'Any word from the Bailey?'

'None. The longer they're out, the less likely we'll get a conviction.'

'Sometimes juries take their time just to show they're doing their job properly,' reassured Leyden. 'You saw them. Did they look like an Essex jury to you?'

'You never know what an Essex jury looks like until they bring in some verdict against all the evidence?'

'Yeah.' The sight of a fish and chip shop reminded Leyden of food. 'Fancy a bag of chips?'

'Don't you ever stop eating?'

'Got to keep up my strength. But you haven't eaten all day. Not on a diet, are you?'

'Why would I be?'

'Just wondered. Fancy a bag of chips, then?'

'No!'

Three hours later, Chalke was sitting in her office, feeling hungry. The wooden man was running at full tilt. Patsy couldn't remember putting him like that.

There was nothing to connect the incident at the funeral director's and murder of Lee Finch but Chalke found herself wondering why someone had taken the trouble to put Stan behind the undertaker's desk and Minicab in the dry-cleaning drum. It was as though the killer wanted to draw attention to the crime.

If the squad had been short-handed before, Minicab's murder stretched them still further. Part of the team looking into the Dim Reaper's associates had been switched to delving into Minicab's life. DI Andy Butterfield had been given day-to-day running of the search for the Reaper while Chalke headed up Minicab's murder.

The lab had found hairs and fibres in the boot of the Dim Reaper's car. The fibres were from garden twine which could have been used to tie the victim's hands. The belt buckle was thought to have been made in eastern Europe. The amalgam from the dental fillings wasn't the sort used in Britain. Both pointed to the victim being a foreigner.

Soon Weaver would have to upgrade the inquiry into a murder hunt, which would release more resources, but it was only last night that Begley had approved the manpower necessary to study footage from CCTV cameras along the Dim Reaper's possible routes into central London. Weaver should have pressed sooner but he'd known Begley would squeal about the budget, and he had no stomach for such fights. Chalke relished them.

The CCTV study had soon paid dividends.

The barrier computer in the underground garage showed that Dave Shine had left at 12.10 p.m. Cameras had picked him up heading along Evelyn Street and through Rotherhithe until the congestion charge camera captured him crossing Tower Bridge Road. He had arrived back at the flats at 9.52 p.m. What had happened in between – where he had gone, who he had met – was still a mystery. And now the manpower devoted to the CCTV search had been cut by half.

There was a knock on Chalke's door. Sue Jones placed a pile of papers on her desk.

'Um, thanks. These are…?'

'Spreadsheets on serious crime and homicide in our area compared with the numbers of officer hours on active policing.' Sue saw the look of incomprehension on Chalke's face. 'It's something the Yard asked for before you arrived. DS Leyden was tasked with it but he's been busy so I've put these together.'

'Bobby Leyden can do a spreadsheet?'

'Not as such.' Sue smiled. 'I thought it might be quicker if I did them.'

'You can handle Excel?'

'It's not too bad once you've got the equations right.'

Chalke could never get the equations right.

Sue was wasted as an admin assistant. She needed a job to match her abilities. That was something Patsy would address in the future. Now she had more immediate things to worry about.

'Are you sure you're all right, Sue?' she asked. 'No delayed shock?'

'I'm fine, honestly,' said Sue in her West Country burr. 'But… I don't understand – why would anyone kill Minicab? I mean Lee. Sorry, I know it's none of my business.'

'No problem. We don't know yet.'

Sue hesitated, then changed the subject. 'I love your perfume.'

'Jo Malone. Black Vetyver Café with a touch of Vintage Gardenia on top.' Chalke dug in her handbag and brought out two small bottles. 'Here, try.'

'It's beautiful,' said Sue. 'Must be expensive.'

Patsy remembered that she had been meaning to ask Sue where she grew up.

'I'm from Plymouth – well, Devonport, originally,' she said.

'Isn't that a naval base?'

'Yes.'

'You've still got your accent.'

'I don't think I'll ever lose it.'

'Don't. It's really attractive,' said Patsy. 'Any men on the go at the moment?'

Sue shook her head. 'Darren and I split a month ago... Sometimes I think men are more worry than they're worth.'

'Tell me about it.'

At that moment Leyden put his head around the door.

'Just had word from the Bailey. The judge is sending the Rich jury to a hotel.'

'Any thoughts on the result?'

'On the quiet, the jury manager reckons it's split eight–four and the four won't budge.'

That was not good. Not good at all.

DAY FOUR

Saturday

PATSY CHALKE HAD woken up after a terrifying dream which she'd abruptly forgotten. Now she found she was unable to go back to sleep for thinking about the case.

Although they hadn't yet identified who had called the Dim Reaper from Cyprus, the location itself was interesting. North Cyprus had become a favourite bolt-hole for British villains because of the lack of an extradition treaty between the two countries.

Polly Peck boss Asil Nadir had flown there after being accused of stealing £150 million. Drug mastermind Brian Wright, known as 'the Milkman' because he always delivered; Gary Robb who skipped bail while facing charges of conspiracy to supply drugs; and 'Maggot' Pete Roberts, sentenced to six years for Britain's most notorious meat scam, had all fled there.

Nadir had returned voluntarily while Maggot Pete and the Milkman had been handed back. But it was still a lottery whose collar the local police decided to feel.

Patsy's sister Caro had wanted to buy a cliff-top villa in North Cyprus until Patsy had pointed out that the vendor couldn't show a legal title to the land. She suspected that he'd simply grabbed it following the 1974 invasion. It was going to be interesting if the Greeks ever returned.

Suddenly Patsy had an idea. She slid out of bed and padded into the living room. She wrestled *The Times Atlas of the World* down off a book shelf.

A map of Cyprus was inset on page 36.

Patsy covered the Greek part of the island with her hand – and saw she was looking at the shape of the cufflinks found on Stan Figgens.

The foreman at the MOT centre on Norman Road was not happy. 'It's Saturday, my busiest day. And I've got a bloke off on holiday. You should have booked.'

'I've never needed to book it in before,' protested Leyden.

'You've never brought the car in on a Saturday before… Seeing it's you… but I won't be able to look at it until this afternoon, and we close at 4.30, remember.'

'Thanks, mate.' Leyden was handing over the keys of the Ford Mondeo when his phone rang.

It was Chalke, very pleased with herself. She wanted him to talk to Lucymar while she tried to get the Turkish Cypriot police to pull their fingers out.

That suited Leyden. He was less than half a mile from the girl's flat. He left the garage to walk along Norman Road, turning left over Creek Bridge. Rusting barges sat in the mud at the bend. They'd been there as long as he could remember – ghosts of the old river. Lucymar's block of flats, built where wharves had once stood, was the future.

Leyden took the lift up to the third floor and knocked on Lucymar's door. He knocked again, louder. A woman poked her head out of a neighbouring flat.

'What you trying to do? Wake the dead?'

'Sorry, love. Do you know if Miss Varenos is in?'

'They were there last night. Heard them on the balcony. And you could smell that wacky baccy.'

'Who's "they"?'

'She had some bloke with her. Who are you, anyway?'

'Police.'

'Why don't you say you can smell gas and kick the door in?'

'That only happens on TV.'

'Just as well. We're electric here.' The woman vanished back into her flat.

Leyden gave the door three hefty blows. Lucymar called in a small voice, 'Who's there?'

'It's Bobby Leyden. I've a few questions for you.'

'Moment.'

The moment became three minutes. The door opened a few inches to reveal Lucymar in a lime green T-shirt. If anything, she looked even more emaciated than last time.

'I was asleep,' she said.

Leyden moved past her into the living room. An empty bottle of Bacardi sat on the floor, next to an overflowing ashtray. The air was heavy with stale smoke and marijuana.

'Must have been some welcome home party,' said Leyden. 'Where is he?'

'Who?'

'Dave Shine.'

Lucymar's eyes widened in fear. There was the sound of a lavatory being flushed. A tall black man with dreadlocks strolled in, totally naked. He ignored Leyden, rooted through the ashtray until he found the remains of a spliff then wandered back towards to the bedroom.

'He's a friend,' said Lucymar as the man disappeared.

'What's his name?'

Lucymar shrugged. 'I met him last night in a club in Deptford. I *needed* to get out.'

Leyden assumed she'd run out of drugs. 'You're taking a risk. If Dave showed up –'

'I can't stay in forever.'

'Did you know that Dave's wife is due to arrive in London tonight?'

'She doesn't know about me. Please – don't tell her.'

'We have to.'

Lucymar thought. 'I know. I tell you about Dave's secret place and then you don't tell his bitch wife about here?'

'What secret place?'

'Is it a deal?'

'Lucymar, love, I can't do that.'

She folded her arms. 'Then I don't tell you about secret place.'

Leyden almost felt sorry for the girl. 'Okay. I'll forget about you for a few days but we're going to have to tell her some time. You know that. This is a murder investigation.'

'No deal.'

'Okay, tell you what I'll do–' Leyden slid his hands deep into his trouser pockets. 'I'll *not* arrest you for being in the country illegally and you'll tell me about the secret place.'

Lucymar considered. 'You help me get new visa?'

'Promise.'

She looked at him, trying to decide if he could be trusted. 'Okay. Dave owns a parade of four shops in Chislehurst. No one knows. Not wife, not taxman. Only me. The shops all have maisonettes above them. I write down address for you.'

'Why didn't you tell us this before?'

'In my country we do not tell police everything straight away.'

Leyden changed tack. 'You remember that phone call that Dave had from Cyprus? What did he say exactly?'

'I told you, he went into the bedroom to talk.'

'Who answered the phone?'

'He did.'

'What did he say?'

'He just say, "Hello".'

'Think harder. What time of day was it? Where were you? What were you doing?'

'It was the evening. We'd been... at it. He was not happy when the phone rang.'

'What *exactly* did he say?'

'He said, "Hello". Then something like, "Glockie! How're you keeping? Where are you? North Cyprus! You sound like you're just down the road." Then he took the phone into the bedroom.'

'Glockie?'

'I think so. Something like that.'

The heavy beat of reggae music started up in the bedroom.

As Leyden let himself out, he realised that Lucymar had still not asked about the Dim Reaper's whereabouts or his well-being.

'Your turn to drive,' Chalke said as they crossed the road to the car park.

'My car's in for an MOT. You should have told me yesterday want me to drive.'

'I didn't know yesterday that we'd be going on a jolly to find the Dim Reaper's secret property empire, did I?'

She climbed into the Mercedes, assumed an expression of fixed concentration, and inched out into Royal Hill. A few hundred yards further on at the top of Hyde Vale, she pulled over with a sigh of exasperation and took a pair of spectacles from the glove compartment.

'I didn't know you wore glasses,' said Leyden.

'I don't often.' Chalke accelerated through the pinch point and onto the A2 ahead of a number 53 bus. 'I couldn't get my lenses in today.'

'You wear contact lenses?'

'Only for long distances. I'm fine reading. Don't tell anyone.'

'Okay... Why not?'

'Because I don't want people to know. Right?'

'If you say so.'

They didn't speak for the rest of the journey – Patsy, furious with herself for being a pompous prick, and Leyden at a loss to know what to say.

It was only as they arrived at the small shopping parade consisting of a florist's, newsagent's, hairdresser's and mobile phone store that Leyden asked, 'Shouldn't we have back-up?'

'You can handle Dave Shine, can't you?'

'Yeah, but–'

Chalke swept out of the car, still angry.

This was a mistake, thought Leyden. They should have cover back and front; an armed response unit in reserve; uniforms in a containing perimeter.

He hurried after Chalke, now striding towards the shops.

'Keep your thumb on my number in your phone,' he called, positioning himself where he could keep an eye on both front and back of the shops. 'Any problems, hit the button.'

He watched as Chalke entered the florist's. She came out a minute later and went into the newsagent's. She was gone some time. Just as Leyden was getting anxious, she appeared on the first-floor walkway to the maisonettes. She waved to tell him that she was safe and headed back.

'No joy,' she told him. 'The shopkeepers live above their stores. They negotiated their leases with the agent. None of them has ever heard of Dave Shine.'

A dead end.

If only it was as simple as on TV when every murder was solved in one hour – minus the time for the adverts – thought Leyden.

Back in the car, Chalke started the engine. She was about to pull away when she paused. 'Um… since we're out in the country, we could go and have lunch.'

Leyden accepted the peace offering. 'I know a nice pub not too far from here.'

'Thought you might.'

Centuries ago, the Blue Boar had been a coaching inn on the old Dover road. Leyden remembered it as a simple country pub with delicious homemade food. But it had changed out of recognition, doubling in size with an ugly extension covering the site of the old apple orchard.

Leyden and Chalke sat at a window table in the bar looking out onto the car park. Chalke had chosen a Caesar salad with a glass of rosé, Leyden a beef and ale pie and chips with a pint of lager.

'Sorry about this,' muttered Leyden. 'It used to be good, honest.'

'This is fine. Nothing wrong with the salad.'

'How can you eat lettuce leaves?' Leyden dipped a chip in his gravy.

'They're good for you. Careful. God, you're mucky. I don't know how Karen keeps up with your laundry.'

'She doesn't.' Leyden dabbed at the gravy on his shirt. 'I do my own washing and ironing.'

'Modern man! You wouldn't like to do mine as well, would you?'

'I'll pass, thanks.'

Chalke glanced out of the window. Two men were smoking in the entrance to the restaurant. 'Well if it isn't Des Weaver. I wonder who that is with him.'

Leyden followed her eye. 'That's Tosh Bibby,' he said.

'How do you know?'

'I used to be stationed around here. Everyone here knows Bibby. Former wide boy with a heart of gold. He does a lot for charities – hosted a celebrity golf match for the police fund last year. He owns a haulage company, taxi firm, pubs, clubs, God knows what else.'

Leyden took a gulp of lager and resumed his attack on the pie and chips.

Chalke winced at the way he was holding his knife like a pen while inverting his fork to shovel up peas. She'd have to have a word about his table manners but after their earlier spat, now was not the time.

They were finishing their meal when Weaver and Bibby emerged through an interior door from the restaurant. Weaver looked surprised to see them. He murmured something to Bibby and headed towards them.

'Hello. What are you two doing up here on a Saturday?'

'We had a lead on the Dim Reaper but it came to nothing so we decided to have lunch,' said Chalke. She was glad she'd taken off her glasses.

'This is Tosh Bibby, by the way.'

Bibby was Weaver's height and age but there the similarities ended. The artificial tightness around Bibby's eyes suggested the surgeon's knife while his tan had not come from being outdoors. Patsy knew a good haircut, and Bibby's was Mayfair standard. He wore a baby blue V-neck golf sweater and matching polo shirt. There was gold around his neck, on his wrist and on four fingers.

'Bobby Leyden,' said Bibby thoughtfully. 'Your brother's not Brian Leyden, is he?'

'That's right.'

'There's someone who's pulled himself up by his bootstraps. His building company must be worth a few million. You don't mind if we join you?' Without waiting for a reply, Bibby pulled up a chair and clicked his fingers. A waitress hurried over. 'Four Remys. The XO. Large.'

'Not for us,' said Chalke. 'We've got to get back to work.'

'It's Saturday.'

'We're still on duty'

'Your loss. Just for me and Des then. We go back a long way, don't we, Des?'

'A long, long way,' agreed Weaver.

'Des once nicked me over a misunderstanding regarding the ownership of a car.'

'Misunderstanding, my foot,' snorted Weaver. 'He was nicking Jags and knocking them out in Germany.'

Tosh Bibby grinned, showing perfect teeth. 'Des put in a good word so I got away with a suspended sentence. I decided to go straight and – surprise, surprise – I found I could make good money without the hassle. I've always been grateful.'

'Goes both ways,' murmured Weaver.

'Yeah, well, what goes around, comes around. The Gypsy code.' Bibby explained, 'I'm from an old Romany family, you see. People think gypsies move around but my lot stayed in Kent, picking hops, fruit, selling charms in winter. Once they were part of the Kent countryside but now no one wants a pikey camp next to them so I had the idea of setting up a site where Romanies can rest up. I started the ball rolling with a charity football match with a couple of England players. They didn't care a shit about the cause but I made it worth their while. Then there were all the TV soap stars, celebs.'

Bibby enjoyed hearing the sound of his own voice, Chalke noted, not doubting that everyone else would be fascinated by everything he did or said. His arrogance annoyed her, but for Weaver's sake she assumed a mask of polite interest – and switched off.

'You never forget your roots,' Bibby was saying. 'I started with nothing, now I've an estate in Kent, a pad in Marbella and a yacht in Greece. Not bad for a teenage tearaway, eh?

'No,' said Leyden, knowing that Bibby expected a response and knowing instinctively that Chalke was not going to provide it.

'Bloody right, son. Now excuse me. Nature calls.'

Bibby left to go to the lavatory as the waitress brought the brandies.

'Tosh takes a bit of getting used to,' said Weaver in the ensuing silence. 'But he's put me on the money a few times. The tip-offs for the Welling shooting *and* the attempted diamond robbery both came from him.' Weaver dropped his voice. 'He called this meet today because he's heard a whisper about the people-smuggling racket. You know Swanson International Haulage–'

'In Norman Road?' said Leyden. 'I walked past their yard this morning.'

'Tosh reckons it's coming out of there. He's going to tip us the wink when the next illegals are expected.'

'The commander will like that,' said Chalke.

'She'll be delighted,' said Weaver. 'But don't say anything. Nothing's definite yet.'

Tosh Bibby rejoined them. He peered at Leyden as if seeing his bruised face for the first time. 'Been in the wars, son?'

'Boxing,' replied Leyden shortly.

'Bobby boxes for the Met,' said Weaver.

'Yeah? Where'd you start?'

'Abbey Wood Boys' Club. It was their trainer Bill Hutt who helped me get into the Job.'

'Bobby's our light heavyweight champion,' said Weaver.

'It's an honour, Bobby.' Bibby rose to his feet and held out his hand. 'It's great the way these boys' boxing clubs help kids turn round their lives. Not everyone can do it on their own as I did. Take Joey Starling, for instance. Joey used to work on the door at my first club. Never had any bother when he was about – one look from him did the trick – but he kept ducking and diving. I made him clean up his act and now the rest is history, as they say. You know he's starring in this film they're making around here?'

'We know all about the film,' said Weaver.

Several times over the past weeks, local police had been called out to investigate shootings and break-ins, only to find they were part of the movie.

Bibby turned to Leyden. 'You into football, Bobby?'

'Love the game.'

'If you ever fancy coming to Millwall, just give me a bell. I've a box there.'

'That's very kind, sir,' said Leyden. 'But –'

'Tosh. My friends call me Tosh.'

'Tosh. That's very kind.'

Bibby hiccupped.

'We must go,' said Chalke. 'Do you want a lift back, Des?'

Bibby answered for him. 'My driver'll take Des back. We have a few things to talk about yet.'

Leyden signalled for the bill.

'It's sorted,' said Bibby,

'Oh no. You can't do that.' Chalke waved to the waitress.

Bibby swirled brandy around in his glass. 'She won't take your money.'

'How do you know?'

'I own the place.'

Leyden spent the afternoon at his desk, getting up to speed with the two inquiries while keeping tabs on the Millwall game against Reading on his phone. A few years ago he wouldn't have missed a game at the Den, never mind how much overtime was going, but now too many coppers and faces in the crowd knew him. He could never take up Bibby's offer.

He forced himself to concentrate on the cases. Minicab's movements since locking up the shop on Thursday remained a mystery. From the contents of the kitchen waste bin, it appeared that he had gone home, cooked himself fried eggs with oven chips, eaten them, and then gone out again – but where?

One neighbour who had driven past Minicab's bungalow at nine o'clock thought he remembered his Vauxhall Astra parked outside, but he couldn't swear to it. It could have been the night before.

They had drawn a blank with witnesses, which was puzzling. Even if Minicab's body had been carried in the back way, someone in the supermarket's loading bay should have seen something.

On the other hand, at least there'd been progress on the Dim Reaper inquiry.

Dave Shine had used a Barclaycard to pay the bill at the Pizza Express in Charing Cross Road at 3.45 p.m. on the Tuesday. Since the bill had come to £42.50, he must have had at least one companion. None of the waiters remembered him.

CCTV had captured his car entering the underground car park at the eastern end of Gerrard Street in Soho at 2.33 p.m. He had left at 4.10 p.m. He'd not arrived at the garage under his flat until 9.52 p.m. Tracking his car during those missing hours was going to be slow, difficult – and very time-consuming.

That reminded Leyden that he had to collect his own car. Chalke had already left, saying she had to get ready to go out for the night.

Leyden returned from Norman Road to find his desk phone ringing. He listened, took the message then steeled himself to call Patsy Chalke on her mobile.

'Sorry to disturb you, guv.'

'Not a problem.' Patsy was not going to tell him that she was about to step into the bath.

'Do you want the bad news or the worse news?' he asked.

'There's bad and worse?'

'We live in a rapidly changing world.'

'Go on. Hit me with it.'

'The judge has dismissed the Rich jury.'

'He didn't give them long.'

'They told him there was no way they were going to reach even a majority verdict.'

'I thought you said it was a bonking jury.'

'Looks as though there's been a falling out. They want to go home.'

'What now?'

'Rich has been allowed bail while the prosecution decides if it's worth going for a retrial.'

'Wonderful,' said Chalke. 'What moron lets a child molester back on the streets?'

'This is the worse bit. He's back on *our* streets. He's been sent to a bail hostel in Catford.'

'Catford! That's not far from where he nonced that first little girl. Fuck. Fuck. Fuck.' Chalke ended the call without saying goodbye.

It was the first time Leyden had heard Chalke swear. He was thinking that he liked her the more for it when he saw a message to call Speed Bump. He groaned.

He'd known Kenny Dibbs, aka Speed Bump, since school, but while Bobby had joined the police, Kenny had turned to labouring and petty theft. He had acquired his nickname after he'd picked a drunken fight with a pub bouncer. The bouncer had thrown him into the road where a car had promptly driven over him. Kenny had got to his feet and had staggered back to continue the fight.

Bobby wanted to get home but he believed in Sod's law. The one time he blanked Speed Bump would be the one time he'd have something useful to say. He called Karen to tell her he'd be late. The landline was engaged, her mobile switched off, so he left a message.

It was almost dusk when Leyden arrived at the British Oak. The nights were drawing in. Soon autumn would give way to winter. He couldn't remember that they'd had a summer.

He knew that Speed Bump had chosen the pub on Old Dover Road because few on the Ferrier could be bothered to come this far. He couldn't be seen drinking with the Old Bill. Bobby liked the Oak. It never changed. The wooden panelling, the bar billiards, even the carpet were the same as always. The only addition was a limited edition of a rugby jersey that the landlordhad bought on the 2005 British Lions tour to New Zealand.

Speed Bump was already at the bar. 'How're tricks?'

'Okay, mate. What are you drinking?'

'I'll go for the San Miguel.'

Leyden noticed that Speed Bump had been drinking from a Carling glass. San Mig was more expensive – but now he had a copper to pay.

'How's young Janna?'

Speed Bump's ten-year-old niece was currently living with the family while her mother was inside for fraud. Her father, Speed Bump's half brother, had done a bunk two years ago.

'Only top of her class, ain't she?'

'That's great.' Considering what the little girl had been through, it was a miracle.

'She wants to become a doctor. We've had to buy a computer for her, special like, because the boys need ours to play games on.'

'And how are Mole and Vomit after that last incident?' asked Bobby, referring to Speed Bump's fourteen-year-old twin sons.

'That headmaster almost got a bunch of fives, know what I mean?'

'That would have helped,' Bobby said drily.

'The boys were just having a bit of fun.'

'They set fire to the chemistry lab.'

'It was never proved they did it deliberately. The science teacher fitted them up.'

Bobby knew better than to argue. Speed Bump's sons were the apple of his eye. To everyone else, especially their teachers, they were the core of everything rotten.

'Just hope they keep their noses clean.' Bobby was bored with Speed Bump's dysfunctional family. 'You phoned, mate.'

Speed Bump lifted his glass in front of his mouth. 'You know that film they're making at the old flour mill, the one with Joey Starling? There's a gang of Somalis nicking off the set.'

'What sort of things?'

'Anything they can lay their hands on: computers, electrical cable, chairs, a whole rack of raincoats. They're stashing the stuff in those lock-ups behind Casterbridge Road.'

'How do you know this?'

'I've seen them stash the gear. Anyway, I'm in the film.'

'What!'

Speed Bump swelled with pride. 'They wanted blokes who looked the part, know what I mean?'

'You actually have lines?'

'Nah, not as such, no. I'm what they call an extra but I've got Joey's autograph. Do you know Joey Starling?'

The second time today that Starling's name had come up. In Leyden's book, Starling was a local thug who happened to have gone into TV and films. The critics who had been won over by the gritty realism of his performances didn't know that he was just playing himself.

'Heard of him, never met him.'

'You know he has a thing for young girls?'

'Who does?' Leyden was thinking he'd pass the Somalis on to local CID.

'Joey. And he likes them damaged.'

'You mean on drugs?'

'Vulnerable.' Speed Bump was proud of his choice of word. 'A bit dependent, like.'

Bobby decided that the film star's sexual proclivities were no concern of his. 'What do you know about Dave Shine?'

'I heard about the dead geezer in his funeral parlour. Who did they burn instead, then?'

'No idea yet. You heard of anyone going missing?'

Speed Bump picked at a pimple on the side of his nose. 'Nah, but if it was one of the Somalis, you'd never know. The family would just send someone else to get his dole money.'

'What's the turnout with Minicab?'

'We was on remand at Brixton together once. Not the sharpest knife in the drawer.'

Coming from Speed Bump that was saying something.

'Nothing you know linking Dave Shine and Minicab?'

'Can't think of nothing. You know Minicab's missus is having it off with Guinness?'

'Who doesn't?' Bobby finished his lager. 'Do you want a lift home?'

Speed Bump's face fell. 'Ain't we having a session?'

'Early doors, mate.'

Speed Bump was lighting a cigarette even before he was out of the bar door.

'You're not smoking in my car,' warned Bobby. Not only had it sailed through the MOT, but the garage had given it a complimentary valeting. It had never smelled so clean.

'Fuck's sake.'

To give Speed Bump time to finish his cigarette, Bobby asked, 'What's happening about the estate being knocked down?'

'My block's coming down in two years, they say.'

'I heard every household's getting 4k for moving.'

'I've already spent it, know what I mean?'

'The council will take your rent arrears out of that.'

'They can't do that.'

'Just marking your card, mate.'

Speed Bump flicked his cigarette away in disgust. 'I'll do a runner.'

'Then you won't get the dosh.'

'Fuck them.' Speed Bump was still simmering with a sense of injustice as Bobby swung into Pinto Way. This was a hollow square of five-storey flats around a car park next to the Ferrier estate.

A black youth was running for his life pursued by a gang of Somalis, Afro-Caribbeans and whites.

It occurred to Leyden that while the teenagers might be feral scum, they weren't racists. They'd attack anyone regardless of colour or creed. He supposed that was progress of a kind.

Speed Bump sank lower in his seat.

Leyden knew that if he intervened he was probably going to get a kicking. If he told them he was a copper, he would definitely get a kicking – and bubble Speed Bump into the bargain. On the other hand, if he did nothing that kid was going to get spread over the tarmac.

He didn't have a choice. No time to call for back-up, either.

The mob broke around the car. One youth in a white hoodie took a flying kick at the door. Another banged his fist on the roof.

'Watch my fucking car!'

Bobby threw the Ford into a three-point turn.

'Please. Just leave it,' said Speed Bump.

'Bollocks I will. Who the fuck are they?'

'The Ferrier Boyz.'

That explained it. A few months earlier, six gang members had been sentenced to a total of forty-six years for beating and stabbing a student who had dared to stand up to them. The rump of the gang was making up in violence what they lacked in numbers.

The black lad had doubled back towards them, the mob closing all the time. They were about to run past the car again, except this time Bobby was going to write the script.

He waited until the quarry was clear then accelerated towards the gang, steering straight at the thug in the white hoodie. At the last second, he swerved and flung open the driver's door. The yob was in mid-air, about to deliver another flying kick, when the door caught him.

Bobby leapt out. The youth was motionless on the ground. The rest of the gang advanced on Bobby. He counted seven.

Speed Bump stayed in the car.

Thanks, mate.

Bobby would have backed himself against two, possibly three, but seven was too many. They'd drag him down, and once on the ground he wouldn't be getting back up in a hurry.

He vectored in on the two largest gang members.

'Right, you fucking little toerags. Get here.' He jabbed his finger at the ground in front of him. 'Now.'

They were coming to get him anyway, so let's plant a seed of doubt. In any gang there'd be one or two who fancied themselves, the rest were sheep. Take out the hard men, and the rest would bleat.

A rangy black boy swaggered up. He was taller than Bobby, with a longer reach. He'd be fast, but he was wearing a hood. It restricted his vision and gave Leyden something to use.

'There're harder guys than me around – except you ain't one of them,' said Leyden.

The boy dropped into a fighting crouch. Another bloody southpaw, noted Leyden. Okay, don't let him settle. Don't give the others time to get behind you. Leyden darted in, grabbed the boy's hood, pulling his body downwards. At the same time, his knee came up hard and fast. Once, twice. Two strikes to the body – anywhere between groin and neck would do. Leyden grabbed the thug's head with both hands and twisted violently. As he doubled over, Leyden locked his fingers around the boy's head, bringing it down onto his rising knee. Heard the crunch of cartilage as the boy's nose shattered.

The gang backed away. Leyden scanned their faces, searching for the next leader. There wasn't one. 'Next time you touch my car, I'll break your fucking legs. Now fuck off out of it.'

The gang picked up the boy in the white hoodie and sullenly withdrew until they were far enough away to hurl insults. Once they were out of sight, Leyden told Speed Bump, 'It's okay, mate, you can get out now. Thanks for your help.'

'It's all right for you.' Speed Bump was already lighting a cigarette. 'If I get burning rags through my letter box, I'll know who to thank.'

'Put a bucket of water behind the door.'

Leyden climbed back in his car and drove off.

Bobby hadn't spoken to Karen since that morning when they'd both been hurrying to get ready for work – Karen complaining about having to go in on a Saturday morning. He remembered that he'd suggested bringing home pizzas. He tried phoning home but the number was busy. It was still engaged as Bobby arrived at the takeaway. Karen's mobile was turned off. He decided to get her favourite vegetarian pizza. He was gambling on her mood. She would either be grateful or else she'd throw a wobbly and demand to know how dare he presume to tell her what to eat.

He ordered an American Hot for himself, thinking that if Karen was going to be awkward, she could have his pizza and he'd eat the veggie one. Anything for a quiet life.

He found Karen on the sofa in the sitting room, legs tucked under her, watching a hospital soap. She'd changed into a sweatsuit.

Bobby held up the pizza boxes. 'I didn't forget.'

'I've already eaten.' Karen continued to stare at the TV.

'I thought we'd agreed to have pizza.'

'I had cheese on toast when I hadn't heard from you. What was I supposed to do? You might have been out till midnight. I didn't know.'

'I've been trying to call you for the last hour. You've been engaged.'

'I've been speaking to my mother, that's all.'

The way that she wouldn't look at him made him suspect she was lying. 'You don't want this pizza?'

'I've told you,' she said. 'I've eaten.'

Bobby felt helpless and frustrated. He could face down a gang of feral scumbags but he had no idea what to say to his girlfriend now. 'I'll scoff this then we can go out for a drink.'

'Don't bother on my account. I'm happy watching telly.'

He didn't understand. Karen was a party animal. The idea of

staying in on Saturday night was anathema to her. He carried the pizzas through into the kitchen, hoping that Karen would change her mind. She didn't.

At least a blazing row would clear the air. This slow abrasion was too painful. Life couldn't go on like this.

Patsy Chalke didn't know if she'd been invited to the Royal Opera House to even up the numbers or if it was her sister Caro's latest attempt to matchmake. She didn't mind either way. It meant she got to see *Don Giovanni*, one of her favourite operas.

She was a bit surprised to see her lover and his wife there – thankfully not in the same party – but she was used to dealing with fraught social situations – and so, luckily, was he.

It was also lucky Caro didn't know about her current man, or she'd have had kittens. Her sister already fretted about what she called Patsy's 'chequered past'. She didn't know the half of it.

Patsy had been born with a silver spoon in her mouth, and had been doing her best to tarnish it ever since.

Her great-grandfather had made his fortune clothing the army during the First World War, accumulating enough money to marry into minor aristocracy. The son had, in turn, married an American heiress. Then more lands, more titles, more money were made in the Second World War – Patsy's ancestors did well out of wars. Now the family was regarded as Old Money, with fortunes in property, banking and shipping channelled through shell companies in tax havens. No one knew how to protect their money like the rich.

Mummy was a silk in commercial law, a part-time judge – one of the great and the good who sat on quangos and the boards of opera houses. Daddy, second son of a marquis, was a successful architect.

Elder sister Caro was the perfect clone. Head girl, respectable upper second from Exeter, married to a merchant banker with political ambitions. Maintaining the family tradition of accruing fortune and social status.

Patsy was the rebellious younger daughter. She had surprised the family by managing to avoid getting expelled from the last of a series of public schools to win an exhibition at Oxford. She had further surprised them by finishing her degree and going on to McGill University in Montreal to start her doctorate in criminology.

In her second year, she'd fallen for an ice hockey pro. Twice they'd set a date for the wedding, and twice he'd called it off – the second time the day before the ceremony. Instead of going off the rails, Patsy had put her head down and completed her research before disappearing around the world. She was twenty-five when she returned to Britain.

The same year as she had inherited the trust fund from her grandmother.

And the same year she had gobsmacked family and friends by joining the Met. She still wasn't quite sure why. She'd thought she'd enjoy the buzz and she had a strong – if individual – sense of right and wrong.

She had been fast-tracked for command rank even though she'd spurned the conventional career path for life on the street. Having adventures, as she put it.

Patsy liked living on the edge. Sometimes she fell off. Knocking out the American senator and trying to drown Rich were just two of her better known escapades.

Her private life was endlessly messy. She enjoyed the thrill of an illicit relationship; the moment when she and her lover would lock eyes across a dinner table – with his wife watching them.

Patsy was drawn to older men, which had led to several affairs with senior police officers, a liaison with a solicitor who absconded with his clients' funds, a fling with a judge who had presided over a trial she was involved in – this last would have been the end of both of their careers if it had got out.

As far as Caro knew, Patsy was currently unattached, and therefore eligible.

There were eight in her sister's party, the guests reflecting her husband Richard's ambitions: junior Home Office minister Barney Ruttle; Paul Tyler, a deputy mayor of London; their wives; and TV historian Alister Simmons who surprised her by being amusingly self-deprecating. The party sat in adjoining boxes, costing £700 each. Caro's husband could afford it.

Patsy had got into her little black cocktail number without any difficulty – good. Although after three days of starvation she hadn't lost a pound – bad.

She was enjoying the performance although she wished her lover wouldn't keep staring at her from the neighbouring box. He was pushing his luck –and making a fool of his wife. Patsy was tempted to go home with the TV historian to teach him a lesson.

At the first interval, Patsy hurried to the loo before going out into the street for the leper cigarette. She was heading back through the Paul Hamlyn room when she was surprised to see Alison Begley. Her boss had had her hair done and had bought a new frock. It made her look provincial, thought Patsy uncharitably.

She was about to make a detour when Begley spotted her.

Patsy tried to sound pleased. 'Hello. Didn't know you were an opera buff.'

'I try to get here when I can,' replied Begley loftily. 'We all have to get out of the office some time.'

'Absolutely,' said Patsy. 'Are you enjoying it?'

'Oh, very much. And you?'

'It's not bad. But don't you think the director seems overly keen to interpose his vision between the audience and the music? When I saw this production back in 2005, it was awesome. I think they're trying too hard to keep it fresh.'

'Um–'

'Also, I'm not sure about Leporello's range,' Patsy continued gaily. 'He's struggling with his projection.'

'Really–' Begley was clearly uncomfortable with a junior officer who looked a million dollars and had brains to match. 'Well, it's nice to have bumped into you. I must get back–'

'Patsy, where's the champagne? Oh, sorry. I didn't see you had company.' Barney Ruttle appeared from nowhere to give Begley his trademark smile.

Patsy tried to hide her displeasure. 'Alison Begley, Barney Ruttle.'

'Enchanted. How do you two know each other?' he asked Begley.

Patsy wanted to kick him. He knew Begley was her boss – and exactly what Patsy thought of her.

'Commander Begley is my superior officer,' said Patsy.

Suddenly Begley clocked who Barney was. 'Mr Ruttle, I believe you're chairing the working party on ethics in policing that I'm attending on Monday.'

'Oh, Lord! Am I?' said Barney. 'No one tells you these things. They just get put in the diary.' He took Begley's hand. 'At least I know there'll be one friendly face there.'

Patsy couldn't restrain herself from making a vomiting sound, only barely disguised as a cough. She saw Paul Tyler and Alister Simmons heading towards them.

'We're trying to find Caro,' said Paul.

The men waited to be introduced to Begley. The bloody woman was still standing there. A minute ago she couldn't wait to get away. But now she'd recognised Alister from TV and no doubt she'd seen Paul Tyler at some London mayoral event.

Again, Patsy did the honours.

'Are you involved in Patsy's cases?' asked Paul. 'Eye-catching stuff. A dead man inside a dry-cleaner's drum!'

'And the mysterious case of the body at the crematorium,'

added Alister in his best TV voice. 'Perhaps I'll take up that offer to front *Crimewatch* after all.'

'I have a… sort of overview,' said Begley.

'Think you'll solve them?' Paul Tyler asked Patsy.

'If we get the manpower.' Patsy couldn't resist saying.

'I've already arranged extra personnel for you,' lied Begley.

The three men left to go and find Caro.

'Everyone's here tonight,' said Begley. 'I saw Mansel Daley earlier. You know – that QC who gave you a hard time over Terry Rich.'

'He's in the next box,' said Patsy. 'He made a point of coming to say hello.'

'Did he mention the Rich case?'

'He did, actually.' Patsy smiled. 'He said he wished I'd drowned the perverted fucker, to use his exact words.'

'It's because of Mansel Daley that Rich is back on the streets.'

'He was only doing his job.'

'I'm glad that you're being phlegmatic about it,' murmured Begley. 'By the way, I heard a rumour that Paul Tyler's joining the Met Police Authority.'

'He's going to be the chair,' said Patsy. 'It's Rubble's idea.

She caught the blank look on Begley's face. 'Barney Rubble, from The Flintstones? No? Anyway, Mr *Ruttle* is fed up with the way the Authority's being run.' She'd probably said too much. 'This is all off the record, you understand.'

Patsy could see other questions forming in her boss's mind. She had often thought that the thirty-minute interval was too long – now she was convinced of it.

'So you're not with any of these men?' said Begley.

'Rubble and Paul are both married,' said Patsy.

Not that it had stopped either of them taking a mistress, she could have added.

DAY FIVE

Sunday

CHALKE WAS UP early for a Sunday. There was nothing – or rather no one – to keep her in bed. After the opera they'd all gone for supper at the Ivy, and then she'd taken a taxi home, sober and alone. She hadn't tried very hard to pull Alister, but then he hadn't tried to pull her at all.

Standing on her balcony, having the final cigarette, she'd concluded that he was a closet gay. She didn't care much either way, but she wished that Caro would take more trouble over her matchmaking.

Patsy drove to Greenwich, taking advantage of the light traffic. She parked in the railway easement and tapped in the four-figure code to open the pedestrian gate to the police station yard. Most officers used the back way to avoid the front desk, where a member of the public would invariably be having a go at one of the civilian staff.

Sunday morning would be no different.

A few of the team were in, grateful for the overtime, together with two new detective constables Begley had sent. One was a finance specialist, so Chalke set him delving into the bank accounts of the dry-cleaner's and the funeral director's.

Chalke was wondering about coffee when Leyden knocked on her door to announce that Crystal Shine was downstairs. Leyden looked as if he'd got dressed in the dark and had then been dragged through a hedge backwards. The side pocket of his jacket was torn, his chinos were creased – not in a good way – and his tie and shirt didn't live on the same colour chart.

Chalke had always found scruffy men attractive.

She made herself focus, hoping that Crystal Shine would throw some light on her husband's disappearance.

Some hope. Mrs Shine turned out to be a sun-bleached blonde, dripping with gold and bursting with anger. She reminded Chalke of Lorraine Finch – but a Lorraine Finch with money.

'Where is she?' demanded Crystal as soon as the detectives entered the interview room.

'Who?'

'That slag he's got in a flat on the river. I want her out. NOW.'

'It's not that simple,' said Chalke, sitting down across the desk.

'What do you mean, not that simple?'

'The flat belongs to a property company owned by your husband.'

'Yeah, *my* husband.'

'You have no rights to the flat,' said Leyden, leaning against the wall.

'Even if he's dead?'

'You think your husband's dead?'

'Nah. No such luck.'

Chalke thought it was time she took control of the interview. 'When did you last see your husband?'

'The night before he left. Dave had to get up early to bring a coffin back so I made him sleep in the spare room.'

'Did you hear from him once he'd arrived in London?'

'He phoned once. He'd forgotten to tell me the Land Cruiser was due in for a service.'

'Does he usually phone you?'

'Nah.'

'Any idea where he could have got to?'

'Not a clue.' Crystal Shine shrugged impatiently. 'I don't know what he does when he's over here.' She gave a bitter laugh. 'Well I do now.'

'You two got along all right?'

'Suppose so. We don't see a lot of each other. He's got his life, I've got mine.'

'He doesn't play golf?'

'Dave? No. That's outdoor stuff, ain't it? He's happier in a bar getting pissed.'

'Does Dave have any business interests in Spain?'

'Not outside the undertaker's.'

'You don't appear concerned for his safety,' said Leyden.

'He'll turn up. He always does.' The thought seemed to depress Crystal then she bucked up. 'But I'll tell you one thing. If he is dead, I'll sell those bleeding funeral parlours tomorrow. Imagine what it's like having to tell friends that I'm married to an undertaker!'

'How long have you been married, Mrs Shine?' asked Leyden.

'Too long. Fourteen years. That's two seven-year itches in Dave's book but he's got a shock coming. I took him back once. This time I'm getting a divorce.'

'That went well,' said Patsy after Crystal Shine had left, threatening to go to her solicitors. 'I need a coffee.'

'I'll bring you one up from the canteen.'

Ten minutes later Leyden appeared in her office with two beakers of coffee.

Chalke put down her wooden man – now goose-stepping – and took the mug. 'What did you make of Crystal?' she asked.

'From the way she was crated with tom, I'd say she's not short of a few bob.'

'Crated with tom?'

'Dripping with jewellery. Keep up, Guv.'

Patsy took a sip of coffee and pulled a face. 'God, this stuff's terrible.'

Bobby tried it. It tasted better than the stuff he drank at home.

Chalke knew the only alternative was the tin of Tesco's instant that Sue Jones kept with the teabags, the brown-stained sugar and iron-furred kettle on the floor behind her desk. Chalke had been meaning to buy a coffee-maker for her office ever since she'd arrived. She wondered whether the kitchen shop in Blackheath was open on Sunday mornings.

While Chalke was thinking about coffee machines, Leyden was mulling over the case. 'What if Crystal and the Dim Reaper have been living beyond their means and he's faking his disappearance for the insurance money?' he said. 'He could be hiding out in Spain in a false moustache and sombrero.'

'I didn't know you could get a false sombrero,' said Chalke. 'Anyway, that does nothing to explain whose body was in the crem.'

Her desk phone rang. Chalke answered it.

'Bring her up,' she said.

Lorraine Finch's large sunglasses failed to hide the best shiner Bobby Leyden had seen in years. Thunderous blues, purple blacks, rich magenta, a smear of pallid yellow. It put his black eye to shame.

'I want him arrested,' began Lorraine. 'He thinks he can get away with murder.'

'Who?' asked Chalke. 'Who do you want arrested?'

'Guinness. The evil bastard.'

From the way Lorraine lowered herself gingerly into a chair, Leyden suspected she'd received a good kicking as well as a black eye.

Chalke leaned forward across her desk. 'Are you saying Tony Yayale killed your husband?'

'Of course not. He was with me.'

'So?'

'Bastard treated me like a human punchbag.'

'When did this happen?'

'Last night, after the fights.' Lorraine began to fold her arms, winced in pain, and thought better of it.

'Any witnesses?'

'Only that scrubber.'

'Why don't you start from the beginning, Mrs Finch?' suggested Leyden.

'He was taking liberties, bringing that tart back to our gym.'

'What tart?'

'Don't know her name. One of those who prance round half naked between rounds.'

'Let me get this right.' Chalke locked her fingers and rested her chin on her thumbs. 'Yayale brought this girl back after he'd been fighting. You'd not been with him?'

'I'd watched him fight and then I'd gone back to the gym, as usual. There're things there he likes... you don't need to know.'

'But he arrived with this other girl?'

'Only wanted a bloody threesome, didn't he?'

'And you weren't having it?' asked Leyden.

'Do me a favour. That tart was a good ten years younger than me.'

'You could have left.'

'No, I couldn't. I was... I didn't have much on and I'd–' Lorraine crossed her wrists and raised her hands over her head.

'You'd tied yourself up?' asked Leyden.

'There are ways... But I couldn't untie myself and they started carrying on. Disgusting it was. When I finally got loose, I grabbed a dumb-bell and clouted him.'

'You hit Guinness... Mr Yayale?'

'Get your retaliation in first is my motto,' said Lorraine. 'Caught him a good one.'

'But then he retaliated.'

'Kicked the shit out of me. I want him nicked.'

Lorraine Finch's husband had been murdered two days ago. Chalke wondered if she even remembered.

'We'll interview Mr Yayale and the witness.'

'That scrubber'll say whatever he tells her to.'

'Strong personality, is he?' asked Leyden.

'He'd have you for breakfast.'

Leyden bridled. 'I'd like to see him try.'

Chalke tried not to smile. 'DS Leyden was asking whether Mr Yayale's a strong character. The type who can bend others to his will.'

'You don't know the half of it. It's not easy saying no to Tony.'

'So if he asked you to lie about his whereabouts, it'd be hard to refuse him.'

'Suppose so.'

'Is there anything you'd like to change in the statement you made about the night your husband was murdered?' asked Chalke.

'Not a bleeding thing. But I do want to know how long the dry-cleaner's is going to be closed.'

'There's still forensic work to be done there.' Chalke chose not to mention that it had been left on hold over the weekend to cut back on overtime.

'How am I supposed to live with no money coming in?'

'It should only be a few more days.'

Lorraine Finch grunted. 'I'm going to have to sell the place anyway. No one'll want their suit cleaned there once they know Minicab's been in the drum.'

'You're going to need a bigger office to keep this in,' said Leyden as they left the kitchen shop in Blackheath.

'I couldn't put up with that coffee any longer.' Chalke lit a cigarette.

'How can you taste anything when you smoke?'

'Don't get on your high horse about my smoking.'

'Haven't you thought about giving it up?'

'Giving up is not a problem. I've done it dozens of times.'

'Seriously.'

'Seriously, bog off.'

'I can't believe that someone like you smokes.' Leyden struggled to adjust his grip on the large box containing the coffee-maker.

'You don't know my other vices.'

Leyden was about to say something about extravagance but bit his tongue. Must be nice to be able to spend £500 on a whim. Like everyone else at the nick, he was curious about Chalke's wealth. He'd tried dropping a few hints but had learned nothing other than that Patsy Chalke was a very private person.

'Think we can get Guinness on assault?' he asked as they crossed Tranquil Vale.

'Lorraine admits she started it but he did give her a good beating. Let's see if we can use this to drive a wedge between them.'

Leyden grimaced and moved the box to his other hand. Served him right, thought Chalke. It was his fault they had to walk all this way back to the car. She'd been going to park outside the shop on the double yellow with a police notice on the sunshield until Leyden had protested. Chalke never had any problems bending rules when it suited her.

'Shit, I don't believe it!' She stopped in her tracks.

'What?'

'Terry Rich. On that bench over there. What the fuck's he doing here?' Chalke ground her cigarette into the pavement.

'There's a girls' prep school just up that lane there,' said Leyden, pointing.

'I'll kill him.' Chalke strode towards Rich.

Leyden hurried after her. 'You two have history, guv. He could claim harassment.'

'Damned right I'm harassing him. Since when did his bail

conditions allow him to loiter near a school, even on a Sunday?'

Terry Rich saw them coming and stood up. He was a big man but his powerful frame was offset by a weak chin and a beak of a mouth in a face both childlike and spiteful.

The sort of face made for smacking.

Rich gave her the same triumphant leer that he had worn in court. 'Inspector Chalke, how nice to see you.'

'What are you doing here?'

'Do you mean here or here?' He pointed to the ground.

'Here, in close proximity to a school,' snapped Chalke, eyes flashing.

'Am I?' For a big man, Rich had a squeaky voice.

'You know you are.'

'Do I?'

'You are literate?' Leyden spoke for the first time.

'Oh, yes. Extremely so.'

'In that case, you can read that sign. The one that says "School".'

Rich pretended to see the sign for the first time. 'Well, blow me.'

'Watch it.'

'Intimidation.' Rich threw up his hands.

'You're in breach of your bail conditions by being here.'

'No, I'm not. I'm allowed to travel within two miles of my bail hostel.' Rich produced a photocopied page of a London street map. There was a circle drawn around a point in Catford. 'There's my bail hostel. This is a two-mile circle. As you can see, I'm inside it. Besides, it's Sunday, so why would the school be open?'

'On your way, sunshine,' ordered Leyden.

'Are you on duty, whatever your name is?'

'DS Leyden. Yes, I'm on duty.'

'In that case, why are you carrying a coffee-maker?'

Patsy Chalke was still spitting feathers as they drove towards Bermondsey to interview Yayale. She had already alerted Greenwich and Lewisham police to step up patrols outside local schools. While it was in Rich's interest to observe his bail conditions and stay away from children, Chalke's evil side was hoping his compulsions would overcome his reason.

The roadworks along Evelyn Street added to her bad mood. The journey from Greenwich to central London was a nightmare. There were 24-hour bus lanes even though there were no night buses and not many daytime ones, single-lane carriageways which had been deliberately narrowed, and traffic lights that stayed red for no reason. It was Sunday lunchtime, yet it could have been the morning rush hour.

'You'd think the planners would want drivers to complete their journeys as quickly as possible,' she said. 'Get traffic off the roads, not have it crawling along them.'

'Mr Weaver told me that when he first worked in Greenwich, thirty years ago, there were just three traffic lights between the nick and Inner London Crown Court,' said Leyden. 'Last time he lost count after twenty-eight.'

The traffic eased as they turned south off the main road. The Stag pub stood on a corner, a tyre-fitter's to one side, a row of fly-blown shops on the other. The external door to the gym was locked. They went into the pub.

The snug, saloon and public bars had been knocked together to form a blighted barn where a core of drinkers were staring at Sunderland play Hull on three flat-screen TVs. The rap music coming from the jukebox drowned out the commentary.

Guinness was standing at the far end of the bar in conversation with a slim man wearing tasselled loafers and a black silk rollneck under a sports jacket.

'Well, well. Ari O,' breathed Leyden. 'Not seen him for a while.'

'Tell me,' ordered Chalke as they paused inside the door.

'Aristaeus Orestikos, aka Ari O. Loan shark. Tight hold on the local estates. He's bent as a nine-bob note but he's the biffer, if you understand. The rent boys are scared of him after he hurt a couple so badly that they had to be sewn up in hospital.'

'Charming. Wonder what he wants with Yayale?'

'I'd say they were fixing next week's fights.'

An ox of a man in dark glasses sidled up to Ari O.

'We've been clocked,' murmured Leyden.

Guinness stiffened. Ari O put down a bottle of carbonated water and left. The minder followed.

'I hope we didn't scare your friend away,' said Leyden, going up to Yayale.

'He's picky who he shares a bar with.' Yayale took a swig from a bottle of lager.

'How did your fighters get on?' asked Leyden. 'Remember, the two we saw training.'

'One won.'

'What a surprise.'

'How's the head?' asked Chalke.

'What do you mean?'

'After Lorraine brained you.'

Yayale's eyes narrowed. 'What's that cow been saying?'

'She wants you banged up.'

'She started it.'

'She's scared of you, isn't she?' asked Chalke.

'You tell me.'

Chalke leaned towards Yayale, keeping her voice low. 'So scared of you that she's sticking to her story about the night Minicab was killed.'

'Bollocks. What we said is the truth.'

'You claim you went straight home after the fight but Mrs Finch told us that you normally come back to the gym for sex.'

'I was fighting in Woolwich. It didn't make sense to come all the way here.' Yayale curled his lip. 'You don't understand, do you? I'm not the one that needs an alibi. She is.'

'Eh?'

'The slapper's been robbing Minicab blind. He only found out a couple of days before he got slotted.'

'How do you mean?'

'Lorraine used to do Minicab's books, go to the bank for him, pay the bills, everything. When he found out she was bleeding him dry, he went mental, threatened to throw her out. But she was out with me the night he died.'

'She could have paid someone to do a number on him,' said Leyden.

'If she did, she didn't say anything to me. But I'll tell you one thing for free. Lorraine was in school with Crystal Shine. They're best mates.'

'Crystal Shine?' Chalke frowned. 'What's that got to do with anything?'

'You tell me.'

'Fancy a bag of chips?' said Leyden as they headed back to Greenwich along the Old Kent Road to avoid Evelyn Street.

'No way.'

'I'll treat you.'

'No.' Patsy made herself sound more assertive than she felt. To change the subject, she asked, 'Wonder why Yayale pointed us at Crystal Shine like that?'

'Dunno, but if you think about it, we have two wives who are close mates. Crystal's husband vanishes, suspected of murdering person or persons unknown. Then two days later, Lorraine's husband is murdered. Bit of a coincidence, don't you think?'

'And you don't believe in coincidence?'

'You've been reading too many detective books. Nothing wrong with coincidence.'

'Glad you think so.'

The sight of a fish and chip shop rekindled Leyden's hunger. 'It's all right for you,' he said. 'You're on a diet.'

'Who said I was on a diet?'

'All you had yesterday at the Blue Boar was a salad.'

'I ate in the evening.' Another salad – Waldorf this time.

Demons wrestled inside Patsy. She always did this – starving herself for days before cracking and stuffing herself with junk food.

She'd have to go back to WeightWatchers, even though one of the programme's main effects was to make you binge drink. Well, the way she did it anyway. Not eating all day to save up her twenty points until evening, then knocking back the vodka because a shot was only one point while a glass of white wine was three.

It was a strange sensation – drinking half a bottle of iced vodka on an empty stomach.

'Chips are the worst thing you can have,' she said.

'You said you weren't on a diet.'

Chalke's stomach rumbled. 'Shut up.'

'Is that me or your stomach?'

'Both.'

Normally Patsy would have ignored the string of down-at-heel chippies, burger bars and kebab houses along the Old Kent Road but now Leyden had mentioned food, she could think of nothing else. Her stomach had taken over her head. She had to eat.

'There's a good Chinese in New Cross,' tempted Leyden. 'You could get a vegetable soup there.'

Vegetable soup. Couldn't be many calories in vegetable soup. 'All right.'

'Eat there or take back to the station.'

'Eat there. I'm starving.'

Tony Yayale lay on the exercise machine in tracksuit bottoms and black sleeveless vest, ankles hooked in the stirrups, pressing the

80-kilo bar set in the slotted frame above his head.

Sunday evening, and while others slobbed out in front of the box, he worked out. Everyone knew the showman; no one saw the sweat. Yayale preferred it that way. He liked his fans to think it all came easy, but nothing was for free.

He thought of Lorraine Finch and the trouble she'd caused. Fuck her. She was no one without him. He hoped those coppers would give her grief. That'd teach her to cross him.

Yayale sensed that he wasn't alone. He glanced down towards the end of the bench. A bare-breasted woman stood there. He was staring in disbelief when there was the sound of a metallic click. Another click. Yayale looked up to see that his hands had been chained to the bar holding the weights. He went to place the bar on its rest, only to find that the rest was no longer there.

The woman glided towards him. She was wearing latex gloves.

'Take that side,' said a man's voice behind him.

Together they repositioned the stand until the weights were directly over Yayale's throat.

'What the fuck are you doing?'

The woman tightened the ankle straps.

'Fuck you–'

A gag was rammed in Yayale's mouth.

'We have things to talk about,' said the man. 'Then we'll let you go.'

Yayale's arms were rigid but he was comfortable. He could hold this weight for hours. They had underestimated his strength if they thought they could scare him like this.

The man started asking questions. The woman removed the gag.

'Fuck off,' snarled Yayale.

The gag was replaced.

The couple moved out of his vision. There was the sound of weights being moved. The bar grew heavier – and heavier.

Yayale became afraid.

He closed his eyes and concentrated, channelling his power into his arms, fighting to ignore the burning sensation spreading in his muscles. For a while he thought he could do it, taking a minute at a time, one minute after another, another…

But there were more minutes than he could endure.

Sweat began pooling in his eye sockets, rivulets trickling down his cheeks. His hands were starting to shake, his biceps screaming out in agony. Yayale nodded his head. The gag was removed.

'What do you want to know?'

DAY SIX

Monday

'IT WASN'T ME.' Lorraine Finch folded her arms across her body and glowered at Leyden from behind her sunglasses. 'I didn't kill him.'

'You have the motive,' said Leyden.

'What? Because he gave me a hiding?'

'Three motives. Guinness gave you a good smacking –'

'Listen, sweetheart, I've been smacked more times than you've had hot dinners. Had them and given them.'

'He dumped you–'

'Not a problem.'

Chalke didn't believe that. Lorraine Finch's face was made to hold a grudge. She said nothing, though. They had agreed that Leyden should lead the questioning, on the assumption that Lorraine would be more likely to respond to a man.

'A key to Guinness's gym was found in your handbag,' said Leyden.

'Forgot to give it back, didn't I?'

Leyden gave her an look. No doubt Lorraine had 'forgotten' because she'd been planning to steal whatever she could from the gym.

'You used the key to let yourself in while Guinness was working out–' said Leyden.

'Bollocks I did.'

'You crept up on him, shackled his wrists to the bar and moved the weights machine so that the bar was directly over his throat.'

'Didn't do much, did I?'

'It's not a lot, taken one stage at a time.' Bobby leaned back. It was warm in the interview room. He'd taken off his jacket, rolled up his sleeves to under his elbows and loosened his tie even further. Chalke didn't think she'd ever seen him with his tie properly done up.

'First, you cuff Guinness to the bar and then fasten his feet. The bar can only go up and down so effectively he's trapped.'

'Got it all worked out, haven't you?'

'You had motive, means and opportunity.'

Tony Yayale's body had not been discovered until the pub cleaner had got round to opening the gym at ten o'clock that morning. Guinness's face had not been a pretty sight – blackened, bloated, eyes popping. The smell of his shit and piss had made Chalke gag. Even Doc Brennan had found it hard to be jocular.

Begley, all sweetness and light after their encounter at the opera, had drafted in a team to run the on-the-spot inquiry. Chalke was grateful. Her hands were full enough with the two investigations already running.

She had been coming round to the idea that Lorraine had killed Minicab with Guinness's help. Placing the body into the dry-cleaning drum had been an attempt at misdirection, she suspected.

But now Guinness was dead.

'You had motive, means and opportunity,' repeated Leyden.

'Yeah, and I also have an alibi. I went to the pictures with a girlfriend. We saw *Mamma Mia!* at FilmWorks on the Peninsula, then went for a chinky at that place under the Holiday Inn.'

'What time are we talking about?'

'The film started at 7.30. Finished around ten.'

'Who's the girlfriend?'

'Crystal Shine.'

Leyden and Chalke glanced at each other.

'Guinness said you two were good mates.'

'Did he now?' Lorraine folded her arms tighter, a ball of smouldering resentment. 'Why'd he say that, then?'

'You tell me.'

'Me and Crystal have known each other for ever. We meet up when she's over.'

'People in the cinema will remember seeing you, will they?'

'How do I know? A dark-haired girl sold us the tickets. There wasn't an usher. There never is in that poxy place. The waitress in the restaurant might remember us.'

Lorraine was very sure of herself. Cock sure.

'After the meal?'

'Crys drove me home. We had a few glasses of Baileys, played some Abba. It must have been about half past twelve when she went.'

'Did Crystal know Guinness?' began Leyden.

'Everybody knew Guinness.' Lorraine played with the cigarette packet. 'I could murder a fag.'

'We've still a couple of things to clear up.'

'Like what?'

'Like why you were bleeding Minicab dry.'

Lorraine didn't miss a beat. 'Was I?'

'Yes,' said Leyden with slow deliberation. 'You've stashed away £20,000 in your bank account and another £30k in the building society. I reckon you've got more squirrelled away somewhere. We'll find it, and freeze it.'

'You can't do that!' For the first time, Lorraine reacted. Fear of losing money clearly touched a nerve that losing a husband didn't.

'You just watch us,' said Leyden. 'You were building a nest egg for when you walked out. What was it, a dowry for Guinness?'

'Fuck off.' Lorraine seemed to huddle in on herself.

'But Minicab found out. Ineffectual little Minicab.' Leyden leaned towards her, keeping his voice low. He had the power of stillness, the ability to slow things down, creating the space for his words to have impact. 'He threatened to kick you out. You laughed in his face. You were twice the man he was. That's when he threatened to bubble you.'

'My Lee wouldn't Bertie anyone.'

'Your Lee had never had anyone deliberately wreck what was left of his business before. But he didn't have the balls to take you on, especially with Guinness on your side, so the only way he could get even was to come to the Old Bill. And that's what he was about to do when he was topped.' Leyden sucked his teeth. 'Doesn't look too good, sweetheart, does it?'

'You're making this up.'

'Then your shag gives you the tin-tack,' Leyden continued. 'All that dosh and he still dumps you. But now you've killed once, you're willing to kill again.'

'No.' Lorraine was sitting upright now.

'It's easier to kill the second time, isn't it?'

'I never killed Minicab. Like I said, I have an alibi.'

'Yeah, Guinness. But then you and Guinness fall out. He was going to blow the whistle on you. You're in egg.'

'Bollocks I am.'

'Remember I said you had three motives. You never let me finish. That was the third reason to kill him – to stop him retracting his alibi.'

'You're fitting me up.' The colour drained from Lorraine's cheeks. 'I didn't do it, gospel.'

Chalke and Leyden left the police station through the side gate, turning down Royal Hill towards the dry-cleaner's.

She had liked the way Leyden had handled the interview, needling Lorraine until he had got under her skin. Her outburst at the end, when she'd finally realised how much trouble she was in, had been interesting.

'What did you think of her?' Chalke asked Leyden.

'Right little charmer. But I don't see how she could have topped Guinness without help.'

'She could have killed Minicab by herself.'

'Yeah, but she'd have had trouble stuffing his body into the drum on her tod.'

'Which means she needed help again. So either Guinness helps her kill Minicab and then she gets a new accomplice to top Guinness. Or the same person's helped her with both killings.'

'The second theory seems more likely,' said Leyden.

'Of course, she could have gone to the gym to make it up with Guinness, but then it all went pear shaped.'

'Possible,' said Leyden, thinking it wasn't very likely.

They halted by the pedestrian lights on Greenwich High Road. Chalke pressed the button to cross although she knew it was a waste of time. The dry-cleaner's was still hidden behind a canvas screen. Minicab's body had been found seventy-two hours earlier. It seemed like weeks ago, thought Chalke.

The detectives were logged in. While Chalke went through into the back room to talk to the SOCOs, Leyden joined Carl Cochrane, who was playing with the automated garment retrieval system.

'Really clever, this,' he told Leyden. 'Look.'

He scanned a ticket on a bar code reader and the rack of garments moved around until the matching ticket, pinned on a coat, halted beside him.

'Let's see if we can find my suit.' Leyden dug in his wallet for the ticket which Sue had given back to him Cochrane scanned it. They watched as the rack clattered around until it stopped at Leyden's M&S suit.

'It's like a train set,' grinned Leyden, reaching towards his suit.

'I hope you weren't thinking of taking that away,' said Chalke, emerging from the back.

'I've only got one other suit. . .'

'Has anyone been through these garments yet?' Chalke asked Cochrane.

'Not yet, ma'am, but I'm sure Minicab would have checked the pockets before they were put into the machine.'

'You're missing the point.' Chalke examined the suits one by one while the two men looked on. A slight bulge in a grey suit jacket caught her eye. 'Look. What's that?'

Leyden leaned over and reached into the inside breast pocket. He pulled out a white business envelope. Inside, a cellophane bag was solid with white powder. Leyden dabbed his fingertip into the corner of the envelope.

'Cocaine,' he said.

Chalke picked up the packet with the palms of her hands, careful not to leave fingerprints. She put it up to her face. 'What's that smell?'

Leyden shrugged. 'No good asking me, guv. I've no sense of smell.'

Cochrane, too, was shaking his head. Chalke frowned. The smell was distinctive, and she'd come across it recently. She made herself concentrate.

It was like formaldehyde, but she hadn't been in any labs. No, it was something to do with Stan Figgens. The funeral parlour. When she'd been shown around. The embalming room.

That smell was embalming fluid.

An hour later Patsy Chalke was arriving at Scotland Yard, the cocaine and samples of embalming fluid from the Dim Reaper's funeral parlour were being blue-lighted to the labs. Meanwhile, Lorraine Finch was being left to stew.

Chalke thought the meeting should have taken place at Greenwich or in Guinness's gym, but Begley did not do crime scenes, feeling more secure behind her desk at Scotland Yard.

She greeted Patsy like a long-lost friend.

'I must say I did enjoy *Don Giovanni*. Although I saw what you meant about Leporello. He struggled in the second half.'

Patsy, who actually thought the singer had improved, just nodded.

'You're so lucky to be able to get such good tickets,' Begley added.

'My sister knows all the right people,' said Chalke. 'I'm sure she'd love to invite you one evening. Shall I mention it to her?'

'That would be very kind. It's not often Hugo and I get out. We both work such long hours.'

'What does your husband do?'

'He's an actuary with Sun Alliance Insurance.'

One of the shortest books ever written – Lives of Famous Actuaries.

Patsy changed the subject. 'I bumped into Terry Rich yesterday. He was hanging around near a girls' school in Blackheath.'

'Steer clear of him, Patricia. Don't give him any excuse to claim police harassment.'

Chalke couldn't remember when she'd last been called Patricia. Probably when she was being expelled from some school or other.

'I was thinking more of the children.'

There was a knock on the door. Weaver entered.

Chalke said, 'We've just found three packages of cocaine bearing traces of embalming fluid in suits held at the dry-cleaner's. Each packet weighs around 28 grams.'

Weaver's eyebrows rose.

'It looks as if the Dim Reaper brought the cocaine into the country and then Minicab distributed it. Of course, we don't know whether Minicab was the only distributor.'

'Clever,' murmured Weaver. 'Drop in your suit to be cleaned and it comes back with the odd package – and all within sight of the nick.'

'What does Lorraine Finch have to say about all this?' asked Begley.

'We'd just finished a long interview with her regarding Yayale's killing when we found the cocaine. It wouldn't be appropriate to go back to her immediately. She's not going anywhere.'

'Let me get this right.' Begley turned a pencil through her fingers. 'A fortnight ago Dave Shine smuggled in cocaine with a body. That body was cremated. Then last week Shine disappeared at the same time as an unknown male was cremated in place of Stan Figgens. We suspect that Shine killed that man and used the crematorium to dispose of the body.'

'We assume he wanted to conceal the victim's identity,' interrupted Chalke.

'Why?'

Chalke tried not to roll her eyes. 'We wish we knew.'

Begley nodded. 'Then Lee Finch – aka Minicab – is battered to death and his body found in the drum of his dry cleaning machine.'

'Seems to me that that putting Minicab's body in the drum could be a way of sending a message,' said Weaver.

'Does that mean that Lorraine Finch is innocent of her husband's murder?'

'Not necessarily,' replied Chalke.

'But it is beginning to look as if Shine killed Lee Finch?'

'It's possible. They could have fallen out over drugs,' said Chalke, unwilling to commit herself further.

'What about Yayale? Lorraine Finch – guilty or not guilty?' asked Begley.

Chalke and Weaver both waited for the other to speak.

'Hard to say,' said Weaver finally.

'She has motive and opportunity,' prompted Begley.

'She also has an alibi,' said Chalke, thinking that Weaver shouldn't wear a pink shirt – it clashed with his florid face and broken veins. 'Time of death is estimated at around 9 p.m. Lorraine and Crystal Shine are on CCTV leaving the cinema at 10.05 p.m.'

'Could she not have snuck out of the cinema and then re-turned?' asked Begley.

'There's only one entrance. She couldn't have avoided the cam-eras,' said Chalke.

'Of course, she might have hired a hit man to take care of Guinness,' suggested Weaver.

'I'm sorry?' Begley sat bolt upright. 'What did you say? Guinness…?'

'Yayale's known as Guinness because he had an Irish mother and a black father.'

Begley gave a theatrical shudder. 'Mr Weaver, I'm disappointed to hear one of my officers using such a name. I spent my time in Diversity Strategy and Citizen Focus working to eradicate that the sort of language.'

'It's Yayale's street name,' explained Weaver.

'But you do not have to repeat it,' said Begley.

'Yes, ma'am.' Weaver's face became even more florid than usual.

Patsy felt a flash of anger. Weaver was ten times the copper Begley would ever be: a noted thief-taker who'd put six murderers behind bars, with priceless informants. How dare Begley!

Weaver continued the briefing as Chalke fought to control her temper. Forensic were taking the gym apart. The place was covered with fingerprints which would take time to identify. De-tectives were working through a surprisingly large number of handcuff suppliers.

'What about this Aristaeus Orestikos?' asked Begley. 'A known criminal seen with Yayale on the afternoon he's murdered. It must mean something.'

Yayale would have been seen with known criminals most after-noons, you moron.

'Word is that Ari O and Yayale were involved in fixing cage fights,' said Weaver. 'The sport's taking off big time. Yayale was trying to expand. If one of the major crime families considered him a business threat, they'd top him in such a way as to send a signal to others not to do the same.'

'Patricia?'

'Sounds plausible, ma'am, but what I want to know is why Yayale went out of his way to tell us that Lorraine and Crystal Shine were friends. Yayale wasn't the sort to inform, but he was doing his best to put the boot into Lorraine.'

'Can't see the importance myself. Now I've got a meeting–' Begley stood to indicate that the conference was over. 'I'm due to see Mr Ruttle this afternoon at the working party on ethics in policing,' she told Chalke.

'Give him my love.'

'Known him long?'

'His wife and I were in college together.'

'Where was that?'

'Pembroke.'

'Why did you go to college in Pembroke?' asked Weaver.

'Pembroke College, Oxford.'

'When I started, graduates in the police force were rare,' he grumbled. 'Now every bobby on the beat has a degree. Did you go to college, too, ma'am?'

'Cambridge,' replied Begley.

And the rest. Come on. And the rest.

Chalke waited for Begley to qualify her answer, but she didn't. Begley hadn't lied, but she had been economical with the truth.

Knowledge was power, Patsy believed. Consequently, she had made it her business to know that Begley had a lower second in politics from Sheffield and had gone to Wolfson College, Cambridge to study social policy and law on a one-year police scholarship while she was an inspector.

Patsy wouldn't have cared if Begley had gone to the University of Longleat to study caravan park administration, but it was interesting the way the woman was reinventing herself.

And careless of her not to do it more thoroughly.

'She's changed her tune towards you,' said Weaver as he and Patsy walked to the lift.

'I bumped into her at the opera on Saturday. She was impressed by the company I was keeping.'

'Be careful. I wouldn't trust that woman further than I could kick her.'

'Nor would I.'

Chalke offered Weaver a lift but he was going on to Guinness's gym. Back in Greenwich, she decided to catch up with her emails before having another crack at Lorraine.

Sue Jones brought in a batch of post. 'I wasn't sure if this was for you. It says Dr P.L. Chalke.'

'That's me,' said Patsy.

'You're a doctor!'

'It's an academic thing. I'm not a medical doctor.'

'Why don't you call yourself doctor?'

Patsy was at a loss. 'I just don't see any reason to.'

'If I was a doctor, I'd want everyone to know.'

Patsy remembered her idea to persuade Sue to go back into education and get a better job. She'd work on her one evening over a bottle of wine. Patsy liked a crusade.

But now it was time to interview Lorraine Finch again.

Lorraine was not glad to see Chalke and Leyden. 'Bloody hell! Are you two lonely for company or what?' she asked.

'Or what,' replied Leyden, sitting down opposite her.

'If you're going to keep me here much longer, I'm going to get myself a brief.'

'That's your right,' said Chalke. 'Although you should understand that if you do, all this will become more formal. At the moment, you're merely helping us with our inquiries. You're not under arrest nor have you been cautioned.'

'Yeah, yeah.' Lorraine backed down.

'Tell me, how well do you know the Dim Reaper?' asked Leyden.

Chalke watched Lorraine closely, but there was no tell; nothing to betray if she was speaking the truth or not. She was a blank piece of paper.

'He's Crystal's husband,' she said carefully. 'I've met him a few times.'

'Did Minicab know him?'

'Yeah, like I said, we all met up.'

'Were they friends?'

'Not that I know of. Sometimes the four of us went out for a meal but Crystal and Dave don't come back to London at the same time much anymore, if you understand what I'm saying.'

'Does Crystal have some bloke over here?'

'How do I know? Why don't you ask her?.'

Leyden nodded, as if accepting the rebuke, not in a hurry to move on. 'Were Minicab and the Dim Reaper in business together?'

'What, an undertaker and a dry-cleaner? Do me a favour!'

'What about the cocaine that Minicab was knocking out for the Reaper?'

'What bleeding cocaine?' Lorraine was immediately alert, eyes flashing.

'The stuff he was dealing from the dry-cleaner's.'

'The little toerag never told me about any drugs.'

Her anger was palpable. Chalke knew why. Lorraine had been milking the business but she'd been siphoning off only his legitimate profits. His illegal takings would have been much greater – and Lorraine had missed them. No wonder she was furious.

Yet… if Lorraine and Crystal were that close…

Leyden felt sure that the Reaper would have told Crystal about his drug trafficking. Criminals kept things in the family; that's how it worked. He would have used his wife to hide profits and assets. And since Crystal and Lorraine were best friends…

It wasn't easy being a copper sometimes.

If Weaver's theory that Yayale's murder was linked to a fight-fixing scam was correct, giving Aristaeus Orestikos a tug was Chalke's next logical step. She knew that she should let the new team interview him but she was prepared to pull rank.

The police psychological test she'd sat in order to be considered for command rank had exposed three weaknesses in Chalke.

The first was an unwillingness to delegate; the second a propensity to cut corners; and the third a belief that the ends justified the means. Patsy had belatedly realised that she'd made a mistake in being honest. Later, she'd done a number on the psychologist, rewritten the answers – and had never been honest in assessments since.

But it didn't change the fact that she was unwilling to delegate.

'Tell me more about Ari O,' she said as she accelerated up Croom's Hill, Leyden wincing as she flew over the speed bumps.

'He's a Bubble–'

'What?'

'Bubble and squeak. Greek. Thirty-six years old. Owns a gay club and a Greek restaurant – sort of place you go to break plates on a Saturday night. His real money comes from loan sharking. Trading Standards have had a couple of goes at him but got nowhere. Don't be fooled by his cultured act. He's the most twisted, sadistic bastard you'd ever wish not to meet.'

They turned onto the Blackwall Tunnel Approach at the Sun in the Sands roundabout. Patsy groaned at the sight of three lanes of slow-moving traffic. A flashing sign warned: 'Lorry stuck in Tunnel'.

'Why didn't they build the tunnel in a straight line, not with all these bends?' she asked.

'Well, there are a couple of theories,' said Leyden unexpectedly. 'One is that the bends were put in to prevent horses bolting when they saw the daylight up ahead at the end of the tunnel – there weren't many cars around in 1897. Another theory is that the builders had to dig around a Black Death burial ground.'

'Fascinating.'

'This was the longest underwater tunnel in the world when it was built. Six hundred houses had to be demolished to make the approach road, including Sir Walter Raleigh's former gaff.'

'You mean he lived out *here*?'

'Before the gasworks was built.'

'Bobby?'

'Yeah?'

'Shut up.'

Patsy put on a CD of Snow Patrol's *Eyes Open*, turning up the volume to deter Leyden from offering any more fascinating facts. The traffic finally speeded up. They exited the tunnel into the East India Dock Road.

'Ari O's expecting trouble,' said Chalke five minutes later, as they came in sight of the Ulysses Grill, sandwiched between a beauty parlour and an empty shop.

On the pavement outside the restaurant, two shaven-headed men in jeans and black leather jackets were giving traffic the hard eye. Two more men were sitting in a car in a side street.

'Cannon fodder. If hostilities break out, those boys will cop it, Ari O'll know the war's started and his real muscle will be intact,' said Leyden. 'By the way, you know how to tell if a Greek is lying, don't you?'

'How?'

'His lips are moving.'

They left the car a few streets away, deliberately not putting police ID on show. Better to get a ticket and go through the hassle of having it cancelled than getting the car trashed.

As they made for the door, one of the watchers blocked their way. 'Restaurant's closed.'

'Not for us, it ain't,' replied Leyden. 'Move aside.'

'Got a problem?'

'Yeah. Scum like you make me want to throw up.'

'Fuck you.' The man reared up like a snake about to strike.

'Don't even think about it, sunshine.'

Chalke stepped in. 'Police,' she said, showing her warrant card.

'Should have known you two was pigs.'

Leyden put his hand against the man's chest and gave him a shove that sent him reeling back against the plate-glass window. 'One day, pond life, one day.'

The restaurant was the size of a small aircraft hangar, filled with oilcloth-covered tables and raffia-backed chairs stretching away to a dance floor. Clay plates were piled in front of a fake fireplace.

A thin boy with masses of black curls and kohl around his eyes came from behind the counter where a doner kebab sat festering by an unlit grill.

'Police,' said Patsy. 'We're here to talk to Mr Orestikos.'

'I'm afraid Mr Orestikos is not available,' said the boy. 'Would you like to make an appointment?'

'No, son,' said Leyden. 'I'd like you to tell Ari O to get his jacksie down here now or we'll get a warrant and spin this drum so hard it'll come apart at the fucking seams. Got me?'

The boy gave a nervous smile and scuttled off towards the kitchen.

'You haven't taken your charm pills today, have you?' said Chalke.

The boy returned. 'Mr Orestikos will see you now. If you'll walk this way.'

'I couldn't walk that way if I tried,' muttered Leyden as they followed the boy up a flight of concrete steps ending at an oak door on a tight bend where it would be difficult to use a hydraulic ram or a sledgehammer. Leyden was willing to bet that there'd be a sheet of steel between the door's wood laminates. Beyond the door the stairs became carpeted.

They entered a large room. Swathes of brightly coloured silks and white gauze fell from the ceiling, creating a tent-like effect. Rich tapestries adorned the walls, cushions and Persian carpets covered the floor. There was the overpowering smell of incense.

'The man's East Ham,' breathed Leyden.

'East Ham?'

'One stop away from Barking.'

'Excuse me,' said a voice to their left. 'I was meditating.'

They turned to see Ari O wearing a royal blue jalabiya with gold silk collar, a cream woven cord belt around the waist. Dark stubble showed through his pale skin. Patsy was struck by his small cupid mouth and his pale, strangely translucent eyes. They reminded her of a fish that had been dead for two days.

'We'd like to talk to you regarding the murder of Tony Yayale,' said Chalke.

'Ah yes, poor Tony,' said Ari O with a hoarse lisp. He indicated the cushions strewn over the floor. 'Please be seated.' He began quoting. *'Here with a loaf of bread beneath the bough, a flask of wine, a book of verse – and thou beside me singing in the wilderness – And wilderness is paradise enow.'*

Two could play that game.

'"How sweet is mortal sovranty!" – think some: Others – "How blest the paradise to come!"' rejoined Patsy.

'Ah! You know the *Rubaiyat of Omar Khayyam*?' Ari O pretended to be delighted.

'It might be more accurate to call it the *Rubaiyat of Fitzgerald*,' said Chalke, 'since it owes its popularity as much to its translator as to its author. Ironically, Fitzgerald's isn't even a particularly faithful translation although it is celebrated for its sublime phrasing.'

Leyden had had enough. He turned to Ari O. 'We saw you with Yayale yesterday afternoon in the Stag. What were you talking about?'

'It's no secret. He wanted me to go into business with him, promoting his cage fighters.'

'You mean, run the book on his hooky fights?'

'You have a poor opinion of me, Mr Leyden. Tony wanted to give his fighters a higher profile.'

'What was in it for you?'

'We didn't get as far as specifics.'

'And eight hours later he was murdered.'

'Sad.'

The boy brought in a tray carrying a long-handled *cevze* and tiny porcelain cups in filigree holders. He handed them round.

'This wasn't about the fights at Streatham on Saturday by any chance, was it?' said Leyden. 'Guinness forget to tell the big boys who was going to win, did he?'

'I don't know what you're talking about.'

'Outside on the pavement there are two tethered goats just waiting to get shot.' Leyden took a sip of coffee. 'Any particular reason?'

Ari O opened his hands palms outwards in a Levantine gesture.

'Why not talk to us on the QT,' said Leyden. 'See if we can help.'

Ari repeated the gesture.

'Ever have any dealings with Minicab?'

'The guy in the dry-cleaning machine? No.'

'The Dim Reaper?'

'No.'

'Why are you lying?'

Ari O assumed a hurt expression. 'I'm not.'

Leyden was losing patience. 'Listen, I don't care how much

blood you spill in the East End but you soil the streets of Green-wich and I'll have your guts,' said Leyden. 'Is that understood?'

'*The moving finger writes; and, having writ, moves on,*' intoned Ari. He turned to Chalke. 'Now if you've finished your coffee, Detective Chief Inspector, I will tell your fortune.' He placed a saucer over her cup. 'Turn the cup upside down and move it in a clock-wise direction three times.' Chalke did as instructed and handed the cup and saucer to Ari O, noticing that his hands had been carefully manicured.

'Shapes pointing towards the handle represent the future; those pointing away, the past,' he explained, staring into the grounds left in the cup. 'Ah, you are wealthy. I didn't know the police paid so well. That wheel means a change in fortune. Perhaps you're go-ing to lose your money. And there's an eye. Someone is jealous of you. A peak. Victory... Hmmm. A complex picture.'

'Do your own,' said Chalke.

'One shouldn't read really one's own future but for you–' Ari O completed the ritual and held out the cup. 'That's an ear – the news of Guinness's death, no doubt. A knife... and a flag. Symbols of danger ahead–' He stopped, scowling at the cup. 'Like I said, one should never try to read one's own fortune.'

He didn't offer to read Leyden's.

Outside the restaurant, Leyden told the two men. 'Put some air between you. You'll make a smaller target that way.'

'Piss off,' said the men, moving apart.

'That was seriously weird,' said Chalke as they walked back to the car. 'Do you reckon Ari O's flipped for real, or was it all an elaborate game?'

'The way he's tethered those goats doesn't suggest madness. Ruthless cunning, maybe, but not insanity.'

'Shouldn't we tell the local force?'

'They'll know soon enough if someone tries to slot those guys,' said Leyden.

'But they could be killed.'

'No big loss.'

Joey Starling couldn't believe his eyes. Jemma Wodehouse. On his film set!

This was the bitch who'd walked out on him – and no one walked out on Joey Starling. He fought to control his temper, breathing deeply, remembering what those anger-management tossers had said.

Jemma had changed since he'd seen her last. Now she was a young woman rather than the teenager he'd known. She'd grown even more attractive – elfin with unruly fair hair tumbling over her shoulders, a diamond nose stud. He wondered if she was still hooked on drugs. No, he thought. Her skin was too good. Still – once a wild child, always a wild child.

She was talking to the first assistant director Freddy Carter. Maybe she was one of the extras. The set – a disused flour mill tucked away off Deptford Creek – was crawling with them. Not that he had anything to do with extras. He didn't mix with little people.

'Ready in five minutes, Mr Starling,' called the second assistant camera.

'Fine.'

Starling hadn't been due on set until the evening for night shots but he wasn't happy with his close-ups. He wanted them reshot; and what the star wanted, the star got.

Jemma had left Freddy Carter and was heading towards the gate. Starling set off around the camera dollies to intercept her.

He could get angry, or he could get even. Getting even was better. This was going to end in tears – Jemma Wodehouse's tears.

'Hi, Jemma.'

She spun round. She didn't look pleased to see him.

'Good to see you,' said Starling.

Jemma stared at him. He'd forgotten how large her eyes grew when she was excited. Or scared.

'How're you doing?' Still she didn't say a word. 'You could say hello.'

She was smaller than he remembered, more vulnerable. Except she wasn't vulnerable. She was a fighter. She was the one who'd walked away.

'Hello,' she said.

'What are you doing here?'

'I live in Greenwich. I'm a student at the Trinity College of Music.'

'Yeah, I remember. You play the sax.' He'd thought it odd that a girl should choose that instrument. A violin or piano, yes, but a saxophone! She'd been good, too, but Starling had had other things on his mind than listening to Jemma play. 'Tell you what,' Starling said. 'How'd you like it if I got you a small part? Who knows, you could become a star.'

'No thank you.'

Polite but cold, and already preparing to leave.

Starling caught sight of the director H. Bruce Montgomery. 'Hey, Bruce! Come over here.'

'I must go,' said Jemma.

'You can't just walk off. We got things to talk about.'

'We have *nothing* to talk about,' hissed Jemma.

'You watch it.' Starling narrowed his ice-blue eyes in a look that usually had people wetting themselves.

Jemma held his gaze, then turned abruptly away to leave.

'Off you go then. At least I've got something to remember you by,' called Starling.

Jemma spun on her heel and marched back. 'I want those back.'

Starling smiled. 'Tell you what, sweetheart, let's meet up later. Talk about it then.'

'Tell you what,' said Jemma. 'Why don't you go and fuck yourself?'

Starling watched her stride away. He let her go. There was more than one way to skin a cat, more than one way to bring Jemma Wodehouse to heel.

No one walked out on Joey Starling.

The scumbag. The fucking scumbag. How dare he.

She would never have come if she'd even suspected that he might be on set.

Jemma headed out through the mill gate, down the cobbled alley and onto Greenwich High Road. She noticed that she was trembling.

For a moment she'd thought that Starling had been going to hit her. It wouldn't have been the first time. She knew his temper, but she didn't care. She'd been through the flames. There was nothing he could do to her now.

Memories of her humiliation returned. God! How stupid had she been? Childish, naive and stupid. He had preyed on her, fed her drugs, made her feel grown up. She'd thought herself a wild child, living in the fast lane with a famous film star. Looking back, she saw it for what it was – tacky and tawdry.

It had been the start of her black time. Her descent into drugs and self-destruction.

Jemma remembered that last night so clearly. Perhaps she hadn't been as high as normal. Perhaps the cocaine hadn't been as pure, the MDMA weaker. For the first time she'd noticed how Starling kept looking at the wall above the bed. For the first time, she'd been aware how he was positioning her body as they'd performed various sex acts. She'd been on her hands and knees, Starling taking her from behind, when she'd spotted the hole – and the camera lens behind it.

She'd freaked, screamed, accused him of being a dirty old pervert. Starling hadn't been able to understand why she'd kicked off. After all the things they'd done together, being filmed was tame.

All the things they'd done while she was off her head on drugs, she'd reminded him. She'd stormed out of his house in Brighton. When he'd tried to stop her, she'd smashed a glass vase over his head. She'd spent the night curled up in a doorway. The start of the black time...

The sight of the approaching 177 bus made Jemma decide to go home. She needed to play music with Bessie. The bus went through the town centre, passing her college. She knew she could use one of the practice rooms there, but she preferred to play at home.

Jemma lived in a basement flat in the triangle between a tatty stretch of the Woolwich Road, Blackwall Lane, which fed into the Tunnel, and the A102 flyover. It was an odd area with streets which didn't join and roads that ended in cul-de-sacs. The triangle was full of students because no one in their right minds would raise a family there. Jemma shared with a fellow student, while upstairs lived an old West Indian couple, mad on jazz, who never complained about the music coming up from the basement. Shame the local pubs were shit.

She got off at the stop near the undertaker's, opposite the site of the old Greenwich Hospital. Ten minutes later Jemma was lost in her own world with Bessie, her beloved alto saxophone. Bessie was a second-hand Conn Ladyface, and at least eighty years old. Jemma had been given a £4,000 Selmer for her last birthday, but she still preferred Bessie.

She spent thirty minutes practising scales and arpeggios, feeling the familiar weight of the sax around her neck and enjoying the challenges, leaping from B flat to E flat and on to G flat. Didn't get much harder. Then she set off on Charlie Parker's 'Donna Lee', enjoying the challenge of the 'fly shit', as the uptempo notes were known. She played 'Billy's Bounce' and 'Confirmation', relishing the difficulty of controlling the wider bore of the Ladyface. She moved on to Bach's 'Minuet in G' then a slight Debussy piece, but she wasn't in the mood for the classics.

She was just starting the bridge in 'I Thought About You' when a clarinet joined in. She hadn't heard Eric come in. He nodded approvingly. She swept into the blues classic 'Round Midnight', Eric playing off her, extemporising as he did so well.

'What's wrong?' asked Eric, when they'd finished.

Jemma unfastened the saxophone strap around her neck. 'Why should there be anything wrong?'

'You only play "Round Midnight" when you're upset.'

'I bumped into Joey Starling.'

'That was careless of you.'

'Not literally.'

'Oh… And?'

'He tried to pick me up. I almost kicked him in the balls.'

'What are you going to do?'

'Nothing. I guess I should've beeen prepared, but I just didn't expect to see him.' Jemma shrugged. 'It was a shock, that's all. I feel better now.'

'You sure?'

'Yeah. I'll live.' Jemma gave a lopsided smile. 'What's for supper?'

'Chicken in a yoghurt crust with garlic and lemon lentils. And–' Eric disappeared to return with a bunch of sweet peas. 'Smell those. Aren't they heavenly?'

'Beautiful. Shall I put them in water?'

'I'll do it.'

'Okay.' That was the advantage of living with a gay guy. Not only were they great cooks, they were also superb at arranging flowers.

Speed Bump wasn't in the British Oak when Leyden arrived in response to another message on his desk. He decided to give him ten minutes – the time it took him to drink a pint of lager – then go home.

Karen was out at another birthday party, this time for a

receptionist at the South Street Clinic. A suspiciously large number of Karen's mates had been celebrating birthdays recently. Bobby had bought Cumberland sausages from Dring's, the butcher's near the nick, and planned to watch the Arsenal game on the box while eating bangers and mash. The more he thought about it, the more appealing it became. He was disappointed when Speed Bump came in, wearing a new Berghaus anorak.

'They must pay film extras well,' said Bobby, ordering two pints of San Miguel.

'From Skaghead's catalogue.'

'Right.'

Skaghead was a local junkie who funded his heroin addiction by shoplifting to order. He did well at Christmas and at the start of the school year when his catalogue clothed half the Ferrier estate.

'Cost me a pony. Sells in the shops for £150. I could tell him to get you one.'

'Leave it out.'

'The film director's made me a sort of member of Joey's gang.'

'Got lines to say?'

'Nah. But I get to stand near Joey. The director said I looked the part.'

'You won't if you're wearing a £150 anorak, will you, dickhead?'

'I'll take it off.'

'Watch those Somalis don't nick it.'

Speed Bump waited until their pints arrived before asking, 'What's happened about that information I gave you?'

'I passed it on to the local boys.' Leyden knew if he told Speed Bump that Greenwich CID were planning to mount a secret Observation Post, Speed Bump would be around the garages trying to spot the camera. 'No fallout from that barney with those toerags?'

'Nah but two of them had to go to hospital.'

'That's not what you've brought me here to tell me, is it?'

'Remember you was asking about Dave Shine and Minicab–'

'Yeah?'

'Something I heard in a pub. I won't tell you who I was talking to. Don't think you know him anyway, but this bloke's been around a bit, if you know what I mean. Well, this bloke didn't know of anything between Minicab and the Dim Reaper. But–'

Leyden drummed his fingers on the bar. Minicab's attempts to be dramatic irritated him.

'... he reckoned Minicab and Guinness were part of the team that knocked over the cash depot in Maidstone about ten years back.'

Bobby remembered. 'They one where they got away with £22 million, never recovered.'

'That's the one,' said Speed Bump. 'This bloke reckoned Minicab was one of the drivers – remember he was into cars? Guinness was part of the muscle.'

'Anyone go down for it?'

'Only the Pike boys. Georgie Locke got a tug but the Bill didn't have enough evidence to charge him.' Speed Bump stared at his empty glass.

'Who's Georgie Locke?' Bobby ordered another pint.

'Came from up north, used to live in Camberwell. Bought a nightclub on the Isle of Wight. Did a runner when the local cozzers were going to do him for supplying E.'

'Where'd he go?'

'North Cyprus.'

Someone pulled the handle of a fruit machine inside Bobby Leyden's head and came up with three cherries.

'He wasn't known as Glockie, was he?'

'Yeah. How'd you know that?'

'Did your bloke say anything about the Dim Reaper being in on the raid?'

'No, but I'll ask around, quiet like, if you want.'

'You do that. Is Georgie Locke still on Cyprus?'

'Don't you read the newspapers? His villa caught fire a week or so ago. He's toast, mate.'

DAY SEVEN

Tuesday

CHALKE ARRIVED IN her office to find the file she'd requested from archives waiting for her.

Leyden was already in. He was fuming because his searches in the Police National Computer for information about the Maidstone raid had set off a tripwire and now he was locked out of the system. He didn't understand it. Every copper knew that trawling for details on minor celebs like Princess Diana's ex-butler would mean a visit from Big Brother demanding how much the tabloids were paying – but a ten-year-old blag!

Chalke also thought it was odd but she managed to reassure the rubber-heelers that Leyden's interest was part of a genuine inquiry before turning her attention to her new coffee-maker. This morning she'd actually remembered to bring in beans to grind.

She removed the machine from its box and sat it in the corner. She poured the beans into the grinder, measured out the ground coffee, tamped it into the holder and locked it in place.

She was pouring water into the reservoir when Leyden came in. He eyed the coffee-maker with suspicion. 'Do you know what you're doing?'

'I used to have one of these. Espresso or cappuccino?'

'White, two sugars.'

'I'll take that as a cappuccino. Get the sugar from under Sue's desk.'

Chalke set the controls and stepped back. The machine began making gurgling noises.

'Have you read the instructions?' asked Leyden when he returned.

'Don't need to.' Patsy was not the sort to read instructions. 'It's child's play.'

They stood side by side, watching steam rise.

'Your old machine was the same as this one, was it?'

'Er… Not exactly.'

'Why's that dial going into the red?'

'Which dial?'

'That one.' The hissing grew louder.

Leyden edged towards the door.

The machine began throbbing. Scalding hot water started spitting out of the top.

'I don't think it should be doing that.'

'Turn it off. Quick. Turn it off.'

Leyden pulled the plug out of the wall socket. The machine subsided, burbling and spluttering.

'Fuck,' said Patsy. 'Make it work, Bobby. Please.'

If only he knew how much she needed a caffeine fix. Her lover, coked up to the eyeballs, had kept her awake most of the night with his amorous demands.

Leyden took the coffee-maker and instructions away. Chalke began to read about the Maidstone raid. She noticed that it would the tenth anniversary in a week's time.

Four men, wearing overalls and balaclavas, had burst into the depot manager's home and threatened to kill his wife and two young daughters unless he cooperated. The manager, Graham White, had been blindfolded and driven to the depot where his arrival in what appeared to be a police van prompted security to open the gate.

Once inside, the raiders had leapt out, overpowering the workers on shift. There were thought to have been eight of them.

Two facts caught Chalke's attention.

That the robbers had known exactly where the security cameras and hidden alarm buttons were located indicated inside information.

And that they'd chosen September, when the cash from the summer sales was returning to the depot, showed they knew what they were doing.

The only members of the gang to be charged were Vinnie Pike and his cousin Johnny. Following an anonymous tip-off, a bank-note wrapper bearing Vinnie's fingerprints had been found in a dustbin at his parents' home in Sidcup. DNA from Johnny, who had been staying with Vinnie on leave from the Royal Navy at the time, was subsequently identified on a glass in the manager's home.

Detectives had concluded that it had been the cousins' job to guard the family while the rest of the gang had gone on to the depot.

Chalke finished reading the file and hoped that Weaver wouldn't be late. The files could tell her the outline of the investigation but they said nothing of the suspects who'd been in the frame at the time, the feeling on the street. That's where Weaver was a walking encyclopaedia. He arrived at nine, complaining of a hangover.

'You look as rough as I feel,' he said by way of greeting.

'Thanks a bunch.'

By now Leyden had coaxed the machine into life so Chalke traded paracetamol and coffee in exchange for Weaver's memory banks.

'What's the interest in the Maidstone raid?' he asked.

'One of Bobby's snouts has come up with a rumour that Guinness and Minicab were involved.'

'There was no mention of them at the time,' said Weaver. 'You sure this is kosher?'

'The informant doesn't have a great track record,' conceded Chalke. 'But he mentioned a guy called Georgie Locke.

Remember Lucymar saying how the Dim Reaper got a call from someone on North Cyprus called Glockie? Within a few days of making that call, Locke burned to death in his villa. Then comes the business at the crem, the Dim Reaper disappears, and Minicab and Guinness are killed in bizarre circumstances. Worth a look, don't you think?'

'Put like that,' conceded Weaver. 'Although I'd still put the murder of Guinness – I am sorry, I mean Tony Yayale – down to fight fixing that went wrong.'

'I could have killed Begley yesterday,' said Chalke.

'I've had worse guv'nors.'

'Still–' Chalke had been embarrassed for Weaver, a copper she respected and admired. 'Now activate your memory banks and I'll make you more coffee.'

Weaver sank back in his chair. 'It was Kent's collar but we got involved because a number of the suspects lived on our patch. Not that we got very far. They must have had a man on the inside but we never found him. We fancied Graham White at first but his life unravelled so fast that we ruled him out.'

'What do you mean, unravelled?'

'His daughters, Josie aged seven and Laurel aged five, both suffered terribly from the experience. The marriage came under a lot of pressure. Graham and his wife separated. Two months later, the elder girl Josie had a panic attack and ran into the road, straight under a lorry. Graham White fell apart. He blamed himself for not protecting his family.'

'And?'

'Went off the rails, drank a lot. The local lads had to take his car keys off him and drive him home more than once. Lost his job. Divorced. We were surprised. He'd seemed a hard nut. Former sergeant in the RAF Regiment, had a bravery award for rescuing some squaddies when a fuel bowser exploded – and had the burns on his forehead to show for it.'

'I wonder what's happened to him.'

'I'll ask a mate in Maidstone if he knows anything.'

'Thanks. No one else in the frame?'

'Kent turned the staff upside down and inside out, including monitoring their bank accounts and the accounts of possible suspects for years afterwards – zilch.'

'Any word on the street?'

'There was a guy... Barry Cowburn. Flash git from Bermondsey. Started showing off with dosh he couldn't explain, bought himself a sports car. But no sooner did we put him under observation, than he got run over. Hit-and-run driver.'

'The gang getting nervous?'

'Maybe. Mind you, Cowburn was as pissed as a parrot at the time.'

'Georgie Locke?'

'Roofer by trade, found in possession of banknotes from the job but we couldn't link him to the depot and he had an alibi.' Weaver rubbed his chin thoughtfully. 'Carl Cochrane was part of the team that investigated Georgie Locke.'

Cochrane arrived in response to Chalke's summons, carrying the *Daily Telegraph* open at the share prices. Chalke saw he'd made marks alongside some shares.

'Any tips?' she asked.

'Stick to horse racing,' replied Cochrane gloomily, before folding the paper.

'You were involved in the Maidstone depot raid, Carlo,' said Weaver. 'Remember Georgie Locke?'

'Nasty piece of work. Moved down here after a run-in with an Asian mob in Bradford. We had Locke as the guy who beat up the depot worker as a lesson to the others but his tart swore he'd been with her at the time. We reckoned if we shook her tree hard enough, she'd change her story, but we didn't get a chance. The CPS decided not to prosecute. We couldn't understand it.'

'What do you remember of Vinnie and Johnny Pike?' asked Chalke.

'First cousins and good mates. Both only children, in their mid-twenties. We reckoned Johnny Pike had been brought into the job at the last minute by Vinnie, a window cleaner with a record of petty crime. Physically they were very similar. Neither said a word after their arrest. It was Mr Weaver who nicked them.'

'Did you?' Chalke was surprised Weaver hadn't mentioned it.

'I was just the arresting officer. I wasn't really involved in the inquiry.'

'Thanks, Carlo,' said Chalke. 'Keep me up to date with the crem inquiry.'

'Will do.' Cochrane was reopening the share pages even as he left.

Weaver played with his mug before saying, 'I remember that there were concerns at the way the Locke investigation was handled.'

'Such as?'

'Locke had burned something in his garden just before the police arrived. We never found out what. Story of the whole inquiry really.'

'Where are Vinnie and Johnny Pike now?'

'They got thirteen years apiece so they're probably both still inside.'

Chalke tapped their names into her computer. 'They came out four weeks ago,' she announced. 'Living at the same parole address in Southend.'

'They always were close.'

'None of the £22 million was recovered.' Chalke began playing with her wooden man. 'You said Minicab once owned a chain of key-cutting kiosks. Do you think he could have bought that chain with his share of the robbery?'

Weaver was not convinced. 'Minicab was always ducking and

diving. And then there were his winnings from rallying.'

'Okay, but the Dim Reaper also bought a number of funeral parlours around then,' continued Chalke. 'When did Guinness buy the Stag?'

'Don't know. He certainly had it at the time of the Giz Washington shooting.'

'I'll get someone to look at the land registry. Any chance you could ask Tosh Bibby about these characters? See if he knows anything?'

'No problem. Now don't forget. Brenda's expecting you for supper tonight,' said Weaver.

'I hope you told her I'm on a diet.'

'Brenda doesn't believe in such things.'

Joey Starling was in a foul mood. He'd been forced to spend the morning publicising the movie at a photo call in Greenwich Park, which meant not only that he'd had to be pleasant to photographers but that he'd be filming until late tonight to make up the time.

Seeing Jemma Wodehouse yesterday still played on his mind. It was the second time she'd walked away from him. Twice too often.

He'd got his PA to track her down through the college. Then he'd sent Jemma flowers and a little something. It was going to be interesting to see if she rose to the bait. If she didn't, he'd have to take a different tack. He'd do whatever it took to get her back under his spell – and then he'd break her.

Back on set, Starling couldn't concentrate, needing retake after retake. He was glad when they broke for lunch. At his trailer he found a note asking for a meet behind the generator trucks. It cheered him up. He decided it must be from an extra. A quick grope with some bird was just what he needed. A blowjob would be even better.

Starling crossed the set, pleased to note that most of the crew were crowding around the catering bus. No one was taking any interest in him. He ducked behind the trucks to find Freddy Carter standing there. Fuck!

'Do me a favour and piss off, Freddy. I'm expecting someone.'

'I left that message,' said the assistant director.

'What?'

'I want you to leave Jemma Wodehouse alone.'

Starling narrowed his eyes. 'Get real.'

'She's clean now.' Freddy blinked uncertainly. 'She's getting on with her life.'

'So?'

'You can have anyone you want. Just leave her alone.'

'What's your interest?'

Freddy was visibly trembling. 'It doesn't matter.'

'Yeah, it does actually. Why should you care?'

Freddy Carter had feared it would turn out like this. He was no match for Starling, who was ten years younger, three inches taller and built with coat hanger shoulders. More to the point, Starling was an aggressive, egotistical lout prepared to trample everyone and everything to get what he wanted. The evil bastards he portrayed on screen merely reflected his everyday life.

But Freddy had to try. And time was running out.

'I'm warning you –' he said.

'You're what? Don't make me laugh. I shit out bigger things than you.'

Freddy pulled the pistol from his pocket.

'You think you're going to scare me with that prop?' mocked Starling.

'It's not a prop.'

'Go on, then. Pull the fucking trigger.' Starling grasped Freddy's hand and jerked the gun up to his forehead. '*Pull it*.'

The pain in Freddy's stomach surged back, making him

stagger. Starling misread it as fear. 'You haven't the balls,' he sneered. He slapped Freddy backhanded across the face.

'Please–'

'Fuck off. Fuck off before I really hurt you.'

Freddy stumbled away, tears of shame mingling with the pain.

But he wasn't finished. Good would prevail over evil – whatever it took.

Ahmed Hiktas of the Judicial Police Directorate of the Turkish Republic of Northern Cyprus was not a man to be hurried – nor a man to apologise.

'We are fed up with your English criminals,' he told Chalke in his suprisingly fluent English, even as she was thanking him for his phone call. 'We don't want your trash.'

Hiktas was getting his retaliation in first, Patsy realised. But what was he was retaliating against?

'And now someone in London is making waves about a telephone number,' Hiktas continued in his deep voice.

Chalke swung her feet up onto her desk. 'It came up in a murder inquiry. We'd really appreciate your help to get the subscriber's name.' She didn't say that they thought they already knew it.

'The telephone belonged to a George William Locke. One of your criminals.'

Hiktas's gravelly voice conjured a man with a lined, suntanned face, grizzled hair, moustache, smoking a cigarette.

'Locke died two weeks ago when his villa burned down,' continued Hiktas.

Chalke realised she was thinking of Omar Sharif. 'Was the fire suspicious?'

'Do you have any reason to think it would be?'

'I just wondered.'

'You are right. Petrol was used to start the fire.'

'Any chance that Locke was killed and the fire started to hide his murder?'

'We don't know. There was very little left of the body.'

'He was alone in the villa?'

'As far as we know. The fire was reported by a fishing boat out at sea. The villa stands by itself on a cliff, you understand. By the time the fire brigade arrived, it had burned to the ground.'

'Right.'

'But I can tell you that Locke was either a frightened – or a very careful – man. There were CCTV cameras all around the villa.'

'I wonder why.'

Hiktas took time to reply. Patsy heard the rasp of a lighter flint.

'Last year, Locke bought a large piece of land and borrowed heavily to build a tourist development. Now the economy's gone bad. The people Locke went into business with are not the sort you'd want to cross.'

'Was he involved in any criminal activity?'

'Someone like Locke could never go totally straight,' said Hiktas. 'Is there anything you wish to tell me?'

Chalke outlined the events of the past week.

'So Locke phoned Dave Shine just one day before the fire,' calculated Hiktas.

'I don't know whether it's relevant but we believe that Dave Shine was smuggling cocaine into Britain from Spain.'

'Interesting.' Hiktas drew on his cigarette, making Patsy wish she was allowed to smoke in her office. 'The Colombians are finding that many of their traditional drug routes into Europe are becoming too well policed so they've started moving drugs through West Africa where corruption makes it easier. The new routes come together in the eastern Mediterranean – in Cyprus.'

'And Locke?'

'He first came to our attention last year when he was seen talking to those responsible for bringing in cocaine from Egypt.'

'So he could have been killed in a drug deal?'

'He could have been killed for half a dozen reasons.'

'You are sure it was Locke's body?' asked Chalke.

'The dental records match and he had a steel plate in his left forearm, the result of falling from a roof.' Patsy heard Hiktas grind out his cigarette. 'So yes, we have been able to identify him. Unlike the Caucasian male found in a forest ravine a mile away just a week later. The animals had got to him. The local police station is getting rather tired of these mutilated corpses.'

'A tourist?'

'Tourists are reported missing within hours. There's always a wife, girlfriend, holiday rep.'

'By the way, remember I mentioned Stan Figgens... He was wearing gold cufflinks in the shape of Northern Cyprus. His widow says they weren't his.'

'Fax me a photo. Perhaps they belong to some club or society on the island.'

'Thank you.'

Chalke rang off. She picked up her wooden man and began thinking.

Why had Locke phoned Dave Shine? Shine had been quiet and thoughtful after the call, said Lucymar. Had there been something in the call which had set off his murder spree?

Rewind.

Hiktas had said that Locke was the type who could never go straight. The Dim Reaper was another. Guinness had a record. Minicab was suspected of having been a getaway driver. Locke had fled Britain because he was about to be busted for supplying drugs.

What if they were all involved in drugs?

She adjusted her wooden man so that he was holding out his hand to stop traffic.

On the other hand, Weaver believed that Ari O and Guinness

might have upset a London crime family. Guinness was dead and Ari O was afraid.

The Dim Reaper had once been an enforcer for the Jolly crime family – perhaps he was working for them again. The type who could never go straight.

Then Chalke had another thought. Surely Johnny and Vinnie Pike must have been on a good promise to stay silent after their arrest. Now they were free, they'd be expecting the money. Their share must come to at least £1 million each.

People would kill for that kind of money.

Jemma was enjoying the morning. Her first lecture was not until two o'clock so she'd had a lie-in and said good morning to Bessie. She was still practising when Eric suggested taking the Pink Peril to the SeeWoo supermarket in Horn Lane to buy food for supper.

'Only if you drive with two hands,' said Jemma, remembering Eric's fondness for playing his piccolo while steering his 125cc scooter with one hand. Eric promised, but that didn't stop him jingling the huge bunch of keys dangling from the ignition as they drove along. He had a thing about keys – and a collection a Newgate gaoler would have envied.

Jemma enjoyed shopping in SeeWoo, savouring the exotic smells that brought back the wonderful month she'd spent in Malaysia, but it soon became clear that Eric had no idea what to buy. He wandered up and down aisles, pushing a trolley while playing his piccolo. He finally halted in front of the fish counter where he entertained the staff with 'Molly Malone' before buying a piece of haddock.

It was one of Eric's manic days, recognised Jemma. She knew better than to try to bring him down. Besides, Eric's good mood lifted her. Perhaps he was putting on an act for her benefit.

Eric scooped up garlic, ginger and pak choi.

'Any idea what you're going to do with those things?' asked Jemma.

'Well, funnily enough I was thinking of making fish with garlic, ginger and pak choi. Actually spring onions would be good too. Run back and get them, would you, there's a cherub.'

When they arrived home they found a woman standing on the pavement outside their flat holding a bunch of flowers.

'Miss Wodehouse?' she asked, even before Jemma had climbed off the scooter.

'Yes.'

'These are for you.'

'Oooh,' pouted Eric. 'No one ever sends me flowers.'

'You can share these,' said Jemma following him down into the basement. As Eric went to put the fish in the fridge, Jemma inspected the flowers. They were beautiful. Orchids, lilies, roses, proteas and cordyline leaves.

'Who're they from?' called Eric.

'Don't know. Doesn't seem to be a card.'

'A secret admirer.'

'Didn't know I had one.' That wasn't true. Half the guys at college had tried to hit on her, but she wasn't ready yet. The scars from Starling went deep. She was still healing.

'They put my poor little sweet peas to shame,' sniffed Eric, eyeing the flowers.

'Don't be silly. I love them. Now, will you arrange these for me.'

Eric picked up his flute and launched into an Irish jig, which quickly morphed into a mad pixie dance. He stopped suddenly in the middle of a bar. 'Just for you.'

He laid the flowers on the draining board and began cutting the stems. 'Open that plant food,' he said, pointing to a small brown sachet that had come with the flowers.

Jemma did as he asked. She found she was looking at half a dozen, small, off-white crystal rocks.

Eric glanced at them. 'Doesn't look like plant food.'

'No,' said Jemma, staring in horror. 'It's crack cocaine.'

'Didn't know Interflora did crack,' said Eric, looking interested.

'They're from Starling.'

'Peace offering?'

'Peace offering! I'm clean now. Clean! It took a lot but I kicked it.' Her voice rose hysterically. 'And what does he send me? Crack fucking cocaine.'

Eric wrapped his arms around her. 'Easy. Easy. Do you want to tell the police?'

'I can't prove it was him. Anyway, that would just open a can of worms.'

'What do you mean, a can of worms?'

'Do you think it's too early to have a drink?'

'It's never too early. We'll finish off that bottle from last night.' Eric poured two glasses of wine, put one in her hand. 'So why can't you go to the police?'

Jemma curled a strand of hair around her finger. 'If I tell you something, will you promise not to tell another living soul?'

'Cross my heart and hope to die.'

'You know I used to... go out with him.' Jemma took a deep breath. 'He used to film us having sex. I didn't know. I swear to you, I didn't. I walked out when I spotted the camera over the bed.'

'What happened to the videos?'

'He must still have them. Probably pervs over them.'

All of a sudden Jemma knew she had to recover those videos. They hadn't seemed important until now. She had shut Starling away in a secure compartment of her memory, and believed she'd never see him again.

Now the bastard was trying to take over her life.

In his dreams. And in her nightmares.

Until she had the original videos he would always have a hold over her.

As if reading her mind, Eric picked up his flute and played the opening bars of the *James Bond Theme*. 'Let's get them back.'

'What?'

'I bet he keeps them on a memory card.' Eric played another couple of bars. 'All we have to do is get inside his pad and "liberate" the card.'

'And you know where he's staying, do you?'

'Matter of fact, I do. That new place on the river, Drake Tower. He's got the penthouse.'

'How am I supposed to break in there?'

Eric gave a cheeky grin. 'It would help to know the hall porter.'

'And you do?'

'You could say that.'

'I quite fancy an afternoon by the seaside,' announced Leyden as they emerged from the Dartford Tunnel and turned onto the A13 towards Southend.

'I suppose you went there as a kid,' said Chalke. 'Sandcastles, candyfloss, donkey rides on the beach.'

'Leave it out. Torremolinos for us, mate. I suppose you vacationed on the Riviera.'

'That's where you're wrong, *mate*.' Getting out of the office had put Patsy in a good mood. Joni Mitchell was playing on the stereo, she was enjoying feeling the power of her car and, if she was honest, enjoying Leyden's company. 'One of the best weekends of my life was spent in a caravan in Porthcawl.'

'You're joking!'

Patsy should have been on a sixth-form field trip to study rock formations or something – she never did find out what before she was expelled. Instead she'd gone off with a boy she was madly in love with at the time. They'd broken into a caravan in Treco Bay to spend the weekend drinking shoplifted cider and going through every position in the sex manual she'd brought along. Six months later the boy had had an epiphany and become a Buddhist monk.

To this day she couldn't enter a caravan with its characteristic smells of stale bread and plastic without remembering how she'd cricked her neck that weekend. She returned to the present, and their trip to interview Vincent Alan Pike, now thirty-three, and John Nathan Pike, thirty-two.

'What are they doing living out in Southend?' she asked Leyden.

'According to the jam reports –'

'Jam?'

'Jam roll – parole. They were left the house and £5,000 each by their paternal grandmother twelve months ago.'

'So they come out of nick and instead of going back to south London, they move straight into their Gran's house in Southend.'

'Actually, it's in Prittlewell,' corrected Leyden.

'Where?'

'Prittlewell. Nowadays it's a suburb of Southend but historically Prittlewell was the original Saxon settlement and Southend was just a fishing village at the south end.'

'Bobby, is there a useless information competition I could enter you in?'

'Just thought you'd like to know,' said Leyden.

They entered a built-up area.

'Directions,' demanded Chalke.

'I haven't got a map. Use your satnav.'

'We're not talking since she told me to do a U-turn on the M2,' said Chalke. 'Then she told me not to swear at her.'

'Don't suppose you've tried reading the instructions, have you?'

'Life's too short–'

'These things are brilliant. I got lost in north London last week. The satnav told me bear left in 200 yards and guess what?'

'What?'

'There was London Zoo.'

'Ha bloody ha.'

Leyden tapped in the destination postcode and the street number.

'If we get lost, it's your fault,' said Chalke.

Five minutes later, they pulled up outside a semi-detached pebble-dashed house in a long straight road of identical semi-detached pebble-dashed houses.

'Fluke,' said Chalke.

The door was opened by a man in new jeans and a V-neck sweater over a white T-shirt. His pallor announced that he had not long been out of prison.

'Mr Pike? I'm DCI Chalke. This is DS Leyden. We'd like a word.'

Pike glanced up and down the road as if to check who was looking. 'Um… yes, of course. Come in.'

When Leyden had read the cousins' records, he'd been struck by their physical similarities – both five feet ten, medium build, brown hair. They'd been all but indistinguishable in the mugshots.

'You Vinnie or Johnny?' he asked.

'Vinnie. Everyone says we're more like twins than cousins.'

The detectives followed him past a grandmother clock and telephone table with a message pad covered with doodles of stick men into the living room. Pike was holding his left arm stiffly across his chest.

'Hurt yourself?' asked Chalke.

'I tripped and landed funny. Nothing broken, but I've pulled some ligaments in my shoulder.'

'They take forever to heal,' said Leyden from experience.

'Tell me about it,' said Pike. 'Would you like a tea, or coffee? Only instant, I'm afraid.'

'I'm fine,' said Chalke, choosing a chair near the electric fire.

'I wouldn't mind a cup of tea,' said Leyden. 'White, two sugars.'

While Pike was in the kitchen, Chalke took stock. China dogs sat on occasional tables while ducks flew up the wall above a glass display case packed with porcelain figures. Chalke guessed the sitting room was as the grandmother had left it – with one glaring exception.

Pike returned from the kitchen.

'You're an artist.' Chalke indicated the watercolour hanging over the fireplace. It showed a distant figure plodding through a forlorn landscape under a lowering grey sky. The painting, executed in drab monotones, reeked of sadness. The signature read V. Pike.

'I did that when I was in Swaleside nick on Sheppey. It won me a £100 Koestler prize. The governor was over the moon – he'd never had a Koestler before. He thought the painting was a metaphor for freedom.'

'And is it?'

'It's the view from the arts and crafts room. You know what a hole Sheppey is. Shame I couldn't recapture the smell of the pig shit. Still, it stopped me being ghosted for kicking up about the food.' He left to go back into the kitchen.

'Ghosted?' asked Chalke.

'Sent to a prison up north.'

'That's a problem?'

'It is if your nearest and dearest live in the south.'

Pike returned to hand Leyden a mug of tea.

'Is Johnny around?' asked Chalke.

Pike collapsed into the chair and stared at the rug. 'He's abroad, I think.'

'You think?'

'We didn't hit it off. He blamed me for what happened. Reckoned I'd cost him nine years of his life.'

'I see.'

'He'd been learning languages inside. French, German, even

Russian. He said he was going to join the French Foreign Legion. I don't know how much was bullshit but Johnny was the sort who liked a… structured life. He'd enjoyed his time in the navy and he couldn't rejoin now he had a record.' Pike caught himself. 'Sorry, I'm going on. What can I do for you?'

'Did you know that Lee Finch and Tony Yayale have been murdered?'

'I read something–' He shrugged. 'So?'

'They were part of the crew that knocked over the banknote depot,' said Leyden, stirring his tea.

'I don't know them.'

'You don't know them!' echoed Leyden incredulously.

Pike shook his head. 'No. And I don't think you can prove they were part of the team, either.'

Both detectives were caught off balance. Leyden recovered first. 'What about Georgie Locke?' he asked.

'I met him a few times around Camberwell.'

'How well did you know him?'

'I didn't really. He was older than me.'

'You didn't know he'd gone to live in Cyprus?' prompted Chalke.

'No.'

'Or that he was dead?'

'No way.'

'What about Dave Shine?'

Pike took his time answering. 'Dave Shine, yeah. I had a cell mate in Durham who used to hang around with him.'

'You're really saying you don't know these guys, Finch and Yayale?'

'That's what I'm telling you.'

'Come on,' said Leyden. 'You were all part of the same mob.'

Pike gave a half smile. 'So you say.'

'You admit taking part in the robbery?' asked Chalke.

'Nine years of my life says I did.'

'But you don't deny it.'

'Nine years of my life says I did.' Pike took a sip of tea.

In the pause that followed, Chalke looked around the room. There wasn't a single recent photograph. Old ones, yes – some in black and white, even – but nothing from the last ten years.

'Look, I didn't bubble anyone then,' said Pike. 'I'm not going to start now.'

'The police must have offered you a deal,' said Leyden.

'And the rest.'

Chalke asked, 'Who tipped off the police about that banknote wrapper in your parents' bin?'

'Haven't a Danny.'

'You must have thought about it. As you say, you've had nine years to think about it.'

'I didn't know there was a wrapper in the bin,' muttered Pike, eyes firmly on the floor.

'You're saying you were fitted up?' When Pike did not reply, Chalke continued. 'But there was other evidence. DNA placed your cousin in the manager's house.'

'So they say.'

He's gone into denial, thought Chalke. It happened to old lags. They protested their innocence during the trial and through appeals procedures, and even kept up the pretence in prison in case they were celled with a grass. After a time, they came to believe it.

'When did Johnny leave the country?'

'Two weeks ago today. He said he was going to get a train to Paris and then make his way to Marseilles. He thought the Foreign Legion had a depot there.'

'I'm wondering if Johnny's collected his money and scarpered,' said Leyden. 'No one in his right mind would join the French Foreign Legion. It'd be like swapping one prison for another.'

'Not for Johnny. I told you, he likes others to do his thinking for him.'

'Like you getting him into the raid.'

Pike didn't reply.

'What about you?' asked Chalke. 'What are you going to do?'

'I've bought a car. That VW outside. I'm going to drive down to Spain as soon as I get my act together.' He rubbed his damaged shoulder. 'There's nothing to keep me here.'

'Not kept in touch with anyone?'

'No way. Clean break.'

Leyden found himself actually liking Pike. All right, he wouldn't talk about his crime but that wasn't unusual. 'What have you been doing with yourself since you came out?'

'Not a lot. A few pints, watched TV, walked. Walked a lot. I had a mate stay, a bloke I met inside.'

'Where were you last Tuesday evening?' asked Chalke. 'A week ago today?'

'Tuesday? My mate was staying then… That could have been the night we had the curry in that Indian by the station.' Pike thought for a moment. 'Yeah, Winston left on the Wednesday and we had a curry the last night.'

'How about Wednesday morning?' That was when someone moved Stan Figgens's body behind Bell's desk.

'Winston was still here. He left around midday to get back to Liverpool.'

'Who's this Winston?'

'Winston Taylor. He looked after me when I was first inside. I was returning the favour. He's not had much luck since he came out.'

'What was he in for?'

'Manslaughter.'

'Thursday night?' That was when Minicab was murdered.

'If that's the night *Hustlers* is on the box, I was watching that. Otherwise I might have gone for a couple of pints in the Railway Tavern. The other pubs around here are crap.'

'Between nine and ten next morning?' When Minicab's body was transferred to the dry-cleaner's.

'That's easy. I was seeing my parole officer. Post-release assessment.'

'Sunday night?' Guinness's death in the gym.

'I don't bloody know. Probably watching TV.' Pike was becoming impatient. 'No, I wasn't. I drove to Shoeburyness and walked along the beach. It was great. No one around but me.'

Two out of three verifiable alibis wasn't bad. Chalke would have been suspicious if they'd been perfect. 'You know we'll check.'

'Do what you like, but listen – I ain't never killed anyone in my life.'

'Someone's going round bumping off your old mates,' said Leyden. 'And if you're not the killer, you could be next.'

'What if there's someone in there?' whispered Jemma outside the penthouse flat.

'You heard what my mate said,' replied Eric. 'Starling's not due back until this evening.'

Jemma took a deep breath and turned the key. They stepped in, closed the door behind them, and stood listening.

Go for it, girl.

They crossed the hall into the living room where they found themselves looking onto the Thames through a smoked glass wall.

'Cool!' said Eric. 'Why can't we live here?'

'Because Starling's a film star and we're music students.'

'One day, babe, one day.'

'Where do we start looking?' asked Jemma.

In the days before digital cameras, there'd have been negatives, prints, maybe a roll of film. Now they were looking for a memory card no bigger than a postage stamp.

'In the obvious places – like the laptop.' Eric picked up the Acer on the dining table and peered into the SD card slot. 'Thought that would be too easy.'

Jemma looked around. Through an open door, she caught sight of an unmade bed. The sight unnerved her. She wondered what young girl had spent the night in there and whether she too had been filmed without her knowledge.

'You take the bedroom; I'll look here,' said Eric.

'I'd rather you looked in the bedroom,' said Jemma.

She began checking the shelves, looking inside ornaments, running her fingers under surfaces. She did the same in the kitchen: pulling open drawers, searching in small pots and utensils. There was no real reason for Starling to hide the memory card, she thought. He would just want it somewhere accessible – and secure.

The longer she searched, the more depressed she became. They were looking for a needle in a haystack. Why had they ever thought they could find the memory card? Why had they thought it'd even be here?

The phone rang. One… two… three rings. The warning signal from Eric's mate that Joey Starling had returned.

Eric came flying into the living room. 'Oh shit, oh dear.'

'What's he doing back here?' wailed Jemma. 'He's supposed to be filming.'

The penthouse was the only apartment on the top floor. They needed to reach the staircase to the lower floors before Starling arrived in the lift. It was always going to be close, and now they had wasted time panicking.

'Hide.'

'Where?'

'There's a walk-in closet in the spare bedroom.'

She and Eric piled in. Jemma hooked her fingers into the louvre door and pulled it shut. The closet faced the open door into the living room.

Eric felt for her hand as she fought to get her breathing under control.

They heard the front door slam. Footsteps on the polished floorboards headed into the kitchen. There was the sound of a drinks can being opened. Jemma peered through the slats to see Starling in jeans and sweatshirt slide back the picture window and go out onto the balcony where he remained leaning on the rail, drinking from a can of Pepsi. The phone rang. Starling glanced at his watch and returned to the living room.

'Hello... Yeah. Nah – taking a break. I've come back for a shower, the one in my trailer's shitty... No problem. I brought the key up from Brighton with me. No chance – I've got it on a chain around my neck... No time at the moment, we're on a tight schedule. Say the weekend... A few days don't matter... You square it... Nah, no idea what the Reaper's up to. If he kicks off on one, I'll kill the cunt.' Starling gave a harsh laugh. 'Yeah, you, too. Take care.'

Starling ended the call, finished the can and crushed it in his hand. He peeled off his sweatshirt to toy with a key on a fine chain around his neck. He pulled the chain over his head, put it on the coffee table and went into the bathroom. A minute later, they heard water running.

Eric touched Jemma on the arm. 'Let's get out of here.'

They crept out of the closet and into the living room. The bathroom door was closed.

Eric headed towards the front door, but hearing Starling talk about the key had given Jemma an idea. She went to the coffee table, picked up the chain and undid the clasp.

She held the Yale key in her fingers. It didn't look anything special.

Eric returned to her side, pulled out his key ring, selected a similar-looking key and put it on the chain. Then he began a jerky dance like a puppet on string. Any second, he'd begin playing his piccolo, feared Jemma. She pushed him towards the door.

Now she had something to exchange.

*

Terry Rich was growing angry. He'd enjoyed getting the better of
Patsy Chalke and her muscle-bound thug on Sunday. But since
then life had gone downhill. Everywhere he went; there were police watching him. He'd be walking down a street and a police
car would coast past; he'd be sitting on a bench minding his own
business, and there'd be a copper giving him the hard eye.

Rich even wondered if they'd planted a tracking device in his
clothing. He checked. They hadn't. But it was eerie how the police
turned up every time he even went near a school. Yesterday he'd
been outside the Ranger's House when a police car had pulled up.
The women officers hadn't believed that he was watching a game
of bowls. He'd been moved on in no uncertain terms.

He'd taken a bus to Eltham, hanging around a park before
strolling towards a small C of E primary school. He was a hundred yards away when a police officer came out of the playground.
Rich had turned down a side street.

Harassment – that's what this was – harassment. He knew the
law. He was innocent until proved guilty. His brief had even said
that he stood a good chance of being acquitted after the way Chalke had tried to drown him.

Rich didn't like his barrister Mansel Daley. He could tell Daley
didn't believe in his innocence, but saw it as his duty to test the
evidence against his client. But at least he was good – which was
just as well, because Rich was as guilty as sin.

But if Rich was going to get his collar felt every time he went
near a school…

Rich applied himself to the problem. He knew the area well.
This had been his hunting ground before that first girl's mother
had gone to the police. He couldn't believe his luck when he'd
been sent to Catford. There were places he had to avoid because he
was known, but that still left a lot of schools.

And he knew the locations of all of them.

He'd considered the problem through Monday night and into Tuesday, until by lunchtime he thought he had the answer.

Rich got off the bus outside Thomas Tallis school, spotting the police car in the B&Q car park opposite. He headed towards Kidbrooke station before turning back through the underpass to the Ferrier estate, where he followed the perimeter road until he saw the prefabricated buildings of Wingfield primary school. It didn't have much going for it as a school, but it had one advantage from Rich's point of view – it was overlooked by flats, many of which had already been vacated as the council prepared to knock down the estate.

Rich scanned the windows of the six-storey concrete slab called Dando Crescent. There were three empty flats next to each other on the fourth floor, all with a clear view into the playground.

He climbed the stairs, anticipation growing inside him.

In a different life, he had trained as a locksmith. Those days were long past, but the skills hadn't left him. He didn't expect council locks would give him any problems.

He was right. Five minutes later he was gazing down at the playground.

Patsy Chalke was surprised to find that Weaver lived on a small estate of semi-detached houses in Bexley. It was the sort of place aspiring young executives bought before they'd made it, then sold immediately they had. But Des and Brenda had moved in when the house had been built twenty years ago, and had never seen any reason to leave.

Patsy paid off the taxi and rang the bell, juggling the bunch of flowers and bottle of wine. Brenda, wearing an apron over a dark green frock chosen to show off a string of pearls, answered the door. She was taking Patsy's coat when Weaver came down the stairs. He had exchanged his tie and jacket for a misshapen fawn cardigan.

Brenda groaned. 'I thought I'd thrown that away.'

'I found it again,' retorted Weaver. 'If I threw away every old thing in this house, you'd be out on your ear.'

'You and whose army! Look at the holes in the elbows. You can't wear that when we have guests.'

'Patsy doesn't mind.'

'It's not a question whether Patsy minds or not. It's impolite.'

'I'll take it as a compliment, Brenda,' said Patsy.

'Go on, back to the kitchen with you,' Weaver told his wife with mock severity. 'Remember your place.'

'I'll place you in a minute.'

Patsy smiled, enjoying the interplay between two people totally at ease with one another.

'Come into the living room,' Weaver told Patsy. 'What'll you have to drink?'

'What are you having?' asked Patsy.

'I like a malt before dinner.'

'I'll have the same.'

Weaver selected a Glenmorangie from a well-stocked cabinet while Patsy inspected the family photographs around the room. Many charted their daughter Annie's progress from infants' to medical school while others showed Des and Brenda in exotic destinations. Patsy was surprised. Des never talked about his holidays, but here were the Pyramids, the Taj Mahal, Sugar Loaf in Rio de Janeiro, Petra, Ayres Rock, whales off Alaska, Sydney Harbour Bridge.

Weaver handed her a large whisky and indicated the armchairs either side of the imitation coal fire.

He began filling a pipe. 'I hope you don't mind.'

'You mean I can smoke?' asked Patsy.

'Of course.'

'Wonderful. For once, I won't feel like a pariah.' She dived into her handbag for her cigarettes. 'Great holiday photos.'

'Brenda loves travelling,' said Weaver. 'No sooner are we back from one trip than she's planning the next.'

'Good for her,' said Patsy.

'It's not easy being married to a copper. She's put up with a lot over the years. The odd hours, the shift work, the temptations.'

Tell me about it, thought Patsy.

'We've been married thirty years last month.'

'Does that explain the beautiful pearl necklace?'

'We'll make a detective of you yet,' smiled Weaver.

The cooking smells from the kitchen together with the whisky began to lure Patsy into thoughts of domesticity. She tried picturing herself coming home after a hard day to find food cooking, her drink poured. But that would need a house husband. Someone who relied on her as the breadwinner. Stuff that.

But if she and her partner both worked, they'd end up with takeaways in front of the TV, eating out a couple of times a week to catch up on each other's news.

What if *she* was the housewife…?

And what about children? Shouldn't her biological clock be running by now? If so, it wasn't ticking very loudly.

Patsy didn't want to think about it.

But the thought had clearly crossed Brenda's mind. Towards the end of the venison casserole, she asked Patsy, 'How are you enjoying Greenwich?'

'Love it. They're a good bunch of people.'

'Bobby Leyden's a character,' said Brenda. 'He's done well to get where he is, coming from his background.'

'It takes all sorts to be a copper,' said Des.

'I'm not sure about Cochrane, though,' added Brenda. 'All he talks about is money.'

'He's all right.' Des was always quick to stand up for members of the team.

'What do you think of Sue Jones?' said Brenda.

'She's sweet,' said Chalke. 'And I love her Devon accent.'

'You know she lost a child?'

'No!' said Patsy.

'Meningitis. Very suddenly.'

'That's awful.' Chalke realised she knew nothing of Sue's past. She should show more interest in her staff, especially people she professed to like.

'A little girl, about five, six years ago.'

'Was there a father on the scene?'

'I'm not sure. It all happened down in Devon,' said Brenda.

'After her child died, Sue moved up here to be near her sister,' said Des.

'We only know because Sue's sister lived up the road,' added Brenda. 'Small world.'

'Sue doesn't talk about her daughter,' warned Des. 'In fact, I'm not sure how many people know.'

'You've never thought of having children?' Brenda asked Patsy.

'They're not high on the agenda.'

'Perhaps you haven't met the right man.'

I've met too many, thought Chalke.

And if I do have children, will I become like Brenda with her gentle plumpness, kindly face, glasses? There couldn't have been much more than fifteen years between the two women, but Brenda seemed to belong to a different generation.

To change the subject, Patsy asked Des, 'So, when are you going to retire?'

'I can't afford to.'

'We've got to see Annie through med school first,' said Brenda.

'And I've got to keep paying for Brenda's holidays.'

'I want to go to Machu Picchu but I'm not sure if Des is up to the altitude. I don't want him pegging out on me.'

'Rubbish, I'm as fit as a flea.' He banged his chest and coughed theatrically. 'You see what I mean.'

'Have you been to Peru?' asked Brenda.

'Years ago I spent a few months bumming around South America.'

'You name it and Patsy's done it,' said Weaver, not unkindly. 'You know, Bren, Patsy's actually a doctor.'

That story had got around quickly.

'Not a medical doctor,' said Patsy, again quickly changing the subject. 'You'd like Machu Picchu. It's an amazing place.'

With Brenda back in the kitchen, conversation turned to work. Weaver agreed with the Cypriot policeman's view that Georgie Locke was not the sort to go straight, and that they should get a warrant to monitor Vinnie Pike's bank account.

'By the way, I did have a chat with my mate in Kent,' Weaver said. 'Graham White tried to have Vinnie and Johnny Pike damaged while they were inside.'

'Really?'

'My mate warned off White, who went to South America shortly afterwards and hasn't been heard of since. His ex-wife Shirley remarried some builder.'

'Any mileage there?'

'Wouldn't think so.' Weaver finished his glass of wine. 'But there were stories that Joey Starling was involved in the robbery.'

'The film star?'

'He was just starting out then and the arty-farty crowd loved the idea of having a real villain in their midst. The possibility that he'd actually taken part in a £22 million raid had them wetting themselves. Of course, he encouraged the rumours.'

'And?'

'He was filming at Shepperton at the time and still living at home. Violet Starling swore her son had spent the evening learning his lines for the next day. Joey wasn't stupid enough to talk himself into a prison sentence.'

Brenda brought in the gooseberry crumble. 'Des, you promised. No shop.'

'My fault,' said Patsy.

Assistant Director Freddy Carter stood still and silent in the shadowy woodland. In the distance, he could make out the glow of lights on the film set. Soon it would be midnight and shooting would end. Filming this late was the price you paid for the director's insistence on using actuality sound, hoping to recapture the realism of classics like *Get Carter* and *The Long Good Friday*. Some hope with the growl of traffic on the A2 audible until the early hours.

It was strange that it should come to this. Sadness and elation competed inside Freddy as he felt the unaccustomed weight of the pistol in his hand.

At least the pain was staying away, allowing him to concentrate on what he had to do.

Soon Joey Starling would come along this lonely path on his way back to his luxury flat. Starling was not one to hang around, especially if there was a girl waiting.

The sound of the shot would be muffled by the trees – not that anyone would take any notice. The locals had become used to hearing gunfire from the movie.

Someone was approaching now, but from over the footbridge – from the wrong direction. Freddy withdrew into the bushes. A couple hurried past. The woman had the hood of her jacket up. He couldn't see the man but by their body language, Freddy guessed that they'd had a row.

He felt sorry for them. Make it up, he wanted to say. Make it up before it's too late.

As if in answer to his unspoken plea, the girl linked her arm through the man's.

Their footsteps receded into the night.

Freddy Carter felt for the safety catch on the Makarov.

DAY EIGHT

Wednesday

PATSY CHALKE WAS having a strange dream involving a circus elephant, a clown and a fire engine. The clown was riding the elephant around the ring. The crowd were applauding. Chalke couldn't see the fire engine, only hear it.

The fire engine had an odd-sounding bell.

It wasn't a fire engine. It was her bedside phone.

She woke with a judder, breaking the surface of consciousness. It was still dark. Patsy reached for the light. Everything was blurred. She remembered she'd taken out her contact lenses. Where were her glasses?

That bloody phone was still ringing.

She scrabbled to pick up the receiver.

'Yes?'

'You're a deep sleeper–'

'Uh.' Patsy recognised the voice of Alison Begley and sat up.

'There's been another killing in Greenwich. I wouldn't have woken you but it's high profile.'

Begley was saying something about a shooting connected to the film being made there but Chalke was finding it hard to concentrate.

'I know you're stretched but give this priority. Press Bureau's sending someone to help the area PR. I'll be down later. I've got meetings at the Yard first, but in the meantime I'll send a couple of DIs with their teams. If you need more manpower just say the word.'

That made Chalke pay attention. Manpower meant money and Begley was fanatical about keeping within budget, irrespective of what the investigation required.

'DCS Weaver will be the nominal senior investigating officer but I'm looking to you, Patricia, to wrap this one up.'

'I'll do my best, ma'am,' said Patsy.

The sun was rising as Chalke parked the Mercedes among the police cars and the fleet of forensic vans. A uniform logged her arrival and pointed her along a pitted tarmac path which straggled through scrub and rosebay willowherb until she came to the footbridge over an arm of Deptford Creek. She hadn't known this area existed – a forgotten stretch of abandoned Victorian mills, grimy warehouses and struggling workshops hidden away around the inlet between Greenwich and Deptford.

The first person she made out among the white-suited SOCOs was Andy Butterfield. She wondered how he'd got here ahead of her. Butterfield lived out in Kent. Begley must have called him first.

'Do we have an ID?'

'Frederick Benjamin Carter. First assistant director, according to the security pass in his pocket.'

Carter, in black jeans, trainers and dark fleece lay face down, his right hand by his side, the other hidden under his body. A dark stain had spread over the tarmac.

'You're seeing his good side.' Butterfield lifted the head. Patsy winced. A pulped mess of blood, gore and gristle occupied where Carter's left temple had been. 'TLD reckons he's been shot at close range.'

Forensic technician Barry Howlett, known as The Living Dead, or TLD for short, was currently taking swabs from Carter's right hand. He'd acquired his nickname through his long pasty face, sunken eyes and tombstone teeth. It was a standing joke that if

TLD didn't keep moving at crime scenes, he'd end up in the body bag.

'Well?' said Chalke.

'I think we're going to get lucky here.'

Patsy waited for Howlett to continue but he was absorbed in what he was doing. She asked, 'Are those powder burns on his temple?'

'They're not burns,' replied TLD without looking up. 'They're powder tattooing or stippling.'

'Whatever.' It was too early to be lectured.

'The fact that the marks are reddish brown shows that the victim was alive at the time of the shooting,' explained TLD. 'If the victim had been dead before he was shot they'd be grey or yellow.'

'Okay.' Chalke appreciated TLD's approach, the way he refused to rule out the unlikely. But she did wish he didn't have the sort of voice that was going to send her back to sleep.

'Powder tattoos are punctuate abrasions, made by the impact of powder grains on the skin,' continued TLD in his monotone drawl. 'Short-barrel firearms and lower velocity cartridges don't normally expel residues as far as, say, a high-velocity rifle, but at shorter distances they deposit greater concentrations. It's clear that the weapon used here was a hand gun.'

'Right.'

'The closer the firearm to its target, the greater the residue concentrations and the smaller size of the pattern.'

'In this case?'

'I'd say less than six inches, possibly less than four, even. If we can find the gun, we'll be able to match it against the residues.'

'Anything else?'

'The barrel of the gun was almost at right angles to the head when the shot was fired. I'll know more when we've hosed off the blood.'

Chalke stood back as TLD gently rolled the body over. With

infinite care, he used a pair of tweezers to remove a black wooden button from the left fist. He dropped it into a cellophane evidence bag and held it up triumphantly.

'Been torn off, by the look of it.' TLD inspected the dead man's hands before covering them in plastic bags. 'There're fibres under his fingernails. He put up a fight.'

Chalke straightened up as a tired-looking Will Brennan in jeans and ski anorak materialised alongside her.

'Why can't people get murdered at a civilised time of day?' complained the doctor.

'Hangover?'

'If I'd known I'd be getting up this early, I might have gone easy on that second bottle of wine. I'd fail the breathalyzer, if I could be bothered to give myself one.'

Patsy suspected that she too would be over the limit after the way she and Des Weaver had got stuck into the Calvados after dinner.

'Reckon Carter was killed on the bridge?'

Brennan suppressed a yawn. 'I'd say so from the blood on the railings.'

'Time of death?'

'It was cold last night, quarter moon, clear skies and full tide around 3 o'clock–' Will Brennan sucked in his cheeks. 'Ooh, I'd say four minutes past twelve.'

'How can you be so accurate?'

'The victim's watch stopped when he fell, but the time's consistent with what I would have said.'

'You're a great help, Will.'

The smell of frying bacon came on the breeze. Brennan turned his head until he had located the direction. 'Ah… Breakfast.'

He left just as Weaver arrived.

'Defence injuries on the left hand, gunshot residues on the right,' Chalke summarised. 'Looks as though Carter was grappling with his assailant when the shot was fired.'

Weaver groaned. 'Why do these things always happen after a long night?'

'You didn't finish the Calva did you?'

Weaver looked pained. 'It seemed a good idea at the time.'

Chalke grinned to herself. The two senior investigating officers and the forensic medical examiner were all suffering from hangovers. Just as well the public never saw this side of a murder inquiry.

'Begley called me out in person this morning,' she said.

'Did she now?'

'But not before she called Andy Butterfield.'

'Watch your back, Patsy. There's nothing that woman can do to me this close to retirement but she could shaft you big time. Don't trust her.'

'I won't,' said Chalke, thinking that was the second time in three days that Weaver had warned her not to trust their boss.

She returned to the bridge, wondering why she hadn't seen Leyden when he appeared from the direction of the mill.

Chalke grunted in greeting. 'What have you got?'

'Carter was forty-one, single, lived alone in Wandsworth. Quiet, steady, even-tempered. Crew liked him.'

'That's not telling us much.'

'Also, he's just had a major row with Joey Starling.'

'What?'

'Two lighting engineers saw them have a right ruck yesterday lunchtime. Starling slapped Freddy.'

'Any idea what the row was about?'

'No, but it happened behind some big generator trucks so I'd say they'd chosen the spot so that they couldn't be seen,' said Leyden. 'Starling's due on set soon.'

'We'll see what he has to say about the row.' Chalke glanced down at the muddy brown water. 'I wouldn't want to swim in there.'

'You wouldn't have to. You could wade across,' said Leyden.

'Sorry?'

'That's how Deptford gets its name. The deep ford over the Ravensbourne.'

'Oh!' Patsy had always thought the ford had been over the Thames – if she'd thought at all. Silly girl.

'Elizabeth I knighted Francis Drake on the deck of the *Golden Hind* a few hundred yards up there,' pointed Leyden. 'Then they left the *Golden Hind* to rot.'

'Too early, Bobby.' The first adrenalin rush was fading. She could murder a coffee. 'Let's go and talk to the film star.'

Jemma Wodehouse had trouble sleeping. By 3 a.m. she was quietly playing Brahms' lullabies. She was starting to regret the impulse that had made her take the key from Starling's. She had no illusions about Starling. He was a nasty piece of work – and he knew some right bastards, she recalled, shuddering at the memories.

She wondered what Starling would do when he found the key had been swapped. Whatever it was would be violent. She hadn't thought this through.

It was a long time before Jemma finally fell asleep, to be troubled by broken and vivid dreams. Twice she woke bathed in sweat. The second time she had wrapped herself in her duvet so tightly that she could hardly breathe.

She reached out and looked at her phone to see the time. Almost eight o'clock.

She was still lying there exhausted when the phone rang. She didn't recognise the caller's number. She held the phone to her ear.

'All right, bitch. I want it back.'

Joey Starling.

Jemma's stomach lurched. 'And you have something I want, something that's mine.'

'Don't fuck around with me.'

'Don't fuck with me, then.' Jemma was amazed how firm her voice sounded. Her hand was trembling.

'You won't be laughing when you haven't got another side of your face to laugh on.'

'What's that – a line from one of your shitty films? No way could you come out with something like that.'

'Don't fuck around.'

Jemma prayed that he wasn't sitting in a car outside the flat.

'I'm not fucking around,' she said. 'I want those videos you took of me. You want the key. Straightforward swap.'

'You don't know who you're messing with.'

'The original recordings, not just the stills,' said Jemma, gaining confidence from somewhere. 'I want everything.'

There was a pause.

'Okay,' said Starling in a voice of barely controlled fury.

In the background, over the phone, Jemma heard banging and a male voice call out, *'Hey, Joey boy. What's your problem?'*

'Bring the key to the set,' said Starling.

'Not until I get my videos.'

'The originals are in Brighton.'

'Not my problem.' Jemma heard the voice say, *'A £10 bag of H is called a joey.'*

'I'll kill the bastard,' muttered Starling.

'What?' said Jemma.

The voice again: *'He's got no bottle. Why's the nonce hiding?'*

'Fuck this.' Starling ended the call.

Chalke found Sandy Wishbourne – a detective constable on loan from Lewisham – being harangued by an angular, honey-blonde woman flanked by two security guards. The rent-a-cops melted away under Leyden's eye but the woman stood firm.

'You can't just march onto a film set and demand to interview the star,' the woman was saying in a mid-Atlantic accent. 'We have a film to make.'

'It's okay, Sandy,' said Chalke. 'I'll handle this.'

'Yes ma'am.'

'Oh, and Sandy, get Health and Safety down here to inspect this place.'

'Hang on.' The blonde was outraged. 'Who are you to come barging in here threatening us with Health and Safety?'

'DCI Chalke. Who are you?'

'Sara Jane Bentley. Press and public relations. This set has been cleared by the Borough of Greenwich. Their film liaison man's on his way.'

'And he'll solve the murder, will he?' asked Leyden.

'No, but –'

Leyden said, 'Don't you want to find out who killed Freddy Carter?'

'Of course we do,' said a deep American voice.

Chalke and Leyden turned to see a barrel-chested man with a shock of white hair. One side of his tanned face was covered by a crazy paving of white scar tissue.

'This is H. Bruce Montgomery, the director,' said Sara Jane.

'Freddy was my friend and colleague,' said the director. 'I want to see his killer brought to justice. We'll cooperate in every way we can.'

'That'll make everyone's life easier,' said Chalke, noticing that the scarred side of Montgomery's face seemed to be completely immobile.

'Sara Jane will do all she can to help. Won't you, Sara Jane?'

'Of course, Mr Montgomery.'

'But we don't really need Health and Safety, do we?'

'All right,' said Patsy.

'If you'll excuse me, I have to talk to my people. Everyone's up-set at Freddy's death, but they need to focus. The show must go on.' Montgomery held up a shovel-sized hand. 'Please don't think I'm being heartless. It's down to Freddy's professionalism that this film is coming in on time and on budget. This'll be his memorial.'

'I understand that Freddy had an argument with Joey Starling yesterday,' said Chalke. 'Any idea what that was about?'

'Lady, not a day goes by without Joey having a spat with someone. Now, if you need me, Sara Jane knows where to find me.' Montgomery limped away.

Leyden looked around. A century ago, grain barges would have sailed up the Thames to unload their cargos here. Now the wharf was covered with sets of lights, camera trolleys and endless yards of electric cable. A double-decker bus served as a canteen.

He was amazed at the number of people on set; most wearing cut-off jeans and with walkie-talkies on their belts. 'Who are all these people?'

Sara Jane went through the production crew, pointing out the gaffer and his team, the focus puller, the key grip, dolly grip, acting first AD, second AD, continuity girl, wardrobe, props master – in this case a young girl – the sound team. 'You should see the American sets. We're running on a tight budget here.'

'You're making a crime movie?'

'Joey Starling plays the local crime boss. Fleur Varndell is the widow of the former leader of the gang who took Joey under his wing. Joey has introduced her son to crime, against her wishes. At the same time, a ruthless Russian mob is muscling into Joey's patch. To survive, Joey's forced to betray Fleur's son to the Russians.'

'How does the mill come into it?'

'It's Joey's headquarters but we've almost finished here. Once Fleur shoots Joey, we move on.'

'That's the end of the film?'

'We shoot all the scenes at any one location at the same time, irrespective of where they come in the chronological narrative.

It's not uncommon for the climax of a film to be shot first. It was Freddy's job to work out the shooting schedule. Next week, we've four days at a pub on the Isle of Dogs. Then we're finished.'

'I don't suppose you know what Freddy and Joey rowed about?' asked Chalke.

'No, but as Mr Montgomery said, you shouldn't put too much emphasis on it. Joey enjoys picking a fight; it energises him somehow.'

'We're told that Joey slapped Freddy.'

Sara Jane sucked her teeth. 'That's not that unusual either, I'm afraid.'

'And he gets away with it?'

'He's the name.'

A slight woman with pale corn hair and dark glasses, hunched up in a quilted anorak, detached herself from a group of technicians.

'Fleur Varndell,' murmured Sara Jane.

Patsy had seen her on screen, usually playing the sexy neurotic other woman. In real life, Fleur Varndell was small and delicate – older, too. But she had the sort of skin and presence the camera loved, and Patsy would have killed for.

Sara Jane introduced them.

'I can't believe this about Freddy.' Fleur clutched a plastic coffee cup in both hands. 'It's terrible. He was a lovely man.'

'Have you known him long?' asked Patsy.

'We were at RADA together.'

'If Freddy went to RADA why wasn't he…?'

'A star? Oh, Freddy was happier on the production side. He was a gifted actor but he suffered terribly from stage fright. That, and a lack of ambition.'

'Can you think of anyone who might want him dead?'

'No.' Fleur Varndell gave a sad smile. 'He was the gentlest of creatures.'

'But he fell out with Joey Starling,' said Chalke.

A stillness enveloped Fleur. 'The less said about that man the better. I have to act with him. I don't have to like him.'

'I gather Freddy normally drove back to Wandsworth after filming,' said Leyden. 'Any idea why he was found on the footbridge leading to Greenwich?'

'I wasn't on set last night. As far as I know, Freddy wasn't due to be either.' Fleur nodded towards a girl with a clipboard and walkie-talkie hovering nearby. 'I'm sorry. I have to go to make-up. And it's going to take even longer than normal this morning.'

'Nice woman,' said Leyden as Fleur Varndell left.

'Was Starling filming last night?' Patsy asked Sara Jane.

'Yes. They were finishing the night shots on the wharf.'

'Were you here?'

'I left early. There was no reason for me to stay. As Miss Varndell said, I don't think Freddy was due to be here either.'

'Where's Starling living while the film's being made?'

'In that new block on Greenwich Reach. The developers offered it free in exchange for the publicity.'

'I take it that Joey has a driver?'

'Yes, although he tends to walk home after filming. I suppose it gives him time to unwind.' Sara Jane glanced at her watch. 'Actually, he should be here by now. He's late.'

'If he'd walked home last night, he'd have gone over the footbridge where Freddy was shot.'

A Jaguar car swept through the mill gates to pull up outside a trailer.

'Here he is. You can ask him yourself.'

The star climbed out. He was on his mobile, face like thunder.

Instantly he was surrounded by aides. He handed one his long black leather coat, still speaking on the phone. When he'd ended his call, Bruce Montgomery limped up. The two glanced towards the detectives, then Starling vanished into his trailer.

'I'd say he doesn't want to talk to us,' said Leyden.

'He doesn't have a choice.'

Montgomery came over. 'Joey'll see you in a minute,' he said.

'I'd prefer to see him now,' said Chalke. 'This is a murder inquiry.'

'I'm aware of that.' Montgomery glanced at his watch.

'Why don't I get you a list of those who were on set last night while you're waiting?' offered Sara Jane.

'We're not going to wait,' said Chalke. 'We have other things to do.'

Montgomery misunderstood. 'You're welcome to come back when Joey's available.'

Leyden stepped forward and banged on the side of the trailer with his fist. 'Hey, Joey boy,' he called. 'What's your problem?'

Montgomery winced. Even Chalke was surprised.

'I wouldn't do that if I were you, sergeant,' warned the director. 'Joey's known for his temper.'

'Did you know, ma'am, in south London a Joey's someone who fetches and carries.' Leyden was speaking loudly so that Starling could hear. 'A £10 bag of H is called a joey.'

Chalke knew what Leyden was trying to do. She just hoped he wasn't going to get hurt doing it. 'Mr Starling, we need to talk to you,' she called.

'He's got no bottle,' said Leyden loudly. 'Why's the nonce hiding?'

The trailer door flew open. Starling exploded down the steps. He thrust his face into Leyden's.

'Say that again. Say that to my face.'

'That's better,' said Leyden. He hadn't moved an inch.

Starling's eyes bulged with rage. 'Don't you ever talk to me like that again. You hear me?'

A grim coldness settled over Leyden. It had ceased to be a game.

'You want respect, you earn it.'

Starling took a wild swing. Leyden blocked it easily. Then he tapped the star on the nose with a short jab.

Montgomery stepped between the men.

'I'll fucking have you,' spat Starling.

'In your dreams.'

'That's *enough*,' said Chalke, her voice like a whip chord. 'We need to talk to you, Mr Starling.'

'Yeah, okay.' Starling was doing his best not to wipe away the tears at the corners of his eyes.

'Can we go somewhere more private?'

'Anything you want to say, you can say here.'

'You did know Freddy Carter was dead?' asked Chalke.

'I got a phone call.'

Montgomery said, 'I called Joey to tell him the sad news.'

Chalke wondered what else he'd told Joey.

She said, 'You had a row with Freddy yesterday, Mr Starling.'

'If you say so.' Joey was staring at Leyden. 'I've got you now. You come from the Ferrier. I knew your aunt and uncle. They were in the iron and steel trade. She ironed, he stole. And you became a cozzer! Fuck you.'

Suddenly, Chalke understood the antipathy between the two men. They were two sides of the same coin. Both had come from sink estates, both had fought their way out. And they hated each other.

Starling was an inch taller with a lean, brutal face while Leyden was stockier and with a thousand-yard stare of his own. She wouldn't like to get on the wrong side of either man.

'Are you denying you had an argument?' Chalke again asked Starling.

'If you say so.'

'And you slapped him.'

'He was out of order.'

'What was the argument about?'

'That's my business.'

'It's our business now that Freddy's been murdered,' said Chalke.

'My client has already declined to answer the question.'

Chalke swung around to see a confident, sharp-featured man in a pin-striped suit carrying a leather briefcase.

'Jez Hart. I'm Mr Starling's legal advisor. You must be DCI Chalke.'

Another phone call Montgomery had made. The director's desire for justice came second to his need to finish his film, thought Chalke bitterly. Montgomery left, not needed now the lawyer had arrived.

Chalke was seething. She asked Starling, 'You were filming here last night?'

'That's public knowledge,' said Hart.

'Perhaps you'd allow Mr Starling to answer the questions.'

Hart gave a mock bow.

'What time did you leave?'

'Around midnight.'

'Where did you go then?'

'Back to Drake Tower.'

'And how did you get there?'

'Sorry?'

'How did you get from here to there?'

'You don't have to answer these questions,' said Hart.

'What Mr Hart means is that you don't have to answer these questions *here*,' said Chalke. 'You can come to the station and do so.'

'I had a lift. Yeah, I had a lift,' said Starling. 'I started walking but I'd only got as far as that road before the bridge when some geezer offered me a ride so I took it.'

Patsy was amazed that he could make up such a tissue of lies and expect to be believed. 'So you were never on the footbridge?'

'That's what I said.'

'What's so important about the footbridge?' asked Hart.

It showed that he wasn't up to speed, thought Chalke. It also showed that H. Bruce Montgomery had pressed the panic button very quickly.

'Freddy Carter was shot dead on the footbridge. Mr Starling was seen heading in that direction.'

'He's already explained that he was given a lift.'

Patsy rolled her eyes. 'And who gave you this lift?'

'Never saw him before.'

'A total stranger?'

'Yeah.' Joey was growing more confident now.

'Can you describe the driver, or the car?'

'It was dark,' smirked Starling.

'There are street lights where the path crosses the road.' Leyden didn't know if there was or not but he was bloody sure Joey didn't either.

'Didn't take any notice. The car was a saloon. Could have been silver.'

Leyden was growing impatient. 'New car, old car? Young guy, old guy?'

'Dunno.'

'Why'd he stop?'

'People know me around here.'

'Wanted your autograph, did he?'

'Really, sergeant, you have a most unpleasant manner,' drawled Hart.

'It rubs off from the ponces I have to deal with,' said Leyden.

Chalke moved on quickly. 'And where did this... man drop you, Mr Starling?'

'At my penthouse.'

'Anyone there who could verify what time you arrived?'

'Mr Starling's relationship with his fiancée Bebee Bedlington ended a month ago, as I'm sure you read in the papers,' said Hart.

'No. Missed that,' said Chalke. 'Did anyone join you at Drake Tower, Mr Starling? Was someone waiting for you?'

'Is this really necessary, Chief Inspector?' asked Hart. 'I mean, it's one thing to have a row with a man and another to kill him.'

'Freddy Carter was shot just after filming ended last night. If it hadn't been for this... lift, Mr Starling would have been in the right place at the right time.'

'Do me a favour,' sneered Starling.

'When you find that driver, chief inspector, I'm sure he'll verify Joey's account of his movements,' said Hart.

'I'm sure he will.' Leyden stared at Starling, his lip curling in contempt. Starling jabbed his forefinger into the detective's face.

'Time you was put under manners.'

'Time you was put under manners,' mocked Leyden.

'Don't rise to it,' snapped Hart, putting a restraining hand on Starling's arm. 'I'll be having words with your superiors about you, sergeant, and about you, too, inspector.'

'Entirely up to you, sir. Would you like the phone number?'

'I believe I already have it.' His tone was glacial. 'Now, as the evidence against Mr Starling is circumstantial at best, and as he is needed on set, I suggest that this interview is terminated.'

There was little Chalke could say. 'Mr Starling needs to make a statement.'

'I'll arrange a convenient time with your superiors.'

Chalke was chewing a mouthful of glass. Hart waved over the dresser carrying Starling's leather coat.

'Here you are, Mr Starling,' she said. 'I've sewed a new button on for you.'

Patsy eyed the black wooden buttons on the coat.

Thank you, God, she thought.

Greenwich police station was under siege. Two TV vans were

parked outside with more on their way, and press photographers were being corralled in front of the old town hall. A couple of dozen fans and casual observers were hanging about.

Two Greenwich University students had come forward to say that they'd seen Starling emerge from the path over the footbridge soon after they'd left Wetherspoon's on Creek Road at midnight, shredding the actor's alibi and putting him firmly in the frame.

Andy Butterfield reckoned it was all cut-and-dried. Freddy had lain in wait for Joey, fronted him up and, in the struggle, Joey had turned the gun on Freddy. This would be consistent with Freddy's defence wounds.

Starling was still refusing to explain what the row with Freddy was about.

A fingertip search of the area around the bridge had drawn a blank, while police frogmen, searching for the murder weapon, were complaining about zero visibility and the treacherous nature of the mud.

'I don't suppose Alison would stump up for a dredger,' said Chalke.

'On our budget?' Weaver gave her a pitying look. 'What's the next move?'

'Search Starling's apartment – or, as Leyden would say, "spin his drum".'

First, though, Chalke phoned Weaver's wife Brenda to thank her for the meal last night.

'It was a lovely evening, thank you.'

'It was good having you here,' said Brenda. 'Des had talked a lot about you.'

'I'm lucky to have him as my boss,' said Chalke. 'I'm learning so much from him.'

'One thing, Patsy. I know this is going to sound silly, but try not to let him work too hard. He isn't getting any younger–'

'I'll do my best. And thank you again for last night.'

Just as Chalke put down the phone, her mobile rang. She checked the caller's identity and braced herself. For her sister Caro to contact her in the office meant that she wanted something. Patsy hoped that she wasn't about to be summoned to make up the numbers at some bash that evening. She was too busy to accept, but if she declined, Caro would get the hump. Patsy began to invent a prior engagement. But she was way off the mark.

'I had lunch yesterday at that new place in St Pancras –' began Caro.

'St Pancras?' Patsy had a picture of filthy windswept roads, constant traffic, lowlife toms, a vicious drug scene.

'On the concourse of the international station. Didn't you see the reviews?'

'Afraid not.'

'It was all right, although the jellied ham was a bit salty,' said Caro. 'Jessica and Emily enjoyed it.'

They would, thought Patsy. Two wealthy, self-indulgent women whose sole function in life was to keep up with whatever was trendy. There was little in London the two didn't see, hear, watch or visit within a week of it opening.

'Gillie Ruttle came along. That's why I'm phoning.' Caro paused for dramatic effect. 'She thinks Barney's having an affair. In fact, she's sure of it.'

'Why?' asked Patsy. 'Has she found an earring under the matrimonial pillow?'

'No, but she has this… feeling. Wives *know*, Patsy.'

'Gillie Ruttle doesn't know how many children she has. I've never known a more self-centred woman.'

'That's as maybe, but Gillie's not the sort to roll over and close her eyes. She won't think twice about wrecking Barney's career,' continued Caro. 'And she'll *really* crucify the other woman.'

'Why are you telling me this?'

'Because I know you. This is one of your little games, isn't it?'
'The sort of thing you find amusing – busting up a marriage and wrecking a promising career.'

'No, I don't.'

'You've done it before'

'That was different.'

'Which time?'

Patsy winced.

'She's going to hire a private investigator,' said Caro. 'And she's going to check his mobile phone.'

'Does she suspect anyone in particular?'

'If you're asking if your name came up – no, of course it didn't. Gillie wasn't going to accuse you to my face, was she?'

'Barney had better be careful, then,' said Patsy.

'That's just like you. Any other woman would say it'd be better if he stayed faithful to his wife. You don't think twice about having an affair as long as you can get away with it.'

'Oh, come on, Caro.' But even as Patsy protested, she thought, you're right. There's nothing wrong with having a fling with a married man as long as nobody gets hurt – or rather, as long as it's only me.

Caro didn't understand that Patsy never wanted to take a man away from his family. Quite the opposite. As soon as a lover began making noises about leaving his wife, she fled.

She couldn't expect her big sister to appreciate that.

When Caro had rung off, Patsy sent a text message to Barney.

'Gillie knows u r hvg affair. Be v careful – and dlt this.'

Patsy closed her phone and stared bleakly out of her window at the backs of the council flats. Her reverie was broken by Sue Jones. 'Are you all right?' she asked softly.

Patsy swung around to see Sue holding a copy of next week's rota. 'Yeah, fine.'

'You look as if you've got man trouble.'

Patsy gave a half laugh. 'What are you? Some kind of mind-reader?'

'Maybe it takes one to know one.'

'I'm fine.' Patsy didn't know what else to say.

'Sorry.' Sue pinned the rota to Patsy's noticeboard. 'I'm speaking out of turn. Do you know where Mr Weaver is?'

'Isn't he in his office?'

'No. I promised to give him back his *Telegraph*. He lets me borrow it to do the sudoku. Do you do sudoku?'

'Not really. I prefer crosswords. Which one do you do?'

'All of them.'

'Even the "fiendish" one?'

'That's the only one really worth doing.'

'Hold on. You have finished the *Telegraph* fiendish sudoku?' Patsy said slowly.

'I do it every day,' replied Sue.

Chalke stared at Sue. Caro was a sudoku addict. She spoke of the *Telegraph* fiendish as a cross between the Holy Grail and Mount Everest. The one and only time Caro had completed it, she'd made her husband take her out for a meal to celebrate.

'Sue, have you ever thought about going to university?' asked Chalke.

'Me?' said Sue. 'I left school when I was sixteen.'

'You must have some GCSEs.'

'I got five, but my mum wanted me out earning money. I was cleaning in the officers' mess in the Guz the week after I left school.'

'The Guz?'

'It's what sailors call their Devonport base. I think it's to do with guzzling cream teas or something.'

'It's never too late,' said Chalke. 'Maybe you could do a foundation course.'

Sue didn't say anything.

Chalke decided not to press the matter. Another time.

*

Chalke and Leyden walked to the car park, unnoticed by the press. They took Leyden's car. As they were driving away, Patsy said, 'Des Weaver's not convinced that Starling's guilty.'

'He's in a minority of one, then,' replied Leyden. 'The Eternal Flame's laying 6/4 that Joey'll be charged by midday tomorrow.'

'What odds is he giving that Starling will walk?'

'Five to one. No takers so far.'

'I'll have that. Can you put on £500 for me?'

'A monkey! Les would have a heart attack. Just put on a score.'

'Twenty quid! Not worth bothering.'

'You'd win a ton,' muttered Leyden defensively.

Shit! When would she ever learn?

'Bobby-'

'Ma'am.'

'Can you forget I said that?'

'Yes, ma'am.' They pulled out onto Greenwich High Road.

'Don't muck about... It's just... Sometimes I don't think. My mind's on the case-' She chose her word carefully. 'I talk to you as a... as a pal.'

God, she was pleading with him.

'Sorry, guv. Yeah, of course.'

'Thanks.' She reached for his hand resting on the gear lever, and squeezed.

A big mistake. A shock of sexual energy surged through her. Glancing at Bobby, she knew that he'd felt something similar.

Just when she'd thought life couldn't get any more complicated.

They cleared the lights in the one-way system and turned down Creek Road. Leyden broke the silence to ask, 'Do you think Freddy Carter's death could be linked to the others?'

'I don't see how,' replied Chalke, relieved they were talking. 'By the way, Weaver doesn't rate your mate's theory that the deaths of

Minicab and Guinness are connected.'

'Speed Bump didn't say their deaths were connected, only that they were rumoured to be part of the same crew, together with Georgie Locke. And we do know Locke and Dave Shine spoke on the phone.'

'Shame Vinnie Pike wasn't more helpful. His alibis check out, by the way, according to Essex. They think he's straight.'

'No news on Cousin Johnny?'

'He hasn't touched his bank account, but he wouldn't need cash if he'd joined the Foreign Legion,' said Chalke. 'Aren't you supposed to be able to join under a *nom de guerre*? Or is that a myth?'

'I'll find out,' said Leyden.

'You mean there's something you don't know?' said Chalke. 'I'm amazed.'

Leyden pulled up outside Drake Tower, the latest addition to the Greenwich waterfront. Lucymar's flat was visible across the creek.

At the doorway, a solitary police officer was being berated by a schoolgirl in a blue uniform. She'd shortened her skirt to mini length, wore black hold-up socks and had an improbably large mouth.

Jailbait.

The officer was saying, 'You can't go up there, love. It's as simple as that.'

'But I've got to get my phone back. I'll die without it.'

'Sorry.'

'But it's got... things on it.'

Leyden nodded to the copper. 'Everything all right?'

'This young lady claims to have left her mobile phone in Mr Starling's apartment.'

'How old are you?' Leyden asked the girl.

'Why?'

'Because I'm asking you, and I won't ask you again.'

'Fourteen,' pouted the girl.

'Why aren't you in school?'

'Because I've come to get my phone. I *need* my phone.'

'When did you leave it in Joey's flat?'

'Last night.'

'You weren't there all night, were you?' asked Chalke softly.

'Why? What's your problem?' The girl was teetering between defence and aggression, trying to work out how to play the scene to her advantage.

'What's your name, darling?' asked Leyden.

'Tinga.'

'That's not your real name, is it?'

'Paris Pratt. I prefer Tinga.'

'Okay, Tinga. I'm Bobby Leyden. This lady here's my boss, Patsy Chalke. We're detectives. Now, what time did you get here last night?'

'Dunno. It was late.'

'Wasn't your mum worried about you?'

'Mum? Not worried, green with envy more like. She wants me to bring Joey home. She'd drop her knickers for him before you could fart.'

'It's not the first time you've spent the night here, then?'

'Third, fourth, something like that. Me and Joey get on well – sometimes.' She was chewing her nails with a vengeance, Leyden noticed.

'Sometimes?' The girl had the munchies. The come-down after a night on drugs, he realised.

'Joey lost his rag this morning.'

'How'd you mean he lost his rag?'

'I was in bed. Joey comes in raving. Wanting to know if I'd taken it.'

'What was 'it'?'

'Some poxy key or something. He got really nasty. That's how I left my phone behind.'

'Let's go and see if we can find it now, shall we?'

Leyden told the uniform to radio for a WPC. He joined Chalke as the hall porter handed over the pass key. The porter – a scrawny youth – looked as if he'd been in a fight. Hardly a good advert for a prestigious new tower block.

The penthouse reeked of cannabis. A mirror on a coffee table bore traces of lines of cocaine.

Tinga spotted her phone on the white leather sofa. Leyden beat her to it.

'That's mine,' she said. 'It's got personal things on there.'

'You mean like photos of you and Joey?'

'Could be.'

'You know you're too young to have sex,' said Chalke.

'I've been shagging since I was twelve.'

'I meant legally.'

'Fuck that.'

Patsy Chalke found it a surreal experience watching Begley being interviewed outside the police station while at the same time seeing the interview live on the Incident Room TV.

Begley began well – if a little schoolmarm-ishly – until her mouth ran away with her. A collective groan rose among the detectives as she told the reporter that the police were confident they were holding the right man for the murder of Freddy Carter. She didn't mention Joey Starling by name.

She didn't need to.

'Jesus! If Joey walks, his lawyers are going to have a field day,' muttered Weaver.

'What was her press officer thinking of, letting her do a live interview?' asked Chalke, suspecting that Begley's hubris was to blame.

A few minutes later Begley hurried in, looking worried. 'I hope the case against Starling is as watertight as DI Butterworth says it is,' she began.

'Well–' Weaver hesitated.

Begley counted off the points on her fingers. 'Starling was in the right place at the right time; his alibi was fabricated; he'd had a fight with Carter just twelve hours earlier; Carter was found clutching a button from Starling's coat; plus there are fibres from the coat under Carter's fingernails. What more do we needt?'

'Paris Pratt says that Joey was behaving normally when he arrived home.'

'So?'

'And there was no blood on him,' added Weaver.

'A bullet from a low-velocity pistol into the head makes a mess,' said Chalke. 'You'd expect Joey to be covered in blood if he'd shot Freddy.'

Begley said, 'So he washed it off.'

'Where did he do that?'

'I don't know. You find out where,' snapped Begley. 'Didn't anyone hear a shot?'

'They'd been filming scenes involving gunshots all evening. No one was taking any notice.'

'What else is this Paris Pratt saying?'

'Let's ask DS Leyden.' Patsy saw Bobby just arriving back from the juvenile suite at Lewisham, where Tinga had been taken with her mother. She repeated Begley's question.

'Not a lot,' said Leyden. 'She's sulking because she's not allowed to smoke in the nick.'

'What about her mother?' asked Begley.

'She's all right. She can pop outside for a fag.'

Patsy managed to keep a straight face. 'Has the girl admitted that Joey gave her drugs?'

'No. She's being stubborn. A hair sample will show what drugs she's taken, except it won't prove that she took them with Joey or that he supplied them.'

'And the videos of her and Starling on her phone?'

'Tinga thinks they're great. Shows that she's got one over on her mother. They've got some sort of shagging competition going.'

'I beg your pardon!' said Begley.

'An extreme form of intergenerational conflict, ma'am, manifesting itself in a sexually explicit competition between mother and daughter,' said Leyden.

'But the girl's made a statement?'

'Yeah. We've got Starling on unlawful sex.'

'What's he saying about the cocaine in his flat?'

'Claims he knows nothing about it. Hart's making noises about it being planted.'

'At least Starling can't deny the photos on his laptop.'

A preliminary search of Starling's flat had unearthed six grams of cocaine, a lump of cannabis resin and a switchblade.

A search of the laptop found in his trailer on set had revealed a collection of photographs featuring the star having sex with a number of teenage girls. Many of the pictures – stills from high-definition film cameras – appeared to have been taken without the girls' knowledge. In others, it was clear that the girls were in on the act, though most had a glassy-eyed look that suggested intoxication.

If it was discovered that the girls were under the age of consent, or that the photos had been taken without their permission, Starling was in the shit.

'If Joey had shot Carter, would he have left this sort of stuff lying around,' he asked. 'He'd have known we'd be all over his flat. Surely he'd have come back and tidied up.'

Even Begley saw that.

News came in that, against all the odds, the divers had found the gun. The Makarov pistol had been tied to a house brick and the string had snagged on submerged pilings.

'I'll get the Fingerprint Bureau to pull out all the stops,' said Begley, gathering up her papers as she prepared to head back to the safety of Scotland Yard.

'Could you ask forensics to do the same with the coat button?' asked Chalke. 'We're still waiting for results on Stan Figgens from a week ago.'

'I'll prioritise both.'

Leyden was called to the phone.

'That was the pathologist,' he reported when he came back. 'Freddy Carter was riddled with cancer. He only had weeks to live.'

Leyden and Carl Cochrane were given an office and the task of logging the eighty pornographic images found on Starling's laptop. Only two prints per image, said Chalke. That sort of photo would get around the nick in minutes.

'The bastard pulled a good standard of bird,' observed Cochrane as the first images appeared.

Leyden grunted. 'I guess the money and drugs make up for what he lacks in personal charm.'

'You don't much like Starling, do you?'

'I don't like him at all, mate.'

'You know Muriel Figgens doesn't want her husband's body back from the morgue,' said Cochrane, connecting the laptop to the printer.

'Why not?'

'She reckons Stan's already had his funeral. One's all he deserved and one's all he's going to get.'

'Has she gone off on her cruise yet?'

'Went yesterday.'

'Reckon Stan's going to be on ice a long time, then, Carlo.'

'You still getting on okay with Patsy?'

'Yeah, we're good.'

'I'd say you were more than good, mate. She's really taken a shine to you.'

'Bollocks.'

Leyden wasn't comfortable talking about his relationship with Chalke. Instead, he said, 'If Lorraine Finch is sticking to her alibi, we're going to have to release her soon.'

'She's at the heart of the murder of her husband *and* her shag,' Cochrane reminded him.

'Perhaps she's innocent on both counts.'

'And perhaps my prick's a bloater.'

'What odds is the Eternal Flame offering?'

'He had her at evens but there were no takers so he's taken it off the board.' Cochrane pointed at the screen. 'Is this the same bird as the last one?'

A girl was sitting astride Starling. The still cut off her head but an indistinct tattoo on her shoulder connected her with the girl they'd seen in the previous shot, kneeling as Joey took her from behind.

Leyden peered at the tattoo. 'What do you reckon that is?'

'Dunno. Cracking body though.'

They scrolled on to the next image.

'If she's sixteen I'm the Lord Mayor of London.'

After a couple of hours they reckoned they'd identified around thirty girls, although since Starling had been primarily interested in parts of their anatomy other than their faces, it wasn't always clear whether the images were of different girls or the same ones shot from a different angle.

Cochrane was fetching teas when Chalke came in. 'How's it going?' she asked.

'You wouldn't believe how many of these girls have tattoos,' said Leyden.

'Oh, I don't know. They're common nowadays.'

'Don't tell me you've got one.'

'You'll never know, sergeant.'

'That's all right, ma'am. I'll just imagine.'

Chalke was working on the ultimate put-down when Cochrane

returned with two teas. 'Sorry, boss, I'd have got you one if I'd known.'

'I don't drink tea. What do we have?'

'An egotistic voyeur with a predilection for young flesh,' said Leyden. 'Unless we can find some common denominator between these girls, we're going to have our work cut out tracking them down.'

'We could try to identify them from the tatts.' Chalke peered at the photograph of the girl with the tattoo on her shoulder. 'What do you reckon that is?'

'A penguin?' guessed Leyden.

'No way. That's a dragon,' said Cochrane.

It didn't look like either to Chalke.

'We'll send the laptop to Sidcup,' she said. 'The techies should be able to enhance these images. Our Alison is throwing her weight around so we might even get a quick result. Blue-light it down and I'll make a phone call.'

It was Weaver who remembered that Starling owned a Georgian town house on Brighton seafront. The photographs were scanned and sent to Sussex police.

Within the hour, local detectives had entered Starling's house, and identified the master bedroom as the location for most of the shots, which were taken with two professional HD digital cameras – one above the headboard and the other at right angles, hidden in a painting. Both their memory chips were missing.

All that remained now was to identify the girls.

Jemma waited for Starling to phone back. When he didn't, she didn't know what to do. After a while she phoned Starling's mobile, only to find the number unavailable.

She decided to go into college. Anything was better than moping around the flat. It was the right decision, although the lecture on music theory and composition largely passed her by.

It was almost lunchtime when she heard the rumour that Joey

Starling had been arrested for shooting some bloke. Jemma hurried to the junior common room.

A crowd was gathered around the TV set. Across the bottom of the screen news ticker was announcing: *Breaking news – Film star Joey Starling arrested in connection with the midnight shooting of Assistant Director Freddy Carter.*

For the first time in her life Jemma thought she was going to faint. The world went black; she swayed, feeling the blood pulse around her head. She needed to get away from the chatter, away from the laughter. She needed to be alone.

In a daze, she wandered out through the gates into Park Row. A reversing car narrowly missed her as she crossed the road and headed down the alley at the back of the Trafalgar Tavern, passing the Yacht pub and the new £1 million dolls' houses.

Jemma understood now why Starling hadn't phoned back.

She emerged onto the riverside. Normally she stopped to admire the ancient Trinity Hospital almshouse, now dwarfed by the vast power station alongside. Today she didn't even see it.

It was only when she was under the disused cast iron coaling jetty that she began to get a funny feeling. She'd walked from sunshine into shadow, but the chill settling over her had nothing to do with temperature. She was sure she was being watched.

Jemma slowed, pretending to watch two coxless fours from the local Curlew rowing club stroking upstream. She follwed their progress until she was facing back the way she had come. A tourist couple with a map; a young mum pushing a buggy; and three men – one dressed in a suit with a backpack, two in jeans. One of them was on a mobile phone.

Jemma picked up her pace and walked onto Ballast Quay. Fifty yards away, up Hoskins Street, a man was leaning on a silver car, talking into a mobile phone. She glanced back. The man in jeans was still talking into a phone.

She thought about going into the Cutty Sark pub. Surely they wouldn't follow her in there and risk being identified. But what then? She'd have to come out sometime. She hurried over the cobbles, icy fingers grasping at her heart, past the Harbourmaster's House. The streets were straighter here, long terraces of artisans' cottages owned by Morden College. She looked back. The bonnet of a silver car was inching into view.

Suddenly there was a sound like a thousand angry wasps and Eric swung around the corner on the Pink Peril. Even before he'd stopped, she'd scooped up the spare helmet and swung her leg over the pillion seat.

'Don't ask. Let's get out of here,' she said.

Eric accelerated away, turning left into Banning Street before starting a crazy zigzag through residential streets that ended with them crossing Blackwall Lane and shooting up a narrow path into their street.

'What was that about?' he said when they were inside the flat.

'I think I was being followed.'

'You know Starling's been arrested?'

'Yeah, I saw on TV. How did you find me?'

'People saw you wandering out of college. They said you looked like death.'

'Thank you. You're a good friend.'

'Now listen, I've got to get back. Got a stand-up performance in half an hour. You relax. I'll be as quick as I can.'

When Eric had left, Jemma locked and bolted the doors, went into her room, turned off her phone, flung herself on the bed – and wept.

It was just after three o'clock. The cardboard box that had held pork pies and sandwiches was empty apart from the fish paste ones, and Andy Butterfield was busy interviewing Starling.

Front desk called up to say there was a man claiming he had information about Joey Starling.

'This'll be the alibi,' forecast Weaver.

Chalke went to prise Leyden away from the computer screen.

'Come on. This one's right up your street,' she told him. 'Get you back in the real world after all that kiddie porn.'

The man in the interview room was in his late twenties with bad skin, chewed fingernails and nicotine-stained fingers.

'I heard you want to speak to the guy who gave Joey Starling a lift home last night,' he began.

Leyden sat down across the table and said, 'Yeah.'

'You're looking at him.'

'Fuck off.'

The man's jaw dropped. 'What d'you mean? I... I've come in here to try to help. And I get that. I ain't standing for it.'

Leyden said, 'Fuck off, then.'

'Don't you want to know what information I have?'

'You want to be nicked, do you? Wasting police time, obstruction, conspiracy to pervert the course of justice, perjury, bearing false witness,' said Leyden, making it up as he went along.

Sweat burst out along the man's scant hairline.

'I hope you're being well paid, mate, because you're looking at five years,' continued Leyden. 'But go on, give us a laugh – and then we'll nick you.'

Now that Leyden had the man crapping himself, Patsy, who had been leaning against the door, said sweetly, 'Let's start again. What's your name?'

'Mark Tyrone Parsons, thirty-three, of 98B Church Street, Deptford.'

Leyden leaned back in his chair. 'Got that off pat, haven't you?'

'What do you do for a living?' asked Chalke.

'I'm a night porter at the Black Dog hotel in Wrotham but I've been off sick this week.'

'Tell us what happened last night, Mr Parsons,' said Patsy.

'I couldn't sleep.'

'Because you're a night porter, right?' mocked Leyden.

'Yeah, right. I thought I'd go for a drive. Just local, like. See if that made me sleepy.'

'So your plan was to drive until you fell asleep at the wheel and killed someone?'

'I just fancied a drive. Roads are quiet, like.'

Leyden gave a mocking laugh.

Parsons looked at Chalke. 'Why's he got the petrol with me?' he whined.

'Because I can't stand lying toerags,' said Leyden harshly. 'Come on then, finish your story.'

Parsons glanced nervously at the door. He looked as if he was about to make a run for it. She would in his shoes, thought Patsy.

'I was driving down Cross Street when I saw Mr Starling. I've always been a fan of his so I asked him if he wanted a lift. He said he was going home so I drove him to Drake Tower. That's it.'

Leyden let the silence build until Parsons looked as if he would collapse under its weight.

Finally Leyden said, 'You're a fucking awful liar.'

'It's the truth.'

'You wouldn't know the truth if it gave you a blowjob.' Leyden took off his jacket, managing to convey menace in the act. 'Who do you owe?'

'What?'

'You wouldn't risk getting yourself nicked unless you owed big time.'

'No–'

'Who did you get a call from?'

'What call?'

'The call to come here and make a cunt of yourself.' Leyden exploded out of his chair to rear over Parsons. 'Because you're not going to make a cunt of us, you poxy moron.'

'I thought I could help.'

'Bollocks you did. What was Starling wearing when you picked him up?'

'Long leather coat and jeans.'

'And you dropped him…?'

'Outside Drake Tower.'

'So you'll have seen the gaggle of girls waiting for him.'

'There were a few girls hanging around. Mr Starling went in the back way. He didn't want to be bothered.'

Leyden said, 'I'd stop talking out of my Aris if I was you, mate.'

Parsons wiped away the sweat on his forehead. 'Okay, forget it. I'll just go.'

'Too late, my son. If you told us who sent you here –'

'I can't do that.' Parson's face scrunched up as though in pain. 'I'm not a Bertie.'

Leyden stared hard at him.

'I can't. Really I can't.'

'Shame.' Leyden stood up. 'Come on.'

'What?' Parsons pressed himself back in his chair. 'Where?'

'The cells, mate.'

'Whoever put Parsons up to it scares him more than we do,' said Chalke as they climbed the stairs back to the Incident Room.

'Tosh Bibby owns the Black Dog hotel,' said Leyden. 'Perhaps he can lean on Parsons.'

'Good point. I'll ask Weaver to give him a ring.'

At five o'clock came the news that fingerprints had been successfully recovered from the Makarov, even though it had been immersed in water. The techies were full of themselves.

'Yeah, yeah,' said Leyden, taking the phone call. 'Just tell us what you've found… Just one set of prints? No possibility that you might have…? Sorry, mate, had to ask.'

'Well?' asked Chalke.

'There're only Freddy Carter's prints on the gun.'

'That fits in with the theory that Carter was lying in wait for Joey,' said Begley when she was told. 'In the struggle, Starling turned the gun on Carter and it went off. We could settle for self-defence.'

When Andy Butterfield put this to Starling, he said, 'Load of bollocks. I told you, I never saw Freddy Carter last night.'

'By the way, your alibi's here,' said Butterfield. 'In a cell, facing a charge of perverting the course of justice.'

'Not my problem. You always get saddos wanting part of the action,' said Starling.

It all started going wrong for Begley just after seven o'clock.

The Forensic Science Service laboratory called to report that although the wooden button had come from Starling's leather coat, it hadn't been ripped off. The ends of the fibres were too regular. The cotton had been cut.

Secondly, a preliminary investigation had confirmed that, while the fibres under the fingernails of Freddy's left hand had come from Starling's coat, the only marks on the coat were on the inside, at the back near the hem. Not somewhere that would be scuffed in a fight. More like somewhere you'd scratch the coat if you wanted to get fibres under your fingernails without the owner's knowledge.

Thirdly, a screen buff contact of Weaver's had been going through all the films Freddy had worked on. He called to say that five years ago Freddy had been assistant director on a low-budget mystery where one character had attempted to frame another by committing suicide and making it look like murder. The character had shot himself on a bridge over a river, tying the gun to a brick before hanging the brick over the bridge so that when he let go of the gun, it fell into the water.

In the film, the shooting had taken place during a snowstorm. Other than that the deaths were identical.

At eight o'clock, as Lorraine Finch was being released on police bail, Chalke watched from the Incident Room as Jez Hart gave a triumphant press conference outside the police station.

Starling had already been smuggled out in a van to go to stay with Montgomery at his home in Kensington.

Weaver was wheeled out to make a brief statement. 'A man helping with inquiries into the suspicious death of Freddy Carter has been released on police bail, pending further investigation into Mr Carter's death and also pending further inquiries into certain matters that have come to light.'

Chalke stuffed documents and files into her briefcase, thinking what a shitty day it had been. Blunt, Leyden and one or two of the other usual suspects were going for a drink, but she didn't fancy one. On the way to her car, Chalke had an idea. Maybe some good could come out of today after all. Ten minutes later, she emerged from the community college on Royal Hill with a clutch of information about the various courses Sue Jones could do to qualify for university.

Now all she had to do was convince Sue it was a good idea.

Sue lived in the bottom half of a small house on Wyndcliffe Road, a long sloping street leading down from Charlton Road towards the Thames and the O2 Arena. Her green Nissan Micra was parked outside.

There were two doorbells in the porch. The lower said simply, 'Jones'.

Chalke pressed the bell and waited. A figure appeared behind the frosted glass door panels.

'Yes?'

'Sue, hi – it's Patsy Chalke.'

'Oh… Right. Just a minute.' Sue vanished to reappear a moment later, wiping her hands on a cloth. 'I was just taking an olive and rosemary loaf out of the oven.' She looked worried.

Chalke apologised for the intrusion, and explained the purpose of her visit.

For a moment she thought Sue was going to ask her to leave, but then she seemed to remember her manners. 'Please – come in. Come in.'

She led the way along the hall, a boxed-off staircase to the right, and through a door into her flat. She showed Chalke into a small warm living room with lots of reds and yellows, smelling of polish and baking.

Sue disappeared into the kitchen and returned with the freshly baked loaf. She cut a slice and handed it on a plate to Patsy.

'Wow! This is the best bread I've ever tasted. Sue, you're wasted in the Incident Room. You should become a master baker.'

Sue didn't seem to be listening. She was leafing through the brochures. Finally she looked up. 'I don't think I could do this.'

'Come on! Anyone who can do the *Telegraph* fiendish sudoku will storm it,' said Patsy.

'No –'

'And look at the way you set out that spreadsheet. I couldn't have done that.'

But Sue was already standing up. She looked as though she was about to cry.

'Thank you for all this… I appreciate it. Really. But… You've got me wrong. Now, if you don't mind, I should get on wtih my baking.'

'Of course… Sorry.'

Patsy was surprised. Sue must be more insecure and unconfident than she'd realised.

She was still thinking about it when she got home. Perhaps Sue would change her mind if she left her in peace. After all, nobody liked being nagged.

It was almost 10.30 p.m. Eric had failed to get Jemma to eat although she had drunk most of a bottle of wine. The local TV news was on with the sound turned low.

'I just don't understand why Starling killed Freddy,' Jemma was saying for the twentieth time. 'What had Freddy ever done to him?'

'Perhaps Freddy was trying to warn him off.'

'Yeah, but…'

All evening, they'd been going over and over the same ground, round and round the same theories. They were getting nowhere, the words growing ever staler in their mouths.

Greenwich police station appeared on the TV. Jemma turned up the sound in time to hear the reporter say: 'Earlier this evening, the star was released on police bail. His solicitor Jez Hart made a statement on his behalf–'

Cut to a man in a sharp suit and gelled hair reading from a piece of paper: 'Mr Starling, who has been helping the police with their inquiries into this tragic affair, has now left the police station without a stain on his character. We are now examining remarks made earlier today by a senior police officer that could be construed as defamatory. Mr Starling is expected to be back on the set of his current film *I'll Take the Bullet for You* tomorrow morning.'

A burly policeman with a drinker's face was saying something but Jemma wasn't listening. She'd been holding herself together in the belief that Starling was going to be made to pay for killing Freddy. Now she could feel herself start to unravel.

She went to find her mobile phone, remembering that she had switched it off that morning. Three missed calls from Starling. From the times, it was clear that he had begun trying to contact her immediately he had been released from police custody.

Jemma did not want to talk to Starling. There was only one person Jemma wanted to talk to. Her mother.

She dialled a number from memory. Her mother answered immediately.

'Yes, I've just seen it,' said Jemma, heading for the privacy of her bedroom. 'No. He's not going to get away with it… Hang on, Mum, let me–'

Jemma closed the door.

Bobby Leyden lay awake, wondering why Carter hadn't simply shot Starling. He had nothing to lose. The cancer would have killed him before he could have been put on trial. Leyden couldn't decide whether Freddy's attempt to frame Starling showed courage or cowardice.

He turned his head to look at Karen. She was asleep, facing away from him.

It was over between them. He'd been avoiding the truth for some time, trying to convince himself that they were just going through a bad patch and that things would get better. That they'd rediscover the magic they'd shared when Karen had moved in.

It had been one of the happiest times of Leyden's life. They'd been on the verge of a great adventure – setting up home, buying furniture, making plans for their future.

He didn't know why it had all gone so wrong so quickly. Why they were now living virtually separate lives. Why the little home life they shared had become an endless grind of silence, sulking and sniping.

There was no spark left in their relationship but neither had the courage to admit it.

The realisation had come after they'd made love. There'd been little animation or desire. It had been something both felt they were expected to do. Neither had tried too hard to please. When they'd finished, Karen had rolled over and had fallen asleep in seconds.

There was nothing between them.

No, that wasn't true. There was misery.

There had to be more to life than this. Bobby just hoped he had the courage to go out and find it.

DAY NINE

Thursday

FLEUR VARNDELL STARED at Joey Starling as if he was something unpleasant she'd found on the sole of her shoe.

'You scum,' she hissed. 'He was worth ten of you. You soil the planet just by breathing.'

'Shut it. You hear me? Shut it.'

Fleur took one, two, three steps backwards, her cheeks streaked with tears, her mouth working soundlessly. She pulled a pistol from her handbag. Her hands trembled as she lifted the gun.

'You don't scare me,' taunted Starling. 'Pull the fucking trigger or piss off.'

Fleur swallowed, nerving herself to fire.

'You haven't got the guts.'

'That's where you are wrong.' Fleur spoke with slow deliberation. A smile lit her face. 'Goodbye and good riddance,' she intoned dramatically.

Her finger tightened on the trigger. There was an explosion.

'Cut.' H. Bruce Montgomery gave a deep sigh. 'Children, children. I know we're upset about Freddy's death but do try to stay professional. Take a break everyone.'

He put his arm around Fleur's shoulders and, limping, led her away from the crew.

'Internalise, darling, internalise. This is for the camera, not the back row of the stalls.'

Fleur nodded.

'And remember – you hate this man.'

'How can I forget?'

'I think I'd have blinked more if someone had pointed a gun at me like that,' observed Leyden from where they'd been watching on the edge of the set.

'I'd have closed my eyes and prayed he'd go away,' said Chalke.

'No, you wouldn't. You've have ripped his throat out.'

'That's your job. I'm the cerebral one, remember?'

'Charming. Here I am, aspiring to be Watson to your Holmes, Lucas to your Maigret, Tommy to your Tuppence, Achilles to your Tendon – and all you want me for is muscle.'

'Achilles?'

'Poirot's first name.'

'That was Hercules.'

'Thought that was the name of Steptoe's horse.'

'Do you live on this planet or are you just visiting?'

'Just visiting.'

This flirting had to stop, Chalke told herself. It would only end in tears – just like Alison Begley's career unless they could persuade Starling to agree to a deal. It was a shabby deal, but it was one that had been approved by the top brass. In return for Starling not pursuing the Met for slander and defamation, the charge of possession of a class A drug would be kept on file and the investigation into the contents of Starling's laptop halted.

Chalke had been sent to put the deal to Starling but she'd been forced to wait and watch as he'd screwed up the scene time after time. And when he got it right Fleur Varndell fluffed her lines. Now Starling retreated to his trailer.

'I'll give him a few minutes. Maybe his mood will improve.'

'Wouldn't bank on it if I were you.'

'And this time I'll talk to Starling by myself, seeing as we're here to broker a deal, not start a war. You stay out of it.'

Leyden wandered over to talk to Speed Bump, thinking that there were even more people on set than normal, when he spotted Fleur Varndell slouched in a canvas chair.

She caught his eye. 'May I have a quiet word?'

'Of course.'

He waited, but Fleur seemed at a loss to know what to say.

To break the ice, Leyden asked, 'Does every scene take this long to get right? Sorry. I know nothing about film-making.'

'Starling was doing a Brando, and I wasn't having it.'

'A Brando?'

'Deliberately screwing up until I was flat then letting rip to steal the scene.'

'I had no idea–'

'Bruce saw what was going on. Starling's got a reputation for it. Some actors won't work with him.'

'I see.'

'I… I wanted to ask you about Freddy Carter.'

'I can't say anything, officially,' said Leyden.

'Of course… I shouldn't have–' She turned away.

Leyden had always liked Fleur Varndell as an actress. Now he was warning to her as a person. There was something decent about her – something fragile, too.

'No, it's all right,' he said. 'It looks as if Freddy committed suicide.'

'But I heard that he'd had a fight with Starling, that he was found clutching a button from Starling's coat.'

'That button had been deliberately cut off, not ripped off in a struggle. It's one of several things that suggests Freddy was trying to set up Starling.'

Fleur looked away, sadness and maybe anger etched in her face. 'But why's Starling still on police bail?'

'A technicality, so we can pull him in on other charges if we want to. Our boss has cocked up big time. Strictly between us–'

Leyden explained the deal they were here to offer.

'What sort of images?'

'Sorry?'

'You said images were found on his laptop.'

'Porn, amateur home-made stuff. But please, Miss Varndell–'

'I promise.' She took his hand. 'Not a word.'

Chalke was being made to wait outside Starling's trailer. She suspected she'd be there until shooting restarted, when she'd be told Starling had no time to see her. Payback for yesterday.

In their dreams.

'Mr Montgomery.' She greeted the director as he left the star's trailer.

'Detective Chief Inspector Chalke. And how are you today?'

'Running out of time – just like you.'

'Excuse me. Why am I running out of time?'

'Because you need your star to complete the shots on the wharf–'

'And?'

'And I'm running out of time because I have two murder inquiries on the go. I can't hang around here any longer. Since I need to speak to Mr Starling, I'm about to revoke his bail and take him back to the police station.'

'You can do that?'

'I can do that.'

Montgomery's smile did not reach his eyes. He disappeared into the trailer to emerge seconds later. 'Misunderstanding. Please go in.'

Chalke put her head in the trailer. It was crowded with hangers-on, all wanting a piece of the man who'd made the cozzers look stupid. Starling was seated at the table, texting. There was a day bed, wardrobe, refrigerator, sink and small cooker.

Hart ordered everyone to leave, forcing Chalke to back down the steps while Starling's cronies filed past, sneering openly.

She went in again. The trailer smelled of plastic and brandy. Chalke remembered Porthcawl and rubbed her neck. She was not invited to sit down.

'Joey wants a full, public apology,' began Jez Hart, dressed for the TV cameras in sharp pinstripes and silk tie.

'That's not on offer,' said Chalke.

'Then we'll have no alternative but to begin legal proceedings,' said Hart. 'We'd expect a jury to award exemplary damages.'

'For what?'

'Damage to reputation and career. We'll be seeking around £1 million.'

'A million – for damages to Mr Starling's career,' echoed Chalke.

'Joey is hot. He is the man.'

'It's a lot to lose,' said Chalke.

'You said it.'

'So what I'm wondering is why Mr Starling is determined to wreck his career – or rather allow you to wreck it for him?'

Starling stopped texting. 'What's she on about?'

'A quantity of a class A drug was found in your apartment –'

'There's not a film star today who's not been in possession of class A drugs, and the fans know it,' said Hart. 'That's not going to hurt Joey.'

'The quantity's at the top end for personal use. Many prosecutors would press for a dealing charge on six grams.'

'Don't try to pull that one.' Hart pretended to get angry. 'We'll be entering a vigorous defence that the cocaine was planted as part of a plot to fit up Joey.'

'Will you be claiming that the pornographic images of Mr Starling in sex acts with young girls were faked in the Met's audiovisual labs?'

'The images were the personal property of Mr Starling. They were seized illegally, and you have no way of knowing that those girls were underage.'

'You're right. But once we set that investigation in train, with the assistance of the Brighton police–' She was rewarded by a twitch from Starling.

'Ignore her, Joey,' urged Hart. 'No judge would allow that evidence to be put before a jury, not the way it was gathered.'

'You're sure about that?' smiled Patsy.

'I'd stake my career on it.'

'It's not your career that you're staking, is it?' she asked sweetly. 'It's Joey's. And, as you say, it's one hell of a career to lose.'

'Is she right?' growled Joey.

'Of course she's not. The laptop was seized from this trailer illegally. Anything found on it would be deemed inadmissible evidence.'

'We'd dispute that, naturally,' said Chalke. 'But in any case, by then the damage would have been done. Mr Starling's sexual penchant for underage girls would have been made public.'

'How come?' asked Starling.

'Some girls may decide to speak out.' Patsy shrugged. 'And the press has a knack of getting hold of sensitive court papers–'

'You mean you'd leak the names.'

'Certainly not. *I'd let Weaver speak to his mates among the crime reporters.* 'Look, I'm offering you a no-lose bet.'

'Nah, you're not. I stand to lose a million quid,' said Joey. 'I'll take the risk. Anything to see plod's face rubbed in shit.'

'My client has spoken,' said Jez Hart.

Chalke left the trailer simmering with anger. Why the hell was she expected to do Begley's dirty work? Begley had got herself in this mess. She should sort out her own shit.

'We're out of here,' Chalke told Leyden.

'Let's just watch them shoot the scene,' said Leyden. 'Maybe they'll get it right this time.'

Starling, wearing his long leather coat, emerged from his

trailer. He went into the mill, ready to make his entrance.

'Positions, everyone.'

The second assistant camera held out the clapperboard. 'Slate 220, scene 22C. Take 17.'

'Action.'

Fleur took a step towards the mill door. Starling strode out.

'What do you want?' he asked coldly.

'To bury my child.'

'Your "child". You wanted him to be a child for ever. He wanted to be a man.'

'A man who was killed thanks to you. He had his life ahead of him. He was decent – not a piece of shit, like you.'

'Shut it or I'll fucking deck you.'

Fleur pulled the pistol out of her handbag. Her eyes filled with tears, her mouth working soundlessly. Her hands trembled as she lifted the gun but at the same time she radiated inner resolve.

Better, thought Chalke. Fleur's character would have known what she was going to do when she went to confront Starling,

'What is it with little people?' sneered Starling. 'If you're going to pull the trigger, do it or piss off.'

Fleur gave a resigned smile which barely lifted the corners of her mouth.

'You haven't got the guts,' taunted Starling.

'That is where you are wrong.' Fleur spoke with slow deliberation. 'This time, you're going to take the bullet yourself.'

They were just four paces apart.

Leyden saw Fleur thumb back the hammer. She pulled the trigger.

There was an explosion and a hole appeared where Joey Starling's left eye had been.

The national murder manual teaches that cases are solved by 'effective early action' when clues are fresh, witnesses are accessible, their memories vivid and intact; when forensic evidence and CCTV film are available and uncontaminated.

Coppers call it the 'golden hour' – while the trail is still hot. It didn't get any hotter than two murder squad detectives actually witnessing a killing.

The first sirens could be heard while the film crew were still gawking in shock.

The cavalry that Begley had brought to Greenwich on the Carter inquiry yesterday were still around, kicking their heels and trying to avoid getting sent back to their home nicks. Two murder squad teams under their respective DIs were at the mill in minutes, followed by a busload of uniforms, a major incident control room, and a police caravan. The mill offices were requisitioned for interviews.

It all seemed pretty straightforward – a speedily-contained crime scene with a finite number of suspects.

Except it wasn't.

The second location unit had been filming in the cobbled alleys around the mill for 'colour' shots before moving to the Isle of Dogs, which explained the large number of extras Leyden had noticed. The additional fifty or so potential suspects had been allowed onto the wharf to use the catering bus. The film company had a list of their names and addresses, but there was no knowing if the names were correct. Extras turned up for a nominal fee, free food and the chance of appearing in the background of a film, but some had already become fed up with hanging around and had wandered off.

'Couldn't get a more public murder,' muttered Weaver as they stood in the mill yard.

'You prefer murders to be private?' smiled Chalke before asking, 'Do you think Starling's death is linked to the others?'

Weaver shrugged. 'Minicab found in his dry-cleaning machine; Guinness murdered in his own gym – now this. All very public.'

'The Dim Reaper?'

'Or an accomplice,' said Weaver. 'But I can't see a motive.'

'Those rumours you mentioned about Starling being involved in the Maidstone job–'

'There was never any proof,' said Weaver.

'But still – thieves falling out?'

'Keep an open mind, Patsy,' said Weaver. 'Keep an open mind until the evidence becomes overwhelming.'

'Fair enough.' Chalke was grateful for advice from the old pro. 'I thought Fleur Varndell was going to faint when she saw what she'd done.'

'She's an actress,' said Weaver. 'She could have faked it.'

'Starling's death gets Begley off the hook,' said Leyden as he joined them. 'Perhaps we should check her alibi.'

Chalke ignored him. 'There's no chance this could be an accident, is there? Someone being careless with the gun?'

'CO19 are on their way,' said Leyden.

'You're firearms-trained, Bobby,' remembered Weaver. 'Have a quick look.'

Leyden examined the Makarov. It was the same model of pistol that Freddy Carter had used. It had held just the one round. Someone had known that Fleur Varndell would pull the trigger only once.

'It's real, right enough,' he told Chalke.

'So the killer either substituted a live round for a blank or substituted this for the prop gun.'

'Either way, the exchange must have taken place during the break.'

'Find if this was the same pistol as used in the earlier takes,' said Chalke.

'Okay.'

Leyden was about to mention something he'd noticed but Chalke had already turned away. In a way he was glad. Maybe it was nothing. Maybe he was barking up the wrong tree. He hoped he was.

The props girl was no help. Between sobs, she managed to say that she'd only been given the job two days ago when the props master had gone down with man flu. Normally she was the assistant continuity girl.

She *thought* the pistol was the same as the one they'd used earlier, but one gun looked like another to her. Miss Varndell had given her the gun at the break. She'd put it on top of the props cart where she'd found it when she went to hand it back to Miss Varndell. She didn't *think* it had been moved but...

Leyden recalled seeing the props cart – a sort of chest of drawers on wheels with plastic crates stacked on top.

No, she hadn't kept a close eye on the gun.

No, she didn't *know* for sure if the pistol was the same one Miss Varndell used before the break.

In fact, she didn't know anything anymore. She burst into renewed floods of tears.

As he was leaving, Leyden spotted the director coming out of Starling's trailer. He thought there should have been a uniform on guard.

Sara Jane came up to him.

'Such a shame,' she said, but without a hint of sorrow. 'As soon as we'd finished shooting, Joey was off to Los Angeles for three months schmoozing the good and the great. He'd booked a suite at the Beverley Wilshire. All right for some.'

'What was he going to be doing there?'

'Trying to break into the Hollywood scene.'

Something in Sara Jane's tone made Leyden ask, 'Have you worked with Starling before?'

'No, I'm glad to say. Starling was a total shit. There was a young dresser he fancied. She didn't want to know so he got her fired.' She clicked her fingers. 'Just like that.'

'He liked his women young, I gather.'

'So I've been told,' said Sara Jane shortly. 'But he could be a shit to men, too. He got the art director sacked as well.'

'We'll need his name.'

'I forget... But I'll make sure I get it to you.'

'What did Starling have on Montgomery?'

'I'm sorry?'

'I've just been watching Joey act, and frankly I've seen more animation in a turnip. Why's he the star?'

Sara Jane twisted an earring between her fingers. 'Joey's role grew during shooting. Fleur was supposed to be the lead but then Joey sort of hijacked the film.'

Chalke rejoined them. She was holding a photograph. 'Starling had this in his pocket when he was shot.'

The photograph, taken at night, showed a man behind the wheel of an open-top sports car. A glamorous blonde girl sat beside him, her arm draped around his shoulders. Both were grinning into the camera. Behind them, you could make out a bar with a poster advertising a band. There was a cactus in the corner of the shot.

'Ever seen this before?' Chalke asked Sara Jane.

The PR took the photo, squinted hard and said, 'That's Bruce Montgomery. And I *think* that could be Cindy Carsons. She was the girl who was killed in the crash when Bruce was seriously injured.'

'What happened?'

'Bruce was directing a film in Mexico about two years ago. Cindy was one of the cast. They got plastered in a bar before setting off to drive to a party – except she drove down a ravine instead. Cindy was killed. Bruce is lucky to be alive. That's why he limps, has scars on his face – all the rest of it. This is his first film since the crash.'

'Was Joey on that film?' asked Chalke.

'He had a small part.'

'So why was Joey carrying this photo around?' asked Chalke.

Leyden watched the light bulb come on in Sara Jane's brain. 'No idea,' she said.

H. Bruce Montgomery stared at the photograph with a mixture of loathing and fascination.

'Don't know what you're talking about.' he managed finally.

'You were wasting your time searching Starling's trailer,' said Leyden. 'He had it on him.'

'Starling could prove that it was you who was driving that night, not Cindy,' said Chalke.

'The crash was fully investigated by the Mexican police.' Montgomery was unable to take his eyes off the image.

'I bet it was.' Leyden took the photograph out of the director's hands, worried that he was about to tear it into pieces.

Montgomery finally looked up at them. 'I honestly have no memory of what happened. I remember being in the bar, then the next thing, I was in hospital in Los Angeles. I was told Cindy was driving.'

'This photograph says otherwise.'

'You don't know it was taken the night of the crash.'

'I reckon we'll be able to date it from that poster in the window,' said Leyden.

Chalke brought them back to the present. 'Where were you during the break in filming?' she asked the director.

'I spoke to Joey in his trailer, as you know. Then I came back here to my office to go through the shooting schedules. My PA was here all the time. She'll vouch for me.'

'I gather he was due to go to Hollywood soon.'

'Joey wanted to talk to some people there.'

'Who was paying for the stay? The Beverley Wilshire isn't cheap,' said Chalke, who knew because she had stayed there.

8

'Joey was funding it himself. He said he was about to come into some money.'

Dr Will Brennan allowed Chalke five minutes with Fleur Varndell.

'Don't put too much store by anything she says,' he said. 'She's in shock. Any admission would be challenged in court.'

Fleur's trailer was identical to Starling's except for the flowers. The actress was lying on her day bed, a damp towel over her eyes.

'How're you feeling?' asked Chalke.

'I keep seeing it happen time and time again. I keep hearing that explosion.' Fleur took a deep breath. 'Sorry… I suppose I should get a lawyer.'

'I only came to see how you were,' lied Chalke. 'But I have to ask – did you know the gun was loaded?'

'Of course not.'

'Was it the same gun as you used earlier?'

'I don't know.' Fleur began massaging her temples. 'It was just a prop.'

'You and Joey didn't say the same lines as you had before the break.'

'He's known for ad-libbing. He does it to mess up other actors.'

'You seemed to be coping.'

'It wasn't a problem.'

'Where were you during the break?'

'I stayed on set.'

'That's true,' said Leyden, entering. 'I saw you.'

Chalke's mobile phone rang. She glanced at the caller ID, apologised and left.

'Thank you for confirming my alibi.' Fleur smiled up at Leyden.

'You're welcome.' Leyden smiled back. 'Just one thing. I don't remember seeing your handbag on the props trolley.'

'The handbag's mine. I prefer to use my own possessions when

I can. It makes things more natural.'

'Fair enough. Now, you must rest or Doc Brennan will be after me.' At the doorway, Leyden paused. 'One last question. I noticed you cocked the gun when you fired the shot–'

'Did I?'

'You didn't do that in the previous takes–'

'Didn't I? I'm sorry… I don't know. Does it make a difference?'

'It does with a Makarov,' said Leyden.

Leyden was examining Starling's mobile phone when he caught sight of Speed Bump trying to attract his attention. Leyden ignored him. The last thing he needed now was one of Speed Bump's half-baked theories. But Speed Bump was becoming more and more agitated, waving to Leyden and then pointing across the set.

No escape.

'Yes, mate, what can I do for you?'

'See that bird there – the one with the sort of wavy hair and funny jacket?'

'The looker with the nose stud? Yeah.'

'She had a right two and eight with Joey on set a few days ago.'

'So? Joey had rucks with everyone.'

Leyden turned on Starling's black Nokia X6 and opened the call log. One mobile phone number stood out. Starling had called the number first at 8 a.m. yesterday morning then at 8.12 in the evening, as soon as he'd been released. He'd tried another four times through the evening before starting again at 7.47 a.m. this morning. The last call was just before he'd been killed.

'Yeah, but when she walked off you should have seen Starling's face,' Speed Bump was saying. 'Reckon he wasn't used to birds turning him down. Him being a star, like.'

Leyden looked again at the girl. Small face, partly hidden by fair tumbling hair, an Afghan waistcoat and jeans. She was talking to a black guy with orange hair and a small flute in his hands.

'Do you know who she is?'

'Not seen her before .'

Leyden hit the redial button on Starling's phone.

'Hey, did I tell you? the director wants me to go to the Isle of Dogs to carry on filming,' said Speed Bump. 'Just me and one or two others.'

Leyden was looking towards the girl, thinking she remind-ed him of someone, when he heard Starling's phone dial out. He tensed.

The girl was taking a phone out of her jacket pocket. She looked at the screen. Her eyes widened. Abruptly, she closed her phone and dropped it back in her pocket. Starling's mobile went dead at the same time.

'Jemma Wodehouse,' she said in reply to Leyden. 'This is Eric Traubenhat. We share a flat.'

Eric put the piccolo to his lips and began softly playing the theme from *Dixon of Dock Green*.

'You and Joey Starling have been talking a lot in the past twelve hours or so,' Leyden said.

'I've not said a word to him.'

'He's been trying to get hold of you,' said Leyden.

'Has he?'

'All last night and again this morning.'

'Oh. Must have been a wrong number.'

'I don't think so.' Leyden turned to Eric, who was still playing *Dixon of Dock Green*. 'Leave it out, mate. Bit before my time, that.'

Eric switched to *Z Cars*.

'So was that.'

Instantly Eric launched into 'A Policeman's Lot Is Not a Happy One'.

'He's got a large repertoire, hasn't he?' said Leyden, grinning in spite of himself.

Leyden's smile gave Jemma confidence. It showed a human side to this bruiser with the severe haircut. She decided she liked him.

'Why couldn't they have been wrong numbers?' she asked.

'Because you called Starling yesterday morning. In fact–' Leyden compared the times of the calls. 'He phoned you. Half an hour later you called back – but didn't get through. Then last night he tried to get back to you. I imagine you'd switched off your phone.'

Jemma looked at the ground and said nothing.

'And you had a barney with Starling here on set.'

'Oh.'

'So why pretend you didn't know him?'

Jemma sighed. 'Starling tried to hit on me. I turned him down. He got angry.'

'A lot of girls would be happy to go out with a film star.'

'I'm not a lot of girls.'

'Nor am I,' said Eric, breaking off playing.

'Shut up.' Leyden turned back to Jemma. 'The phone calls?'

'Starling was trying to get me to go out with him.'

'He was trying bloody hard,' said Leyden. 'What was he, infatuated with you?'

'I don't think he was used to people saying no.'

Eric started playing *Peter and the Wolf.* Leyden failed to see the relevance.

'Ever go to Starling's house in Brighton?'

Two red patches appeared on Jemma's cheeks. 'No,' she said.

'You're not very convincing.'

'I'm not an actress.'

'What are you doing here on set?'

'Eric is friends with one of the crew.'

Eric nodded while continuing to play.

'What's he playing?' asked Leyden.

'Prokofiev's *Peter and the Wolf*.'

'I've got that far. I mean, what's the instrument.'

'It's a piccolo.'

'He's good, isn't he?' Leyden realised they were talking about Eric as if he wasn't there.

'We're students at Trinity College of Music.'

Chalke was waving him over. Leyden summoned the nearest uniform. 'I want you both to make statements.,' he told Jemma. 'This officer will look after you.'

Jemma and Eric turned to accompany the uniform, Eric now playing 'The Dead March' from *Saul*.

'Sorry, forgot to ask,' called Leyden. 'What time did you get here?'

'After Starling was shot,' said Jemma.

'They've finally got hold of the props master,' Chalke told Leyden. 'He says the prop gun was a replica. It couldn't fire a live round.'

'So someone swapped guns,' said Leyden.

'Not necessarily today, though,' said Chalke. 'It could have been done any time since the prop master's been off sick. All the killer needed to do today was to load it with a live round.'

'Even though you and I were on set?'

'I think we're missing something. Let's go for a walk.'

'Okay, but why do we need to walk?'

'I want a cigarette, dumbo.'

They strolled together away from the mill along the creek.

'Right,' said Chalke. 'What did we witness?'

'Fleur Varndell shooting Joey Starling.'

'The entry wound was consistent with Fleur firing the shot,' agreed Chalke.

'You think that someone might have fired a simultaneous shot?'

'Not really,' said Chalke. 'But I'm sure we're missing something.'

She glanced around. When she was sure she wasn't being watched she whipped out a cigarette from the open packet inside her jacket with her left hand while at the same time flicking open her lighter with her right.

'How did you do that?' asked Leyden.

'Years of practice at school.' Chalke exhaled. 'My first since breakfast.'

'I thought it *was* your breakfast.'

'Huh.' Chalke let the smoke drift from her nostrils. Heaven. 'Let's go through this. Who wanted Starling dead?'

'Easier to say who didn't. Starling was turning the screw on Montgomery, and he was the one who called for the break.'

'But why would Montgomery kill Starling now? He must have had opportunities in the past.'

'The Reaper?'

'It does have his hallmarks,' said Chalke, remembering what Weaver had said.

She gazed down at a supermarket trolley sticking out of the brown sludge of low tide. A pipe dripped green slime into the creek opposite. The windowless back wall of a warehouse blocked out the light. Not a view to inspire.

'Tell me about the pistol.'

'It's a standard Makarov PM, made in Bulgaria,' replied Leyden.

'How do you know it was made in Bulgaria?'

'The figure 10 inside the circle stamped beside the slide release is a Bulgarian military proof mark. The best Maks come from Russia or East Germany. The ammo's interesting. The rounds are shorter and wider than the Nato Parabellum round, designed to stop Nato troops using Russian ammunition in time of war.'

'Fascinating,' said Chalke. 'But how do you fire a Makarov? Just pull the trigger?'

'No, first you've got to pull back the slide to put a round in the breech,' explained Leyden. 'You can then carry the gun with the

hammer down and safety engaged. The safety lever is up for on –
the opposite way to a Walther.'

'So you take off the safety and just pull the trigger?'

This was the moment Leyden had been fearing. 'To fire the
first shot, you either cock the hammer with your thumb for a
single-action shot or pull hard on the trigger for what's called a
double action,' he said. 'The hammer stays up for subsequent
shots.'

'It must be difficult to aim if you have to pull hard on the
trigger.'

'Yes.'

Patsy flicked her cigarette butt into the sludge. 'I wonder what
Fleur did?'

'She cocked the gun,' he said.

Patsy turned to face him. 'Wasn't easy to say that, was it,
Bobby?'

'No, guv.'

'I was wondering if you were going to mention it.'

'You mean, you –?'

'I'm a trained observer, *mate.*' She started to head back. 'Come
on. We'll keep it to ourselves for the moment. Don't want the pack
heading off on the wrong scent, do we?'

'Um–'

'Look, I don't think Fleur did it either, but let's you and me try
to work as a team, eh?'

'Yes, guv.'

Weaver cam hurrying towards them. 'One of the missing extras
matches the description of Graham White, the cash depot manager,' he announced. 'Same burn scar on the forehead.'

'You're joking.'

'I would be, except I've just heard from my mate in Kent. White
arrived from Caracas a month ago, according to Immigration.'

'Do we have an address for him?'

'He's gone off radar, but his ex-wife Shirley lives with her daughter and new husband in a large house near Westerham.'

'Shit!'

White had sworn vengeance for the death of his daughter, recalled Chalke. And the spate of killings had started soon after he'd returned to Britain. Joey Starling was rumoured to have been in on the Maidstone raid.

Had they just witnessed a revenge killing?

What if the previous murders weren't part of a drug war?

What if they weren't down to the Dim Reaper?

What if…?

Chalke thought her head was going to explode.

At least, thanks to Begley, they weren't short of boots on the ground.

'Bobby, go and see White's ex-wife. Take that WDC from Lewisham with you.'

'Yes, ma'am.'

'And remember. We're a team.'

When Begley's order had gone out for extra hands to be sent to Greenwich, Sandy Wishbourne, dark and pretty with a cheeky grin, had been one of the first to be transferred. Usually coppers got the hump when they were shifted to other nicks without being consulted, but Sandy had had a severe falling out with her boss in Lewisham's child protection squad. Her new job was a godsend.

Bobby had known her for years, and had always fancied her. But his plan to chat her up in the car came to nothing. All Sandy wanted to talk about was Patsy Chalke.

'She's cosmic. Those stories about her – the way she decked that Yank, tried to drown that ponce Rich. I wish I just had half her looks or her brains. What's she like to work with?'

'All right,' said Leyden guardedly.

'I bet she sets a high standard.'

'She's actually very human.'

'You must fancy the pants off her.'

Leyden hadn't thought about it. Apart from the electric moment when their hands had touched, he considered Patsy Chalke to be so out of his league that it was pointless even to dream. He was the only one in the squad who didn't.

He applied himself to finding Shirley Grey's house, which was tucked away among the spider's web of unmade roads on Limpsfield Chart. They finally arrived at electronic gates which swung open to reveal a large modern red brick mansion at the end of a gravel drive. They glimpsed a swimming pool before parking next to an Audi TT.

A casually elegant woman was waiting at the portico doorway.

'Shirley Grey?' asked Leyden.

She nodded. 'You must be the police officers.'

Apart from her Yorkshire accent, Shirley Grey was the epitome of southern chic. Slim with large breasts and carefully tousled ash blonde hair, she wore black leather booties, designer jeans and a silk shirt. Her finger nails were painted bright red. She had silver parrot earrings, and a cold sore partially hidden under lip gloss.

'We spoke on the phone,' said Leyden. 'This is WDC Sandy Wishbourne.'

Shirley Grey led the way into a large room with French windows. A grand piano sat next to a harp. Fashion magazines were carefully arranged on various coffee tables.

'You said it was urgent.' Shirley flopped onto a sofa. 'Don't tell me you've had a breakthrough.'

'Breakthrough?'

'With the raid.' She spoke as if the robbery had been last week.

'There've been a number of murders that *may* be connected to the raid,' replied Leyden carefully. 'Can you tell us what happened that night? As much as you remember.'

'Oh, I remember all right. There's not a day passes that I don't remember.' Shirley sat up, wrapped her hands around her knees. 'We lived in this nice little bungalow outside Maidstone. It was too small, really; the girls had to share a bedroom. But we liked it. We bought it when Graham came out of the RAF Regiment.'

'How did you meet your husband?'

'He was stationed in Yorkshire near where I lived. We were wed inside a year. They wanted Graham to put in for a commission but I couldn't take to service life. It was like us wives were expected to take our husbands' ranks.'

Leyden nodded.

'Anyway, we decided that he'd come out. He walked into the job at the depot. He understood security, was positively vetted, used to management. We were in that bungalow almost two years. We'd put down roots. There were other young families nearby. We had two girls Laurel and Josie. The girls had a sandpit in the garden–' Shirley faltered; seeing something in her mind's eye from long ago. 'In this place you don't get to see a soul from one week to another.'

'Your husband works long hours?' asked Leyden.

'Don's out from seven in the morning until God knows when. He's got jobs all over Surrey and Kent. I never know what time he'll be back. At the weekend, he's either watching Chelsea or playing golf.'

'His business is doing well?'

'He works hard. I trained as a bookkeeper so I look after that side of things. You know what they say, behind every successful man there's a woman.'

Leyden was letting her run. Sandy was doing her part – sitting rapt and nodding in encouragement whenever it seemed Shirley might dry up. But Shirley never would dry up, thought Leyden. She was bored and lonely, and delighted to have someone to talk to.

'The night of the raid–' he reminded her gently.

'It happened so fast. I'd cooked a Lancashire hotpot – Graham always loved that. He'd been working late. The girls were in bed asleep by the time he came home. He was disappointed. He liked to read them a bedtime story. We'd watched the news and weather forecast and we were thinking about going to bed ourselves when there was a knock on the door. I remember thinking, who can that be this time of night? The next thing, Graham was in the doorway, white as a sheet. There was a policeman with him but the policeman was wearing a balaclava with slits for eyes. It was weird. I was thinking, this doesn't make sense. Then I saw he had a sawn-off shotgun to Graham's head. Then a second man pushed his way into the room and he was in a balaclava. I'd never seen Graham scared before. I went to scream. I couldn't help myself. The man came flying at me and clasped his hand over my mouth. I heard Laurel cry out. Graham went to turn but the other man hit him with the gun. Graham fell to his knees. He tried to get up but the man hit him again. There were other men in the hall but they'd turned off the light. Someone said, "Get those fucking kids to shut up or we'll slit their throats." It was a rough, common voice. I'd recognise it to this day. Someone pushed me into the girls' room. Josie had her arms around Laurel. They were both terrified. I tried to comfort them, tried to be brave for their sakes. But then a man came and grabbed Josie and took her away. I tried to stop him but he hit me with his shotgun. You can still see the scar.' Shirley pointed to a mark beside her right eye. 'I held Laurel… it was awful. I didn't know what they were doing to Josie. I was helpless. That was the worst part – being helpless–' Shirley swallowed, blinking away tears.

'You all right?' asked Sandy gently.

'I'll live.' Shirley produced a handkerchief from her sleeve and blew her nose. 'I found out afterwards that the man who'd hit me had put a shotgun to Josie's head to make Graham do what they wanted. Josie never spoke about it. She wasn't the same after–'

Shirley gave a sob. 'Nothing was the same after. The girls had counselling but it was Graham who needed help. He blamed himself for not standing up to the bastards, but there was nothing he could've done. Then your lot started. They all but accused him of being in on the raid. Graham! After all we'd suffered!'

'I'm sorry,' murmured Sandy.

'Our lives fell apart. You couldn't imagine the pressure. The girls had nightmares. Both started wetting their beds, stopped eating. We were worried sick. The rows started. Graham began drinking. I asked for a trial separation. I suppose I was trying to shock him into getting his act together… but then Josie was killed… Graham became a different person. He'd explode at the slightest thing. He became obsessed with revenge. He gave up everything he enjoyed. He'd been an instructor at the local karate club, and we both enjoyed amateur dramatics, but he lost interest. In one night, our world ended.'

There was the sound of someone coming down stairs, two at a time.

'Laurel,' said Shirley, composing herself by kneading her cheeks with the heels of her hands.

A faired-hair girl with a ponytail, wearing jodhpurs, burst into the room.

'Laurel's off school with a cold,' explained Shirley.

Leyden guessed that Laurel frequently had days off school to keep her mother company.

The girl gave the detectives an insouciant wave. 'You'll never guess what Tamsin's put on Facebook,' she told Shirley.

'Not now, love. We're talking.'

Laurel pretended to be disappointed. 'I'll go and tell Firefly then. He listens to me.'

'Walk him round the yard. His left hind wasn't right this morning… Firefly's a horse,' Shirley explained as Laurel disappeared.

'Good-looking kid,' said Leyden. 'She must be… fifteen.'

'Fifteen going on twenty-five. My fault. I've always treated her as a grown up. There're only the two of us really.'

'You remarried not long after the divorce,' said Sandy quietly.

'I used to do Don's company's books. Not that they took very long.' She picked at the handkerchief. 'Laurel needed a father. We needed a home. Don's done well out of it. He wasn't employing fifty men when I married him.'

'We won't keep you any longer,' said Leyden, rising.

'Thanks for talking to us,' said Sandy.

'By the way,' said Leyden as they were at the door. 'Do you ever see Graham?'

'No.' Shirley folded her arms tightly across her chest. 'He went abroad before the divorce. I've not heard from him since.'

'We gather he's back in Britain.'

'News to me,' said Shirley.

'Well?' said Leyden as they drove out of the gates. 'What did you think of our Mrs Grey?'

'Definitely more grey than white,' said Sandy. 'She's not quite the weeping willow she pretends to be.'

'Why do you say that?'

'Listening to her syntax, watching her body language. She's a very strong-willed woman. Remember how she said, *we* decided that Graham should leave the RAF; *I* was giving him a chance to get his act back together. And the way she claimed responsibility for the success of her husband's business?'

'I'll ask my brother about Donny Grey.' Leyden pulled out his mobile phone.

'I'll tell you another thing,' said Sandy. 'Shirley was lying when she said she hadn't seen Graham.'

'Sorry?'

'You saw how she fidgeted throughout the interview, that dis-jointed way of speaking? The one time she was completely still was when she said that she hadn't seen her husband. That was the *only* time she made sustained eye contact. She was lying.'

'How can you be so sure?'

'Because people are more eager to be believed when they're lying. That's when they try to impress you with their honesty,' explained Sandy. 'I specialised in kinesics in my social psychology degree at Portsmouth. You know – cognitive questions, decoding body language.'

Leyden didn't know. He hadn't known that Sandy Wishbourne was a graduate. He should have expected it. Everybody had been to university except him. He was getting sick of it.

'I thought it'd be helpful in the police force,' continued Sandy. 'But I haven't had much chance to put theory into practice.'

'And this kinesics thing works?'

'I think so.'

'Do you practise on fellow officers?'

'All the time.'

'And in relationships?'

'It's probably why I'm not in a relationship. What technique do you use?'

'Me?' The question took Leyden by surprise. They'd had basic interrogation training at police college but that was a while ago. He relied on gut feeling, but he didn't want to admit it.

'You know research has shown that the traditional baseline technique – comparing the suspects' reactions in pre-interview small talk and the interview itself – doesn't actually work?' said Sandy.

'Really?'

'And once a suspect is believed to be lying and then subjected to the accusatory technique, the chances of a false confession are much higher?'

'I'll tell *you* something,' said Leyden. 'Shirley wore that scar like a badge of pride. She could easily have hidden it with make-up.'

Before Sandy could reply, he was dialling a number on his mobile phone. Even talking to Brian would be better than being lectured to.

From the noise in the background, it sounded as if his big brother was standing next to a concrete mixer. Despite having built up a multi-million pound business, he was never happier than when on site. If happy was a word that could be applied to Brian.

'Donny Grey? Yeah, I know him,' shouted Brian. 'What about him?'

'Just interested. He seems to be doing well for himself.'

'Yeah. If I remember, it came together for Donny about six year or so back. About the time he kicked out his first wife and remarried.'

'He kicked her out?'

'He was having it off with his bookkeeper. She'd been the wife of the manager in that big Maidstone raid. Is that what this is about?'

Leyden ignored the question. 'So Donny Grey was small-time when he married?'

'I used to pass on small jobs I didn't want to him. You'd be doing me a favour if you banged him up. The bastard's just undercut me on a big contract.'

'You should be more competitive.'

'I don't have a load of eastern Europeans working for peanuts.'

'I thought the Poles were going back home.'

'Bugger the Poles. Donny's got Bulgarians, Kosovans, God knows what. Don't know where he finds them.'

'How did he get into the big time?'

'Mystery to me. He's not the sharpest knife in the box. His missus is the brains.'

'Thanks, mate.'

'You're welcome. Hang on… *Oi. Not that way.* Jesus! Got to go.'

'Sure. Thanks for –'

But the line was already dead.

Leyden bumped into Chalke as he walked back into the Incident Room.

'How was Mrs Grey?'

'Sandy reckons she was lying when she said she hadn't seen her ex.'

'How would Sandy know?'

'She studied kinesics as a student.'

Leyden was hoping Chalke would share his jaundiced view of the science, but she only said, 'Interesting.'

He slung his jacket over his chair and went down to the canteen to get a toasted sausage and egg sandwich and a mug of tea. He stayed there talking to Les Blunt for fifteen minutes before heading back to the Incident Room. There was a note on his desk that Chalke wanted to see him.

'Where've you been?' she demanded as he entered her office.

'In the canteen.'

'I tried phoning you–'

'Left my phone in my jacket.'

'I know. I heard it ring. We all heard it ring. Interesting choice of ring tone – the *William Tell* overture.'

'I thought it was *The Lone Ranger*.'

On the windowsill, the wooden man looked as if he was about to leap into the air.

'You've spoken to Sandy about Shirley Grey?' he asked.

'Yes, but if – and it's a big if – Graham White is responsible for these killings, why's he waited until now to act?'

'Perhaps he's been banged up abroad and he's only just got out,' said Leyden.

'That's worth checking.' Chalke made a note to run the query past Interpol liaison.

'Any news on the guy on the film set matching White's description?'

'Not so far. The film people are still tracking down the new extras.'

Leyden had a thought. 'Remember how the Dim Reaper's business took off after the Maidstone raid. Well, Donny Grey's building firm did the same.'

'No one's ever suggested Donny Grey was part of the team.'

'I'm not saying he was,' said Leyden. 'But you're ignoring the link between the raid and Donny – Shirley.'

'If you're saying that Shirley and Graham White were in on the job then they've paid a hell of a price.'

'They wouldn't have known how things would turn out.'

'How does this explain Donny Grey's business success?'

'What if Graham signed up as inside man on the under-standing that the money would be stashed for him. That way, he wouldn't change his lifestyle or pattern of expenditure – things we'd monitor. But it all goes pear-shaped. His daughter is killed; he cracks, does a runner. His missus, who's been in on it all along, collects. Second husband benefits.'

'If that's the case wouldn't the first person on Graham's hit list be Shirley?'

'She's still the mother of his child,' Leyden said. 'That must count for something.'

Chalke thought. They needed to have a closer look at Shirley Grey, and they needed to find Graham White.

Her brain was aching. Too many questions, too many pieces of the jigsaw. And none of them fitted.

Christ. If she was honest, she didn't even know if they were pieces of the same jigsaw.

She picked up the wooden man and rearranged his arms and legs so that he became a fast bowler in his delivery stride. Then she wondered why she'd done that.

'Here's the smoked salmon and cream cheese on rye,' said a voice from the corner. No one had noticed Sue Jones come in. 'Sorry, I've been a while. There was a queue.'

'Thanks, Sue,' said Chalke. 'Would you like a cup of coffee?'

'Would you mind?'

'What would you like? Espresso, cappuccino, latte, Americano?'

'Cappuccino would be nice. And don't worry, I can make it.'

The detectives continued to discuss the case while Sue sorted out the coffee.

'That girl's got no self confidence,' said Chalke when she left. 'She's a walking bloody doormat.'

Leyden agreed, though he didn't think Sue was quite as helpless as his boss did.

Once Leyden had left, Chalke began her sandwich and let her mind wander to the evening ahead. Dinner with her lover. His wife was away and while the wife is away, the dog and bitch do play. But where to play? London could be a surprisingly – a terrifyingly – small place. They couldn't risk eating in any of the better-known restaurants. And Patsy was too exhausted to cook. Perhaps they'd go to one of those gastro pubs along the river. That should be safe. Then again, why bother to eat anything at all? Why not cut straight to the chase – and rut?

Because she was tired and brittle and needed romancing. A gentle evening first – then saw-blade sex.

Mal Topper wore a dark suit, white shirt and conservative tie, as befitted a member of the local Round Table. He thought of himself as a businessman, owning a fleet of ice-cream and burger vans. The ice-cream vans could be found in summertime in parks throughout south-east London, at tourist spots along the river, at carnivals and fetes, music events and sporting occasions. They haunted the council estates, always playing the same tune – 'Colonel Bogey'.

The burger vans worked in winter and at night in town centres, outside late-night pubs and discos and near major railways stations.

The vans were properly licensed and all had passed scrutiny by local health inspectors.

And they were all – police intelligence believed – used to push drugs.

The vans drove the local drug squad crazy. Whenever they stopped one, it'd be as clean as a whistle – even though the previous day, undercover surveillance teams would have witnessed the van knocking out more coke than cornets.

Now in his mid-forties, Topper no longer mixed with known criminals, but he and Ari O went way back. So when Ari O called a meet, he'd agreed.

He looked up from the booth to see two shaven-headed goons come in, peer around the deserted restaurant, and leave. A moment later they returned with Ari O.

Topper suppressed a sneer. You had to be careful with Ari O. He might be a poser but he was a poser who'd blow your head off if he thought you were taking the piss.

'Ari, mate, how you're doing?'

'Fine. You keeping well?'

'Can't complain.' Topper was relieved that Ari was wearing normal clothing. He'd heard stories that he'd taken to going round dressed as an Arab sheik.

'I didn't know this place was open in the afternoon.'

'They wanted to do me a favour.' Topper nodded towards the minders. 'Tell your lads to relax. Have a steak. It's on the house.'

'Okay, boys, enjoy.' Ari O sat down opposite Topper.

The restaurant was in Trafalgar Road in Greenwich, traditionally a neutral zone between the east London gangs like the Krays and their south London rivals such as the Richardsons. Because it was in the villains' interest to keep their no man's land trouble-free, Greenwich had become popular with criminals wanting somewhere safe to live. The £23 million Brink's-Mat gold bullion heist had been planned a quarter of a mile from Greenwich police station. However Greenwich began to lose its safe-zone status with the arrival of Russian and Kosovan gangs whose idea of opening negotiations was to mow down rivals with a machine-pistol.

'You want to try the rump steak,' suggested Topper as a waiter brought menus.

'I don't touch meat.'

'Since when?' The last time they'd met, Ari had been on a high-protein diet of duck breasts and oysters.

'Red meat causes imbalances in the blood,' lisped Ari in his hoarse voice. 'Listen to your body. It'll tell you what's good for it.'

'My body's telling me to have a rare steak and chips.'

'A Greek salad,' Ari O told the waiter. 'And make sure it's washed in bottled water.'

'Anything to drink, sir?'

'Bottle of the Merlot, thank you, mate,' said Topper. 'What are you having, Ari?'

'Still water.' Ari waited until the waiter had left, before saying, 'You've heard that Glockie's toast?'

'Yeah.'

'The cozzers reckon the fire was started deliberately.'

'Glockie always had a flair for making enemies.' Ari O leaned forward. 'Do you get the feeling that something's going down?' he whispered.

Topper suppressed a groan. If Ari was going to go mystical on him, he could fuck off. 'What do you mean?'

'These killings. And the way the Dim Reaper's fallen off the planet.'

'So?'

'You two have dealings.'

'I don't know where he's got to,' said Topper. 'The coppers are tearing up London looking for him.'

'Word is that he topped Minicab because he caught him with his fingers in the till,' continued Ari O. 'The Reaper wouldn't take kindly to being ripped off.'

'No.'

Topper was well briefed about the police investigation, but he wasn't going to tell Ari O that. He'd been taken aback to learn that the scheming little git had been knocking out cocaine through the dry-cleaner's. It showed what a conniving bastard Dave Shine was. Topper had thought he'd had the exclusive arrangement to distribute the drugs Shine brought into the country. He was going to have words with the Reaper when – or if – he surfaced again.

But if Ari O was right then the Reaper had killed the wrong one. It was Lorraine Finch he should've topped, not her ineffectual husband.

The waiter brought red wine and water. The minders were drinking Corona Extra by the neck, slices of lemon in the tops of the bottles.

'Still talk to Shug Jolly, do you?' inquired Ari O casually.

Topper smiled to himself. Ari O was coming to the point. 'Sometimes. Why?'

'Guinness.'

'Heard he was shagging Minicab's missus,' said Topper, deliberately going off at a tangent.

'Yeah, but that's not what I'm on about.' Ari O played with his glass. 'Look, when you speak to Shug, tell him I accept Guinness was out of order. It was nothing to do with me. I'm out of the fight game.'

'I didn't know you were ever in it.'

'Guinness wanted me to go in with him.'

'You reckon Shug –?'

'Guinness was pushing his luck, trying to see how far he could go.'

'Now he knows.'

Ari O giggled. 'Only if there's life after death.'

The food arrived. Ari began picking fastidiously at his salad.

After a while Topper murmured, 'You know you said you thought there was something going on?'

'Yeah.'

'The copper in charge thinks it might have something to do with Maidstone.'

'That wouldn't be DCI Chalke, would it?'

'Know her, do you?'

'She turned up a few days ago. She had that Leyden with her. Unpleasant piece of work.' Ari scowled at the blood oozing from Topper's steak. 'How can you eat that?'

'You don't know what you're missing, mate.' Topper dipped a chip in the blood. 'You should see my piranha when there's claret in the water. Sends them absolutely mental.'

They ate steadily until Ari O said, 'Maidstone. Nah. Too long ago.'

'Yeah, but think – Glockie, Minicab, Guinness, now Joey Starling.'

'What do you mean, Joey Starling?'

'You not heard? He was shot dead on the film set this morning.'

'Shit.' Ari O put down his knife and fork. 'Anyone in the frame?'

'Not yet. I'll get a steer when there is.'

'There was bad feeling over the way the loot was divvied up,' said Ari O. 'The Reaper always reckoned he should have got more.'

'He should be a happy man next week then. With Minicab, Glockie, Guinness and now Joey gone, there's going to be more for the rest of us.'

'You think they were all down to the Reaper?'

'He's a bastard. If there's one person in the world who'd hold a grudge–'

'It'd be the Reaper.' Ari O looked worried.

'I reckon we'll get over a million each,' said Topper.

'If only the cash hadn't been turned into industrial diamonds.'

'We have this every time there's a divvy-up. Look, the boss got it right. It was genius getting rid of the cash so soon after the raid. The coppers haven't been able to trace a penny.'

'Fair point. And always said the hardest part would be spending the money,' said Ari O.

'But he set it up proper, didn't he? We've not gone short – and not one of us has had ever so much as had his collar felt.'

'Still, the Reaper's never liked it.'

'That's why the boss kept one key and gave the other to Joey. The Reaper trusted Joey – as much as he trusted anyone. More to the point, he knew better than to mess with him. The boss knew that.'

'Hang on, if Joey's been slotted–'

'Don't worry. The key's hidden in Joey's Brighton pad. The boss knows where.'

'So who's going with the boss to the safe deposit place?' asked Ari O.

'Don't know yet, but we need to let the dust settle around Joey before we move. Not desperate for money, are you?'

'Nah.' Ari O took a drink of water.

'Any thoughts how you're going to spend your share?'

'I'm going to buy a club in Punta del Este.'

'Where?'

'Punta del Este. Uruguay. There's a big scene out there.'

Topper assumed Ari O meant a gay scene.

What about you?'

'I've got plans,' said Topper guardedly. 'But listen. There's a couple of things you don't know.'

'Like?'

'Like the Pike boys got out a month or so ago.'

'So?'

'So, they never got paid, did they? Maybe they're after their share.'

Ari O thought about it. 'Nah, they ain't got the clout. They don't worry me.'

'Okay. Also, the depot manager Graham White's back in the country. Remember he swore revenge after his daughter died? The coppers can't find him.'

'Why's he kicking up suddenly? Anyway, how can he know who was in the team. The coppers don't.'

'Maybe if someone told him.'

Ari O was quiet a long time. 'Who?'

'Don't know. Who did the Reaper put into the crem?'

Topper's mobile rang. He put it to his ear, listened, eyes clouding. He closed the phone.

'That was the boss. Joey's key wasn't in Brighton. He had it on him. Someone's taken it.'

'But without the two keys, we can't –'

'Don't worry. We'll find it. If we've got to crack every fucking head in south London, we'll find it.'

Patsy Chalke stood in front of the whiteboard thinking that the Eternal Flame's odds of 10/1 against an arrest in the Starling case by noon tomorrow was pretty miserly. She'd have offered 200/1.

There were just too many lines of inquiry for a quick result, despite all the manpower that had now been allocated. Starling's murder was featuring prominently on TV and radio news. No doubt it would be splashed all over tomorrow's tabloids. A bank of flowers from fans was growing at the gates to the mill.

Dozens of statements had been taken and there were extras still to be interviewed. A handful – including Graham White's lookalike – could not be traced. This worried Chalke because while Starling's murder had been carefully planned, the moment of its actual execution had been opportunistic. Was the lookalike really in the frame?

The killer must have known the plot of the film. Did that point to an inside job rather than an extra? Maybe not. There was no reason why an extra couldn't have picked up detailed information about the film by chatting to the more permanent actors or crew.

A team was running the names of everyone who had access to the film set through the NPC to see if anything turned up.

NABIS – the National Ballistics Intelligence Service – was checking if the Makarov had been previously fired in a crime, not just in Britain but throughout Europe and the United States. They were also trying to trace the ownership of the pistol since it had emerged from the clutches of the Bulgarian army.

Les Blunt was in his usual position in his glass-fronted office, resting his head in his left hand and shielding his eyes. At first Chalke had suspected that he did it to catnap, but since he'd proved brilliant at spotting lies in statements she wouldn't have cared if he'd curled up on the carpet.

A search team was going through Starling's flat in Greenwich while Sussex police were taking apart his Brighton home. As well as finding more porn, they'd come across a homemade video of a man and a woman crossing a street in an American city, arm in arm. Neither the couple nor the location had been identified. More blackmail victims?

There was still no sign of the Dim Reaper. The detectives had hit a dead end tracking his car from the West End, so they'd begun to work backwards, checking CCTV cameras from the time of the BMW's return to the underground garage. As Weaver had forecast, it was a slow, laborious and costly exercise. And fraught with pitfalls. It only needed one copper to be thinking about last night's row with his wife to miss the one vital frame.

There were reports that Dave Shine had been seen drinking in the Queen's Head in Fitzrovia the night before last. The Queen's Head was a known villains' pub so when follow-up inquiries drew a blank, no one was surprised. The manpower needed on the Starling killing meant had made Weaver decide he couldn't afford to put the pub under surveillance.

The fact that Shine's credit cards had not been used since he'd paid for the pizza meant nothing. He had more plastic than you could shake a fist at, his wife Crystal told them – and not all in his name, know what I mean?

Then there were Minicab and Guinness…

'Lonely at the top, eh?'

Chalke turned to see Weaver, even more florid than usual, standing behind her. She hadn't heard him approach.

'I keep wondering if I've missed something,' she said.

'You'll always miss something,' replied Weaver. 'Everyone does.'

'Thanks a bunch.'

'But the secret is knowing that you'll miss something.' Weaver sniffed the air. 'Is that coffee?'

'It could be. I'll make you a cup.' Chalke headed for her office followed by Weaver.

'I've sent the video of the man and woman to the FBI to see if they can identify them – or at least the location,' he said.

'Good idea.' Chalke fired up the machine and motioned for Weaver to sit down. 'You don't think Fleur knew there was a live round in the gun, do you?'

'No. Not really.'

'Just wondered.'

'So you should. Never ignore the improbable, as Sherlock Holmes says.'

Leyden put his head around the door. 'Actually, sir, what he said was, "When you have eliminated the impossible, whatever remains, *however improbable*, must be the truth."'

'Thank you,' said Weaver drily.

'He also said, "Eliminate all other factors, and the one that remains must be the truth."'

'Thank you, Bobby,' said Chalke. 'What do you actually want?'

'I thought you'd like to know that they've found the fingerprints of both Dave Shine and Johnny Pike at Guinness's gym.'

Leyden phoned Vinnie Pike's home in Southend. When there was no reply, he tried Vinnie's mobile. Pike answered. He was in Erith, getting his car fixed before he left for Spain. Leyden suggested meeting at the Running Horses in Erith High Street, between the station and the river. Pike said he'd find it.

It was rush hour, and Leyden decided that it would be quicker to take the train. He regretted his decision as soon as he squeezed into the crowded carriage and found himself listening to MP3 players and commuters on their mobiles announcing that they'd be home soon.

The Running Horses was a large modern pub with an expensive jukebox and Sky TV screens. Leyden ordered a pint of lager and leaned on the bar watching golf being played somewhere sunny. The advertising breaks were more interesting. After ten minutes, Pike walked in, his arm still hanging awkwardly by his side.

'What do you want to drink?' asked Leyden.

'Just orange juice and lemonade. I'm off to France this evening on the nine o'clock ferry.'

'You're going to have fun driving with that shoulder.'

'I'll manage.'

'Do you have a contact number?'

'The mobile will be on. What do you want?'

'You said your cousin Johnny left the country a fortnight last Tuesday.'

Vinnie shrugged. 'I didn't see him get on a train or anything.

I told you, he said he was going to Marseilles to join the Foreign Legion.'

'There's no booking in his name on any ferries, Eurostar or flights out of the country. He hasn't joined the Foreign Legion, either.'

'He could have joined under a different name.'

'Not nowadays.' Interpol liaison had done its stuff. No Brit had joined the Foreign Legion – under any name – in the past three months. 'You've not heard from him?'

'I told you I hadn't.'

'You told us you hadn't on Tuesday. Things have changed.'

Vinnie took a pull of his drink. 'Like what?'

'Like Johnny's fingerprints being found at a murder scene.'

'You what?'

'Johnny's prints were found in the gym where Guinness was killed.'

'Straight up?'

'Straight up.'

Vinnie rubbed his shoulder. 'Doesn't mean Johnny was involved in anything dodgy. They could have been from years ago – before he was inside. Don't suppose Guinness has a regular cleaner go over the place.'

'The gym was given a coat of paint three years ago.' It wasn't true but Leyden wanted to see how Vinnie reacted.

Vinnie didn't react.

'Can't help you, then.'

But maybe there was a reaction. Something was worrying Vinnie, and he was trying hard not to show it.

'Is your cousin the vengeful type?' asked Leyden.

'Wouldn't say so, but prison can do strange things to a man's mind.'

'You'd better watch your back. You're the one who got him into the shit.'

'This time tomorrow I'll be halfway to Spain. Can't fucking wait.'

'Anywhere special in Spain? Alicante, maybe?'

'Why Alicante?'

'To see your old flame, Crystal Shine.'

For a second, Leyden thought Pike was going to lose his temper.

'You people never let up, do you? We were in school together, okay, but I haven't seen Crystal for years. I didn't even know she had a place in Spain. But if you'll give me the address, I'll be happy to call in. It'll be somewhere to doss for a few days.'

'As long as the Dim Reaper doesn't come back when you're there. You don't want to fuck him around.'

'Not a problem.'

'That's good. Because there's something else you should know. The manager of the depot you robbed is back on the scene. Johnny's not the only one who might be bent on mischief.'

'What?'

'Graham White wanted to have you damaged while you were in the nick. He's after the people he blames for the death of his daughter. You're going to need eyes in the back of your arse, mate.'

Crystal Shine's home on the Cator estate was less than a quarter of a mile from the Ferrier as the crow flew, but it might have been in another county. Centuries ago, the Cator estate had been the grounds of Wricklemarsh House, one of the finest houses in Kent, before London bullied its way out into the country. Now St Michael's church stood on the site of the house, surrounded by wide leafy ways where listed buildings sat next to £3 million architect-designed houses. Not that Crystal Shine's home was in that league. Her 1930s detached house in Brooklands Park wasn't worth much more than £1 million. A Mini convertible sat in the drive while a blue Mazda was parked at the kerb. The Mazda belonged to Lorraine Finch.

Birds of a feather were flocking together.

Lorraine and Crystal were closer than they'd let on. Husbands, lovers and boyfriends all came and went, but their friendship remained constant.

Chalke wished Leyden could have accompanied her into the dragon's den. But he'd gone to Erith, and she'd had to bring Cochrane as first substitute in the growl stakes.

Crystal Shine opened the door, sneered and led them wordlessly back into the living room where Lorraine was sprawling on the sofa in tight jeans and an FCUK T-shirt. The remains of a bottle of wine sat on a table.

Crystal dropped into a TV chair, picked up a bottle of varnish and continued to paint her toenails. The detectives were not asked to sit down.

'Don't tell me you've found Dave,' began Crystal.

'I was going to ask you if you'd heard from him,' said Chalke.

'Nah. Wish you'd hurry up and find the fucker. I can't divorce him until you do.'

'How well did your husband know Tony Yayale?'

Crystal curled her lips. 'They met.'

'When was the last time?'

'The four of us went out for a meal when we were both over earlier in the year.'

'Did Dave ever go to Guinness's gym?' asked Chalke.

'Wouldn't have thought so. Dave wasn't one for exercise. Unless it was a bit of horizontal jogging with that fucking tart of his.'

'Stay away from her,' warned Chalke. 'You have no right of access to the flat.'

'Fuck access. I… I'll–'

'Your solicitor will tell you the score'

Chalke turned her attention to Lorraine Finch, who, she realised, still hadn't asked a single question about the murders of her husband and her lover.

'Minicab never did anything for me,' said Lorraine when Chalke pointed this out.

'And Yayale?'

'That ended when he brought that slapper to the gym. Anyway, I've put the dry-cleaner's up for sale.'

'Lorraine's coming back to Spain with me,' said Crystal.

'Neither of you is leaving the country just yet.'

'Sorry, sweetheart,' said Crystal. 'I'm booking the flights tomorrow.'

Chalke was getting bored. She missed Leyden. He'd have been in their faces, winding them up. They'd be shouting the odds, and who knew what they might blurt out. Cochrane didn't have Leyden's edge. Then again perhaps he was nervous about messing up in front of his boss. Chalke changed tack.

'Tell me about Vinnie Pike,' she asked Crystal.

'Vinnie!' said Lorraine. 'Remember him, Crys? He was the love of your life when you were sixteen.'

'Randy little sod.' She grinned at Lorraine. 'Remember when I thought he'd got me up the duff?'

The women burst out cackling again.

'You've not seen him since he came out of prison?'

'Nah. I've no time for losers. Talking of which, why don't you just fuck off out of it?'

'Thank you for your time,' Chalke said sweetly. 'By the way, if you go near that flat, I'll do you for conspiracy to pervert the course of justice, action likely to cause a breach of the peace and criminal trespass.' She opened the door. 'And if you do try to leave the country, you'll be arrested at the airport.'

Chalke closed the door, thinking that she who laughed last, laughed longest.

But what did she know?

Leyden got back to Greenwich police station to find that most of the squad had left. It had been a hell of a day and enough was enough. Yet again, he'd meant to go for a run – but the pint in Erith had given him the taste for more. He was in no hurry to go home, so he was actually pleased to find a note on his desk saying that Speed Bump had phoned.

Bobby couldn't be bothered to let Karen know that he'd be late. Life couldn't go on as it was, but he would let her call the shots. She could move out in her own time.

He didn't know if he was doing the decent thing, or just being cowardly.

Leyden arranged to meet Speed Bump in the British Oak but first he had to tidy up the day's loose ends. He sent emails, wrote up the interview with Vinnie Pike, put in his expenses and, with time still to spare, began reading an intelligence review on the recent post office robberies in south-east London.

The gang were thought to be professionals building a war chest for a big job, according to the report. An ice-cream van had been seen in the vicinity of three of the raids. Intelligence suspected that the ice-cream seller acted as a lookout and repository for the gang's money and weapons. That got Leyden thinking, and when he next glanced at the Incident Room clock he found he was running late.

It was impossible to park near the Oak this time of evening. Leyden had to cruise almost to the end of Bowater Place before he found a space. He was surprised to see Carl Cochrane's grey Lexus parked next but one. This wasn't Carlo's normal stomping ground.

Leyden walked into the lounge and up to the bar. From there, he could see through a doorway across the public bar where Cochrane was talking to a man in a suit with a thick neck and sparse sandy hair.

Mal Topper.

Just then Speed Bump came in. Leyden moved to one side so

that Cochrane wouldn't clock him if he turned around.

'How're things?' asked Leyden, ordering a pint of San Miguel for Speed Bump.

'I've had to hang around the mill all bleeding day waiting to give a statement.'

'Thanks for helping the police.'

'But I didn't see anything, did I?' Speed Bump sounded disappointed. 'Tell you what, though – everyone feels really sorry for Fleur Varndell. Something like that could scar you for life.'

'Suppose it could. No word on the set about the shooting?'

Speed Bump shook his head. 'Not a dickie bird.'

'What's the latest on Mal Topper?'

'Why?'

'Because he's in the other bar... Don't look,' said Leyden as Speed Bump started to turn around.

'He's a bit off his manor. He normally drinks out Bromley way. My nephew drives one of his vans. That's why I never touch his burgers. I know where they come from.'

'If they're that bad, why don't local food standards close him down?'

'Money.' Speed Bump rubbed his thumb and forefinger together. 'But Topper's a funny fucker. He keeps crocodiles and all sorts of nasty things at his place in Kent. He's got a swimming pool full of piranhas.'

'Yeah?'

'Word is more than one person's fallen in that pool and never got out again. Nothing left of them either, if you know what I mean.'

'Right.' Leyden knew how gullible Speed Bump could be. He wouldn't notice if a mate put a key in his back and turned it. 'You left a message.'

'Just wanted to say that your blokes should be more careful where they set up an OP. Everyone on the estate knows about it.'

'What are you on about?'

'That empty flat in Dando Crescent, overlooking the garages where the Somalis stash their stuff.'

'News to me.' Leyden thought the local guys had been planning to install cameras to monitor the garages. They didn't have the manpower to run an OP. Things were stretched to the limit.

'And tell your bloke he's wasting his time getting there at half past eight in the morning,' continued Speed Bump. 'The Somalis never get up before ten.'

'Okay. How's the family? Mole and Vomit staying out of trouble?'

'Yeah, they're all right. But what about Janna, eh?'

'What about Janna?'

'Her teacher said that she's got a reading age of thirteen – and she's only ten,' said Speed Bump proudly.

'Still wants to become a doctor?'

'Either a doctor or a detective, she says.'

'God help her,' said Leyden.

Leyden had just dropped off Speed Bump when his phone rang. He pulled over. It was Bill Hutt, calling from the Abbey Wood Boys' Club.

The club was Bill's life. Now in his sixties, he still worked seven days a week, coaching boxing as a way of encouraging self-discipline, self-reliance and respect for others. But the club was going through hard times. The local authority grant had been cut, commercial sponsorship had dried up and the wealthy individuals who'd once identified with boxing now found sexier things to spend their money on. Leyden felt guilty he hadn't been in touch.

'Hi, Bill, how you're doing?' he said.

'All right, son, all right. Not heard from you in a while.'

'Sorry, Bill, I'm run off my feet. You've read about these murders–'

'Thought you might be tucked up.' A pause. 'You're not forgetting to train, are you?'

'No, I'm fine,' lied Bobby.

'Keep running. Keep those legs strong, maintain lung capacity. That's the secret.'

'I'm working at it, Bill.'

'Heard you had a difficult bout against that RAF geezer. You always did have a problem with southpaws.'

'We'll work on it next time I'm in, as soon as the pressure's off,' said Leyden.

'You know where to find me, son.'

'Yeah, of course. Thanks, Bill.'

The trainer chuckled. 'It's all right, Bobby. I'm not giving you a hard time. I'm phoning to say thank you. I didn't know you had such generous friends.'

'I don't.' Leyden didn't have a clue what Bill was on about.

'Gentleman by the name of Tosh Bibby called in. He said how you'd mentioned the club. Then he started on about how he'd been a tea leaf who'd mended his ways and how young tearaways needed something in their lives.'

'Yeah?'

'He was a bit flash for my taste but when I said we were in danger of having to shut down, his ears pricked up. He asked if I was on the level. I said, on my mum's grave.'

'Go on.'

'To cut a long story short, he sent an accountant bloke round yesterday to look at the books. Then, not half an hour ago, Mr Bibby comes on the dog. Guess what he's going to do?'

'Tell me,' said Bobby.

'Only give us sixty big ones, ain't he?'

'What?'

'Twenty grand a year for the next three years to tide us over until the economy picks up, he said. And that's not all. He wants to set up a youth tournament with cups and holidays abroad for prizes. It's all down to you, my son.'

'Leave it out.'

'You must come round soon. Any fights lined up?'

'A match against the army in November, but –'

'I know, you're snowed under. Just remember where we are, eh, son, and do me a favour. Give Mr Bibby a ring and thank him.'

Shirley Grey knelt to rearrange the roses she'd found on the grave. It was dusk, and the churchyard of St James the Great was deserted. Josie had been the first to be buried in this new part when the churchyard was recommissioned. The solitary grave had seemed lonely then; now the plot was almost full. Shirley was glad that Josie had company.

Shirley went to sit on the bench facing the grave. She'd paid for the bench and the gravel path and contributed handsomely to the upkeep of the new cemetery. On the other side of the old church with its sturdy tower, graves were in danger of disappearing in the long grass and weeds. Not here. Not while Shirley had breath left in her body.

The visit from the two detectives had unsettled her. She'd told them the truth when she'd that said there wasn't a day went by that she didn't remember that terrible night.

That was about the only truth she'd told them.

She hadn't mentioned the British gangster movie that Josie's father had seen in an English-language cinema in the Venezuelan capital of Caracas just three months ago. She also hadn't mentioned that Graham had heard the villain use a threat on screen, and recognised it as the same threat in the same voice that one of those bastards had made that night.

Thank you, God, for a miracle.

'Sorry I'm late, darling. Mummy had visitors.' Sometimes Shirley spoke aloud. Other times she talked to Josie in her head.

Frequently, she couldn't tell which was which. 'Two detectives, a man and a woman. They said that some men who'd been murdered recently could have been involved in the raid.' Shirley paused. 'Payback time at last, sweetheart.'

A swift swooped low over the grass, banking steeply before disappearing like a dark comma into the gloom. A man stepped out from behind the yew trees. She heard his footsteps approaching on the gravel. She half-turned her head.

'Josie always had a thing about red roses.'

'Remember the time we found her squeezing drops of blood onto the white roses so they'd become red?'

'She was very brave. Didn't seem to feel pain.'

'Not like Laurel.'

'No.'

The man was very close now. Still Shirley did not move.

'I heard the news about Joey Starling,' she said.

'I was–'

'I don't want to know.' Shirley held up her hand. 'The police called today.'

'I heard you tell Josie. What did they want?'

'They knew you were back in the country.'

'Doesn't matter.'

'They're looking for you.'

'No worries.' Graham White put his arms around his ex-wife. 'Not long now.'

She sighed. 'Shame we don't know the others.'

'Listen–'

'An eye for an eye. That'll do.' Shirley's eyes returned to the headstone.

'What about Donny?'

'H doesn't have a clue – bit like those detectives.'

'Let's keep it that way.'

'Is there anything you want to tell me?' Bobby asked Karen as they sat in their small living room. He'd been watching soccer on TV while Karen read a magazine.

The Real Madrid sweeper was rolling on the ground as though someone had ripped out his intestines with a pair of rusty pincers. Tosser. There was no way that was a penalty.

Karen didn't reply. Leyden repeated the question. Karen still didn't look up from her magazine. Leyden saw that she had iPod ear buds in. He leaned forward and waved. She took out the nearer earpiece.

'Is there anything you want to tell me?' he said again.

'About what?'

'Dunno. Anything.'

'Not really.'

Karen replaced the earpiece and carried on flicking through the magazine.

Leyden glowered at the TV. Even Bill Hutt's good news couldn't lift his evening. Soon, he knew, Karen would stop pretending to read and slide off to bed, saying she felt tired. He'd have another beer and watch whatever was on the box.

Karen had been in the shower when he'd arrived home. The sight of her mobile phone lying on the table next to her handbag had finally proved too great a temptation for a copper.

According to her call log, a large number of Karen's outgoing and incoming calls were to and from someone called Chris.

His first impulse had been to question Karen but then he realised that he didn't care. And that was the part that really hurt.

'Do you fancy going down the Crown for a drink?' he asked.

At least then they'd have to talk. Karen didn't reply. He suspected that she could hear, but chose not to.

He mimed having a drink and then a crown on his head.

Karen turned a page of her magazine. 'I'm okay here. You go.'

You might be okay, Leyden wanted to say. I'm dying inside.

Leyden pulled up his emotional drawbridge and retreated behind a moat of indifference. He couldn't decide if Karen was being deliberately cruel or just thoughtless. He wondered if she was behaving this way because she felt guilty. Unlikely, he decided.

He switched off the TV and went upstairs to the box room where he kept his punchbag, weights and a cross trainer. He began to beat the shit out of the punchbag.

Chalke smiled down at her lover, lying naked on his back, arms stretched behind his head. His eyes were closed, but she knew he wasn't asleep. Patsy was grateful for the respite. It had been a long day, a long evening, and an even longer night – ending in a bravura performance in bed.

She thought back over the evening's events.

First, there'd been the call from Weaver. Patsy had been getting ready for dinner. She'd put on a skirt for a change, and a different scent from her usual. It was another Jo Malone blend – she kept that company in business single-handed – this time pomegranate noir with blue agava. Patsy had been inspecting herself for the last time in the mirror when the phone had rung.

'Have you heard from Begley?' Weaver had begun.

'No.'

'I've just had a call from her demanding to know how the inquiry's going. When I asked her which inquiry, she said, "Quite." Any idea what she's on about?'

'Not a clue. Do you think there's shit flying around?'

'If there is, it won't be sticking to Begley.'

'I'd have thought she'd have learned to stay out of it after that business with Starling,' said Patsy.

'She'll have forgotten about that already,' said Weaver. 'I'd get in early tomorrow if I were you. I've got a bad feeling about this one.'

Patsy had managed put Weaver's call to the back of her mind by the time she reached The Grapes, a gastro pub on the river where she'd agreed to meet Barney Ruttle. He'd said he wanted to pick her brains about a new post he'd been offered in a ministerial shuffle.

It turned out Rubble had been offered a position in the Northern Ireland Office. He was agonising about whether to accept it. Not only from a career point of view – he was also worried about the effect close protection officers might have on his hitherto unconstrained and very colourful love life.

Patsy and Barney had once had a short fling, but now they were just friends. Not that it stopped them flirting like hell, especially after a glass or two. Patsy had just promised she'd give Rubble another chance as a lover if he reached Number 10, when she'd spotted her sister Caro walking towards the table.

Naturally Caro had assumed the worst. Once she'd made her disapproval quite clear, she mentioned that she'd had a phone call from 'some woman called Begley' about opera tickets. She'd been 'a little short with her', she said.

Patsy had seen Caro being 'a little short' with people. This wasn't good. She reminded her sister that Begley was her boss, and that Caro had promised to help her get tickets to the Royal Opera House.

Not that there'd been any point. Her sister didn't do apologies. And judging from Weaver's call, the damage had already been done.

Her lover finally stirred. 'Mmm. That was majestic,' he murmured.

'I wondered how long you were going to lie there with that silly grin on your face.'

'Tectonic plates shifted.'

'That was the neighbours banging on the ceiling to complain.'

He gave a dreamy smile. 'I've been thinking about Terry Rich.'

'God! You really know how to turn a girl on.'

'Sorry.' He opened his eyes, crinkled in an apologetic smile. 'You know how one's mind drifts… I think he'll walk on a retrial.'

'It'll be your fault if he does.'

'Strictly speaking, darling, it'll be yours. You shouldn't have tried to drown him – or rather, you should have succeeded.'

'Darling–'

'Yes?'

'Shut the fuck up about Rich. You are in no position to annoy me.'

'Actually, now that you mention it, could you take these cuffs off? My arms are going numb.'

Patsy sat astride Mansel Daley QC, leaned forward so that her breasts were touching his face, and began massaging his arms, shackled by her handcuffs to the brass bed head.

'I suppose you're going to rough me up in court again,' she said.

'I'm afraid I'm going to have to.'

'I'd better get my retaliation in first, then.' She flicked her finger into his balls.

'Ouch. That hurt.'

'It was intended to.' Patsy held her hand, with her middle finger cocked behind her thumb, before his eyes and then slowly withdrew it out of sight.

'Christ, Pats!'

'The defence case isn't as strong as you thought it was, is it?' Another flick of her finger.

'Ow! If you think I'm going to throw a trial just because… Yowww.'

'Oh. He's gone hard again. You public school types really do enjoy pain.' She climbed back astride and slid his cock inside her.

'Now, this trial–'

'You are a witch… You know that.'

'Yes,' said Patsy.

DAY TEN

Friday

THE PHONE CALL came at 7.05 a.m. It was the Greenwich duty officer. Full review presentation in twenty-five minutes. Sorry for the short notice, ma'am, but he'd just been told by Commander Begley.

'Anyone else in yet?' asked Chalke, wondering why he'd said presentation and not conference.

'DI Butterfield's been in for an hour,' said the duty officer, trying not to yawn.

'Thank you,' said Chalke.

God, she felt ill, but at least she was already dressed. Mansel Daley had left twenty minutes ago – looking as rough as she felt. Served him right.

She phoned Weaver as she waited for the lift. He was already in his car.

Leyden was out on a training run. Luckily he'd taken his mobile with him. He turned back for home even as they were speaking.

Chalke decided to take the Docklands Light Railway rather than drive in and risk getting stuck in the Blackwall Tunnel. The DLR would be more reliable. Except it wasn't. She arrived at Heron Quays to find an impatient crowd of commuters on the platform opposite and signal failure at Canary Wharf. It was ten minutes before the first train arrived.

Chalke ran up the escalator at Greenwich Maritime station,

pushing past the crowds who insisted on lining both sides. It was only when she was outside the NatWest – 300 yards from the nick – that she made herself slow down. Better to arrive late and cool than on time and in a muck sweat.

The Incident Room was packed. From the doorway, she made out Weaver and Begley at the front by the whiteboard, and Andy Butterfield, smooth-faced, smartly dressed, clutching a thick folder at Begley's side. Leyden was near the window, still flushed from his run. The Guinness inquiry team was there, together with two other DIs and a dark-haired man she didn't recognise. In fact, now she looked around there were a number of unfamiliar faces.

Begley saw Patsy – and blanked her.

A few days ago, Begley had been fawning over her as the best thing since sliced bread. Now it seemed she was a stale crust.

She wondered if the change had anything to do with Caro's brusqueness. It would be petty, but it was possible.

Chalke was debating whether to push her way through to the front when Andy Butterfield cleared his throat and began summarising the Dave Shine inquiry.

The CCTV team had identified Shine behind the wheel of his 6-Series BMW coming through the Blackwall Tunnel at 8.56 p.m. accompanied by a male passenger. A camera at the Tiger's Head junction in Lee had captured the BMW again at 9.12 p.m., turning left towards the funeral parlour.

The next image, from the same camera taken at 9.39 p.m., showed the car heading straight over the lights coming from the parlour towards Blackheath on the way to Greenwich. The CCTV camera at the garage itself, where the car ended up, hadn't been working for a month.

The traces of blood and hair in the BMW's boot were type O. Shine was AB. The fibres found were from the sort of green twine sold in garden centres. Interviews with Shine's wife, mistress and business associates had led nowhere; a watch on airports and ports had drawn a blank. The belt buckle – the only item to survive the cremator – had been made in Bulgaria.

Butterfield moved on to the death of Lee Finch, who had been killed by two blows from a blunt instrument to the back of the head. The murder weapon had not been found; the place of death was still unknown. Time of death was put around midnight. CCTV cameras and a canvass of potential witnesses had drawn a blank. The drugs found in the dry-cleaner's indicated a connection with Dave Shine.

Finch had been making inquiries about acquiring the London franchise for a souped-up kit car made in Korea. That indicated that he had a bundle of readies stashed somewhere and was seeking to launder it.

At the same time, Finch's wife Lorraine had been stealing from the business while conducting an affair with cage fighter Tony Yayale. Yayale had given her an alibi for the time of Finch's death but then Yayale himself had been murdered.

Chalke noted how Butterfield was careful not to refer to Yayale as Guinness.

Weasel.

Butterfield nodded towards a rather saturnine man standing near the front. 'DI Thomas from S&O.'

Chalke hadn't known that Serious and Organised Crime were involved. As well as dealing with kidnapping, hostage negotiation and major Heathrow crime, S&O ran a specialist intelligence service targeting known big-time villains.

Thomas cleared his throat. 'Two days before Yayale's murder, one of his fighters, going by the name Mad Max the Mutilator, ignored the Jolly family's orders to take a dive. Instead Mad Max won his bout, collected his winnings and left through the dressing-room window. He's now hiding abroad with his girlfriend. This was a very public two fingers to the Jolly family which they couldn't ignore. They were already getting agitated about Yayale's plans to expand; this is probably why he'd tried to form an alliance with Ari O. Since Yayale's murder, the Jolly family has taken over his stable of cage fighters together with his promotion business.'

Butterfield then began droning on again but Patsy wasn't listening. Thomas's intelligence supported the theory that Guinness's murder was a gangland affair and nothing to do with the Maidstone raid.

And if she was wrong about that, what else had she got wrong?

She had a gut feeling that the murders of Minicab and Guinness were linked. But, looked at objectively, what was there to connect them other than the word of an unreliable informer? Okay, the cufflinks on Stan Figgens were in the shape of Northern Cyprus but did they have to have something to do with Georgie Locke?

Chalke returned from her thoughts to hear Butterfield talking about the Starling shooting. Starling was believed to have been blackmailing the film's director. If they could find he was blackmailing others then they'd also have a motive for his murder. The scar-faced extra still hadn't been found. Photofit technicians had put together a likeness that could be Graham White.

The missing man hadn't spoken to anyone. He'd kept himself to himself, always on the fringes. He wasn't visible in any of the film shots. Strange sort of extra.

Finding Graham White was becoming a priority. It was also hoped that Fleur Varndell could be formally interviewed today although she was not the prime suspect.

Chalke saw that Begley had now stepped forward.

'Because of the geographical spread of the killings, I have decided to reorganise the inquiry,' she announced. 'DI Butterfield will remain actions allocator regarding the suspicious death at Falconwood Crematorium, the disappearance of Dave Shine, and the Lee Finch murder. DI Lakeman will head up the inquiry into the murder of Tony Yayale, liaising with S&O. DIs Peter Smith and Will Freeman will handle the Joey Starling investigation. DCS Weaver remains SIO, with DCI Chalke taking an overview.' She glanced at the wall clock. 'Sorry. No time for questions.'

Begley and Weaver headed for the door, the crush of bodies parting before them. Patsy made her way to her office and closed the door. She felt sick in the pit of her stomach. She was Pasty Chalke, legend. She was also Patsy Chalke, little girl who wanted to curl up on the floor and pretend none of this was happening.

She'd been shafted.

She thought about going off sick. Others had gone off sick for less. No. It wasn't her style. Fighting was her style.

Take the positives. Begley had given her an overview brief – that meant she could go anywhere, interview anyone.

And God help any fucker who stood in her way.

'You're sure you want to do this?' asked Leyden.

'Of course.' Chalke climbed out of Leyden's Mondeo, smoothed down her jacket and lit a cigarette.

She'd believed that she knew Roman Road well. Many Sunday mornings she'd come to the colourful street market here in Bow. She hadn't known the Jolly family ran their crime empire from their drinking club in the same street.

'We'll be stepping on S&O's toes,' warned Leyden.

'Then they should wear steel-capped boots.' It occurred to her that she could be damaging Leyden's career. It didn't do to make enemies in Serious and Organised if you were a mere detective sergeant.

'Maybe it'd be better if you stayed here,' she said. 'I can do this.'

'In your dreams. I'm not letting you go in there alone.' Leyden set off towards the anonymous black door.

'Bobby, I'm a senior police officer. I'm also a woman. I'm a damned sight more likely to come out of that club unharmed than someone like you who's likely to start a fight.'

Leyden grunted his disagreement.

'When is your next fight, anyway?'

'November – if I ever get the chance to train, that is.'

'Shame – just as your face was healing.'

'Can I ask you a question?'

'As long as you don't expect an honest answer.'

'What happened back there, at the nick?'

'I wish I knew.'

Chalke pushed open the door of the drinking club to reveal a long narrow room with a bar on the right. The walls were filled with signed photographs of boxers, footballers, TV soap stars and C-list celebrities. Even though it was just eleven o'clock, all the bar stools were taken.

'DCI Chalke, DS Leyden. We're here to see Shug Jolly,' Leyden told the men at the table by the door.

'Yeah? And why do you think Mr Jolly wants to see you?'

'Because we're asking politely,' said Chalke, feeling Leyden tense beside her.

'Wait a minute.'

Aware of the drinkers' hostility, Leyden strolled into the room and began inspecting the photographs. He stopped before a large black and white image of two boxers. One lay flat on the canvas; the other, fists clenched, stood over him.

Leyden was still looking at the photograph when the drinkers rose from their seats. A man had appeared at the far end of the bar. The man was in his sixties with a melon-shaped head. He wore a purple silk shirt buttoned to the neck and walked with a roll that came with bad knees. His flattened nose and the scars around his eyes told that he'd been a fighter.

'Polite is good,' said Shug Jolly.

Leyden pointed up at the photograph. 'That's when you decked Terry Spinks.'

Patsy was surprised to hear the respect in Leyden's voice.

'Third round. Albert Hall. Then Tel got off the floor and battered me,' chuckled Jolly in a thick Glaswegian accent.

'You got the better of him at Wembley the next year.'

'You know your boxing, Mr Leyden, but you never really got the better of Tel. You just managed to beat him on the night.'

'Was he the hardest you fought?'

Chalke frowned. They weren't here to talk about Jolly's boxing career.

'They're all hard, son. You don't get to fight for the championship by being a softie. But Howard Winstone, if you really want to know.He was missing the tips of three fingers on his right hand. That's why his left cross was something special. Lovely man.' He pointed up to a signed photograph of the Welsh boxer. 'Box a bit, do you?'

'Um–'

'Bobby's the Met's light heavyweight champion,' said Chalke as Leyden struggled for a suitably modest answer.

'I started at the Abbey Wood Club with Bill Hutt,' he explained.

'A good man, Bill Hutt. But I take it you're not here to talk about boxing.'

'Tony Yayale,' said Chalke.

'Och. What a way to go, eh? Killed by the weight of his own expectations.'

'You've taken over his fighters.'

'Me? No.'

'Someone in your family has.'

'I'm not responsible for the actions of everyone in my so-called family, hen.'

'As head of the family concern, you're responsible for the consequences of their actions. You joke that Yayale died under the weight of his expectations. Don't you worry that one day you'll suffer under the same pressing weight of responsibility?'

Jolly regarded Patsy Chalke thoughtfully. 'That's some speech, hen. Let's take the air.' He jerked his head towards the doorway.

The detectives accompanied Jolly over the road and through an iron arch into a small park. Two large men followed.

It hadn't rained for a fortnight, and the weather was about to break. The atmosphere was growing oppressive. You could almost smell the sulphur.

A few yards into the park, a small fountain played at the junction of two paths. Jolly leaned against the lip of the fountain and folded his arms.

'What do you want?'

Chalke could have told him that flowing water didn't affect modern listening devices, but that wouldn't go down well if one of her colleagues was listening.

'You – or someone in your family – have taken over Guinness's fighters,' she repeated.

'If we hadn't, someone else would. Just business.'

'And Mad Max disobeying orders?'

'He doesn't have the brains to stay hidden for long. His bird'll hand him over when he runs out of dosh. He'll get a good beating.'

'You won't kill him?'

'It would be a disproportionate response.' Jolly saw the surprise on Chalke's face. 'When I gave up the ring, I went a bit mental. Ended up serving six years for robbery. I spent those years studying. Do know the most important thing I learned?'

Patsy shook her head.

Jolly's smile vanished. 'Never get caught. And I haven't been. For all the listening devices and the informers and intelligence-led operations, I've never been convicted of so much as speeding since I came out. Proportionate response, you see.'

'Was it a proportionate response topping Guinness?'

'I didn't kill Guinness.'

'You might not have killed him, but what about a member of your family or someone who works for them?'

Shug Jolly laughed, showing teeth that were not his own. 'You're a caution. How shall I put this – neither me nor mine had anything whatsoever to do with Guinness's death. And that's the truth.'

'Truth is relative, Mr Jolly.'

'Not always. Sometimes it can be absolute. Whether you believe me or not is up to you.'

'So why is Ari O running scared?'

'Probably because Ari O is a paranoid sociopath, terrified of his shadow each time the moon's full.'

'Okay. But if you didn't kill Guinness, who did?'

'You're the detectives.'

'The way he was killed suggests a public warning,' said Leyden.

'Son, I conduct my business in a narrow stratum of society where a wink is as good as a drill bit through the knee.'

'As long as people know that you're prepared to use extreme violence, you seldom need to, you mean?'

'Exactly.'

'The Dim Reaper,' said Chalke. 'He's one of yours.'

'Was one of mine. Past tense. Not seen him for years.'

'You know he's gone off radar?'

'I've heard.' Jolly pushed himself upright. 'So, are you going to believe me or not?'

'I reckon we might,' said Chalke. 'Although you have clearly benefited from Guinness's death.'

'I'll not deny that.' Jolly winced as he took his first step. 'This bloody knee. There's nothing else I can help you with, hen?'

'Like what?'

'Terry Rich. It'll be a scandal if he walks on retrial.'

'Thanks all the same.'

'That's the difference between you and me, you see, hen.'

'You mean you'd have succeeded in drowning him?'

'Och, no. That would have been a disproportionate response – especially with witnesses present.'

In the east, storm clouds were gathering. It was getting more and more humid.

'Heavy, isn't it?' Chalke said as they walked away.

'My mum used to get terrible headaches on days like this,' said Leyden. 'She used to hate them.'

'I can understand that.'

A traffic warden was taking a close interest in Leyden's car.

Leyden shouted, 'Oi, you. Leave it.'

'Are you over time?' Chalke knew that Leyden hated feeding parking meters.

'Probably.' He waved at the traffic warden. 'Leave it. I'm a police officer.'

The warden appeared not to have heard. He was opening his pocket book when a piercing whistle came from behind them. The warden's head jerked up. He stared past Leyden, raised his hand in acknowledgement, and put his book away. Leyden spun around to see Jolly and his minders. One gave an ironic wave.

By the time Leyden had turned back, the warden was disappearing down a side street.

When they'd reached the car, Chalke hesitated. The last thing she wanted to do was to go back to Greenwich after her humiliation.

Leyden was a mind reader. 'I don't know about you, guv, but I haven't eaten all day. How about an early bite?'

'Good idea.' She saw Leyden eyeing a nearby pub. 'As long as you're not thinking of a pie and a pint.'

'I don't fancy fizzy water and a lettuce leaf.'

Chalke had a brainwave. She pulled out her mobile phone. 'I know. I'll take you to St John's – if we can get a table.'

'Is it posh?'

'Don't be silly. It does have a Michelin star, though.'

'What?'

'Hello, this is Patsy Chalke… Hi, Emily. Just wondered if you had a table for two… No, for lunch… Excellent. We'll be with you in twenty minutes or so. See you then.'

'Am I going to enjoy this?' asked Leyden.

'You'll love it. Oysters, snails, offal–'

'Great.'

'Don't be a wimp. To Clerkenwell, driver. This is my treat.'

'No way.'

'You can get the tab next time.' The prospect of a good lunch had cheered Patsy. She asked, 'Do you believe Jolly?'

'Yeah, reckon so,' said Leyden, making an illegal right turn into the Mile End Road.

'So do I.' Chalke settled deep in the passenger seat and returned to wondering why Begley had turned against her. She continued thinking as Leyden cut through the back streets of Shoreditch towards the Barbican.

They parked in a multi-storey and began to walk up the street, Leyden glancing enviously into the pubs they passed. Suddenly he stopped.

'Christ!' He darted into the pub. Patsy followed to find Leyden staring at the TV above the bar. 'Look.'

The screen was showing a dozen or so bedraggled Chinese standing by a Swanson International Haulage wagon watched by police officers. Alison Begley and Des Weaver were visible in the background.

The newsreader was saying: 'This morning, off the A20 in Kent–'

'So that's why they hurried off,' said Chalke.

'That was going to be our bust!' said Leyden.

'There's obviously been a change of plan.'

'Hasn't stopped Begley or Weaver grabbing their share of the glory, though, has it? That was set up for TV.'

'You think so?'

'No, guv. A TV crew just happened to pull up as Kent police made the collar.'

'Point taken.'

The presenter moved on to the next item, a man believed to have drowned after vanishing on a ferry in the English Channel. There was a picture of an unclaimed VW car on the ferry's car deck.

At least that wasn't their problem.

Chalke wondered why Weaver had thrown in his lot with Begley. It felt like a betrayal. Her mobile rang. It was Les Blunt.

'Hello, Les.'

'Thought you'd like to know that there're discrepancies in the stories of Jemma Wodehouse and Eric Traubenhat, ma'am. You know, the two Leyden flagged up.'

'Yes?'

'According to their statements, they were in different places when they heard the shot that killed Starling.'

'Didn't they say they were together?'

'They did. But in his statement Eric says he was right at the mill gates, while Jemma says she was still a few hundred yards away.'

'Thanks, Les. Who else knows this?'

'No one.'

'Okay. We'll go and see them. But do me a favour. Don't say a word to anyone. I'm going to have lunch first.'

'We've got a gig,' said Eric, waylaying Jemma on the steps of the college. 'Saturday.'

'Great. Is that tomorrow or a week tomorrow?'

'Dunno. Belinda didn't say.'

'Where?'

'Belinda knows.'

Such practical details didn't matter to Eric. He just turned up and performed. Brilliantly.

Eric skipped away playing a snatch from 'Money Makes the World Go Around'.

Jemma wished she had asked Eric for a lift home. She was still nervous, still looking over her shoulder ever since she'd been followed. She hadn't spotting anyone acting suspiciously. Two days on, she was daring to hope she'd imagined it.

Jemma threw her gig bag containing Bessie over her shoulder and made for the bus stop outside college. A 177 came along. Jemma climbed up to the top deck and again began thinking what to do about the key she had taken from Starling's flat.

She didn't know what the key opened but she did know it was important. Starling wouldn't have worn it around his neck otherwise. Then there were all the calls he'd made to try to get it back.

Now Starling was dead. But from what she'd overheard in his flat, she knew others were involved with the key in some way.

They'd come looking for it. And they wouldn't be the sort to mess around.

She was in trouble.

Okay. How to get out of trouble?

Try to be logical. Options. Throw away the key?

No. Starling's friends wouldn't believe she'd got rid of it. She could end up being tortured. Killed, even.

She couldn't hand the key to the police without admitting that she'd broken into the flat and dropping Eric's mate Jimmy the Porter right in it.

No, she'd keep the key safe until she could give it to Starling's underworld mates. They could have it and good riddance.

She'd have never have taken the bloody thing if she'd known how things were going to turn out.

Jemma was so lost in thought that she missed her stop and had to go on to the one opposite the Wing Wah buffet.

She walked back along Woolwich Road and into the triangle. She let herself into the flat and went into her bedroom. She took Bessie out of her case, having to shift the chair to make room to put her next to the Selmer. Odd – Jemma couldn't remember moving that chair.

She opened her bedside drawer, and the icy hand returned to clutch at her heart.

Normally the drawer held a random clutter of junk: jewellery, tissues, sets of spare reeds, passport, hand cream, packet of condoms, diary, old ballpoint pens.

Now everything was laid out with military precision.

Jemma sat on the bed and felt very scared.

Her mobile phone began to ring.

'Well, did you enjoy that?' asked Chalke as she and Leyden drove over Blackfriars Bridge.

'It was different,' conceded Leyden.

Chalke looked at him out of the corner of her eye. 'Different good or different bad?'

Leyden didn't like to say that if that was how the other half lived, they were welcome to it.

'I've never had liver and onions like that before but the rhubarb crumble was good – though I could have done with more. Hardly fill your plates, do they?'

'You should have stuck with the fish,' said Chalke, who'd had brown crab meat and sole slips.

'Can't see the point of going to a meat market and having fish,' he said. 'Anyway, thanks. But I'll pay next time.'

Chalke's insistence on picking up the bill rankled with Leyden. He couldn't remember a woman ever buying him a meal before.

To avoid further talk about the restaurant, Leyden called Jemma's mobile. She was at home and he arranged to drop by in twenty minutes, traffic permitting.

In fact, it took nearer half an hour. On the doorstep, Leyden introduced Chalke. He wondered why Jemma looked glad to see them. That wasn't the welcome coppers normally got.

Jemma, in a sleeveless vest under a thin cardigan, showed them into the living room where a cello sat in the corner next to a viola. A few feet away a slide trombone, a French horn and a cornet stood together.

'You've enough instruments for an orchestra,' observed Leyden.

'They're Eric's. He can play anything.'

'And you?'

'Saxophone, basically. Bit of clarinet and piano. Everyone plays the piano.'

'I don't,' said Leyden.

'I think Jemma means everyone musical,' said Chalke.

'Can you?'

'I've had lessons.'

'And?'

'Let's get on, shall we?'

Jemma sat upright in a chair, holding the saxophone in her lap.

'We've been comparing the statements you and Eric made regarding Starling's murder,' began Chalke, wondering who Jemma reminded her of.

'Yes?'

'You claim you were some distance from the mill when you heard the shot.' Chalke sat down opposite Jemma while Leyden continued to prowl around.

'Yes.'

'But according to Eric's statement you were both at the mill gate when the shot was fired.'

Jemma knew she should have worked harder coaching Eric. He had the attention span of a butterfly. The truth was they'd arrived on set well before the director had called for the break. When Fleur had fired the shot, they'd been blending in with a crowd of extras.

'I didn't take much notice where we were, to be honest,' stammered Jemma. 'I mean, you can't remember everything. But you shouldn't take Eric's word – he doesn't… um… take a lot of notice of what's going on round him.'

'If you say so,' smiled Chalke.

Jemma didn't like that smile. The policewoman was altogether too glamorous and clever. That smile had all the warmth of a deep-freeze. At least Leyden was a regular sort of guy – number one haircut, rearranged face, high street suit. She could relate to him more than this film star.

But just as Jemma was mentally preparing her next line of defence, Leyden said, 'Tell me about you and Joey Starling.'

'I told you. There's nothing to tell.'

'Are you sure?' Leyden deliberately stood behind her so she had to turn to look up at him.

'Sure.'

'Jemma, that tattoo on your shoulder–'

'My penguin?'

'I've seen it before.'

'You can't have done.'

'Two days ago – on Starling's laptop.'

Jemma dropped her head. 'Oh.'

'Anything you want to tell us?'

'No.'

'Starling had a collection of pornographic images on his laptop,' said Chalke softly. 'We're tracing the girls involved.'

'There're two images of you,' said Leyden.

Jemma gave a strange laugh. 'Only two? I thought there'd be more.'

'Want to tell us about it?'

'What's there to tell?' Jemma cradled her saxophone like a child. 'Joey fed off girls like me. I was a fool.'

'Did he give you drugs?' When Jemma didn't answer, Leyden

added, 'Most of the girls in the videos look out of it.'

'I was still at school when I met him. By the time I came to my senses, I was hooked on crack. I celebrated my eighteenth birthday in a drug clinic with an overdose.'

'You're clean now?'

'No thanks to Joey fucking Starling.'

'Why did you lie when you said you didn't know him?' asked Chalke.

'It's not a time I'm proud of,' said Jemma. 'But it's in the past. Finished.'

'And Starling's dead,' said Chalke.

'Bloody good riddance. The world's better without him.'

Again Jemma reminded Chalke of someone – a fleeting resemblance that faded the harder Chalke tried to nail it down.

'But –'

'Come on. If you'd been me, would you have said anything?' interrupted Jemma.

No, Patsy wouldn't. Bloody right she wouldn't. Patsy wouldn't admit what she'd done to anyone, sometimes not even the guy she'd done it with.

'You'll have to give a statement about the videos,' she told Jemma. 'It'll be in confidence. I'll send a WDC.'

'I'd rather talk to Mr Leyden, if that's all right.'

'Okay.' Leyden looked pleased. 'I'll be round tomorrow. I'll give you a bell first.'

This was all getting too cosy, thought Chalke. Time to rattle Jemma's cage. 'What were you and Eric doing on set the morning Starling was killed?'

Jemma put the sax to her lips and blew softly. A deep mellow sound filled the room. 'I was going to confront him. I was going to spit in his face.'

'Do you know anything about guns?' asked Chalke.

*

Back in Greenwich, Leyden remembered that he hadn't called Tosh Bibby. Leyden didn't particularly want to speak to Bibby. For all his generosity, he didn't like the man, but he owed it to Bill Hutt.

When Bibby didn't answer, Leyden left a message, thanking him for helping the boxing club. Then he started on his paperwork with a clear conscience.

Five minutes later, Bibby phoned back. He was in Greenwich on business. Why didn't they meet up?

Why not, thought Leyden. It was past five o'clock, and he'd been in since 7.30 this morning. And it would keep Bibby sweet.

Bibby suggested Davy's Wine Vaults in Greenwich High Road. In ten minutes.

Leyden would have preferred a pub but decided to let Bibby call the shots.

The atmosphere had become even more oppressive. It was building up to one hell of a thunderstorm. Leyden turned the corner by the old town hall, all thirty-two million bricks of it, passed the Carnegie library of West Greenwich, or what was left of it, and glowered at the ugly new hotel, totally out of proportion, which had been built next to the listed station, once the terminus of the world's first passenger railway line.

Leyden suspected he was becoming a grumpy old man. He didn't care. How could the bloody council have allowed such an eyesore?

It was the first time Leyden had been in Davy's. There was sawdust on the uneven flagstone floor and mismatching chairs, a concept which had spawned a successful chain of wine bars across London. Leyden didn't have a clue what to order. He knew that red wine went with meat and white with fish, although Patsy Chalke had confused him at lunch by pointing out exceptions to the rule. The information had gone in one ear and out of the other. Now he wished he'd listened.

He was pretending to study the special offers on the black-board when Bibby swept in. They shook hands. Bibby picked up the wine list, stabbed a finger at some name at the bottom on the page and paid with two £20 notes. He didn't appear to get much change. He picked up the bottle and two glasses and led the way to a table.

'I wanted to thank you for being so generous,' began Leyden.

Bibby poured a little wine into his glass, swirled it around, sniffed, took a sip. He said, 'That'll do.' He poured Leyden a glass and topped up his own.

Leyden tried it. It tasted like any other wine. 'Very nice.'

'So it should be for that money.'

Leyden glanced at the label. Pommard 1er Cru Jarollières Nicholas Rossignol 2000. He was never going to remember all that to tell Chalke.

'As I was saying, thanks for helping Bill Hutt.'

'It's not Bill Hutt I'm helping, son. It's the kids on the streets. I'm where I am today because Des Weaver gave me a second chance. That's what I want to give kids on estates like the Ferrier – a second chance.'

'It's very good of you.' Leyden took another sip of wine. It still tasted like the stuff Karen got from Tesco.

'I thought of what you've achieved. You're another me in a way,' said Bibby. 'Des has high hopes for you – you know that?'

'No.'

'You done your inspector's exams yet?'

'Not yet,' said Leyden.

'You should, son.' Bibby took a large drink. 'Would you call yourself ambitious?'

Leyden had never thought about it. 'Not particularly,' he said.

'You'd like your own team, wouldn't you? You'd like to be in charge of your own investigation.'

Yes, put like that, Leyden would. Chalke had got onto him over lunch about sitting the exams, but then she wanted to improve everyone. Look at how she banged on to poor Sue Bigtits.

'I suppose so.'

'You put your head down and work, my son. You won't regret it.' Bibby topped up his glass. 'Anything I can do to help, just let me know.'

Leyden had hardly touched his wine. Bibby appeared not to notice.

'Thanks.'

'In fact, with Des coming up to retirement, and all the things I get to hear–' Bibby took another gulp. He was using his left hand, no doubt to show off the gold Rolex Oyster on his wrist. 'Des built his career on my information.'

Leyden didn't know what to say. Clearly an informant like Bibby would be a massive boost to his career, but there were two sides to any deal. Bibby was repaying Weaver for the chance he'd given him years ago. What would he want from Leyden?

'Sorry that people-smuggling bust didn't happen on your patch,' Bibby was saying.

'What happened?'

'I found out that they were planning to switch to another wagon in Kent. Did you see the bust on TV?'

'Yeah, I caught it.'

'They like to get in on the act, don't they? Kent Police, that Begley woman, Immigration. They'll all claim a slice of the credit but everyone knows it was down to Des.'

'Was the driver running a solo operation?'

'Was he hell! Alfie Swanson's in it up to his neck. I couldn't work out how he kept managing to undercut me and afford new wagons every year.'

'Of course, you own a haulage company,' Leyden recalled.

'Biggest in south-east London, my son. Wasn't going to have a toerag like Alfie Swanson come along and wreck me, was I? Not when he was as bent as a nine bob note.' Bibby took another glug of wine. He was drinking faster by the glass. 'Got any further finding the Dim Reaper?'

'A few sightings here and there.'

'He's done a runner,' said Bibby confidently. 'He'll pop up in South America in ten years or so, mark my words.'

'It's a thought,' said Leyden. 'But who did he slot?'

'Not a clue, son. Never had any dealings with the man.' Bibby emptied the bottle into his glass. Leyden thought that it was just as well he didn't like wine himself.

'Did you ever find out who put Mark Parsons up to giving that false alibi for Starling?' he asked.

Bibby struggled to place the name. 'I've got you. No. I threatened him with the tin-tack as well. In the end, I let him off with a warning. His bird's in the club so they need the money.'

'Someone went to a lot of trouble to protect Starling when they thought he'd killed Freddy Carter.'

Bibby checked his watch. 'Hell. Didn't realise it was so late. Going to hit rush hour.' He drained his glass.

'You're not going to drive?' asked Leyden as Bibby stood up.

'No way. Got my driver outside.'

Leyden hurried to finish his wine.

As they walked towards the door, Bibby took Leyden's arm. 'Remember, that was a kosher offer. Think about it.'

'I will, Mr Bibby,' said Leyden.

This time, he noticed, Bibby hadn't once said to call him Tosh.

Chalke wrote up her interview with Shug Jolly, knowing that her visit would show up on S&O's radar. She suspected she was going to catch flak for going where angels feared to tread, but how much worse could things get? Even her wooden man looked depressed. She tried to get him to give a high five but he didn't look very convincing.

The Incident Room was buzzing with energy, every desk occupied. Detectives she'd never seen before were busily talking on phones and tapping away at keyboards. The whiteboard was crammed with new actions and lines of inquiry. A hive of industry. The world was getting on without Patsy Chalke.

There was no sign of Weaver. The fact that the two new DIs were installed in his office suggested he'd be out all day.

Patsy needed an ally. The most obvious one was Paul Tyler. Patsy picked up the phone and called Barney Ruttle's mobile.

'Rubble? Patsy. How are you enjoying high office? Good… How well do you know the woman who's succeeded you at the HO? Really? Biblically… and you're still friends? We need to meet up… you're a sweetheart. See you there.'

Chalke had two other phone calls to make.

Ten minutes later, she walked through the Incident Room feeling happier than she had all day. Les Blunt came up to say that some of the old team were going for a pint. Would she like to join them? Patsy declined. She had places to go and people to see. But first she had to order a case of port for her brother-in-law's birthday the following week. Taylor's Vintage 1966 – the year of his birth. That should mend a few fences at almost £100 a bottle. Then she'd take the DLR home.

The sky was preternaturally dark. Flickers of lightning split the air over the city. The storm would soon be upon them.

Leyden was thirsting for a pint to take away the taste of the wine. He was just about to head out to join the rest of the team when Sue Jones appeared at his side.

'Can I ask you something?' she said.

'Of course. What is it, Sue?'

Sue hesitated. 'Is Mr Cochrane in some kind of trouble?'

'Carlo? Not that I know of. Why?'

'It's just that he's been whispering into the phone a lot the last few days, and then I saw him on his mobile in the passageway with a face like thunder. I wondered–'

'Knowing him it's probably something to do with money. Probably just one of his shares falling a few points. I wouldn't worry about it, love.'

'Okay… Thanks'

'Not a problem. You coming to the pub?'

'Could I? That'd be lovely.'

The pair reached the Prince Albert, Leyden's spirits lifting at the prospect of beer. The Tolly was Weaver's pub, but they weren't sure about Weaver at the moment. If he was going to turn out to be a two-faced git they'd boycott his pub. It didn't make a lot of sense, but that was the way coppers thought.

Sandy Wishbourne, Cochrane, Brian Peel and Les Blunt were already at the bar. No one offered to buy drinks for Leyden and Sue which suggested that it was Cochrane's round. Leyden bought Sue fizzy water and himself a pint of lager, and they joined the group.

Leyden sat next to Sandy. 'So what have you been working on today?' he asked.

'Liaising with Kent, looking for Graham White. He's been seen in the Maidstone area again. What's more, Shirley Grey's been clocked hanging around Maidstone's red-light district.'

'Maidstone has a red light district?'

'You'd better believe it.'

'I wonder what Shirley's doing there. It's not as though she needs to go on the game.'

'By the way, Sussex have traced another six of Starling's girls. They all attend the same film school in Brighton and they're all terrified their parents will find out.'

Cochrane was complaining about the people-smuggling bust. Feelings were running high. Everyone in the old squad was united in their condemnation of the way Begley had treated Chalke.

Some maintained that Weaver would have protected her if he hadn't been tied up in the people-smuggling operation. Cochrane disagreed. He seemed to have it in for Weaver. Must be the weather making him quarrelsome.

Leyden offered Sue a lift home but she insisted on taking the bus. As he walked out, one of the new DIs and his team walked in. Leyden was tempted to stay. It would be worth paying money to watch Cochrane wind himself up, but he decided he'd had enough for the day.

Workmen's vans were a common sight in Leyden's road so there would have been nothing suspicious about the white van parked outside his home. Except it was seven o'clock in the evening and his front door was wide open.

Leyden pulled in fifty yards away on the other side of the road. He thought about calling for back-up then changed his mind. It was nothing he couldn't handle himself, and this way he'd get to give the intruders a good thumping before summoning arresting officers.

He slid lower in his seat as a man emerged from his home carrying a suitcase and two carrier bags which he put in back of the van. Leyden took a mental picture of the burglar – white, about thirty years old; five feet nine, average build; short brown hair, two days' stubble; stud in left ear; wearing grey cargo trousers and a green sweatshirt, Nike trainers.

No problem. But he'd have a mate.

It was a misconception that burglars struck at night. Only a crackhead got a buzz from opening a bedside drawer with someone snoring a few feet away. They were the sort who left turds in the spare bed.

Most professional burglars worked in the daytime and relied on the indifference that permeated big cities. After two years, Leyden still hardly knew his neighbours, although he'd run CRO checks on them in case he found himself in a compromising situation. He was friendliest with Vic and Phyllis next door. Every night, Vic, who'd worked on the Woolwich ferry for thirty years, went to their local pub to watch football. Leyden had often invited Vic in to watch the big games but he preferred the pub. Mrs Winforton, a garrulous retired schoolmarm desperate for company, lived on the other side, while opposite were Simon and Suzi who worked at an insurance broker's in Bromley. And that was about it.

Leyden wanted to get a look at the accomplice, but when no one came out, it struck him that they might be trashing his home.

He hurried along the road and up his path. He took the three steps in one bound, through the open doorway and into the living room.

The guy he'd seen was just picking up his laptop. A black guy in Matalan gear and bling was going through the CDs and DVDs.

'Can I help you?' asked Leyden.

The two men froze.

'I don't want any trouble, mate,' said the white guy.

'I'd put that computer down then, for a start,' said Leyden.

'You don't understand.'

'No, mate, of course I don't.'

Karen appeared from the kitchen. She was pale and hostile.

'I'm moving out,' she announced. 'You can't stop me.'

So that was it. He wasn't being burgled after all. He was being left.

'Why would I want to?' he said.

Karen moved closer to the black man. 'It's not what you think.'

'You don't know what I think.' He wanted to ask Karen why she hadn't had the courage to tell him she was leaving, why she felt she needed these hit men from Mothercare – but he wouldn't waste his breath.

'No bother, man,' said the black guy.

'No bother at all. Just don't take anything that belongs to me – like that laptop.'

'You don't use it,' said Karen.

'I'll have more time now,' said Leyden. 'Which one of you is Chris?'

A statuesque black woman – six feet one, cropped hair, cheek bones like razors, beer bottle shoulders – appeared in the doorway holding Karen's jewellery case. Leyden made a bet with himself that she was the pan-African ladies' kick-boxing champion.

'I'm Dr Christina Obasanjo.'

Karen ran to her side. Outside there was a prolonged roll of thunder.

'This is my brother and his friend,' said the Amazon. 'Karen was worried that you'd cause trouble.'

'Just shows how well Karen knows me.' Rain began drumming on the roof. Karen was going to get wet beginning her new life. 'I've been waiting for her to leave.'

'Karen has struggled to acknowledge where her true feelings lie,' said Christina Obasanjo.

'Be happy,' said Leyden. 'Now put down that Stones CD. It's mine.'

Philip was pretty – not handsome, pretty. Girls called him pretty. He called himself pretty. Men called him effeminate, or worse. Philip – known as Pippin – preferred girls but he'd found from the age of sixteen that his dark curly locks and snub nose attracted a certain kind of man. Pippin liked money, liked to receive presents, and over the years had acquired a liking for cocaine that had become an addiction.

He was also an ingrate. He couldn't give a flying fuck about the debt he owed the guy who had saved his arse that time in prison, but he did care about the 5k the guy was offering for something that Pippin spent his time doing anyway.

Picking up rich men in clubs.

Pippin had never been to the Lowlights Club in Stratford, east London. He'd heard of it but it was outside his normal haunts around Chalk Farm and Highgate. He didn't need to travel to attract business. He was pretty.

He made his way down the steps into the club to see two brutes clocking everyone who came in. Pippin knew that he wasn't their type and wondered why they were there. He moved towards the bar, giving clubbers the chance to get a good look at him. Pippin never put his hand in his pocket. It wouldn't be long before someone offered to buy him a drink.

He took in his surroundings. Every club was different, but every club was the same – the strobe lighting, the tiny dance floor, not crowded this early in the evening, the dark recesses.

Pippin accepted a glass of wine from a bespectacled businessman in his mid-forties, suit but no tie. Pippin knew his sort; he could even see the pale band on the man's finger where he normally wore his wedding ring. The businessman was attempting to find out in a roundabout way if Pippin had a place they could go.

Pippin made vague conversation and peered around, trying to penetrate the shadows. He made out a man sitting by himself in the corner, a location that suggested money and power. He appeared to be wearing some sort of Arab robe. He could be the one.

Pippin was about to let the businessman buy him another drink when one of the brutes came up to say that the corner guy wanted Pippin to join him. The businessman vanished like the morning mist. The invitation was couched as a request but one that Pippin knew he would be ill-advised to refuse.

He had no intention of refusing. This was when he began earning his money.

DAY ELEVEN

Saturday

CHALKE TOOK HER time getting in on Saturday morning, lingering over her half a grapefruit and then resisting the temptation to buy a Danish pastry from the M&S store near the DLR station in Greenwich. She was making herself a cup of coffee in her office when the phone rang.

'DI Ball, Dover, ma'am. It's regarding a person missing, believed drowned, from the Channel ferry.'

'Yes?' Patsy wondered why Dover was contacting her.

'We've identified him as Vincent Alan Pike of Cherry Drive, Prittlewell, Southend.'

Vinnie Pike!

'Hang on,' she said. 'What took you so long? Wasn't that car found the day before last?'

'The car left on the ferry was registered to a Paul Crickley of Erith, ma'am. Turns out he's a small-time car dealer who hadn't bothered to register change of ownership. Nor had Mr Pike. Met officers called at Crickley's address to find it was a car lot. Since no one in the neighbourhood had seen him for a couple of days, local officers assumed that he was the one lost overboard.'

Chalke understood. The Met had screwed up but Ball didn't dare rub it in too much. 'And?'

'Luckily, an officer was in a pub last night when Crickley walked in,' said Ball. 'He'd been in south Wales buying cars. Crickley could show that he'd sold the VW to Pike,' continued

Ball. 'When we tapped in Pike's name, you came up as an interested party, ma'am, which is why I'm giving you a heads-up.'

'What's the thinking on this?'

'We're not ruling out foul play. The weather was calm and the ferry company says it's impossible to go overboard without trying hard. Pike changed £20 into euros on the ferry so it doesn't look as if he planned to commit suicide. We're checking internal CCTV footage and we'll recover data from the external cameras when the ferry docks again this morning.'

'Thank you. I'd be grateful if you'd keep me in the picture.'

'A pleasure, ma'am.'

Chalke was thinking what a greasy twerp when Weaver put his head around the door. He had phoned the previous evening to apologise for the carve-up, which, he said, had come as much as a shock to him as it had been to Patsy. Talk in the morning.

'Sorry I couldn't phone you earlier yesterday,' he said. 'Begley wouldn't let me out of her sight. Any idea why she's got it in for you?'

'None at all,' Chalke lied. She was starting to think it was down to Caro, ridiculously petty as that seemed. Either that, or some of the brass had been dripping poison about her in Begley's ear.

Her boss had a surprise coming.

Chalke's plan was on course. Barney Rubble was working on his successor to back Paul Tyler as chair of the Met Police Authority, and seemed to be making progress. Meanwhile Patsy had rekindled an old flame. How fortunate that she'd had a thing with the current mayor a few years ago, between his marriages.

If the Metropolican Police Commissioner was as politically astute as he was said to be, Patsy would be figuring on his radar quite soon.

At that point Begley was going to be feeling pretty sick.

Weaver promised to keep Patsy up to date with developments.

'Look on the bright side,' he told her. 'This overview gives you *carte blanche*. Make the best of it.'

Chalke intended to, but first she spent the morning clearing her in-tray, determined not to give Begley anything to complain about.

At least office chat had moved on from her humiliation. The news that Bobby Leyden's bird had left him for woman had swept the nick like wildfire.

Chalke had seen Leyden and Bibby leave Davy's together yesterday afternoon. She was waiting for Leyden to explain what that had been about, but his mind was clearly elsewhere this morning. Still, the memory prompted Chalke to do something she'd been meaning to do for a few days – put in a high-security trawl to other Operational Commands on Bibby – just to see what, if anything, emerged. She hoped Weaver wouldn't find out. He would see it as ingratitude at best, back-stabbing at worst.

In the meantime, Leyden was having a shit-awful morning, trying to get on with his worka and ignore the jibes whizzing around the nick like mosquitoes.

He had found the house quiet after Karen and her removal team had left. Which was odd, considering that he and Karen had hardly spoken for weeks. He'd phoned for a takeaway Chinese, turned on Sky and watched football with a couple of cans of 1664 lager. Then he'd celebrated having the house to himself by lying diagonally across the bed. How sad was that?

Still – now life could move on. He found himself wondering if Sandy Wishbourne was available.

At midday Chalke suggested an early break. It was partly to cheer him up, but mostly to prevent him thumping the next copper to take the piss.

Chalke sat on the wall outside the Cutty Sark pub, lit a cigarette and inhaled deeply. Last night's storm had cleared the air, so that Greenwich – a pollution black spot – now felt fresh and clean. Downriver, the new apartment blocks in Silvertown appeared almost within touching distance. The clarity of the air was positively Alpine. It wouldn't last.

A snub-nosed tug was hauling barges of rubbish downriver towards the Essex marshes. Patsy often wondered why the Thames wasn't used more. A huge river ran through the heart of the capital and yet at the same time London's roads were filled to bursting.

Leyden handed her a glass of rosé. Aware that she was avoiding coming to the point, Chalke said, 'I've been wondering why Vinnie Pike only changed £20 into euros.'

'Perhaps he'd needed euros to spend on the ferry.'

'The ferry would take sterling.' Chalke paused before deciding it was silly to beat about the bush. 'I'm sorry about Karen.'

'I'm glad it's over,' said Leyden, relieved that Chalke had finally mentioned it. 'It's just that I never knew she was that way inclined.'

'Everyone's that way inclined, as you put it. Just some more than others.'

'Get away.'

'You should try getting in touch with your feminine side some time.'

'I need to get in touch with my trainer and start preparing for the next fight. I've not been sparring since we found Stan Figgens.'

'Seems a long time ago.'

'Too long for DAC Branson. I had him on the phone this morning asking why I hadn't been to the gym. He said he could get me a transfer to a quieter job if I wanted.'

'And?'

'I told him I liked it here.' Leyden took a gulp of his lager. 'He can't make me move, can he?'

'Not just like that.' Chalke was pleased.

After a moment Leyden said, 'I'm glad Mr Weaver's back on side.'

'It can't be easy for him.' She knew that following the demands of superior officers while remaining loyal to the troops could be a difficult balancing act.

Chalke's phone rang. Speak of the devil.

'Hello, Des.'

'Just thought you'd like to know that Ari O's been found dead.'

'Go on.'

'His body was found naked in a rubbish skip with a firework up his rectum.'

'A firework?'

'A rocket.'

'Christ! Where did this happen?'

'The body was found off Hanbury Street, E1.'

'That's Jack the Ripper territory,' said Chalke.

'DCI Chalke. Are you sure you should be here.' Shug Jolly stood in the doorway of his club, a mug of tea in his hand. 'Your east London oppos aren't going to be happy having you stomping all over their manor.'

'Let me worry about that,' said Chalke. 'You told me you weren't involved in Guinness's death.'

'Aye.'

'But now Ari O's been murdered. Strange how anyone who upsets your family finds themselves dead.'

'Och, come in. You too, Bobby.' Shug Jolly turned to a minder. 'Go and find Rita. Tell him that Merc's one of ours.'

The detectives followed Shug Jolly into the club. He was having even more difficulty walking today, rolling like a sailor on land for the first time in months.

'You've been to the scene?' Jolly waved a hand and four men rose from a table as if lifted by invisible wires. He lowered himself awkwardly, indicating for the detectives to join him.

'Yes.'

The naked and bound body of Ari O, a large rocket protruding from his rectum, was still lying where it had been found, on a pile of rubbish in a rusting skip. The skip was at the rear of a warehouse that was being converted into flats – or had been until the credit crunch came. The body had been found by a totter on the hunt. It could have lain there for days if he hadn't reported it.

'Was he really killed by the rocket up his arse?' asked Jolly.

'Marks around the neck suggest he may have been strangled,' replied Chalke. 'But it's possible he was still conscious when the rocket was inserted.'

'It had been lit though, hadn't it? It did go off?'

Jolly was like the coppers at the scene – fascinated by the rocket. Chalke had had to listen as senior officers debated at length whether it was possible to aim a rocket up an anus. What was it about men and their arses?

'There were burns on the backs of his legs,' she said.

Jolly's melon face creased in laughter. 'It couldn't have happened to a nicer man. Though I have to tell you, his death was nothing to do with us.' Jolly held up a hand as Chalke went to protest. 'Hen, it's not often I give my word to the police, but you have it now. It's nothing to do with me or mine.'

'Even though the killer left something to tie the murder to Guinness's?'

'Did he?' Jolly looked interested. 'What?'

'You mean you don't know?' Chalke was not going to tell Jolly that an admission ticket to Guinness's last cage fight had been attached to the rocket stick. A fact which had convinced Weaver that Ari's death was the second part of the warning to those in the cage fight game – cooperate or else.

'I wouldn't ask you if I did, hen. Though I can find out soon enough.'

'I'm sure you can but you won't find out from me.'

'Och, Missy Chalke, when will you learn it's better to cooperate?'

'Okay, you cooperate. What do you know about Ari O's murder?'

'Not a lot. Ari left the club with a boy before anyone could warn him about Ari.' Jolly chuckled again. 'Turned out it was Ari who needed warning.'

'What about Ari's minders?'

'They stayed at the club.'

'Was that normal?'

'How do I know? Do I look the sort to hang around poofter clubs?'

Chalke raised a hand in apology. 'Sorry.'

'Apparently, Ari didn't usually spend much time with these boys–'

'You said you didn't know what happened.'

'I said, *I* didn't hang around the club. I have someone do it for me.'

'Did you have a man there last night?'

'May have done. Why? Having trouble finding witnesses?'

They were. So many punters claimed to have been in the lavatory at the time that Ari O left with the boy that the investigating team had christened the loos the Tardis.

'Any description of the boy?' asked Chalke, wondering why the head of London's leading crime family was being so helpful. Shug wasn't normally a friend of the police.

'Dark and pretty. Early twenties. Do you want help finding him?'

'The police are always grateful for assistance, Mr Jolly, you know that.'

'Aye, but gratitude can take many forms, hen. Did you know, for example, that Joey Starling lost something important before he was shot?'

'What sort of something?'

Shug ignored the question. 'His people are trying very hard to find it. Offering good money, too.'

'So what was lost?'

'You're the detective.'

Jemma stood on the grass in a simple black frock, her back to the rhododendron bushes, and fought to keep up with Eric, who appeared to be attempting a world speed record playing 'The Sailor's Hornpipe' on clarinet. No sailor had ever danced that quickly. She glared at him to slow down but he was impervious to her looks.

They were playing at the Greenwich Society's summer party, in a small garden under the Observatory. There hadn't been time for a rehearsal. Fortunately, the music was middle of the road – intended not to challenge the punters as they chatted among themselves, sipping their glasses of wine.

The previous evening Eric had come home drunk at midnight, which had annoyed Jemma because she couldn't go to sleep until she'd bolted the door. She'd spent most of the evening talking to her mother on the phone. Then, to avoid thinking about the intruders, Jemma had practised with Bessie until Eric had staggered in.

But now she was enjoying herself.

She felt safe. The sun was shining, the gardens were beautiful and the trio were being well received – even tourists who'd come to be photographed standing astride the Prime Meridian were stopping to listen.

Jemma didn't notice the two men watching from the path. Sullen men with hard eyes, trying to blend in with the sightseers.

She didn't notice a man with sandy hair and a look of grim authority stop to speak briefly to them. His name was Mal Topper, not that that would have meant anything to Jemma. Topper had taken a look at Jemma and Eric before going on to position two more men near the statue of General Wolfe where Eric had left his scooter.

A fifth man was driving the body of Jimmy the Porter to the man's home. Topper's pets were going to feed well.

At the end of the first set Belinda went off to the loo. It was the first chance Jemma had had to talk seriously to Eric. With his hangover, it would have been a waste of time earlier.

She began by telling him how the detectives had spotted the discrepancy in their statements.

'But you told me to say we were by the gates,' said Eric.

'I told you to say we were *outside* the gates.'

'But I saw Starling being shot.'

'Forget about that. If the detectives come back, remember we were a couple of a hundred yards from the mill when we heard the shot.'

'If you say so.'

Eric's attention was already wandering. The next piece of news should make him concentrate. 'Listen, I don't want to worry you... but someone's got into the flat.'

'What do you mean, someone's got into the flat?'

'Yesterday morning. I don't know how. They wanted to scare me, send me a message.'

'What sort of message?'

'They rearranged all the things in my bedside drawer.'

'Tidy is better,' muttered Eric, beginning to play the adagio from Mozart's Clarinet Concerto in A Major.

'What do you mean – tidy is better?'

Eric kept his eyes firmly on the ground. 'It's easier to find things.'

'What are you saying, Eric?' Jemma slapped her hand over his fingers to stop him playing. '*Eric!*'

'Thought you'd like things tidy.'

'It was you?' Jemma didn't know whether to hit him or hug him. 'I've been so worried.'

'Sorry.' He peeped up from the corner of his eye. 'Forgiven?'

Jemma waved her finger under his nose. 'This time – but never again. Promise me that you'll never do that again.'

'Promise.'

Belinda returned. Jemma went to pick up her bottle of water when she saw Eric's mobile on the grass next to his flute. He had forgotten to switch it off. Naughty.

'Eric, turn off your phone.'

'It's okay. It's on silent.'

Now that he thought about it, Eric realised the silent setting was probably the reason why he hadn't been getting any calls or messages the last day or so. He picked up the phone. One text message. From Jimmy the Porter.

They no uv got it – run

What? That didn't make any sense to Eric. He turned off the phone. He'd ask Jemma about it later – if he remembered.

Chalke and Leyden stood at the door of Starling's penthouse flat and surveyed the wreckage. The flat had been totally and systemically destroyed.

The bedrooms, the kitchen, the bathroom. Chaos. Paintings had been pulled off walls, drawers emptied in a frenzy of devastation. Even floorboards had been pulled up.

'At least they didn't find what they were looking for,' Leyden told Chalke.

'How do you know?'

'If they had, they wouldn't have wrecked the whole place. They'd have stopped looking and some parts would be untouched.'

'Seems logical,' said Chalke. 'But how did they get past the hall porter?'

'We don't know when this was done,' said Leyden. 'Once you're up here, no one's going to hear you.'

A relief porter was on duty, drafted in because Jimmy the day porter was off sick. Leyden remembered the scrawny youth with the black eye of a few days earlier.

When they went to check the CCTV cameras, they found they had been wiped cleaned the day before. That would have been when Jimmy was here, the relief porter said.

Chalke phoned Weaver to tell him of their discovery. There was no more they could do here. And she wanted to get out of Greenwich.

'Fancy a trip into Kent?' she asked Leyden.

'Sure, why?'

'We've still not found Graham White. We could have a look at the girl's grave and then go and see Shirley.'

They set off down the A2 with Leyden pointing out the speed cameras. Chalke had driven along this road that first morning, trying to find Falconwood Crem. It seemed a long time ago. As she passed the last speed camera and hit the open motorway, Patsy switched to autopilot and began thinking about the case. The killer had been busy. Very busy.

Vinnie Pike one night, Ari O the next. How had the killer – or killers – known that Vinnie was going to be on that ferry? That Friday was Ari O's night on the pull in his club? And whoever had planned Starling's murder had to have known the details of the movie script, down to the exact scene when he was shot.

The more she thought about it, the more it seemed unlikely that the same person had killed Vinnie and Ari O. It was just too much for one person to do.

What the fuck was going on?

Chalke found she was doing 90mph, overtaking an articulated lorry.

'Any speed cameras along here?' she asked Leyden.

'Don't think so.'

'Good.' Chalke floored the accelerator. The car leapt forward, pinning Leyden back in his seat. 'There was an odd smell the last time I took her over 130. Don't know what it was.'

'I do. I'm sitting in it.'

'Don't you trust my driving?'

'Patsy!' A white van swung out ahead of them. She hit the brake, throwing them against their seat belts.

'Moron!'

'You were doing over a ton ten,' said Leyden, aware that he had called her by her first name.

Chalke too was aware of this. No big deal. Or was it?

She slowed to eighty and returned to her thoughts.

Why couldn't they track down the Dim Reaper? How was he managing to avoid the police hunt? He had to have an accomplice. Maybe he was just calling the shots, his accomplice doing the leg work.

Then there was Johnny Pike to consider. His fingerprints had been found in Yayale's gym. They were reasonably certain that he hadn't gone abroad when he said he had. Chalke corrected herself – when Vinnie said Johnny had. But he hadn't been seen since he'd left Southend.

Chalke had a thought.

What if it had been Johnny's body in the coffin? What if the Dim Reaper had killed Johnny and then burned his body?

Her mobile was ringing. It was DI Ball in Dover again.

'Sorry to trouble you, ma'am, but I thought you'd like to know that we've found a Barclaycard in the name of David A. Shine down the back of a seat on the ferry,' he reported.

'Strange place to find a credit card,' muttered Leyden after Chalke had thanked Ball.

'That's what I'm thinking,' said Chalke.

In the last two days, there'd been several reported sightings of Shine – though none was rock solid. And there had been no one matching the Reaper's description on set when Starling had been shot. That could support Chalke's theory that the Reaper had an accomplice. And now this bank card. Surely that was a plant? Or had the Dim Reaper left it on the ferry on purpose, to send some kind of message? If so, to whom? And why?

Oh God! Her head was going to explode.

'Are we going to get something to eat?' asked Leyden as they arrived in East Malling. 'Just because you're back on a diet –'

'No I'm not,' said Chalke, annoyed that Leyden had seen through her. 'Why didn't you eat at the Cutty Sark?'

Leyden stared glumly ahead until they pulled up at the lychgate of St James the Great next to an Audi TT.

'That's Shirley's,' he told Chalke.

'I had a feeling we'd find her here,' said Patsy.

There was no immediate sign of Shirley Grey but there was no doubt which grave was her daughter's. Fresh red roses lay at the headstone. The grave itself was surrounded by a border of wild flowers set in a manicured greensward. The bench facing the grave bore a plaque in Josie's memory.

This wasn't a grave. This was a shrine.

'I wonder where she is?' mused Chalke.

'Perhaps she's in the village shop,' said Leyden. 'I'll just go and look.'

'If you're that hungry–'

Shirley Grey came around the corner of the church, carrying a trowel and a watering can. She was wearing old jeans and a sweater. She didn't look pleased to see them. Leyden introduced her to Chalke who lied that they'd been on an inquiry nearby and had come to pay their respects to Josie.

'You tend the grave beautifully.'

'I come most days. I like it here.'

'Does your husband ever come with you?'

'Not really. He doesn't have much time–'

'What about Josie's dad. Does he come here?'

'I wouldn't know.'

'When we last spoke, you said you hadn't heard from Graham,' said Leyden. 'That's not true, is it?'

Shirley swallowed. 'He wanted to know how Laurel was doing. She is his daughter. It's only natural.'

Her eyes drifted towards the yew hedge that marked the edge of the graveyard.

'Did he tell you where he'd been?'

'I didn't ask.'

'Weren't you curious?'

Shirley fell to her knees and began working at the flower border.

'He was in Venezuela,' said Chalke. 'What was he doing there?'

'As I've said, I didn't ask.' Shirley picked at an imaginary weed before glancing again towards the hedge.

Leyden moved so that he was facing roughly in the same direction.

'How many times have you seen Graham?' asked Chalke.

'Just the once.'

'That's not true, is it?'

'Two or three times.'

'Do you know where he's staying?'

'No. He phones.'

'How did he know where to find you?'

'I don't know. He just did.'

'Did you know he was on the film set in Greenwich at the time Joey Starling was shot?'

The colour drained out of Shirley's face. 'No.'

Leyden could tell she was lying. He might not have Sandy Wishbourne's training but he knew when someone was telling porkies – especially someone who was such a bloody awful liar as Shirley Grey.

'Where were you last night, Mrs Grey?' asked Chalke softly.

'Last night?' Shirley stopped weeding to look up at Chalke. 'I was at home. Laurel was having a sleep-over at a friend's and Donny was in Southampton – some construction industry get-together. Chelsea are playing there today so he stayed on to watch the game. It was nice to have the place to myself.'

An unnecessary amount of information, thought Leyden.

'And the night before? Thursday night?'

'I went to see a friend just outside Dover.' Shirley began worrying another patch of non-existent weeds.

'You stayed the night?'

'No. I... I'd got mixed up. My friend wasn't in. She was expecting me the next Monday. Why do you want to know?'

'Because on each of those nights a man was murdered.'

'Oh!'

'We can't help remembering how Graham swore to be revenged for Josie's death,' said Leyden.

'He had nothing to do with these killings.' Shirley was now looking everywhere but towards the hedge.

Leyden suddenly thought he saw something move in the shadows. He drifted away, pretending to read the headstones. There was definitely someone behind that hedge. As he got closer, he heard footsteps receding on the gravel. He lengthened his pace, then broke into a run. He sprinted through the lychgate, took a hard left back around the church wall and a left again following the graveyard. A path ran between the yew hedge and the gardens of modern houses. There was no one in sight. Leyden jogged on to where the path joined the High Street.

It was only as he was returning that he saw that the yew hedge, which had appeared to be unbroken, was actually in two parts overhanging a gate into the churchyard.

Someone had been standing there. And Leyden was pretty sure that person had been Graham White.

'Don't worry. I'll wait until we get to Greenwich to eat,' said Leyden as they headed back into London.

'Is that all you think about – your stomach?'

'Don't you ever feel hungry? I mean, it's not natural to go this long without food.'

'All right. If you really want to know, I am a little peckish.'

If she was honest, she was bloody starving. And she was not looking forward to the prospect of a Saturday night by herself. She'd turned down Caro's invitation to a concert on the South Bank to spend time with Mansel Daley – only for his wife to return home early. Patsy forced herself to be positive. It had been a long week. She could do with some quality time. A bottle of wine, watch a DVD, bed early.

She came out of her reverie to hear Leyden say, 'Do you fancy a ruby?'

'Sorry?'

'A Ruby Murray – curry.'

'A bit early, isn't it?' Chalke slowed for the speed camera on Sidcup Road. 'Curries don't taste right before half past ten at night.'

'Okay. Noodles, then. I'll treat you.'

As soon as Leyden spoke, he regretted it. Tai Won Mein with its communal tables and benches wasn't what Chalke was used to. His usual meal there cost around £12, the price of four lettuce leaves in that restaurant yesterday.

'I don't know.' Chalke didn't want to commit herself. 'I might have things on.'

'No problem.' Leyden tried to hide his relief.

'I can't see any benefit bringing Shirley Grey in for questioning,' said Chalke almost to herself.

Leyden guessed why. If Chalke did bring her in, Shirley would be given a nominal, which meant her name would appear on the whiteboard, the new teams would follow up, perhaps make a breakthrough. By keeping Shirley out of the system, Chalke was keeping her to herself.

His boss was playing a dangerous game. If the murders continued and the finger came to point at Shirley or Graham White then Chalke would have a lot of explaining to do.

'It's your call.'

'I could be dropping you in it.'

'I'm always in the shit – only the depth varies.'

'Don't forget you're meant to be taking a statement from Jemma Wodehouse.'

Shit. Leyden had forgotten. 'I'll give her a ring. With a bit of luck she'll be going out, seeing it's Saturday night.'

'That was good timing,' said Jemma. She'd just switched her phone on after finishing the gig. They were packing up now. She'd be home in twenty minutes or so.

Leyden closed his phone and swore.

Chalke was approaching the traffic lights with Eltham Road. She had a choice – via the Tiger's Head and Blackheath or through Kidbrooke. 'Which way?'

'Kidbrooke,' said Leyden. 'It'll take forever getting across the lights at Lee.'

Chalke moved into the outside lane, put her foot down and made the lights on amber. 'So where's this noodle house?'

'In the one-way system, on the corner with Creek Road. You must have seen it. The local Chinese restaurant families set it up to give their kids something to do. Now it makes more money than all their parents' places combined. Hang on. Slow down. That's–'

Ahead, a bus was pulling away to reveal a tall, stooped man carrying a green M&S plastic bag. He was heading towards the Ferrier estate.

'Terry Rich,' said Chalke.

'Turn left,' said Leyden. 'Pull in by the golf driving range.'

Chalke smacked her fist onto the steering wheel. 'What's that bastard doing here?'

'Give him a minute. Let's just make sure he's… yeah, he's heading into the estate.' Leyden pulled out his mobile phone and made a call.

'What are you doing?'

'You'll see. We need to stall him.' Leyden began talking quietly into the phone while at the same time signalling Chalke directions.

'There he is,' he said, as they rounded the corner. 'Let's give the pond life a tug.'

Leyden relayed their location to whoever was on the end of the line and ended the phone call. He and Chalke climbed out.

First shock, then fear crossed Rich's face before he hooded his eyes.

'Surprise,' said Chalke.

'Are you following me, detective inspector?' Chalke noted how he'd dropped her rank to annoy her. *Try harder, scumbag.*

'We picked up this unpleasant smell.'

'What are you doing?' asked Leyden.

'Minding my own business.'

'You should have drowned the fucker,' Leyden told Chalke.

'I'll do a proper job next time, I promise you.'

'I'm writing that down.'

Leyden was fighting the urge to thump Rich. 'What's in the bag?'

'Why should I tell you?'

'Because if you don't, I'm going to rip it out of your hand.'

Rich reluctantly held out the bag. 'A few groceries.'

Leyden looked inside to see crisps, semi-coated chocolate biscuits, tea bags, a packet of pork pies, scotch eggs.

'Don't they feed you in the bail hostel?' asked Leyden.

Rich shrugged.

But Leyden was thinking. Despite the M&S bag, the food had come from a Lidl supermarket. But there wasn't a Lidl around here. In fact, the nearest one was near the bail hostel. Why was Rich buying food there and then carrying it around?

'It's a free country,' replied Rich in answer to Leyden's question.

He gathered confidence. 'I'm going to tell my brief about this harassment.'

'You do that, sunshine.' Two boys in hoodies had begun to kick a ball on the patch of grass across the road.

'My QC will have something to say about this.'

Not if he values his balls he won't, thought Chalke.

'That went well,' shouted Jemma, clinging to Eric's back as they hurtled down Vanburgh Hill.

'Suppose so.'

'Listen, that detective is coming round so you'd better disappear or he'll ask you where you were when the shot was fired.'

'Why is this so important?'

'Please, Eric. For me.'

'Okay.'

Jemma didn't want Eric anywhere near a policeman until she had had time to work on him, and today wasn't the day. She needed to have Eric happy and receptive, not hungover and monosyllabic. Still, at least he wasn't trying to play his piccolo as he rode, which was one blessing. The hill was steeper than Jemma had remembered, and scary – especially the bump as they crossed the railway bridge. She wished she'd gone with Belinda and the instruments, but Belinda had had to go back to college first.

They were approaching Woolwich Road when Jemma first glimpsed the VW Passat with tinted windows. She thought nothing of it until Eric turned right and then left into their street. Looking in Eric's misaligned wing mirror, she saw that the car had followed.

'Eric, there's a car following us.'

Even as she spoke, the car accelerated alongside. Eric braked and tried to weave outside the VW. The driver wrenched the wheel over, forcing Eric into the side of a parked car. The Passat's doors flew open. Two burly men with stockings over their heads leaped out. Jemma half-fell off the bike and ran towards their flat. The men gave chase. Eric flung himself on the rear one, sending them both crashing to the ground. The man scrambled to his feet, kicking Eric in the head. Jemma had reached the gate leading down to the basement when she was grabbed from behind. She lashed out, catching the man across the face. The second man arrived, grasped her other arm. One punched her in the stomach, kicked her legs from under her. They began carrying and dragging her towards the car, Jemma struggling and screaming. The Passat reversed back towards them at speed. Eric charged head-first, butting one man in the back before he was hurled aside. Jemma caught an elbow in the face. Everything became an unreal blur.

There was the screech of brakes then Leyden was sprinting towards them. Chalke was standing by her sports car, talking urgently into her phone, while Leyden was felling a man and getting scythed down from behind, hitting his head on the railings. He struggled to rise. The men were running back to their car. The VW roared off, doors still open. A siren sounded in the distance.

Jemma slid onto the pavement and closed her eyes.

Thirty minutes later Leyden was sitting in the basement flat, drinking tea and thinking that if the paracetamol didn't kick in soon his head was going to explode.

The stolen VW had been found abandoned in Woolwich. Eric had been taken to the Queen Elizabeth hospital suffering from concussion. Leyden was resisting Chalke's attempts to get him to follow. Belinda had dropped off the instruments, and Jemma was now cradling Bessie. Chalke was somewhere outside.

'Well?' asked Leyden softly. 'What was that all about?'

'Don't know,' muttered Jemma.

'Jemma, love. No one gets kidnapped for no reason. Why were those men trying to abduct you?'

'Don't know,' she repeated.

'I assume you don't owe money to the wrong people?'

'No.'

'Upset someone in the criminal fraternity?'

'Don't be silly.'

'It has to be something.'

'Something to do with Joey Starling,' said Chalke from the doorway.

Jemma winced. She was afraid of Chalke in a way she wasn't of Leyden.

'How's Eric?' she asked.

'He'll live. They're keeping him in overnight for observation.'

'Can you make sure that he gets his flute and his bunch of keys or he'll go mad?' Jemma corrected herself. 'Actually, he'll drive everyone else mad.'

'Okay. Talking of hospitals–' Chalke held a finger in front of Leyden's face and moved it slowly towards his eyes and then away. 'Here's another one who needs a check-up.'

'In a while,' said Leyden He didn't want to leave without trying to get to the bottom of the attack.

Chalke shook her head at his stubbornness. 'Do you reckon those guys were professional?' she asked.

'They were hard, I know that. That guy should have stayed down when I hit him.'

'Guinness's cage fighters?'

'Could be.' Leyden fell silent, massaging his temple where a duck egg was growing.

'Those phone calls, Jemma,' said Chalke. Jemma's heart plummeted. 'Starling was trying very hard to get hold of you just before he was killed. Why?'

'Don't know,' muttered Jemma.

'You said he was trying to pick you up and wouldn't take no for an answer,' Leyden reminded her.

Jemma shrugged. 'If you say so.'

'But you phoned him back,' pointed out Chalke. 'What did you talk about then?'

Jemma sighed. Time to tell a version of the truth.

'I wanted the photos he had of me but there was someone in the background calling him a nonce. Joey got furious and put down the phone.'

'Ah,' said Leyden.

Chalke needn't have worried about having a boring Saturday night. By the time Scotland Yard's finest had got in on the act, forensics had finished going over the car, witness statements had been taken from neighbours, and Leyden finally bullied into going to hospital, it was mid-evening.

Jemma refused to go for a check-up. She also refused to leave the flat, despite Leyden's efforts to persuade her that she wouldn't feel safe there alone.

Speed Bump called to say that after the detectives left, Rich had caught a bus towards Lee. Vomit and Mole, whom Leyden had detailed to follow him, hadn't done so because they hadn't had the bus fare.

Leyden's EEG scan revealed no obvious damage but the A&E doctor told him to come back to see a neurologist and take two weeks off work. He shouldn't touch alcohol or even think of sparring for at least a month.

As they left the hospital Chalke said, 'I'm up for those noodles if you are. Even though I still think you should be lying down.'

'Noodles sound good to me.'

Tai Won Mein wasn't as busy as Leyden had expected. They managed to get a table to themselves against the wall, from where Chalke curiously regarded the mixture of students and tourists.

'Are you sure you're all right here?' asked Leyden.

'Fine. What do you recommend?'

'Depends what you like.'

'What do you normally have?'

'Spare ribs or butterfly prawns for starters and then ho fun – they're the big flat noodles.'

'Okay. Let's share some ribs, prawns, pickled cabbage – I'm partial to pickled cabbage – and then veggie soup with noodles for me.'

'Hungry?'

'Just a little.' Chalke's smile began in the corners of her mouth and spread slowly, creasing her eyes, lighting up her face.

Christ, she was gorgeous. And she was his boss.

'Jemma must know why she was attacked, mustn't she?' he said for want of anything else to say.

'I'd say there's a lot we still don't know about that girl,' said Chalke.

'Do you think she could be in the frame for killing Starling?'

Chalke sighed. 'Jemma, the Dim Reaper, Graham White, H. Bruce Montgomery. Who knows? Now relax and stop talking shop.'

'Sorry.'

'And stop apologising.'

The prawns arrived. Chalke dipped one in hot sauce. 'These are good.'

'Honest?'

'Mmmm.' Patsy attacked the food, stopping now and then to drink Tiger from the bottle.

She was doing it again, she knew, making the same mistake she always made – starving herself for days then having a God Almighty blowout.

The main courses arrived. 'Weren't you meant to be doing something tonight?' asked Leyden.

'My sister wanted me to go to a concert but she'll have no problem getting rid of the ticket.' That was true, except Patsy had declined on Thursday. 'What were you planning?'

'Nothing.'

'Getting used to living alone?' As soon as she'd asked, Patsy regretted the question. 'Sorry, that was intrusive.'

'No, it's all right. Me and Karen hadn't been getting on for a while. I don't have much luck in relationships,' he said.

'Me neither,' said Chalke.

Leyden was surprised. Normally Chalke was as tight as a duck's arse about her private life. 'You could have any man you wanted,' he said.

'Every man I fancy is either married, inappropriate or a nasty piece of work. Frequently all three. If there were ninety-nine good men and one absolute bastard in a room, I'd leave with the bastard.'

'I don't believe you.'

'It's true.' Chalke nodded, an almost comically sad look on her face. 'Anyway, what you see isn't what you get.'

'You mean you have hidden depths.'

'More like treacherous shallows.' Chalke looked at Leyden. 'There are worse ways of spending a Saturday night.'

'You mean, you don't mind coming here?'

'Of course I don't mind, you idiot.' They were just two feet apart, leaning towards one another. Leyden found he was holding his breath.

He noticed how diners entering the restaurant all stared in their direction. It wasn't him they were looking at.

'Listen.' Chalke looked up almost shyly. 'I want to say thank you.'

'What for?'

'For standing by me. Many others wouldn't have.'

'Then they'd be cowards and fools.'

'You know, I'm getting fed up with all the office politics. This isn't why I went into the police force. I'm thinking of bailing out once we've caught our killer.'

'You wouldn't!'

'I might, but I don't want your career to suffer because of me.'

'What career?'

'Sit your inspectors' exams, Bobby. You're too good to stay a sergeant.'

The rest of the meal was spent in pleasant small talk. Chalke twice reminded Leyden that the doctor had told him not to drink, only to order him another beer to show she wasn't nagging.

Leyden paid the bill.

Chalke drove him home. Leyden thought about asking her in for coffee or whatever, but he was too timid.

He would have been surprised to learn that Patsy was asking herself what she'd say if he did. If Bobby Leyden had been anyone but her sergeant and closest colleague, she'd have taken him back to her place, locked the door and thrown away the key.

It would have been brilliant at the time. But in the morning...

She drove away feeling virtuous.

Good girl. Saint Patsy.

A very frustrated Saint Patsy.

Leyden switched on the hall light and leaned against the door. He didn't know if it was the bang on his head or the company or both, but he felt a wonderful sense of euphoria. Patsy Chalke had told him he was special, too good to stay a sergeant. And they'd chatted like old friends, comfortable in the silences, neither of them pushing the conversation, just letting things happen.

Was he falling for his boss?

No way. She was out of his league, but...

It was almost half past ten. Perfect timing for *Match of the Day*. He brought a beer from the fridge and switched on the television. He swung his feet up on the sofa, plumping a cushion under his head. The lingering taste of Chinese food mixed with the lager. Memories of a great night.

Five minutes later he was drifting off to sleep when his mobile phone rang. He was tempted to ignore it, but it might be work. It might be Patsy. He stood up, zapped off the TV sound and went to get his phone out of his jacket pocket.

'Hello, sorry–' A female voice. Nervous, unsure. 'Mr Leyden?'

'Speaking.'

'It's Jemma Wodehouse. I'm sorry to bother you, but... well... you were right.'

'Sorry?'

'When you said that I wouldn't feel safe in the flat by myself. You were right.'

'There should be a police car outside–'

'But what happens if someone comes round the back, through the gardens?'

'If you're really afraid, go out to the police car. I'll make a call to let them know.'

'There's a problem with that.'

'Yeah?'

'I couldn't stand being at the flat. I had to leave. I almost freaked. Sorry.'

'Don't worry. Just tell me where you are.'

'I'm outside your front door.'

DAY TWELVE

Sunday

'DANISH, PAIN AU raisin, croissants,' said Chalke, emptying the assortment of breads and pastries onto Leyden's kitchen table.

'How many are you feeding?' he asked.

'I enjoy breakfast on Sundays. It's usually the only chance I have all week.'

Leyden, too, enjoyed Sunday breakfast but he preferred a late fry-up followed by a session in the local and an afternoon doze. And now Karen had gone, he'd been planning to grill kippers which she'd claimed she couldn't stand the smell of. He was feeling gladder that Karen had moved out by the day.

'Okay, where is she?'

'Upstairs, asleep, in the spare room.'

Chalke gave him an old-fashioned look, wondering why Leyden had made an effort this morning – smart slacks and dark green polo shirt. He'd shaved and smelled as if he'd just come out of the shower. It made Chalke suspicious. All she'd done was throw water over her face, pull on old jeans and climb into her car, eyes still closed.

'Where's the coffee machine?'

'What do you mean, coffee machine?'

'Percolator, cafetière, jug, whatever you use.'

'Karen had instant.'

'I despair.' Chalke wished she'd picked up a coffee from Starbucks on the way over. 'I would have come last night, you know.'

'No need. Jemma was a perfect gentleman.'

'Don't tell anyone else she stayed here. Did you stand down the car outside her flat?'

'Forgot.'

'No harm done.'

'But I do have news for you.'

Jemma's arrival with her saxophone had wrong-footed Leyden. He'd offered her a cup of tea.

'Is that all you have?' she had asked.

'There's no wine.' That had been Karen's department. 'I've got some lager.'

'Lager'll be fine.'

Leyden opened a can of 1664 and handed it to Jemma. She'd sat in the corner of the sofa. Like Karen, she'd kicked off her shoes and tucked her legs up under her. Unlike Karen, Jemma looked vulnerable and frightened. The sax rested next to her.

'Love the house,' she said. 'It's... knacky.'

'You mean small.'

'It's got a good feel.'

'Jemma – what are you doing here? How did you know where I live?'

'You gave me your card, remember.'

'That only had a phone number.'

'One of your colleagues told me.'

Leyden didn't believe that, but he let it pass.

Jemma picked at her watch strap with a fingernail. 'I wasn't as brave as I thought.'

'We could put you up in a hotel for the night.'

'I need to have someone around at the moment. Believe me.'

Leyden looked into her pleading cornflower-blue eyes, and lost the struggle. 'I'm going to have to tell my boss that you're here.'

'Why?'

'Because I'd be in the shit if I didn't.'

Jemma rolled a lock of hair around a finger. 'If I'm going to land you in it, I'll go.'

'Let's see what my boss says.'

'I could give you that statement about Starling and the photos. You could say that's why I'm here.'

'It's not that simple, love.' Leyden took his mobile phone out into the kitchen so that Jemma couldn't earwig. He knew what Patsy Chalke would say, and he was right. She started with *'Christ Almighty!'* and ended a three-minute tirade with *'Jesus Christ!'*

In between she'd pointed out the impropriety of having Jemma under his roof, called into question his moral judgement, asked if he really did want a career in the police, and warned him to keep his hands to himself.

'Oh, come on, Jemma's perfectly safe.'

'It's not Jemma I'm worrying about.'

'I'll lock my bedroom door – promise.'

'Seriously, Bobby, there are people who would be queuing up to hang you out to dry if they found out.'

'Stuff them.'

'Okay, if you're sure. I'll bring over breakfast tomorrow and then we'll take her to the station to give that statement.'

Jemma looked up as Leyden returned, hope vying with fear.

'You can stay,' he told her.

'Thank you.' Jemma swallowed back tears. 'I promise I'll pour the shit over Starling.'

'Too late for that. But tell me – how did you ever get involved with him?'

'I was a film groupie. There're a lot of girls like me.'

'So it seems,' said Leyden before he could help himself.

'I didn't know I was being filmed – honest.'

'Did he ever try to blackmail you?'

'No.' Jemma sounded surprised. 'Why should he?'

'Some of the other girls are terrified in case their parents find out. We know Starling was a blackmailer. Two and two could have made four.'

'Not in this case.'

'Fair enough. Although, I've been wondering... where are your parents?'

'I'm... I was adopted. I wasn't told until I was sixteen. Then both my adoptive parents died within six months. Mum tripped over on the pavement, hit her head, had a brain haemorrhage. Dad died of a heart attack – fallout from Mum's death, I suppose. That was when I sort of started to go off the rails.'

'Understandable,' said Leyden.

'I searched for my birth parents but I could only find my father.'

'What happened to your mother?'

Jemma looked down. 'There's no trace of her,' she said quietly.

'But you found your birth father.'

'He was wonderful.'

'Where's he now?'

'He died recently,' said Jemma in a tight voice. 'That's another reason why I didn't want to be alone tonight. There's too much going on in my head.' She gripped the beer can in both hands, gave a heavy sigh. And made a decision. 'You'll find out anyway–'

'What will I find out?'

'Freddy Carter was my father.'

'Freddy Carter?' Leyden struggled to work through the implications. 'That row Freddy and Starling had hours before Freddy's death. Was that over you?'

'Could have been,' said Jemma. 'I'd told Freddy that Starling had pestered me. When I heard that Freddy was dead, I thought Starling had killed him. I couldn't believe it when you let Starling go.'

'Was that why you were on the film set when he was shot?'

'I wasn't on set, I was outside the mill,' she said, not falling into the trap.

'And those men who attacked you this afternoon?'

'I don't know. Honest, I don't.' Jemma yawned as a wave of tiredness engulfed her. 'Sorry, I'm knackered. Can I go to bed now, please?'

'And that was it.' Leyden said, as he finished recounting the events of the previous evening. 'She slept in the spare room. She was there when I got up. I checked.'

The stairs creaked. A moment later, Jemma appeared, tousle-haired and stretching, wearing a purple T-shirt that hung halfway down her thigh.

She saw Chalke and smiled uncertainly.

For a moment, Chalke almost succeeded in placing who Jemma reminded her of. Then, infuriatingly, the likeness faded away like morning mist.

'Morning. Did you sleep well?' asked Patsy.

'Like a log, thank you. Is it all right if I have a shower?'

'Help yourself,' said Leyden.

'I've brought breakfast,' said Chalke.

Jemma's eyes lit up at the sight of the pastries. 'Oooh! Can I take a Danish? I'm starving.'

Chalke's phone sounded in her pocket. She read the message. 'It seems Lucymar's under siege ' she said. 'We'd better get over there.'

'Lock the door,' Leyden told Jemma as he headed out after Chalke. 'Don't let anyone in. And *don't* eat all the breakfast.'

'Here comes the fucking cavalry,' sneered Lorraine Finch as Chalke and Leyden pushed their way through the crowd gathered in the hallway outside Lucymar's flat.

The two young policemen guarding the door looked relieved to see them. Leyden could understand why. On one side, they faced a finger-stabbing Crystal Shine, Lorraine bawling the odds by her side, while behind them, from inside the flat, Lucymar could be heard hurling abuse in Spanish.

'Okay, okay. The show's over,' yelled Leyden.

Chalke ordered the uniforms to get the neighbours back in their homes, then dismissed them. They couldn't wait to leave.

'Lucymar,' called Chalke. 'You're safe now. Open the door.'

'I can still see those bitches,' shouted Lucymar, peering through the spy hole in the door.

Chalke glared at Crystal Shine. 'I told you about coming here.'

'My solicitor says I've a legal right to see if there's anything of mine in the flat.'

'Your solicitor didn't say anything about making an appointment?'

'Yeah, well. Maybe we'll do that tomorrow.'

Lucymar, dressed in a yellow and green cotton print dress, her legs bare, opened the door a fraction. She looked frightened.

Chalke walked into the flat, followed by Crystal and Lorraine. Leyden wondered if they'd find another stoned, naked Rasta – or maybe the same one. Lucymar sidled up close to him.

'Is this her? This scraggy cow?' mocked Crystal.

'Either you shut it or you leave now,' warned Leyden.

'See if there's anything you can prove is yours, then go,' instructed Chalke.

'What do you mean, *prove*? I ain't got any receipts or anything.' Crystal caught sight of the view over the river. Her face darkened with anger.

'That's my DVD player,' said Crystal, pointing.

Lucymar threw her hands in the air. 'Dave brought it. Take it. Why don't you take everything? Everybody want to look through the flat. I'm fed up of it.'

'What do you mean, everybody wants to look through the flat?' asked Chalke. 'Who else has been here?'

'Don't matter.'

'Tell me, or we'll leave you with these women.'

'He said he was a mate of Dave's. He was looking for a safe, but there isn't one.'

'What was his name?'

Lucymar thought. 'Mol Tapper maybe. Something like that.'

'Do you mean Mal Topper?' asked Leyden. 'Shor, well-built, bulging eyes, in his forties.'

'Could be.'

Leyden remembered the calls from Dave Shine's home in Spain that had been traced to a pay-as-you-go mobile phone bought for cash in the Bromley area. Shine's calls to the mobile increased in frequency each time just before he accompanied a coffin back to Britain. Topper lived out Bromley way.

'Do you know Mal Topper?' Chalke asked Crystal.

'He used to sell ice cream outside the school – you remember, Lorr?'

'Yeah. Ain't seen him in years.'

'When did he come here, Lucymar?'

'Maybe Thursday.'

'Why didn't you tell us?'

'What is there to tell? Man comes, looks for something, man leaves. No big deal.'

'What did he give you?'

Lucymar stuck out her lower lip. 'My business.'

Whatever it was had either gone up in smoke or up her nose, thought Leyden.

'Trollop,' hissed Crystal. 'When I'm finished with you, you'll be out on the doorstep without a fucking penny to your name.'

'Huh! What do you know?' Lucymar patted her belly. 'Dave's baby. Dave father, baby gets money.'

Chalke and Leyden arrived back at Leyden's house to find Jemma dressed and tidying up the kitchen.

Leyden described Lucymar's revelation. 'I thought Crystal was going to pass out when Lucymar said she was pregnant,' he grinned.

'Who legally gets the flat – the child or the wife?' asked Jemma.

'Not a clue,' said Chalke.

Leyden put the coffees they'd bought in the microwave as Jemma laid out plates.

It hadn't taken Jemma long to find her way around the kitchen, Chalke thought. 'We're not going to have time to take your statement now so do you want a lift back to your flat?' she said.

The question took Jemma by surprise. She looked around in panic. 'I don't know. I'm not –'

'We could put you in a safe house for a few days.'

'Isn't this house safe?'

'You don't want to go back to the flat?' asked Chalke.

'I couldn't face it. The hospital's keeping Eric in so I'd be by myself.'

'Have you thought about who was trying to abduct you?'

'I haven't got a clue, honestly.' Jemma's eyes were open wide. It wasn't an altogether convincing picture of honesty.

'Do you have friends you can stay with?'

'Not really.'

It was clear that Jemma wanted to stay at Leyden's. Chalke was uncomfortable with the idea. Apart from anything else, she was starting to feel jealous.

Christ! Patsy Chalke jealous. That was a new one.

Leyden said, 'You can stay here if you don't mind being cramped.'

'It's not cramped. It's lovely,' said Jemma.

'Is that all right?' Leyden asked Chalke.

No, it's not bloody all right.

'Yes, of course, no problem.'

Saint Patsy.

*

'There're a lot of people in today,' said Chalke, surprised at the full car park at the nick. She wondered whose budget was funding this Sunday spree. She didn't care anymore.

Cochrane had grabbed one of the bays directly in front of the building. In spite of notices asking drivers to park with their bonnets facing it, so that exhaust fumes didn't seep into the basement cells, Cochrane had reversed in. Chalke knew she should tick him off, but now wasn't the time to make new enemies.

'Once we've got the lie of the land, we'll go and interview Mal Topper,' she told Leyden.

'Okay.'

Chalke realised that she hadn't asked him if he minded working on Sunday.

'This is taking up your day off,' she apologised. 'Did you have anything planned?'

'Not really,' he lied.

Chalke pushed through the door into the Incident Room. Sue Jones was at the photocopier, a pile of statements on the table next to her. Chalke wondered vaguely what she was doing here on a Sunday, but she still felt awkward after her visit to Sue's house so she just said a friendly good morning before going into her office and shutting the door.

She fired up the coffee machine, then noticed that her wooden man was looking sorrowful. She put him in a high kicking pose – or was he goose-stepping? – and went in search of Weaver.

She found him in his office in a short-sleeved shirt. More red veins had appeared in his cheeks in the past week. He must be hitting the bottle, she thought.

'Brenda's not best pleased I'm in today,' he said. 'We're supposed to be booking our South America holiday but I got a three-line whip from Begley. How's Bobby's head?'

'Fine – though he won't be boxing for a while.'

'And Jemma Wodehouse?'

'Keeping a low profile. There's a police car outside her flat.' Chalke told herself that she wasn't lying – not strictly. 'Anything new on Starling?'

'We've not heard back from the FBI on that couple in the video,' said Weaver. '

'Graham White?'

'Still off radar. No sign of the Dim Reaper either.'

'But you fancy White?'

'He's sworn revenge, someone matching his description was on set when Starling was shot, he's staying off radar,' summarised Weaver. 'Why is he playing hide-and-seek if he's on the level? I've asked Kent to step up the search for him.'

'You've definitely ruled out Fleur Varndell?'

'I interviewed her myself. Lovely woman. I mentioned that Brenda was a fan of hers and straightaway she invited us for coffee at the pub where they're filming.'

'Brenda must be thrilled.'

'Not half. We're going tomorrow. Almost made up for me coming in today,' said Weaver. 'Anyway, what are you doing here?'

Chalke explained about Lucymar and the discovery that Topper had searched the Dim Reaper's flat. Did Weaver know of any link between the Reaper and Topper?

'I can't think of one,' he said. 'They'd move in the same murky world but I'm not aware of Shine and Topper ever working together.'

'What about Shine's calls to the mobile? We know the phone was bought in the Bromley area where Topper lives.'

'Lots of villains live out that way.'

'Okay... What do you know about Topper?

'Small-to-medium-time career criminal, peaked at armed robbery. Won his first ice-cream van in a bet eleven, twelve years ago. He saw the van's potential as a way of getting drugs onto the streets. Bought another van, expanded into burgers and started to do well legitimately. Plays the part of the successful businessman – member of the Round Table, etc. Topper's always managed to stay one step ahead of us. I don't think for a minute he's clean, but he's smart.'

'What's this about him having a swimming pool full of piranha and crocodiles?'

Weaver laughed. 'So they say. Story is that he feeds those who cross him to the fish.'

'You believe it?'

'We've never found any victims.'

'Topper and Ari O had a meal together in a Greenwich steak house a few days before Ari O was killed,' said Chalke.

'I saw that report.' Weaver said. 'They'd do business, even though they're poles apart in lifestyle.'

'What do you mean?'

'Topper's a great family man. His two young teenage girls are in some posh private school in Hertfordshire. He keeps them well away from any potential grief.' Weaver smiled. 'In fact, the only plausible story about the piranha concerns a Kosovan who tried to muscle in on Topper's patch. The guy made the mistake of threatening Topper's missus and kids. The Balkan way of doing business.'

'And?'

'The Kosovan disappeared.'

There was a knock on the door.

'Sorry to disturb you, guv,' Leyden said. 'But I thought you'd like to know that the day's suddenly got much better.'

Leyden explained that it had started with an indignant call from Speed Bump.

'Yes, mate,' Leyden had said, still reading the Mal Topper file. The desks around him were filled by detectives from other teams.

He felt like a stranger in his own nick.

'You know that bloke you asked Mole and Vomit to keep tabs on yesterday?' began Speed Bump.

'Yeah.' Leyden turned a page.

'Well, what's your game?'

'What do you mean?'

'The geezer's a cozzer.'

'Why do you say that?'

'Because Mole clocked him this morning, carrying the same bag. He went up to the observation post in the empty flat.'

Speed Bump had Leyden's attention now. 'In Dando Crescent?'

'Yeah, overlooking the garages.'

'And this geezer's in there now?'

'Too right he is.'

'Keep an eye on the flat. If he leaves, follow him. I'll be there in ten minutes.'

Five minutes later, Leyden was directing Chalke across Blackheath, while also pointing out the Princess of Wales pub.

'That's where the teams changed for the first England–Wales Rugby international in 1881.'

'Amazing,' said Chalke.

'Thought you'd be interested,' said Leyden.

They sped into Pond Road, turning left at St Michael's church, then into Blackheath Park and right down Brooklands Park, passing Crystal Shine's home.

'This is an odd way to go,' commented Chalke.

'Quicker than driving all the way to Kidbrooke,' said Leyden.

They pulled up outside a convenience store on Casterbridge Road. Leyden darted inside, then reappeared with the Asian owner and the owner's son.

'Ahmed will keep an eye on your car,' Leyden told Chalke.

'You don't honestly think someone will try steal it, do you?'

'No, but some toerag might be tempted to run a knife over the paintwork.'

Leyden led the way towards a six-storey slab on the edge of the Ferrier estate. From the general state of dilapidation and the few curtains on the windows, it was clear that much of the block was unoccupied.

As they skirted a line of garages, Leyden hit a button on his phone. 'Okay, mate, where are you?'

Speed Bump appeared from the stairway of the block opposite and scurried over.

'You saying that this geezer's not a copper?' he asked Leyden.

'He's a nonce called Terry Rich awaiting retrial for raping an eleven-year-old girl.'

'How come he's getting a retrial?'

'His brief claims that his confession was made under duress. DCI Chalke here tried to drown him.'

'Fucking brilliant! Sorry, miss, didn't mean to swear.'

'Rich has previous,' continued Leyden. 'You remember Angie Bartles, seven-year-old from Eltham?'

'Course I do.' Speed Bump bristled with anger. 'And this filth is here, on our manor. Fuck that!'

'Where's he hiding?' asked Chalke.

'Fourth floor. Middle one of the three flats. He's put a piece of lace curtain up at the window.'

Chalke and Leyden peeped round the corner.

'He can see the garages from there,' Speed Bump went on. 'That's why I thought he was keeping a watch on the Somalis, know what I mean?'

'What else can he see?' asked Leyden.

'There's the school, the playground... Fucking hell.'

'Is the playground open at weekends?'

'No. But the kids play on the grass next to it. Our Janna's out there now. Christ! I'll rip his fucking throat out.'

'Hang on.' Leyden grabbed Speed Bump's arm as he started towards Dando Crescent. 'You must have mates with kids at the school.'

'I can sort out this fucker.'

'Listen to me,' said Leyden. 'You go in there one-on-one, you'll be done for GBH. Get a crowd together then scarper before the police arrive. No one's going to be looking too hard for you.'

'Jesus, Bobby!' Chalke was aghast.

'Perhaps you could wait back at the car, guv. Don't you have some shopping to do in Blackheath? Part for the coffee machine, maybe, a pair of shoes…?'

'I –'

'You ain't seen us, Speed Bump, okay?' said Leyden, wishing Chalke would just go. 'You ain't seen us.'

'Ain't seen you since Thursday, mate.'

'Good boy. Now don't kill him, and let the women get stuck in.'

There was nothing lowlife hated more than a child molester. Thievery was condoned; robberies winked at; prison and violence, were a way of life. But a nonce was the lowest of the low. The authorities recognised this by segregating sex offenders in prison under rule 43.

But it would be worse if the women on the estate got involved. The men would kick the crap out of Terry Rich. The mothers would cut off his balls with a rusty knife. In these matters, the female was the deadlier of the species.

Speed Bump scuttled away. Leyden began steering Chalke back towards her car.

'I'm not sure about this, Bobby.'

'Speed Bump and his mates will just pick up where you left off.'

'Why not just arrest Rich for criminal trespass, being in breach of his bail conditions, conspiracy?'

'Yeah, yeah. I'll do all that – after he's had the shit kicked out of him.'

'I don't know.'

'Look, Rich is clearly planning to pick up another little girl. Now he won't. When he gets out of hospital, he'll go back inside on rule, and after this you'll have no problems at retrial.'

'Suppose so,' said Chalke.

There was an angry roar in the distance. 'Shit! That's kicked off quickly. Please, guv, go. You can't be seen anywhere near this.'

'What about you?'

'This is my turf. I belong here. If *you're* seen, there'll be questions.'

'Okay. Get this sorted and then we'll go and see Topper.'

'Will do.'

'Call me.'

Chalke squeezed Leyden's hand. He'd never know how close she came to kissing him. Then she spun on her heel and walked quickly back to her car.

The roar came again, louder this time. Leyden hurried across the sparse grass towards Dando Crescent. A few locals were standing in the foyer, listening to the shouts from above. Leyden took the stairs three at a time.

He arrived on the fourth floor to find a baying mob cramming the corridor. Leyden battled his way through to the flat. The door hung off its hinges. In the living room, two men were holding Rich while others fought to punch and kick him.

'That's enough,' shouted Leyden. The mob ignored him. 'I said, that's enough. Let the fucker go.'

Reluctantly the men holding Rich released him. He sunk onto the floor, groaning softly. Mole darted out from the crowd and kicked him in the back.

'NO!' Leyden threw Mole away and took a hard, measured kick at Rich. 'The kidneys are lower. About… there.'

The nonce would be pissing blood for a month.

'Anyone see that?' asked Leyden.

'Ain't seen nothing,' replied Speed Bump on behalf of the mob.

'Okay. Listen. I'm going to call an ambulance and then I'm going to call for back-up,' said Leyden. 'Don't be here when they arrive.'

There was a scramble for the doorway.

Once he was alone, Leyden brought out the kiddie porn he'd brought from the evidence room, pressed Rich's fingers on the pages, then dropped it under the chair.

Bring it on. Mal Topper cradled the glass of vodka and ice and checked – yet again – that the electronic protection surrounding his home was functioning. Blinking green lights on the control panel showed the circuit of hidden sensors. The monitors capturing real-time images from hidden CCTV cameras showed nothing untoward.

Topper wished the killer would make a move. He was ready. The killer was going to walk into a trap. Piranha feed.

Reassured that there was no immediate threat, Topper returned to the poolside where he finished the bottle. It had been full when he'd started drinking four hours or so ago.

Topper blamed it on the bad feeling in his gut.

And Topper trusted his gut.

He had already moved his family out of possible danger. His daughters had gone straight from school on Friday to stay with their mum in a London hotel for a shopping weekend with a musical thrown in. The girls were returning to school this evening while his wife was going to stay with her sister in Romford.

The alarm vibrating in his pocket sent him shooting to his feet. It meant that a car had crossed the cattle grid.

He weaved his way back indoors. A monitor showed a Mercedes sports car coming slowly down the track towards the house.

Topper pulled the short-barrelled pump action shotgun from its clip under his desk. The gun was licensed and legitimate. The Smith & Wesson pistol hidden in the ankle holster was not.

*

'We've had a busy morning,' observed Chalke as she accelerated past a camper van.

'Tell you what,' said Leyden as they took the next bend at speed. 'Let's live to see the afternoon, shall we?'

'You're a very nervous passenger, aren't you?'

'Not usually.'

'I've just had a thought. How's Lucymar managing for food and drink – and drugs?'

'I'll find out.' Leyden pulled out his mobile. 'Lucymar. Bobby Leyden. Just wanted to check that you're all right... Yeah, they won't bother you again... By the way, how're you managing for money?' He grinned. 'How much? Fine. Take care.'

'Well?' asked Chalke.

'She found £3,000 in the Dim Reaper's underwear drawer.'

Leyden's phone rang. 'Hello, Sandy... Terry Rich? What, no one? Thanks for calling. Cheers, love.'

He turned to Patsy.

'Rich has regained consciousness. He's got a broken nose, fractured cheekbone, lost a few teeth, three cracked ribs, dislocated wrist, possible internal injuries. Lewisham hospital's keeping him in for observation. And do you know what? No one on the Ferrier heard or saw a thing. According to Sandy, the borough commander's already decided not to waste resources on the assault. He knows no one's going to bubble.'

'I'm not proud of this, Bobby.'

'Rich was spying on a school playground. Christ knows what the sick bastard was planning. This is for the best.'

'I suppose so.' Chalke was still not convinced. 'How far to Topper's place?'

'Dunno. It's somewhere the other side of Biggin Hill.'

'You mean you're going to let me use the satnav?'

'Probably the only way to find the place.' Leyden hesitated. 'Listen… I think you should know, I saw Carl Cochrane with Topper in a pub a few days ago. He's not registered as one of Carlo's snouts. I checked.'

'Why didn't you tell me?'

'No reason to, but Sue Jones says Carlo's been really bad tempered recently, making sneaky phone calls in the corridor. That sort of thing'

'Christ!'

The satnav told them to turn off the lane, over a cattle grid and down a potholed track. Leyden guessed the potholes had been left deliberately to stop unwanted guests arriving at speed.

Topper's sprawling ranch-style bungalow sat in a hollow, a curtain wall protecting the outbuildings. They drove through an arch flanked by a pair of cartwheels to park beside a Land Rover Freelander.

Chalke and Leyden were approaching the front door when a metallic voice ordered, 'State your business.'

Leyden glanced up to see a CCTV camera trained on them. The voice was coming from a tannoy under the guttering.

'Police.' Chalke and Leyden held up their warrant cards towards the camera.

'Wait there.'

Chalke and Leyden waited. After a lengthy interval, the door opened and Mal Topper appeared. Chalke was struck by his broad shoulders, his bulging eyes – the man must have an overactive thyroid – and the short-barrelled pump action shotgun in his right hand.

'We need a word with you,' said Chalke.

'Yeah? What about?'

'Murder.'

'Also, why you appear to be crapping yourself,' added Leyden.

'Who says I am?'

'People don't generally answer the door carrying a shotgun,' said Leyden.

'It's legal. Twenty-five inches. Want to measure it?' taunted Topper, referring to the minimum length of a shotgun before it was deemed to be an illegal sawn-off.

'I believe you,' said Leyden. 'But still I want you to break the gun and make it safe.'

'I've a licence. I'm on my own property –'

'I don't give a shit,' said Leyden. 'The way you're holding that gun represents a threat to human life. Carry on like this, mate, and you won't have a licence this time tomorrow. Then what will you do when the big bad wolf comes calling?'

'Fuck off. I know about you, Leyden. You're not so hard.'

'Want to put down that gun and find out?'

'Oi, you two!' said Chalke. 'When you're done.'

Topper gave up the staring match with Leyden. He led them through an ultra-modern kitchen out into the swimming pool area with a bar, tables and sun loungers. An empty vodka bottle sat on a table next to a packet of cornflakes and a bowl. Past the swimming pool, a lawn with flower beds and ornamental trees led down to a stream. 'You want a drink?'

'We're on duty.' Topper must be out of his tree if he'd drunk all that, thought Leyden, though he was hiding it well.

'Suit yourself.' Topper brought another bottle of vodka out of a small fridge.

'You searched Dave Shine's flat,' said Chalke. 'What were you looking for?'

'That's my business.' Even drunk, Topper was very sure of himself.

'Does Shine owe you money?' asked Leyden.

'Like I said, my business.' Topper threw a handful of peanuts down his throat. 'I did nothing criminal, so you can't touch me.'

'You had lunch with Ari O the day before he was killed,' continued Chalke.

'Christ! I suppose you can tell me what time I had a shit this morning.' Topper dropped ice cubes in his glass and topped it up with vodka.

'What did you want with Ari O?'

'It was more what he wanted with me.'

'And that was?'

Topper took time to answer. 'It's fair to say that he was a worried man. Turns out he had cause to be. A rocket up his arse! What a way to go.'

'You're not worried you could be next?'

'Not a chance.'

'The Dim Reaper doesn't scare you then?'

'Who?'

Chalke changed tack. 'Why was Ari O worried?'

'Let's just say something he and Guinness were involved in had gone toxic.'

'Cage fighting.'

'Could be. He wanted me to smooth things over, if you know what I mean.'

'And did you?

'Did what I could.'

'Is it true that you keep some strange pets?' asked Chalke.

'You want to see?' Topper picked up his glass and set off unsteadily around a corner to a concrete pit under a Dutch barn structure. The pit was filled with brackish water with a mud bank in the middle. Lying motionless on the bank were two ten-foot long alligators.

'Ronnie and Reggie,' said Topper proudly. 'Florida Swamp 'gators. They had a good feed last night but you should see them move when meat's thrown in. They can cross that water before you can blink.'

The pit had vertical sides. Once in, no one could climb out.

'Follow me.' Topper set off towards a breeze-block building under a corrugated iron roof. He slid back the metal door and flicked a switch. Arc lights clacked on above a pool surrounded by a raised walkway. There was a guard rail between the walkway and the pool, with a gate set in the railings.

'These are my favourites.' Topper went to a metal bin, picked up a pair of tongs and brought out a slab of bloody meat. 'Watch.'

He tossed the meat into the cloudy water. For a second, there were only ripples – then the pool erupted into boiling maelstrom.

'You wouldn't want to fall in there with a cut finger.'

'No.' Chalke suppressed a shudder.

'You want to see my snakes?' asked Topper. 'I've a python as thick as your waist. It can eat a young goat in one. Fucking awesome.'

'Not if you're the goat,' said Chalke.

'Yeah, but I'm one of life's pythons, ain't I?'

'I can't see how crocs and killer fish are going to protect you,' said Leyden.

'I clocked you as soon as you crossed that cattle grid.'

'Yeah, but someone bent on mischief isn't going to come down the drive, are they?'

Topper led the way outside. 'You see those hedges up there on the hillside? There're all sorts of cameras and electronic tripwires hidden up there. Anything moves in this valley, I know about it.'

'What if they came from the far side?' Leyden pointed to the slope across the stream flowing at the end of the garden.

'Same again. Every barbed wire fence contains a sensor and there's another beam along the riverbank. I've got remote control cameras to check out any false alarms.'

'Get many, do you?'

'Foxes set off the alarms. That's why I have the cameras.'

'Sounds as though you're well protected,' said Chalke.

'State of the art, this lot. You want to see?'

It was exactly what Leyden had been hoping for.

'Like Fort Knox,' he complimented Topper ten minutes later, as he finished showing off his security set-up.

Topper smirked.

As they were about to leave, Chalke said, 'I was thinking, you know things about Ari O's murder that aren't in the public domain. You must have mates in the force.'

'Lady, I have mates everywhere.'

'Of course! You know Carl Cochrane, don't you?' said Leyden.

'Do I?' Topper wasn't that drunk. Leyden could almost see the man's defence shields go up. 'Nah, don't think I do.'

Chalke made one last effort. 'Mr Topper, it's clear that you're expecting unwelcome guests. Let us help. We could pool resources. We want to catch the killer as much as you do.'

'That's where you're wrong, lady. I don't want to catch him. I want to slot him.' Topper hiccupped loudly.

Back at Leyden's, they found Jemma cleaning the kitchen. A bunch of flowers sat in a beer mug on the living-room table.

'I couldn't find a vase anywhere,' she said.

'That's because I haven't got one,' said Leyden. 'What are you doing?'

'The place was filthy. If you'd been a restaurant, you'd have been closed down.'

'But I'm not a restaurant.'

'I've put a load of your things in the wash. The laundry basket was overflowing.'

Chalke burst out laughing at the look on Leyden's face.

'I was going to do it tonight,' he said.

'I've saved you the trouble,' said Jemma firmly. 'There's hardly any food in the house. The supermarket's open until four. Shall I go shopping?'

'Um–'

'I'll cook you an Italian meal.'

'I was going to get a takeaway.'

'I'll go shopping,' said Jemma, as if it was all agreed.

'Yeah, fine.'

Leyden fled.

'It's good to see Jemma's making herself at home,' said Chalke innocently when they were back in the car. 'Wonder how long she'll be staying.'

'Not long,' said Leyden.

Chalke wouldn't put a bet on that. She couldn't help noticing that she hadn't been invited to Jemma's Italian night.

The Incident Room had thinned out. No one wanted to work Sunday afternoons, not even for the overtime. There was a message for Chalke that Ahmed Hiktas had phoned from Cyprus. He would try again at five o'clock. Meanwhile Weaver was about to take Sue Jones to the Tolly Shop. Chalke decided she had time to join them. It'd been another long day, and it wasn't finished yet.

Chalke walked up the road with Sue, with Weaver and Leyden following behind.

'I'm surprised you were still working,' Chalke said.

'What else have I got to do? Also, this new lot don't know how the system works so they keep asking for help. I don't mind.'

In the pub, they took their drinks into the garden.

'So how was Mal Topper?' asked Weaver when they were seated around a table.

'Heavily into the vodka,' replied Chalke. 'He was pissed enough to show us his pet alligators and piranhas.'

'You should see the electronic stuff he's got protecting the place,' said Leyden. 'Really impressive.'

'What sort of stuff?' asked Sue. 'Sorry. I don't mean to be nosy, it's just that I've always been fascinated by security systems,' she added in explanation.

'State of the art. A sensor on the cattle grid, electronic beams along the hedgerows feeding back to monitors in his study–'

'He's even got infra-red cameras to track intruders,' added Chalke.

'Sounds as if the place is impregnable,' said Sue.

'Nowhere's impregnable if you have the keys to the castle,' said Leyden.

'So did you see any way in?'

Leyden was happy to display his expertise. 'Along the stream behind the house,' he told Sue. 'Topper's had to position the beams two feet above the ground because foxes kept setting them off. It'll be simple to crawl under a beam and then come down the stream itself. Easy-peasy.'

'I'd say Topper's hoping to lure the killer into having a go at him on his home turf,' said Chalke.

'Yeah, he's like a spider waiting for the fly to walk into his trap,' agreed Leyden. 'Trouble is, we'll never know if he succeeds in killing the fly.'

'What do you mean you'll never know?' asked Sue.

'Topper'll feed the body to the piranhas or the crocs.'

'We'll know,' said Chalke. 'If the killings stop, then Topper will have got him. Are you all right, love?'

Sue Jones had turned pale. 'I'm fine. Sorry. I've just got a bit of a thing about crocodiles,' she said.

Ahmed Hiktas was as good as his word. Chalke's direct line rang dead on the stroke of five.

'Good day, Patsy,' came the gravel voice.

Patsy, now. Perhaps Hiktas had had a good lunch. 'İyi günler,' she replied. 'Good day.'

'You speak Turkish?'

'Just a few phrases. I once spent a month in Istanbul.'

'Istanbul is not Turkey. It is a mongrel city – its head in Europe, its belly in Asia.'

'That's very profound,' said Chalke.

'We are a profound people,' said Hiktas. 'By the way, I was surprised to hear that you are working on Sunday.'

'You are,' she countered.

Chalke heard the rasp of a match and Hiktas inhale deeply. It wasn't fair. Why wasn't she allowed to smoke in her own office? What harm would she do to anyone but herself?

'Saturday night is a bad time here. We spend Sunday sweeping up the pieces. I have Monday off. A moment, please.' There was a gunfire burst of Turkish, then a laboured whirring sound. 'That's better. It is over thirty degrees here. My fan has failed so I ordered my assistant to liberate the chief's.' Hiktas sighed. 'Of course, he will steal it back tomorrow.'

'Right.'

'Those cufflinks in the shape of Turkish Republic of Northern Cyprus–' continued Hiktas.

'Yes?'

'We've failed to match them to any association or club.'

'Well, thanks for trying. Any further developments on Locke?'

'Not yet. But something will come to light – we are a small island, people talk. I will know who killed Locke. I may not be able to bring the case to court, but I will know.'

'And no more half-eaten corpses found up in the hills?'

Chalke heard Hiktas draw on his cigarette. 'One is enough. By the way, he was one of yours.'

'Ours? You mean a Brit?'

'We identified the body yesterday. One Vincent Pike.'

'Surely you mean Johnny Pike?' asked Chalke.

'Vincent Alan Pike,' repeated Hiktas. 'We're quite certain.'

Normally Shirley Grey enjoyed dusk but today it was making her sad. The close of the day, another day since Josie died.

The churchyard held a solemn stillness; the hum of a drowsy bee; the last swallows swooping around the grey stone tower.

Shirley was on the verge of tears. She was trying to convince herself that the grave itself wasn't important. Josie lived in her heart; her daughter's memory would travel with her wherever she was in the world.

She leaned forward on the bench, elbows on knees, hands together as if in prayer.

'Donny excelled himself today,' she murmured. 'We had to go out to a lunch party with people Donny knew in the building trade. He got drunk again. Then he and his cronies disappeared to watch football on TV. I didn't know a soul.'

Donny had given her a pitying look when she'd said that she was leaving to visit the church. No doubt he'd told his cronies that she had a screw loose, that she was obsessed with her dead daughter.

'Still, not much longer, love.' Shirley picked a blade of grass. 'I've arranged for Mrs Sheldon to come to see you. You remember Mrs Sheldon – lived two doors down, always had a soft spot for you. She'll come every week and I've given her money for fresh flowers. And I will be back – I promise you, Josie, one day I will be back.'

The ghostly white shape of a barn owl glided by.

'Laurel thinks I'm doing the right thing. She's already taken some of her clothes – not that Donny would notice if she emptied her entire bedroom. They've never got on. Poor Laurel's been very good about leaving the pony and her friends. She hasn't said a word to anyone.'

The twilight was deepening, the outline of the church tower growing stronger against the amber lights of the village. Warmth came off the weathered stone.

Shirley's eyes brimmed with tears. She had to be strong – for all of them. She rose reluctantly. 'God bless. You'll always be in my heart. Goodbye, darling.'

Shirley Grey left the churchyard as though walking to the gallows. She did not look back.

'You're a fast worker, son,' his neighbour Vic said to Leyden as he was getting out of his car.

'Sorry?'

'Right little homemaker you've got there. She's had the Hoover out all afternoon. If she hasn't been playing that saxophone, that is. I had to turn up the telly.'

Leyden grasped that Vic was talking about Jemma. He changed the subject. 'You off to the pub?'

'Too right.'

'There's no football on Sunday evening, is there?'

'Italian Serie B. Ancona and Rimini.'

'Right. Enjoy.'

Leyden opened the front door to be greeted by unfamiliar smells. After a second, he identified them as furniture polish and cooking. There were now two bunches of flowers in the living room, both in vases. Leyden walked into the kitchen – and stopped dead.

Jemma – in the apron that he'd been once given as a joke – had her back to him, chopping something. Every inch of the work surface was filled with sliced onions, diced bacon, egg yolks sitting upright in their shells, a pot of cream, potatoes in one saucepan, broccoli in another. Two plates covered in cling film sat next to a bottle of wine.

Jemma saw Leyden and removed her iPod earphones.

'I wasn't sure what time you'd be home.'

'Fine,' he stuttered. 'Where did you get all this lot from?'

'The supermarket. I told you I was going.'

'And the vases?'

'Phyllis, next door. She's very sweet.' Jemma wiped her hands. 'Are you ready to eat or would you like a beer first?'

'I could do with a beer.'

'Go and sit down and I'll bring you one. We're having prosciutto and melon to start, then tagliatelli carbonara followed by veal chop and thyme roast potatoes. And the veal is not Dutch, before you say anything. Oh, and a bottle of Barolo. Will that be all right for you?'

'Um… yes.' Leyden didn't know what was wrong with Dutch veal. He thought it better not to ask.

He found himself in the chair by the fireplace with a beer, a bowl of peanuts and the day's newspapers. Tempting smells wafted from the kitchen where Jemma was singing. All that was missing were his slippers.

This was scary.

Johnny Pike lay in the long grass and looked down on Mal Topper's sprawling home. Pike's black overalls, balaclava, parachute boots and black gloves made him virtually invisible in the darkness.

He had spent the past hour crawling along a ditch, inching beneath the electronic beams before squeezing under a barbed wire fence. So far he had managed to penetrate the Topper's first ring of defences without setting off the alarms.

Pike decided to rest before pressing on. He rolled onto his back to gaze up at the stars.

The sight brought back memories of another night on a different hillside three weeks before. Another night spent waiting and watching.

Tonight, the stars were distant silver pinpricks. In Cyprus they'd seemed larger, golden in a softer sky. There'd been scents of rosemary and wild thyme, the murmur of the sea.

As he lay resting on the silent Kent hillside, the memory returned as vividly as a hallucination.

*

He looked down at Georgie Locke's villa, set on the low headland, flanked by rocks and a shingle cove. The lights of Kyrenia glowed behind the hills to his left. Nearer, all was blackness.

A full hour had passed since Locke had turned out the villa's lights before moving. In Devonport Johnny learned the importance of proper preparation and planning. Then his time in prison had instilled patience.

But patience was not a virtue that his cousin Vinnie had shared.

The night before Vinnie had gone by himself to have a look at Locke's villa.

He had never returned. Johnny had to know what had happened to him.

The sliver of moon dipped towards the sea, casting mellow beams over the inky water. It was impossibly beautiful.

He made his way carefully down the barren slope, avoiding the patches of scree, clinging to the sparse bushes before crossing the rough coast road that petered out a mile further at a pebble beach.

He ran towards the high garden wall and leaped for the top, got a handhold and pulled himself up, grateful for the hours he'd spend working out in the prison gym. He'd jumped down and frozen in the wall's shadow, listening.

He crouched before the kitchen door, and sensed something swing at his head.

Bright lights flashed on.

'Vinnie last night. Now you. Get in the house. Go on.'

It was Locke, a baseball bat grasped in both hands.

With Locke behind him, Johnny stumbled into an open-plan living room with a picture window looking out to sea.

'Sit.' Locke pointed to a low sofa. He went to a refrigerator and brought out a can of Tuborg lager.

'Where's Vinnie?' asked Johnny.

'Vinnie forgot himself. I had to put him under manners.'

'Where is he?'

'Up in the hills. The animals will have got to him by now.'

It took a moment for Locke's words to sink in. 'You killed him.'

'He was trespassing.' Locke took a pull of his beer. 'You and Vinnie were always losers.'

'I asked for your help while I was inside,' said Johnny desperately. 'With my girl. What happened?'

'Never got round to it, did I?'

Hatred surged through him. 'Where's my money?' he asked lamely, knowing it was useless.

'What money?' Locke weighed the baseball bat in his hand. 'Don't you understand? You aren't getting any money. You never were getting any money. You was fitted up, you tosser. Fitted. Up.'

In his heart, Johnny had always known this. Through all those years in prison he'd known, but he hadn't been able to face the truth. The banknote wrapper in the bin, his DNA on the glass – none of it had made sense.

Vinnie had refused to believe it. That's why they'd come out to Northern Cyprus to see the man who'd recruited them. To get their share of the money.

'Then Vinnie came here to my house and threatened me. Me. Georgie Locke. I've shat out bigger fuckers than you two for breakfast.'

'But –'

'Why do you think we never let you see anyone else's faces?' continued Locke. 'Why do you think you was kept apart?'

'I wouldn't have said anything. I didn't say anything.'

'Not much you could say, was there? You didn't know anything.'

'Was this your idea?'

'No. It was down to the bloke who set it all up. I don't have a clue who he is. But he's a class act, I'll tell you that.'

'Who recruited you, then?'

'What's it to you?'

'Curious.'

'You know what that did to the cat. Those animals up in the ra-vine are going to have a feast.'

'So what harm's it going to do?'

'You know Dave Shine, the undertaker they call the Dim Reaper?'

'Heard of him. Don't know him.'

Locke crushed the beer can. 'And now you never will. Let's go.'

'You don't have to do this, Glockie.'

'You don't have to do this, Glockie,' mocked Locke. 'You're wrong, my son. I do.'

Johnny Pike understood. Locke was going to kill him, he'd al-ways been going to kill him. He and Vinnie were loose ends. With them dead, the circle was closed.

'Come on,' ordered Locke. 'I'm taking you to see your cousin.'

Johnny took a step towards the door, stumbled and put out a hand to a coffee table to steady himself. Locke glanced away, look-ing for his car keys on the counter that separated kitchen and living room.

Johnny's hand closed around a heavy ceramic ashtray.

He hurled it back-handed at Locke's head. Locke saw the ashtray at the last moment, and flung up a hand to protect his face. John-ny threw himself forward. He caught Locke in the chest. Locke fell backwards, Johnny on top. There was a crack as Locke's head hit the tiled floor, then he was still.

Johnny pushed himself away. A thick dark substance leaked from Locke's skull. His watery blue eyes were wide open.

He was stone dead.

Now on the English hillside, Johnny again smelled the petrol. He recalled how he'd thrown match after match trying to get it to light, the heart-stopping whoosh as it had finally ignited, how he'd almost been trapped by the flames.

Recalled how he'd sworn an oath.

His phone vibrated.

Showtime.

'So where are you supposed to be?' Patsy Chalke asked Mansel Daley.

'Chambers. I told her I had to prepare for a hearing tomorrow.'

'And if she phones chambers?' asked Chalke.

'She'll get the answer phone. The system only works when the secretaries are in.' He leaned out of bed, picked up the bottle of Sancerre and topped up their glasses. 'I thought you'd be pleased.'

'I am.' Patsy let herself drift. Boccherini on the BeoSound, the lights of London spread out through the open window, sandalwood and myrrh in the burner. It was a pleasant way to spend Sunday evening, even if her lover had to go soon.

Sometimes she preferred to sleep alone. Other nights she enjoyed feeling the warmth of a man's body. She wouldn't know which she was in the mood for this evening – until she had no choice. The lot of the mistress.

Mansel Daley dipped a finger in the wine and drew a circle around Patsy's left nipple.

'I hope you're going to lick that off.'

'Never entered my head, your honour,' he said, bending over her breast.

Patsy murmured in pleasure.

After a few moments, Mansel Daley asked softly, 'What are you thinking about?'

'Vinnie Pike's body being found on Cyprus.'

'You do have the most romantic thoughts.'

'You can talk. The other day you were thinking about Terry Rich in bed. No, listen. The body's been there for three weeks. That means that we've been talking to Johnny – not Vinnie – all this time.'

'If you say so.' Mansel Daley was doing his best not to encourage Chalke.

'Shit.' Patsy sat up so violently that she almost sent Mansel Daley tumbling. 'It was there all the time. Those stick-man doodles by Pike's phone. Anyone who'd won a prize for painting would have been more artistic. Why didn't I see it?'

Mansel Daley let her explain. 'Not even the Baker Street Boy himself would have spotted that,' he said. 'Did Johnny know that his cousin had died in Cyprus?'

'He must have done. But why did he take Vinnie's identity?'

'Isn't that tomorrow's problem?'

'Suppose so.' Patsy closed her eyes and let him stroke her body with his fingertips. 'And now it turns out that Jemma Wodehouse is Freddy Carter's daughter.'

'Patsy!'

'Sorry… It's hard to switch off completely. I am trying.'

'You managed it a few minutes ago.'

'That was lovely. Thank you.'

'Since we're talking shop, I don't suppose you know anything about Terry Rich getting beaten up earlier today?'

'Ah–'

'Ah?'

'I'll only tell you if you promise not to stop doing what you're doing.'

'Promise.'

'Rich set up a lair in an empty flat overlooking a school playground. The locals found out,' explained Chalke. 'A swift retrial and fifteen years, wouldn't you say?'

Mansel Daley sucked his teeth. 'What Rich does while on bail doesn't affect the facts of the original case and I'd oppose any attempt to put such information before a jury.'

'Oh, come on.' Patsy sat up again. 'You get Terry Rich off and he'll attack another little girl. He won't be able to help himself. The man needs medical help.'

'You mean castration.'

'Castration would do. Can't you get him to plead guilty on grounds of diminished responsibility and cut a deal so that he serves his time in a psychiatric hospital?'

'I can't see Rich buying that,' said Mansel Daley. 'He thinks he's going to walk.'

'You could point out that he's going to be held on remand pending retrial, and that there are probably more guys from the Ferrier estate in prison than out. They won't take kindly to the idea that Rich was planning to nonce one of their own kids. Being on rule won't help him. He'll be living in fear every second. The screws'll want a quiet nick, so they'll turn a blind eye–'

'You want me to threaten him for you?'

'You've got it in one.'

'Patsy, Patsy, what am I going to do with you?'

'Hopefully the same as you did a quarter of an hour ago.'

'Come on, give me a breather… Though I will have a word with Rich, see what I can do.'

'That's my boy.' Patsy ran her hands slowly down his body. 'There. Better again.'

But as they began to make love, Patsy found herself thinking of Bobby Leyden at home with Jemma. She had to force herself to concentrate.

'That was amazing,' said Leyden as he spread the last of the Gorgonzola onto a biscuit. 'Really amazing.'

'Thank you.'

'No. Thank *you*. Now, sit,' ordered Bobby as Jemma started to get up. 'I'll take the dishes out. Just give me a minute. I'm too full to move.'

It was the best meal he'd ever eaten at home, possibly the best anywhere. Certainly better than that lunch with Patsy Chalke.

'Where did you learn to cook like that?'

'I did an Italian cookery course as part of my rehab in the

States. It's great to be able to put it to use. Eric won't let me near the kitchen.'

'How is Eric, by the way?'

'He says he's found a way of playing his key ring.'

Leyden laughed. 'He seems a character.'

'He is but… "

'What are you doing about clothes and things?'

Jemma twisted a lock of hair around a finger and chewed the end. A habit, Leyden was coming to recognise, that indicated she felt uncomfortable.

'I got a couple of things from the flat this afternoon. I hope you don't mind.'

Leyden noticed that she was wearing a different top from the one she'd had on this morning. Great detective he was.

'No… Course not.' What could he say after she'd cooked a meal like that? And cleaned the house. 'Fine.'

'Did I tell you I'm thinking of going to Australia for Christmas? Freddy's brother lives there.'

'You can afford it?'

'Freddy left me everything, including his house in Wandsworth.'

'You're a wealthy young lady.'

'I'd rather be penniless and have Freddy alive.' Tears weren't too far away.

'You had some time together.' Bobby couldn't stand women crying. It made him feel helpless. 'What I don't understand is why you can't track down your real mother. She can't just have vanished. What's the name on the birth certificate?'

'Jasmin Jobbins.'

'You could check if she's changed her name by deed poll. Of course, she may be dead.'

'She's not dead,' said Jemma quickly.

'How do you know?'

'I just know.'

*

Shirley Grey let herself into the house. The downstairs lights and the television were on. Donny was snoring loudly on the sofa. No doubt, true to form, he'd have come in, brought out a bottle of Chivas Regal from the fridge, collapsed in front of the TV, and fallen asleep within minutes.

Soon he'd snore so loudly that he'd wake himself up. And the first thing he'd do would be reach for his glass and take a gulp of whisky.

Once, she'd found it amusing. Now it disgusted her. Donny disgusted her. He lay there like a beached whale – a large man with too much flesh on his red potato face, crumbs on his shirt and strewn over the carpet.

She'd never loved him. She'd married him for Laurel's sake. In recent years she'd ceased even to like the man.

Shirley went around closing the floor-length curtains, turning down the sound on the TV set, switching off lights. Only then did she take out the small wrap of paper containing the fine white powder. She poured the powder into the glass of whisky, stirred and added ice cubes.

The powder would make the whisky taste odd but Donny wouldn't notice. He couldn't tell good whisky from bad, despite always insisting on ordering the most expensive – annother thing that annoyed her.

'Donny,' she said quietly. 'Donny.'

He gave an almighty snort, jerked upright, stared at her with unseeing eyes, reached out, took a hefty swig of whisky and flopped back.

'Top you up?' asked Shirley.

Donny grunted his assent.

Ninety busy minutes later, Shirley left the house. The boy had slipped away shortly before, with his fare back to Thailand and £2,000 in his pocket. It was worth it.

When Donny finally woke, the first thing he would see – when he could focus – was a photograph of the naked boy giving him a blowjob.

Then he'd see the other photos – Donny in suspenders and black stockings, Donny in a maid's dress that didn't reach down to his groin, Donny and the boy in a variety of poses.

All lit so that you couldn't fully see Donny's face, couldn't see that he wasn't fully conscious – but lit enough so you knew it was Donny.

Gamma-hydroxybutyric acid, or GHB – also known as G-juice, bedtime scoop, cheery meth and by a dozen more names. The date rape drug.

Shirley had originally thought of getting a local prostitute for the part. She'd even gone trawling for the right girl until she'd re-alised that Donny was the sort who'd happily show his mates the photographs. He wouldn't be showing anyone these shots.

Maybe when he came round he'd be so befuddled that he'd think that Shirley had found the photographs and had walked out in disgust.

That would give her a bit of breathing space until he discovered that his bank account had been almost emptied. Almost, but not quite. Shirley had left him enough to pay next week's wages. If he was clever, the business would survive. But he'd need another Shirley White.

Graham was waiting at the end of the drive. Laurel was already at the hotel near Gatwick. Tomorrow they flew to Caracas.

A new life, or rather a rekindling of an old one with Graham on the tourist ranch he was running near Angel Falls.

Shirley was looking forward to it, but she'd come back one day. She had promised Josie.

Almost midnight. Mansel Daley had left an hour earlier, leaving Chalke unable to sleep. She kept wondering why Johnny Pike had pretended to be his cousin, and whether his fingerprints in Guinness's gym had an added significance.

She thought about phoning Leyden. She wondered how the Italian meal had gone. She hoped Jemma had cooked him Spaghetti Bolognese. A weak, watery, tasteless spag bol with a bottle of Valpolicella and a frozen gateau to follow.

It was what Leyden deserved. She was still waiting for him to tell her he'd had a drink with Bibby. Chalke didn't like the fact that he hadn't mentioned it. She'd been going to raise the subject in the noodle house but the evening had been going so well that she hadn't wanted to risk spoiling things.

She hoped – she really hoped – that Leyden wasn't going to let her down.

Patsy got out of bed, went out onto the balcony and lit a cigarette. Her landline rang. Who'd call at this time?

The duty officer with another murder?

Barney Rubble with mistress problems?

Leyden with indigestion?

'Hello?'

'Patricia. It's Alison Begley. Sorry to trouble you so late. I hope you weren't asleep?'

'No, I was reading,' lied Chalke.

'I know it's late but… well… I'd like to clear up any misunderstanding that may have arisen between us.'

'Yes?'

'I hope you don't feel that you've been sidelined by the structural changes in the current investigation.'

Patsy didn't reply.

'That was never my intention,' Begley went on. 'I simply wanted to free you up, to give you the widest possible remit. So that your talents could have room to unfurl.'

Patsy was starting to enjoy this call.

'I happened to be at an event with the commissioner earlier this evening,' said Begley. 'I didn't realise you knew each other?'

'Just socially. You know how it is–'

Smiling, Chalke put down the phone. At least that was one thing sorted. She only wished there was someone there to share the good news.

DAY THIRTEEN

Monday

SIX HOURS LATER, Chalke was woken by a phone call from a former lover, currently a senior officer in SO15 – Counter Terrorist Command. Following a tip-off, an anti-terrorist team had raided a room in a Paddington hotel where four stripped-down M16 assault rifles had been discovered in a golf bag in the wardrobe.

If that wasn't unusual enough, what was really strange was that the guy they'd arrested wouldn't stop talking. He'd gone into motor-mouth mode in the hotel room, hadn't shut up in the car on the way to Paddington Green, and was still gobbing off.

He claimed to be in the process of hiring foreign bodyguards for a businessman called Tosh Bibby. The former – and hoping-to-be-reinstated – lover had spotted Chalke's high-security trawl on Bibby so he was giving her an early heads-up. She'd hear through official channels later. Sorry if he'd spoilt an early morning shag.

He hadn't spoilt anything, said Chalke. In fact, he'd just earned himself a slap-up meal.

'Just a meal?' he'd complained.

'We'll see,' said Chalke, already distracted by the plan that had begun to form in her head.

It would take some favours, but wasn't that what new best friends were for. She picked up the phone and called Begley. It was the first of many calls before she left for Greenwich.

Knowing that it was going to be a big day, Chalke chose a

charcoal grey Armani trouser suit with a white heavy cotton shirt, a Mojave pendant on a leather thong around her neck, a different Jo Malone blend – sweet lime and cedar – and a careful application of eye make-up, partly to hide last night's excesses.

It was past nine o'clock when she climbed the stairs to the Incident Room.

Weaver appeared. He, too, was smartly dressed. 'I'm taking Brenda to meet Fleur Varndell later this morning,' he reminded her.

'Great. By the way, Begley phoned. All is sweetness and light between us again.'

Weaver grunted. 'I still wouldn't trust her,' he said.

'I won't.'

On the way to her office, Chalke tapped Leyden on the shoulder for him to follow her. She tried to adjust her wooden man into a thoughtful pose, but only succeeded in turning him into an obsequious waiter. She tried again.

'How's Jemma?' she asked casually.

'Still in bed when I left.'

Chalke resisted the temptation to ask which bed. 'What did she cook you last night, spag bol?'

'Let me think. Prosciutto, tagliatelle carbonara, veal chop with all the trimmings, followed by Gorgonzola cheese. And a bottle of a red wine called Barolo. Ever heard of it?'

Chalke raised her eyes to heaven. 'So what's she planning to do today?'

'She can't go back to college or anywhere too public so she's going to reline the kitchen cupboards and practise the sax.'

'Bobby?'

'Yes, guv.'

'Don't you think that she's rather getting her feet under the table?'

'What can I do?' Leyden opened his hands in a gesture of helplessness.

Chalke bit her tongue. 'Get hold of Mal Topper. Let's see if he's still scared.'

Leyden was back in two minutes. 'Topper hasn't arrived at his yard. His foreman has tried his home and his mobile. No reply.'

Chalke and Leyden looked at each other.

'Ronnie and Reggie?'

'Or the piranhas.'

This was going to scupper Chalke's plans but she couldn't help that. She snatched up the phone. 'Get the locals to meet us there. I'll get an area car.'

The journey was a nightmare. It was Leyden's fault: he'd told the driver he should be able to get to Topper's in fifteen minutes, and now the man was determined to get there in thirteen. Patsy cursed the tradition that placed the senior officer in the front seat, holding her breath as they flew through red lights, screeched on burning tyres the wrong side of bollards, missing oncoming buses by inches. And all the time, a siren wah-wooing inches above her head. By the time they arrived at Topper's home, her nerves were shredded. Two local bobbies were waiting for them.

'Anything?' asked Chalke, noting the Freelander parked in the same place as yesterday.

'No, ma'am. The house appears to be empty.'

Chalke rang the doorbell. A snatch of music came from deep in the house.

'What's that?' inquired Chalke, thinking the tune was familiar.

'It's the theme from *The Good, the Bad and the Ugly*,' said Leyden.

'No, it's not. It's from *A Few Dollars More*,' retorted a uniform. 'It's the music the watch plays – you know, the one the baddie keeps opening.'

'The one he got when he raped the guy's sister?'

'Yeah. Bet you can't name him.'

'Eli Wallach?'

'No, he was the Ugly in *The Good, the Bad and the Ugly*. Gian Maria Volonte.'

'Excuse me,' said Chalke.

'Who was the one with the long-barrelled pistol, then?'

'Lee Van Cleef.'

'I thought he was the villain in *The Good, the Bad and the Ugly*.'

'He was Angel Eyes but in *A Few Dollars More* he played Colonel Mortimer.'

'EXCUSE ME,' said Chalke.

'Iconic, though,' murmured Leyden.

Chalke gave him a warning look.

The uniforms went to start searching the bungalow.

'Watch out for Ronnie and Reggie,' warned Leyden.

'Ronnie and Reggie?'

'Topper's killer crocs. If he's dead, they could well be on the loose.'

The uniforms edged back towards their car.

'I didn't want them trampling all over a possible crime scene,' Leyden explained. 'Best if it's just the two of us for the moment.

'Very sensible.'

The house was locked. They followed the wall until they came to a metal gate opening onto the pool area. The gate was open.

Some things were the same. The bottle of vodka and the glass were on the table with the ice bucket.

Some things were different. The pile of clothing and the shotgun hadn't been there before.

The door into the house was ajar.

'Doesn't look good.' They walked around to the alligator pit and peeped over the top. Ronnie and Reggie lay motionless on the mud flat.

'Can't see anything,' murmured Chalke.

'I'm not sure what there'd be to see.'

'They couldn't eat a whole person, could they?'

'They could if he was chopped into pieces.'

Chalke shuddered.

'Let's go look at the piranhas.'

They saw the splatter of rust spots as soon as they climbed the steps to the walkway around the pool.

'Blood,' said Chalke.

'There's more here,' said Leyden. 'And look' – he pointed to the edge of the pool – 'That looks like faeces.'

They looked down into the water. A pale rope with tassels at either end floated on the surface of the still water.

Chalke examined the splatter pattern. 'I'd say someone was brought up here, cut to draw blood, and then thrown into the tank.'

'And they were conscious at the time, which is why they were crapping themselves,' added Leyden.

'Topper or his victim?'

'Topper.' Leyden suddenly recognised the rope. 'That's the belt Ari O was wearing around his Arab robe thing. Whoever killed Ari O killed Topper.'

Patsy pulled out her mobile. The tank would have to be drained and the contents of the piranhas' stomachs examined. She wondered how quickly piranhas digested their food. She put in an urgent request for a fish expert and a veterinary surgeon. Hopefully there would be sufficient flesh in the fishes' stomachs to identify Topper's DNA.

'All that protection turned out to be useless after all,' said Leyden.

'What were you saying to Sue? That you could get into this place from the stream?'

'Yeah, but you'd have to know where all the electronic beams and all the alarms were. I wonder if Topper was taping everything.' Leyden turned to walk into the house.

'No. Wait until the SOCOs get here.'

Chalke's phone rang. Not a number she recognised. 'Hello.' Chalke listened, a frown forming on her brow. 'Say again. *They know you've got it. Run.* From Jimmy. When was it sent? Saturday afternoon. Thank you.'

'Sounds interesting,' said Leyden.

'Jemma's friend Eric has just remembered he had a message on his phone.'

'That porter at Starling's flats was called Jimmy,' recalled Leyden.

'And the message came just before Jemma was attacked.' Chalke checked her watch. 'That young lady has a lot of explaining to do.'

Seats 5–8 in carriage G of that morning's 10.13 a.m. Paris to London Eurostar were occupied by four former members of the Russian special forces.

The men from Spetsnaz Vympel squadron, specialising in counter terrorism, fell asleep within minutes of the train leaving the Gare du Nord.

Officers from the DCRI – *Direction Centrale du Renseignement Intérieur* – had interviewed them at Charles de Gaulle airport, when they had arrived the previous afternoon from Kiev. The men claimed they were en route to Britain to work close protection for an exiled Russian oligarch. It sounded plausible, following in the footsteps of other former Spetsnaz.

They had lied.

French intelligence officers secretly photographed the men and followed them to their hotel on the Rue Lafayette near the train station in the 10th arrondissement.

They watched the Russians check in and then left, flagging the men to the British Special Branch officers working out of the Gare du Nord monitoring passengers to London.

The men had been ordered to keep a low profile while in Paris;

to do nothing to attract attention and to split up into pairs. They ignored their orders. Paris was different from the Kola peninsula where they'd spent months training; different from their last post in Yekaterinburg; different from Moscow. More fun.

They spent the night in Pigalle's sex district, drinking brandy and ogling strippers. Running out of cash, they had befriended and then mugged a rich Ukrainian.

Each picked up a prostitute and each demanded their money's worth, which was why the men fell asleep as soon as the train left the station.

They didn't notice the unscheduled stop at Folkestone.

'They know you've got it. Run,' repeated Chalke.

Jemma stared down at Leyden's kitchen table.

'You wouldn't like to tell us what "it" is, would you?' asked Leyden.

'It's a key,' said Jemma in little more than a whisper. 'I wanted to make Starling give me back those videos of me.'

Chalke glanced at Leyden.

'Jem, love,' he said not unkindly. 'What key? I don't have a clue what you're on about.'

'I broke into Starling's flat to try to find the videos. I thought they'd be on a memory card of some kind. Eric knew the porter, Jimmy, so I sort of borrowed the key to the flat. But Jimmy didn't know,' she added quickly.

'Was Eric was with you?'

'No.' Jemma twirled a lock of hair around a finger.

Two lies in two sentences, thought Leyden. It seemed Jemma was determined to carry the can herself.

'But then Starling came back. I hid in a cupboard,' continued Jemma. 'He had a phone call from some guy talking about the key. Starling told him not to worry, he had it on a chain around his neck, so I knew it had to be important. When Starling took off the chain to go and have a shower, I swapped the key for another one.' The words were tumbling out now. 'I was going to get Starling to give me my videos in return for the key.'

'Starling wasn't wearing a chain when he was shot,' said Chalke.

'I'd say he noticed the key had been swapped first thing that morning. That's why he went mental at that girl Tinga. Remember?'

'But then he was killed.'

'I... I didn't know what to do,' stuttered Jemma.

'Someone else found out you had the key?'

'I guess so.'

Starling had been speaking to Jemma from his trailer while they'd been waiting outside to interview him. The next day the porter had had a black eye. It fitted.

And once Starling was dead, others would have followed in his footsteps. That was why the flat had been trashed.

They needed to find Jimmy the Porter – if he was still alive.

'Where's the key now?' asked Chalke.

Leyden would have bet she'd say on Eric's key ring. He was wrong.

'Bessie's been looking after it.' Jemma picked up the alto sax. She twisted off the bell, reached into the body and brought out the key which had been held in place by tape.

'And no one knew?'

'Eric did. He recognised the sound wasn't the same. No one else.' Jemma handed the key to Leyden.

'Why didn't you tell us sooner?'

Jemma shrugged. 'I was waiting to give it back. I knew I'd bitten off more than I could chew.'

Chalke and Leyden looked at one another. Chalke said, 'Would you wait upstairs, Jemma? We have things to talk about.'

'I won't run away.'

'Good girl.

'What do you think it's for?' asked Leyden once Jemma had left.

'Don't know. Maybe a safe deposit box.' Chalke turned the key in her fingers. 'We need to know who phoned Starling.'

'We can check phone records but I'd bet the call came from a pay-as-you-go mobile.'

'Someone wants this key badly enough to try to snatch Jemma in broad daylight.' Even as she spoke, small bells began ringing at the back of Chalke's brain. 'Listen–'

Leyden put his head on one side. 'Can't hear anything.'

'No... Listen. Think about it – the Reaper was about to buy two new funeral parlours abroad, Minicab was looking at acquiring a car franchise, Guinness was moving into cage fighting big time. Even Starling planned to spend three months in the Beverley Wilshire. It all takes money.'

'So...?'

'None of the Maidstone raid money was ever recovered. What if this was a divvy-up among the robbers?'

Leyden was sceptical. 'They've been bloody patient. Not like most villains.'

'But they haven't been like most villains,' said Chalke. She felt sure she was on the right track. 'Apart from the Pike cousins, no one's ever been caught. All the financial monitoring – bank accounts and so on – produced zilch. Remember how the Reaper's funeral business expanded after the raid. And Minicab bought his chain of dry-cleaners. Guinness bought his pub. Perhaps they were given some money – but not so much that it would show up. And the one guy who did start splashing cash about... what was his name?'

'Barry Cowburn.'

'Barry Cowburn was killed.'

'It's an idea,' said Leyden.

'Thanks for your support,' said Chalke.

'No, I mean it's worth thinking about. But it doesn't take us any nearer to the boss man, does it?'

'Funny you should say that.' Chalke hadn't told Leyden about the dawn phone call about Tosh Bibby.

Leyden waited for her to enlighten him. When she didn't, he asked, 'So what about Jemma?'

'We could start with breaking and entering, withholding information, conspiracy.'

'She's had a hard time,' said Leyden. As if on cue, upstairs Jemma began playing 'Nobody Knows the Trouble I've Seen'. 'You could put in a word with the CPS.'

'You saying you want me to go easy on her?'

'Prison could send her back onto drugs. You know how much of it there is inside.'

'I suppose Starling could have planted the key on Jemma,' said Chalke in a flat, neutral voice.

'Planted?'

'He could have been planning a double-cross. Jemma didn't know the key was there.'

'But how could Starling have planted it?' asked Leyden.

Chalke didn't have a clue. 'We'll work something out.'

'Um–'

'Not a word about this to anyone. We'll keep it to ourselves until we know the key's significance. Okay?'

'Okay.'

Jemma was summoned back to the kitchen. She looked even paler than normal.

'You did the right thing handing over the key,' began Chalke.

'But –'

'Perhaps you'd like to give some thought to how it came to be in the sax,' Chalke continued. 'Did you ever take Bessie on the film set?'

'No, I –'

'No need to go into it right now. Just get a story. Okay?'

'Thank you.'

Leyden was afraid the girl was going to burst into tears. 'Keep your head down.'

'Can I stay on here, then?'

Leyden glanced at Chalke.

'I suppose so,' she said reluctantly.

'What would you like for dinner tonight?' Jemma asked Bobby.

'Nothing. Really, it's all right,' stuttered Leyden, aware of Chalke's death stare.

'You said you liked steak. Would that be all right – with mushrooms, tomatoes, onion rings?'

'I love onion rings,' said Leyden in spite of himself.

'Sorted,' smiled Jemma.

In her car on the way back to Greenwich, Chalke decided she could no longer put off confronting Leyden about Tosh Bibby. She didn't understand why he hadn't told her about their meeting. Bloody Leyden confused her. Their relationship confused her.

Everyone said that Bobby was as straight as the day was long. Chalke was about to find out if winter was approaching.

'I saw you with Tosh Bibby on Friday evening coming out of Davy's,' she said abruptly. 'You never mentioned it to me.'

'Sorry. He was offering to feed me the same sort of information he's been giving Mr Weaver once the chief super retires,' said Leyden.

'Why didn't you tell me?'

'I was going to – but I've not had time to think it through.' Leyden turned to look at her. 'I don't trust Bibby.'

'I think you're right not to,' said Chalke. 'I reckon Bibby's been using the police to do his dirty work. Every tip-off he gave Weaver was for his own benefit.'

'You mean like the people-smugglers?'

'Exactly. Swanson was a competitor in the haulage trade.'

'I should have told you.' Leyden held up his hands in apology. 'But where does that leave Mr Weaver? Do you think–'

'Don't know.'

Back at the police station, Chalke went straight to her office, telling Leyden, 'Get Carlo in here.'

Cochrane came in looking like a man with a guilty secret.

'You were seen drinking with a man under investigation for drug trafficking,' began Chalke. 'You didn't report the meet.'

'Who?'

'Mal Topper.'

'Who said I met him?'

'I was in the British Oak that evening you two were in the bar,' said Leyden, feeling guilty for fingering his colleague.

'I've known Mal Topper for years. He came up with the odd tip.'

'Now he's been murdered, you know we're going to be crawling over his affairs like a plague of locusts,' said Chalke. 'Going to find anything there on you, are we, Carlo?'

'No way.'

'Good. But do remember to log meets with contacts in future,' said Chalke. 'Right, matter closed.'

Once Cochrane had left, Leyden muttered, 'That denial wasn't the most convincing I've ever heard.'

But Chalke had a faraway look. 'What if I was on the right lines with the murders all along?'

'How do you mean?'

'Think about it. Your man said the word was that Guinness and Minicab had been on the Maidstone raid. Georgie Locke was suspected of being involved but it couldn't be proved. He phones the Dim Reaper. There's the Reaper's prints in Guinness's gym. Johnny Pike's too. We saw Guinness and Ari O together. Ari O met Topper in a Greenwich restaurant.' Chalke's voice rose in excitement. 'They all know one another. God, I've been thick.'

'Never mind, guv. It could happen to anyone.'

'That was not the reply I was hoping for.'

She grinned. Leyden grinned back.

'Okay, what now?' he asked.

'Now we go talk to Tosh Bibby.'

The four gaunt-faced men with hair cut to the bone stood on the concourse of St Pancras International station forcing other travellers to walk around them. The man who would claim to be James Harding, but who was in fact Johnny Pike, had been watching them from the window of the coffee shop. Finally he approached.

'I'm James Harding. Welcome to London.' He shook hands with each of the men. 'Come. I have transport.'

The Spetsnaz men threw their bags into the back of a people carrier. The leader, Yuri, sat up front.

The car headed down Farringdon Road and cut along the river, pointing out the Tower of London and Tower Bridge before continuing east along the Highway and through the Limehouse Link.

The traffic was heavy, drivers slowing for the speed cameras through the Link. Emerging into daylight, the car skirted the skyscrapers of Canary Wharf and turned down into the Blackwall Tunnel.

Tosh Bibby was expecting them.

As if to prove that crime did pay, Bibby lived in an eighteenth-century country house, complete with walled garden, orangery, tennis court, indoor swimming pool and golf driving range. There were two orchards and a large paddock. The tall iron gates to the grounds bore a coat of arms – three inverted black chevrons on argent surmounted by a crow. The arms of a former lord of the manor.

'It's Harding,' said Johnny Pike into the intercom. 'I'm here with the Russians.'

The gates opened electronically.

The drive, flanked by ancient beech trees, ended in a gravel forecourt. Steps led up to an iron-studded wooden door, out of character in the soft yellow stone facade.

Bibby appeared. He looked drawn and nervous. 'So,' he said to the Russians, 'you reckon you can make this place secure?'

Yuri gave a Slavic shrug. 'We'll see. You got cameras? Alarms?'

'I'd rather have men with guns.'

Yuri nodded. 'Guns is better.'

'Good friend of mine relied on electronic gadgets,' continued Bibby. 'Got topped last night. Fed to his own piranhas.'

'Could we have a word,' said Pike to Bibby.

'Yeah, come in.'

Pike ordered the Russians to carry out a security assessment of the grounds. The men split into pairs and set off.

'You're the first people I've let through those gates today,' said Bibby, leading the way into the house. 'I'm not trusting anyone.'

'I'm afraid the Russians are asking for their money up front.'

'No problem. What about the guns?'

'They'll be delivered them later. I didn't want to travel with the Russians and the weapons.'

Johnny Pike followed Bibby along a high dark corridor and into his study where French windows opened out onto the croquet lawn. A large globe on a tripod stood on the polished floorboards next to an old-fashioned desk, two leather armchairs and a huge plasma TV. Bookshelves reached up to the ceiling. A brushed steel refrigerator sat in the corner.

Bibby swung out the copy of Hals' *The Laughing Cavalier* behind his desk to reveal a wall safe. He began turning the dial.

'How much do you want?'

'Two million pounds.'

Bibby froze. 'Come again?'

'Two million pounds.'

'That wasn't the deal.'

'Yes, it was.'

Bibby squinted, looking properly at the intruder for the first time. 'Bloody hell! You're Johnny Pike! What happened to Harding?'

'He's been lifted by the cozzers.'

'How did that happen?'

'Doesn't matter. You owe me. That crap about my DNA on the glass in the manager's house. I didn't touch any glass. You set us up.'

'All right, son. But I haven't got two million here. The loot's in a safe deposit box in industrial diamonds. Unfortunately that tosser Starling managed to lose the other key.'

'Not my problem.'

'If you'd hang on –'

'You're joking. How much have you got?'

Bibby produced a bundle of £50 notes from the safe. He tossed them to Johnny.

'There're fifty large ones there,' said Bibby.

'Keep them coming.'

Bibby reached into the safe, brought out a similar bundle and lobbed it towards Johnny, deliberately letting it fall short. Bibby turned back to the safe. Johnny moved sideways and crouched down behind the globe.

Bibby spun around. There was a pistol in his hand.

Johnny heard voices. The Spetsnaz were returning.

'They can bury your fucking body.' Bibby thumbed back the hammer, his finger tightening around the trigger.

Johnny fired first. The round passed through the globe and hit Bibby in the chest. Johnny fired again. Bibby stumbled back. He sank to his knees, opened his mouth to speak, slid sideways to rest against the unread books, and died.

Johnny was about to replace his gun in the ankle holster – both liberated from Mal Topper – when the Russians burst in. Only now they were carrying automatic pistols and wearing blue baseball caps that said *Police*.

'Drop the gun,' shouted the man he knew as Yuri. 'Armed police. Drop the gun.'

Johnny didn't understand. The Spetsnaz guys were police officers? It didn't make sense.

Patsy Chalke appeared behind them. They really were police officers.

A poem he'd read in prison filled his head.

He balanced all, brought all to mind. The years to come a waste of breath. A waste of breath, the years behind. In balance with this life, this death.

Or something like that.

He had killed seven men. He would die in prison.

The coppers were fanning out, crouching, each holding a pistol in a two-handed grip, pointing at his body.

In his mind, he said, *'I couldn't do the time; I couldn't go back in there again. Sorry, love.'*

Johnny Pike stood up and raised his arm.

And waited to die.

'One death, maybe, but we never expected it to end in *two* deaths,' said Begley down the phone.

'Let's take the positives. The house is a crime scene,' said Chalke. 'We have access to Bibby's laptop, all his files. His safe is open, and I've found a key in it which I believe will lead to what's left of the money from the Maidstone job. Happy days.'

'There'll be an inquiry.'

Begley was bottling it. It was true, the operation had gone slightly tits up. Still, looked at most ways it was a good result.

It was time to play her trump card.

'We'll have the Police Authority behind us,' she said.

'You don't know that.'

'I do, actually.' Chalke walked up and down the mansion's fore-court, her shoes crunching on the gravel. 'My friend Paul Tyler is becoming the chair after all. It's being announced this afternoon.'

'Oh, I see,' said Begley quetly.

Patsy's phone bleeped to indicate that she had an incoming call. She checked the number.

'Speak of the devil,' she told Begley. 'He's trying to get through now. I'd better answer.'

Chalke lifted her middle finger in farewell, as she hung up on her boss.

'Congratulations, Paul.'

'Thanks. Rubble says I have you to thank, but that's not why I'm calling.'

You could always rely on a politician to put gratitude to the back of the queue, thought Patsy. 'Yes?'

'I'm with the commissioner at a children's bravery award at Mansion House. Reporters here are hearing reports about Russian special forces killing someone at the home of a master criminal,' said Tyler. 'Apparently, you're involved.'

'Paul –'

'The commissioner has gone off to find out what's happening. I thought I'd give you a ring. *Are* you involved?'

'I can see the bodies from where I'm standing,' lied Patsy. 'Listen, Paul. I'll tell you and then you can pass it on to the commissioner. How's that?'

'Sounds good.'

'Okay.' Patsy collected her thoughts. 'Early this morning, following an anonymous tip-off, Counter Terrorist Command arrested a mercenary recruiter called James Harding. In his Paddington hotel room they found a cache of automatic weapons. Harding told SO15 that he'd hired four former Spetsnaz to run protection on a businessman called Tosh Bibby. My pal tapped

Bibby's name into the PNC and saw that I'd been making inquiries about him. So he called me to give me the heads-up. Okay so far?'

'I think so.'

'Harding was due to meet the Spetsnaz at St Pancras and take them to Bibby's home. I came up with the idea of substituting them with our guys. The Russians were taken off the train at Ashford and four officers from CO19, the specialist firearms unit, took their place. We even managed to find four who spoke Russian.'

'Right.'

Patsy could imagine Tyler struggling to remember all this.

'We were amazed when a guy called Johnny Pike turned up impersonating Harding. Up to that point we had believed that Pike had been murdered on a Channel ferry.'

'How did he know about Harding?'

'I don't want to say just yet.'

'And for that matter, who is he – this Johnny Pike?'

'The guy responsible for the recent spate of killings. Do keep up, Paul.'

Tyler tried to digest the facts. 'Right,' he said finally. 'The commissioner's on his way back over here.'

'How about you tell him that not only have I solved the series of recent murders and identified the man behind the £22 million Maidstone raid ten years ago, I also reckon I might be able to recover some of the money. Not bad for a Monday morning.'

'Yes. Um... no.'

'In return, I want you and the commissioner to head off any crap that may be thrown in my direction.'

'Would you like to speak to God in person? He's next to me now.'

'No, his vicar on earth will suffice. Take care.'

She ended the call and compared the key she had just found in Bibby's safe with the one Jemma had given her. The same make, but slightly different.

'Well?' asked Leyden, joining her.

'The safe deposit box must require two keys. Starling had one, Bibby the other.'

'So it was Bibby's thugs who tried to snatch Jemma,' said Leyden.

'Yep.' All they had to do now was to find which safe deposit centre the keys fitted. Might take a while, but they'd get there in the end.

'Shame Johnny Pike's dead,' she said.

'The firearms guys had no option,' said Leyden. 'He pointed a loaded weapon at them.'

'It was suicide.'

They stood aside to allow yet another forensic team into the house. The firearms officers had already left to be interviewed. Chalke felt sorry for them. It couldn't be easy killing a man.

'The Dim Reaper?'

'Dead, I'd say,' replied Chalke. 'We've been chasing ghosts. I'd bet it was his body in the crem.'

'So all these deaths were about Johnny and Vinnie getting their hands on their share of the loot from the raid.'

'Not all of them. I think there's more to it than that.'

'Okay. By the way, Graham White's being held at Gatwick,' said Leyden. 'He was on the way to Venezuela with Shirley and their daughter.'

'Tell Gatwick to let them go. Graham and Shirley have nothing to do with this.'

'We still don't know if it was Graham on the film set,' objected Leyden.

'I reckon it was,' said Chalke. 'But someone got to Starling before him.'

'Right.' Leyden blinked in incomprehension. 'Still, I'm sure Shirley won't be going empty-handed.'

'Get them on a plane before Donny Grey realises what's happening.'

'You sure?'

'There's been enough grief for one day.'

Chalke's jaw dropped open. Waves of shock, irritation and finally delight passed over her face.

'You all right?' asked Leyden.

The memory of Jemma as she'd appeared in Leyden's kitchen yesterday morning had just entered Patsy's head. Jemma – tousle-haired, yawning, looking lost and alone.

The brain was a strange thing. For days she'd been trying to place who Jemma reminded her of, and had failed. But all the time, subconsciously, her brain had been working away – and now she had the answer.

But first they had unfinished business.

'Come on. We've got to get back to Greenwich. Johnny Pike couldn't have done all this by himself.'

The Incident Room was buzzing. Chalke and Leyden walked in to be greeted by cheers. The Eternal Flame slapped Leyden on the back, Cochrane gave him the thumbs-up, Sandy Wishbourne blew a kiss.

Chalke felt sad that no one showed her the same affection. Her team still clearly regarded her as unapproachable. They didn't know how much she'd have appreciated a hug just then.

Weaver had already been taken away by officers from the Directorate of Professional Standards. They would go over his relationship with Bibby with a fine-tooth comb. Starting, no doubt, with the arrest of the Pike brothers ten years ago. No one would want to be in Des Weaver's shoes – even assuming he was innocent.

Chalke had spent the journey back from Bibby's home wondering if the way Weaver had steered her away from the Maidstone tie-in and towards Graham White had been deliberate. She hoped not. She hated the idea that Des Weaver was bent.

Her phone began ringing as she entered her office.

She was surprised to hear Brenda Weaver's voice.

'I'm sorry to trouble you, Patsy, but I can't get hold of Des,' Brenda said. 'He's not in his office and he's not replying to his mobile.'

'He's had to go to Scotland Yard,' said Chalke.

'Oh, blow. He was supposed to take me to meet Fleur Varndell. I suppose I should be used to this by now.'

Chalke didn't know what to say. 'He'll call you when he can.'

'Thanks, Patsy. See you soon.'

Chalke put down the phone, relieved to end the conversation. She went back into the Incident Room to see Sue Jones emerge from the corridor to the washrooms. It was clear she had been crying.

'Can I have a word?' called Chalke. She beckoned to Leyden and returned to her office.

Sue followed.

Chalke sat behind her desk. She motioned for Sue to sit down. Leyden closed the door and leaned against it. Chalke fiddled with her wooden man until he looked as if he was directing traffic. Leyden's stomach rumbled.

'Sorry.'

'Never mind, Bobby. Steak tonight,' said Chalke tartly. She put down her wooden man, raised her eyes to meet Sue's directly, and asked, 'So. Do you want to tell me about Keeley?'

'Why?' she stammered. 'What's there to tell?'

'Your daughter died of meningitis,' prompted Chalke.

'She was only three and a half.' A cloud of pain crossed Sue's face.

'When you were living in Devonport.'

'Yes.'

'Was that where you met Johnny Pike?'

Sue started. She looked up at Leyden in silent appeal.

'Was it?' he asked.

'He was a young seaman on HMS *Monmouth*, one of the ships based there,' she said softly.

'And you started going out?'

'Yes.'

'Did he know he was the father?' asked Leyden softly.

Sue said nothing.

'Keeley was born eight months after Johnny was arrested for his part in the Maidstone raid,' prompted Chalke. 'Did you know you were pregnant when he was arrested?'

'Perhaps Johnny wasn't the father?' said Leyden.

Sue pulled a crumpled white handkerchief from her sleeve. The silence grew and grew like a gentle fall of snow, changing the outline of everything in the office.

'Johnny was her father,' said Sue finally, twisting the handkerchief around her fingers.

'Did he know?'

'I wouldn't write to him. I couldn't believe what he'd done. He was only supposed to be going up to London for a couple of days to see his rotten cousin. We were supposed to be going to Land's End camping when he came back. But he never came back?'

'But you did tell him in the end?' persisted Chalke gently.

'He'd heard I'd had a baby–' Sue stared at the forms in her lap. 'Keeley was the spitting image of him. She had his way of looking at you that made you smile. I took her to see Johnny in prison. He couldn't take his eyes off her.'

'And?'

'He said he'd see that me and the baby were looked after – get the word out – but I never heard anything. When Keeley fell ill, I had no one to turn to, no money for private treatment. Who knows? It might even have saved her–' Sue gave a choked sob.

'Then they wouldn't let Johnny attend her funeral because he wasn't registered as her father.'

'I'm sorry,' murmured Chalke.

'What happened when Johnny came out of prison?' asked Leyden.

'He was angry. He wanted to know why no one had helped me. Or Keeley. He and Vinnie had just this one name – a man called Georgie Locke who'd gone to live on Cyprus.'

'Hang on,' said Leyden. 'What do you mean they only had one name?'

'They only knew the bloke who'd recruited them. On the raid they hadn't been allowed to see anyone else's faces. Everyone wore balaclavas. They were told it was for security.'

'Okay. Tell us about Georgie Locke.'

'Vinnie went to see him and never came back. The next day, Johnny went to find out what had happened. Locke told him he'd killed Vinnie. There was a fight, Locke hit his head. Johnny didn't know what to do, so he ran away.'

'And torched the villa,' added Leyden.

'He panicked,' said Sue. 'But Locke did give him the name of another member of the gang.'

'Dave Shine,' guessed Chalke. 'The Dim Reaper.'

'All Johnny wanted to do was to get to the boss.' Sue wrapped the handkerchief around her hand like a bandage. 'Dave Shine was a nasty piece of work.'

'You mean Johnny killed him.'

'Johnny said he didn't have a choice. It was either Dave Shine or him.'

'How did he kill him?' asked Leyden.

'I don't know,' said Sue. 'I didn't ask.'

'You helped put his body in the coffin in place of Stan Figgens, didn't you?'

'No.'

'It'd be too much for one man,' said Chalke. 'Johnny would have needed help.'

'All Johnny wanted to do was to find out why they'd let our daughter die.'

'And get his share of the £22 million,' said Leyden.

'I don't know anything about that,' whispered Sue.

'But one name led to another,' said Chalke.

'I suppose so.'

'To Minicab?'

'Yes.'

'Why did Johnny plant that cocaine in the dry-cleaner's?'

'To put you on the wrong track, I suppose.'

'You suppose–'

'I don't know anything about it.'

'That's not true though, is it, Sue?' said Leyden. 'You used information you picked up in the Incident Room to help Johnny.'

Again Sue turned to look up at him. 'No.'

'You know how the system works. You know our sign-ons. You could access the inquiry, get into the Police National Computer and look at intelligence reports,' pointed out Leyden. 'That's how you knew about Guinness's gym. That's how you knew Friday night was Ari O's club night. That's why you've been doing so much overtime recently.'

'No,' said Sue.

'Don't lie, Sue.'

Sue looked Chalke in the eye. 'I didn't kill anyone.'

'Johnny wasn't a big bloke. How could he overcome a monster like Guinness?'

'He said he'd found Guinness on an exercise machine, listening to music,' replied Sue. 'Johnny managed to creep up and shackle him.'

'You were there?'

'No.' Sue was sounding more and more desperate. 'Johnny just told me.'

'Tell me about Ari O's murder.'

'Johnny knew someone from prison. A rent boy who owed him. I think he lured Ari O outside. I don't know–'

'Do you have a name for the rent boy?'

'No.'

'And Joey Starling?'

Sue looked straight at Chalke. 'I don't know anything about Joey Starling,' she said. 'I swear I don't.'

'I believe you,' said Chalke, to Leyden's surprise. 'But you were on the ferry the night Johnny – or, as we thought at the time, Vinnie – vanished.'

'I smuggled Johnny into France in the boot of my car. Then we caught the next ferry back together.'

'And Johnny stayed with you after that?'

'Yes.'

God, no wonder the investigation had been such a mess, thought Chalke. Sue had been feeding Johnny Pike everything the police knew.

'Mal Topper,' Leyden was saying. 'You asked me how his home was protected when we were in the pub garden, then you passed on the information to Johnny.'

'Yes.' Sue spoke in barely a whisper.

'And you two killed him,' said Chalke.

'Not me. I wasn't there.'

'How did Johnny come to turn up at St Pancras this morning?'

'Topper told Johnny that Tosh Bibby was the brains behind the Maidstone raid. It was Bibby's idea to set up Johnny and Vinnie.'

'Go on.'

'Before he… died… Topper told Johnny that Bibby had just hired four Russians to protect him. So Johnny knew he had to act quickly if he was going to get to him.'

'And you tipped off the police where Harding was staying,' said Chalke. 'So Johnny could substitute himself and get to Bibby.'

'Yes... But I don't understand – what happened?'

'Harding talked. We substituted police commandos for the Russians.'

'And they killed Johnny.'

'Sue, love, Johnny killed himself,' said Leyden. 'He pointed a loaded pistol at firearms officers. They had to make a split-second decision.'

Sue seemed to shrink into herself. 'What will happen to me?'

'You'll be interviewed by officers from outside Greenwich. You'll be offered legal representation and asked to make a statement.'

Sue looked at Chalke. 'I never did get around to signing up for any of those courses.'

'They're keen on education in prison,' she said. 'And you'll have plenty of time.'

There was a knock at the door. Leyden opened it to reveal a man and a woman who could only have been detectives.

'Susan Hillary Jones,' intoned the woman. 'I am charging you with conspiracy to murder, aiding and abetting a felony, with-holding information–'

It didn't seem right to go to the Tolly Shop without Weaver, so the whole task force, plus anyone else who could slip out, crowded into the Prince Albert.

Leyden walked up the road by himself, leaving Chalke on the phone to Begley. Most of the team had gathered at the far end of the bar but Leyden needed something to line his stomach before getting stuck into the booze.

He was halfway through a pasty washed down by a pint of la-ger when a voice behind him said, 'I hope that's not going to spoil your steak dinner.'

'I've not eaten –'

'Since breakfast,' smiled Chalke. 'I know.'

'Nor have you.'

The day had been too hectic to think about food. Now Chalke realised she was hungry. 'What's that pasty like?'

'Fine. Try one.'

'No, thanks.'

The party was warming up. Blondie was pumping out on the jukebox; Butterfield was chatting up Sandy Wishbourne next to the fireplace; Ben Lakeman and his team were getting heated over Saturday's Chelsea–Liverpool game; and a pool competition was starting in the back room. Les Blunt had just won £20 on the electronic poker game bearing the sign, 'For Amusement Only'.

An argument had broken out over the motif for the special tie to be commissioned, which those involved in the case would be eligible to wear.

Cochrane favoured a piranha while the others wanted flames from a crem oven.

Leyden bought Chalke a glass of rosé wine. 'Do you think Sue was telling the truth?' he asked.

'On a scale of one to ten – three.'

'Jesus!'

'I reckon she went to the dry-cleaner's on purpose that morning to cover her tracks. Remember how many of her prints we found?'

'Then she refused to go home even though she seemed in shock,' recalled Leyden. 'She wanted to keep tabs on the investigation.'

'Just as well she confessed, though. We had nothing on her.'

'I imagine we'll find Johnny's fingerprints in her home.'

Chalke pulled a sad face. 'I had plans for her.'

'I feel like we've been betrayed.'

'It could get worse yet,' said Chalke.

There was a moment's silence as each waited for the other to broach the unspeakable. 'He must have known, mustn't he?' said Leyden finally.

Chalke shrugged. The idea of Des Weaver as a corrupt copper didn't bear thinking about. At the same time it was hard to believe that Weaver didn't know he was being used. Maybe it had suited him not to look too closely.

Weaver had supped with the devil, that much was certain. But had his spoon been long enough?

The barmaid began loading the remaining pasties onto a plate.

'There goes my lunch,' muttered Chalke.

'I thought you didn't want one,' said Leyden, before charming the barmaid into letting him have the last pasty.

'You never know what you want until you can't have it.' Chalke took a large bite.

'You said you believed Sue when she denied knowing anything about Joey Starling's murder,' said Leyden.

Chalke, who suspected that Leyden had deliberately waited until she had her mouth full before asking the question, continued chewing.

The argument over the tie was becoming heated. Two crocodiles rampant over an oven was currently competing with a rocket up a rectum. Some were asking how they'd depict a rectum.

Leyden drained his pint and held up the glass to be refilled.

Chalke placed a hand on his arm, finally swallowed and said, 'Not yet. We've got to places to go, people to see.'

'You mean we're not finished?'

'Can you hear the fat lady singing?'

Chalke parked in Ferry Street on the Isle of Dogs and looked back across the river to Greenwich, wondering how it had taken so long to drive such a short distance. Bring back the ferry.

The Ferry Inn could certainly do with the custom. With its peeling paintwork, grubby windows and general air of neglect it had the appearance of somewhere with more of a past than a future. Which was exactly why it had been chosen as a location for the film.

Sara Jane Bentley spotted Chalke as she was showing her warrant card to a surly security guard.

'Where's Fleur Varndell?' asked Chalke.

'She's between takes, out the back in the garden. I'll tell her you're here.'

'I can find my own way.'

'You can't just walk onto a film set.'

'You see a film set, I see a public house.'

Chalke picked her way through the clutter of cables, reflective light shields, boom mikes and a camera gantry on rails.

Fleur Varndell was in the garden, sitting at a rusting metal table in a lightweight blue raincoat reading a book. 'I was expecting Mr Weaver and his wife,' she said.

'He's been detained,' said Chalke.

Fleur's pale face held a fragility that Chalke hadn't seen before. She searched for a sign of the ruthlessness that Fleur would need to kill in cold blood – and found none.

'Please sit down. Sara Jane will get you some coffee,' said Fleur.

'I'm fine, thanks.' From the looks Sara Jane was giving her, Patsy wouldn't trust her not to spit in it.

'Thanks, Sara Jane.' Fleur dismissed the PR.

Chalke sat down and pulled out her cigarettes. 'Do you mind?'

'It's your funeral.'

'True.' Chalke lit a cigarette, inhaled and said, 'I have a question for you.'

'Yes?'

'Why doesn't Jemma Wodehouse want anyone to know that you're her mother?'

'Why do you say I am?'

'I could order DNA tests but they're not needed.' Chalke let the smoke drift out of her mouth. 'Are they?

'No.' Fleur closed her eyes, gave a slight shake of the head. 'Jemma is my daughter.'

H. Bruce Montgomery burst into the garden. 'What do you mean forcing your way in here and upsetting people?'

'I didn't force my way in,' said Chalke calmly.

'We've hired the pub, so it's now private property. You don't have a warrant –'

'I'd hoped that this could have been done informally but–' Chalke stood up. 'If you're ready, Miss Varndell.'

'Fleur is going nowhere,' shouted Montgomery.

'Please, Bruce,' said Fleur. 'We're just talking. I'm fine.'

Montgomery glowered at Chalke who regarded him without blinking.

'Really, we're fine,' said Fleur. 'Just leave it. *Please!*'

Montgomery limped off, muttering to himself. Sara Jane stayed.

'This is private, Sara Jane,' said Fleur.

For the second time, the PR girl reluctantly left.

When they were alone, Chalke asked, 'You admit you're Jemma's birth mother?'

'Apology for a mother would be more accurate,' sighed Fleur. 'May I have one of your cigarettes?'

'It's your funeral.' Chalke pushed the packet and lighter across the table.

Fleur lit her cigarette, coughed.

'Freddy wanted us to keep the baby and get married. He had romantic ideas of two struggling actors living in a garret, bringing up their child. I didn't see it that way. I was going to be a star and nothing was going to stand in my way.' Fleur gave a harsh laugh. 'I've never regretted anything so much in my life. How could I give away my daughter? But I did. Freddy had no say in it. I went to Hollywood. The waif look was in. I did well. I didn' see or hear from Freddy for some years until we found ourselve working together on the same film. It reminded me of what could have been.'

'I see,' murmured Chalke.

'Do you?' Fleur leaned forward. She was desperate to be understood, Patsy realised. 'Have you ever had children?'

'No.'

'I couldn't have any more.' Fleur began to cry. 'And I gave away the one child I had.'

'You made up for it.'

'I owed her.'

'We're not talking about that,' said Chalke briskly. 'How did Jemma manage to find Freddy but not you?'

'There was some foul-up with the birth papers.' Fleur dabbed at her eyes. 'I'd changed my name – twice, in fact. And it was some time before Freddy told me that Jemma had been in touch. He said he didn't know how I'd take it.' She shook her head in disbelief. 'Take it! I was delighted. But then Starling got his claws into her. I couldn't believe how quickly she... Freddy did what he could, but it was like trying to hold back the tide. In the end, I virtually kidnapped her and packed her off to the Betty Ford clinic in California.'

'She didn't tell me that,' said Chalke.

'It's not a time she talks about. I don't blame her. I was away filming a lot. She joined me for a month in Malaysia but then I had to finish the film in Hollywood so she came back to the UK. She stayed with Freddy and we spoke every day.' Fleur stared into the middle distance, forgetting her cigarette. 'It was going well; Freddy and I were talking about getting back together. Jemma was all for it, then Freddy got cancer, the first time. It put everything on hold. Freddy got better, we... then it came back.'

'And Starling started chasing Jemma again?'

'I wanted to kill him–'

Fleur started in surprise. Jemma was standing in the doorway, Leyden behind her.

The actress recovered quickly. 'Come and sit here, Jemma.' She patted the seat next to her, moving up to make room.

Now Chalke saw the two side by side, she wondered why it had taken her so long to make the connection. They were two peas from the same pod.

'How on earth did we miss the family resemblance?' she asked Leyden.

'Just shows what sort of detectives we are.' Leyden pretended to scowl at Jemma. 'You told me a load of porkies, young lady.'

There was a moment's silence, then Chalke said, 'I wanted to tell you that I know who was responsible for the murder of Joey Starling –'

Fleur gave a resigned smile. 'Freddy gave his life... I –'

'No.' Jemma tried to interrupt. 'I –'

Chalke spoke loudly over the two women. '– a man called Johnny Pike, who was killed this morning in a shoot-out with police. I'm satisfied that he was responsible for Starling's death. We will not be pusuing the investigation further.'

Chalke's eyes met Fleur's.

'Now that you're officially mother and daughter, no doubt you'll have a lot to talk about,' said Chalke. 'In fact, Fleur, don't you think it'd be a good idea if Jemma moved in with you? It would give you the chance to get to know each other again.'

Fleur asked Jemma, 'What do you think?'

'I'd like that – if it's okay with you.'

'It's okay,' said Fleur wiping away her tears. 'It's better than okay.'

'Sorry, Bobby,' said Jemma. 'You'll have to cook your own supper.'

'Not a problem. Brilliant. Over the moon for you.'

Chalke and Leyden stood looking across the water to Greenwich Lucymar lived in the sandy-coloured flats to the right of the creek mouth, Joey Starling's penthouse was directly ahead.

It was getting dark, the street lights flickering on. There was rain in the air.

'You happy with that?' Chalke asked Leyden.

Leyden stared ahead. 'You're the boss.'

'You said yourself there was no point in sending Jemma to prison,' said Chalke, surprised at his reaction.

'I wasn't thinking of Jemma.'

'You want to arrest Fleur?' When Leyden did not reply, Chalke pressed, 'Well, do you?'

'We could have let a jury decide,' he muttered.

'You trust juries?'

'No, but –'

Chalke realised had made a mistake. She'd assumed that Leyden shared her view of right and wrong.

They stood in silence side by side.

Chalke turned towards him, not knowing what to say or do. She looked up into his face, wanting to undo the moment, wondering how she could undo her decision.

Leyden was still gazing stony-faced at the Thames.

'I'll go back if you like,' she offered in a small voice.

The corner of Leyden's mouth twitched. He regained control instantly, but it was enough for Chalke.

'You sod. You bloody sod.'

She began thumping Leyden's chest until he grasped her hands. He was grinning broadly.

'Never do that to me again,' she said.

They were standing very close.

'It's the right thing,' he said. 'There's been enough grief for one day.'

'You're sure?' Chalke stared hard into his eyes. She needed Leyden to have reached the decision himself – not just to be saying it to please her.

'All down to Johnny Pike.'

'Thank you.'

'What are you thanking me for?' said Leyden. 'It's bleeding obvious.'

'Bleeding obvious,' repeated Chalke as they turned their backs on the river.

They were near the cars when Chalke asked, 'Did Jemma ever get round to buying that steak?'

'Yeah. I found her on the way back from the supermarket. Her shopping's in the boot of my car. I suppose I'd better go and give it to her.'

'Then again, I cook a mean steak.'

'You do?'

'Mushrooms, tomatoes, baked potato–'

'Onion rings?'

'Onion rings are my speciality.'

'Right.'

'And I could open a bottle of 2001 Château Margaux Premier Grand Cru Classé to celebrate.'

'No lager?'